The

BLACK VELVET
COAT

Published 2015
Printed in the United States of America
ISBN: 978-1-63152-009-9
Library of Congress Control Number: 2015938463

Book design by Stacey Aaronson

For information, address:
She Writes Press
1563 Solano Ave #546
Berkeley, CA 94707

She Writes Press is a division of SparkPoint Studio, LLC.

The

Black

Velvet

Coat

A Novel

JILL G. HALL

SHE WRITES PRESS

This book is dedicated to my mother,
who I now know did the best she could.

PROLOGUE

—

*S*ylvia rolled over in the bumpy bed and tried to sleep. *Hotel Monte Vista* blinked in pink neon through voile curtains onto the bedspread. The clock ticked. She cuddled her beagle-basset, stroked the satiny fur, and whispered, "Do you think they'll find us, Lucy?" The puppy hummed and grew quiet.

Every time Sylvia closed her eyes, she had that vision again: waxing moon, waves splashing, a body bouncing on the ocean toward the beach. A nightmare or a premonition? Either way, it was no good. Had they found her coat with the pin? It could be traced back to her. Would salt water rinse off fingerprints? Guns sink, don't they? What if Ricardo's body washed up on shore?

Sylvia switched on the light and sat up. Her shaky hands pulled a Lucky Strike from its pack. She lit it, inhaled, and blew the smoke out through her nostrils. She reached for the *Life* magazine from the bedside table and studied Grace Kelly's smiling face, cool blue eyes and smooth blonde hair. People had compared her own beauty to the movie star's, but Sylvia didn't see the resemblance, and Grace had found her prince.

Lucy crawled from beneath the covers and plopped at the foot of the bed with a sigh.

Sylvia attempted to smile at her. "You can't sleep either, girl?" Returning to the magazine, a recent one, she tried to calm her jittery thoughts and flipped through ads for phonograph needles, beauty creams, and Playtex Living bras. She turned a page and stared at a picture.

"Oh my God!" The photo of her with Ricardo leaving their engagement party filled the entire page. Such a wreck that night, her hair in shambles and mascara smeared, as if she'd been through a wind tunnel. Of course, Ricardo appeared perfect with his neat hair slicked back. He had been sauced, but the picture didn't show that. Sylvia slapped the magazine shut and tossed it across the room, not wanting to remember the last time she had seen him.

She had been certain it was love the way her heart loped every time he was near. When he smiled at her, she thought she might fly. So naive. She closed her eyes and held back tears. But in the end, right before she pulled out the gun, she realized it must not have been love at all.

I

———

A fall wind blew off the bay and licked Anne's tall body as she hiked up California Street, full auburn hair flying behind her. She shivered and wished she had worn more than jeans and a T-shirt. In the window of Rescued Relics Thrift Shop, she spotted a swing coat that forced her to stop. Her heart chakra felt as if it actually glowed with white light. She just had to try on the coat.

As she wandered inside, a musty smell overwhelmed her, and she waited a moment for her eyes to adjust to the blink of the fluorescent lights. The shop was stuffed with racks of clothes, old toys, and household goods.

A clerk behind the counter snapped her gum. "Hi, doll."

"May I try on that coat in the window?" Anne asked.

"Help yourself. Just came in this morning." The woman continued to unpack multicolored beads from a shoebox.

Anne returned to the window and reached for the black velvet coat. "Oooh, '60s. My fave." A rhinestone snowflake pin with a hazy film on it, as if splashed by the sea, rested on the rounded collar.

Slipping on the coat, a whiff of White Shoulders perfume enveloped her, and a peaceful calm spread through her whole body. In search of a mirror, she stepped around chipped blue-and-white plates, silver trays, and a plaid couch.

With head to one side, she tried to view her image in the cracked mirror, but it was hard to see through the dust. She caressed the coat's sleeves. Luscious and soft. Anne tugged off the coat and gaped at the Dior label. "Lah-de-dah," she whispered. There must have been some mistake. The price tag pinned to the sleeve read $65, but it was worth more like $650. She looked over at the woman at the counter, who returned her gaze with a wink. Anne dug in a pocket for her money. If she bought the coat, she wouldn't have enough to cover the rent, let alone all those outstanding bills. But she had to follow her instincts. She grinned, tossed the coat over her arm, and moved to the cash register.

The man in line ahead of her set down a mountain of neckties. Waiting her turn, she flipped through a stack of magazines, but none of them were old enough for collage fodder. Only vintage photos inspired her work. One series featured movie moguls—Hitchcock, Kazan, and Mayer. The most recent pieces were about political divas.

The clerk removed the tag from the coat and snapped her gum again. "Good bargain, sweetie. And with a pin too." She nodded, causing her dangle-ball earrings to wobble back and forth under a beehive hairdo.

Anne paid and tossed the jacket over her shoulders. As she exited, the cashier yelled, "Honey, you look like a million bucks in that coat!"

Anne smiled and waved goodbye. Back out into the cold, she jumped a cable car and sat on the wooden seat. Snuggling into her plush purchase, she felt confident with her buy, but what about the rent and all those other bills? Four years ago after college, she'd moved here with such high hopes. She had become enamored by the big-city energy and never wanted to move back to the stifling Midwest. But she felt as if life was passing her by and the real world now seemed a lot harder than she had ever imagined. Even though she had gotten good grades it had still taken her six years to finish college. The first year she had frittered away at the community college, and then at the university it had taken her awhile to get the hang of how to sign up for the right classes in order to graduate. She hadn't expected to get into San Francisco's Museum of Modern Art, but at least thought she would have found gallery representation by now.

The cable car scraped underneath her as it ascended the hill. They passed Chinatown, and she looked down Grant at the red and gold lanterns, then dialed her cell. "Hi, Mom. I hate to ask you, but I'm in a bind. Could you lend me some money?"

"Again?"

"Just a little to tide me over?"

Her mother paused. "Your room is still here for you."

Anne thought about the two-story yellow craftsman on Maple Lane in Oscoda. "I'll sell some more pieces soon." She tried to keep her voice upbeat.

"I know, dear. But you're going to move back sooner or later. Stop torturing yourself."

Anne's phone beeped. "Hurry! I'm losing power. Please?"

"Okay. My Avon sales have been slow this month. I can only send $50."

"Anything will help." It wouldn't be enough, though. Anne tried to call the hotel to ask for an extra shift, but her cell had run totally out of juice.

The cable car reached the peak and passed Grace Cathedral. The spires appeared to be reaching toward God and the heavens, a sign that she had chosen the right metropolis. She hopped off at the corner of California and Polk, her stop, then walked uphill toward her apartment. The flower shop located below her apartment teemed with pink roses, magenta gladiolas, and white stargazers.

"Hi, Tony!" She waved to the vendor, pulled more bills from her mailbox, and tiptoed up the steep stairs. She didn't want to see Mrs. Ladenheim, the landlady, who lived on the first floor. Even so, the woman's door opened a tad, and her Siamese cat skittered out.

Anne passed Val's door as he started his vocal warm-ups, probably to prepare for tonight's *Beach Blanket Babylon*. "Ke, kae, ke, kae, koo."

On the third floor, she unlocked her door and stepped inside, almost tripping on a pile of newspapers and a pair of shoes. What a mess! Squished paint tubes, adhesive jars, wrinkled tarps, and magazines were strewn about. Not an inch of floor or table or counter space had been left uncovered. Even the walls had works-in-progress plastered on them. Anne knew this clutter instilled bad feng shui and made a promise to clean up later. When tidy, it could be quite sweet: a room with a kitchenette, daybed, and art studio all in one.

The place felt as cold as Antarctica. She turned on the heat for once and picked up the phone to call work, but it was dead. The phone company must have finally caught up with her. She planned to cancel it anyway. Slamming down the receiver, she plugged in her cell and called the St. Francis.

"Valet Service. How may I help you?"

"Howard, any extra shifts available this week?"

"Sorry. See you tonight, though. Afterward I'm going to Rhinestone Ruby's. Hope you'll come too."

"We'll see." Last week she had joined him at the disco-western bar. She had followed behind his rust-colored chaps but kept bumping into the guy on her right and then the guy on her left. Dancing had never been her forte. She couldn't even keep step with the Oscoda High drill team and had been asked to quit.

Anne took off the coat, grabbed a rag from the sink, and polished the snowflake pin until it shone in the light. Then she slipped the coat on again, closed the bathroom door, and inspected herself in the full-length mirror hanging on the back. She batted hazel eyes, twisted sorrel hair above her head, and considered an updo.

"Oh, I am so gorgeous!" She posed, as if a beauty queen, all five foot eight of her, with an outstretched arm. Model-like, she dipped her hands in the jacket pockets. The tip of her finger touched something cold. Funny—when she had checked the pockets at the store, she was sure they were empty. She pulled out her hand. The key was brass and as dull as an old penny.

She carried it over to the kitchenette to see it better through the bay window over the sink. A ray of light hit the key. It grew warm and shimmered around the edges. She could have sworn that a puff of salty sea air leapt into the room. Tickling her palm, the key glowed, began to flitter like a lightning bug's wings, wavered, and then stopped. Was she going crazy? She stared at it for a full minute and hoped it would glow again, but no such luck.

She put it back into her pocket and wondered if she had imagined the key's energy. A faint memory of warm vibration against her skin remained. Not able to resist, she pulled the key out again, but it just sat there in her hand. She wanted to call Karl, Dottie, or even her mother to tell them about it, but they'd think she had gone off the deep end.

Attached to the key hung a round tag, where the name *Sea Cliff* was faded, barely legible. It could be from somewhere down near Ocean Beach. She stared at the key again. Could it really be magic?

2

———

1963.

*M*ilo pulled the Rolls Royce around Bay Breeze's circular drive and coasted down the street. A foghorn's deep bass sang. Shadows shifted and fell across the road ahead. "It's thick this mornin'," the chauffeur said.

From the backseat, Sylvia nodded. "Better go slow."

"Sleep well?" In the rearview mirror, Milo's face glowed dark and shiny as the Rolls's hood in the misty fog, his gray hair trimmed short as could be.

"Fine, thanks." She didn't want to tell him she had had a restless night. He worried about her.

"Where to? The usual?"

"Yes, Tiffany's." She had an itch, a craving for something dazzling. A charm that when touched would keep her composed tonight. She sat back on the black leather seat, used a compact mirror to apply Hollywood Red lipstick, and played with the graduated pearls around her neck. Buying something new usually calmed her.

The Rolls continued down the street. She really shouldn't buy anything new right now, but this was an emergency. That blind date scheduled for seven o'clock had her stomach tied in knots.

Milo stopped for a cable car to pass. As they approached Union Square, she put on dark glasses, placed a pale pink chiffon scarf over her blonde hair, and flipped the ends around to the nape of her neck. The Rolls glided to the curb in front of the store and parked. Milo exited and opened her door. He took her hand, and she swung her long legs out, planting blue-and-white spectator pumps on the curb.

She smiled at him and stepped out. "I won't be long."

A man passed by, turned around, and glanced at her. She looked down and smoothed the jacket of her navy suit. At almost twenty-one, she wanted to look grown up.

Tall and erect, she walked as she had been taught years ago in charm school. Pushing through the revolving door, her body tingled with excitement. Tiffany's: where glass cases gleamed under chandeliered lights, a fairyland filled with shiny objects and temptations of delight. It was her favorite place in the world.

The silent store smelled of fresh gardenia that wafted from a bowl on a pedestal. No other customers were present, but staff stood ready behind counters. Sylvia removed her dark glasses and scarf, slipping them into her handbag as a salesgirl approached, her brown hair pulled back and fitted suit just so.

"Miss Van Dam. What can I show you today?"

"I'll just browse, Ruth," Sylvia said with her voice just above a whisper. She gazed at a pair of sapphire earrings. In the perfect ensemble, her blind date might not notice her soft voice and shaky hands.

No one seemed to understand her shyness. She had overheard people at the club refer to her as a snob. But that wasn't true. When someone new tried to talk to her, she could think of a million things to say, but her tongue would twist, her throat would go dry, and she just couldn't get the words out.

At the next counter, she examined brooches, shimmering

emeralds, topaz, and rubies. She wanted something a bit more understated and pointed to a snowflake pin.

"I'd like a closer look at that."

"Isn't it lovely?" Ruth took it out of the case. "Crystal rhinestone."

"Not real diamonds?"

"No. I know it's not our usual fare, but they're all the rage." Ruth placed a velvet tray on the counter and set the pin on top.

Sylvia had never bought an imitation. She peeked at the tiny tag hanging from the pin. The price was a reasonable $500, but even so, she shouldn't buy it. Paul was a lenient guardian, but he had warned her not to exceed the $1000 monthly shopping allotment again, and this purchase would push it over. She hated to disappoint him, but she really wanted it.

Ruth placed the pin in the palm of Sylvia's gloved hand and stepped back. About the size of a silver dollar, it was almost as light as a real snowflake might be, but this one certainly wouldn't melt. She squeezed it in her palm, the permanence comforting.

She wiggled her hand toward the light and observed the glistening rhinestones. They sparkled as brightly as diamonds. You couldn't even tell the difference. She held the pin up to her lapel, glanced in an oval mirror on the counter, and imagined how it would look on her black coat.

Ruth moved next to her. "That really suits you, Miss Van Dam."

Sylvia smiled then frowned. The desire to buy the pin tapped, knocked, and then pounded a hole in her stomach. "Put it on my account, please."

"Of course." Ruth put the pin in a blue box and tied a white bow around it. She handed the package to Sylvia and walked her toward the door.

A glint caught the corner of Sylvia's eye, and she paused.

Alone in a glass case rested an exquisite tiara that somehow seemed familiar. A chill ran down her spine.

Ruth explained. "That's been in our vault for years. Just put it on display."

Sylvia stared at it and tried to catch her breath.

"Would you like to try it?"

"Oh, no!" Sylvia shuddered and rushed out the revolving door. How eerie. She was certain she had seen that tiara before. She seemed to remember its weight on her head and the feeling of the jewels on her fingertips.

Outside, the fog had cleared to reveal a lapis blue sky. The sun reflected on high white clouds. Sylvia squinted at the glare and donned her dark glasses again. Milo, at attention, cap in hand, opened the car door for her. She slid in and relaxed back. He started the ignition and peered in the rearview mirror. "Just that one little package?"

"That's it."

They drove up the hill, where Coit Tower floated in the distance. The tightening in her belly returned. What if Mr. Bonner tried to hold her hand tonight, or worse yet, kiss her? How horrible that would be. She wouldn't know what to do. "Milo, please stop ahead at that liquor store."

He nodded, slowed down, and pulled over.

She handed him some change from her pocketbook. "I'd like a *Vogue* and pack of cigarettes."

"When did you start to smoke?"

"Today," she said with a firm voice. It might make her appear more sophisticated and confident, like Marilyn Monroe.

"You know what Ella would say."

"Doesn't matter," Sylvia mumbled, and she looked down.

Milo ambled into the store. He returned with a scowl on his face as if angry, then grinned and passed over the magazine and a pack of Lucky Strikes. "Don't worry. No one needs to know."

"You're the best." She smiled at him.

They continued up the hill toward home. She put the magazine aside and slid the cigarettes into her purse to try later. The tangle in her stomach twisted. She eyed the Tiffany package beside her and picked it up. Her fingers itched. She untied the white ribbon, opened the box, and stared at the snowflake pin. She clutched it. The knot inside her dissolved into calmness.

At home, Ella met her at the door. Underneath her lace cap, wispy curls had begun to turn the same gray as the uniform she always wore. "Shopping again?"

"Only a bauble."

"Just what you need." Ella stuck her hands in her apron pockets. "And don't even think of breaking your date tonight."

"I won't." Sylvia's throat felt dry.

"You need to start dating."

Sylvia looked down. "I'm only twenty."

"Yes, and it is high time you became more social."

"I'm trying." Sylvia ran past Ella up the stairs.

"Your parents would practically have wanted you married by now!" Ella called.

Yes, but they weren't here anymore, so it really didn't matter. In fact, if that painting didn't hang above the landing, Sylvia might not even remember what they looked like. She thought back to that day shortly after the funeral, hiding in her usual spot beneath the stairs, when she overheard Paul talking to Ella and Milo. "I think we should send Sylvia to boarding school."

Ella disagreed. "Mr. Paul, you know she's fragile by nature. Right now she doesn't need any more disruption. She's only thirteen and needs our care."

"At least the two of you could move into one of the upstairs bedrooms."

"No, thanks." Milo said. "Our home has been down here for years, and that's where we'll stay." So Ella and Milo continued to live in the little room next to the kitchen and continued with Sylvia's day-to-day care and supervision.

What a relief. It would have been a nightmare to live with strangers. At the time, she didn't really grasp the finality of death but somehow understood her parents were never coming back.

Now from a box on her canopied bed, Sylvia pulled out the velvet coat and clasped the snowflake pin on it. She donned the jacket and looked in the mirror. A lovely and confident woman stared back, at least for a moment, then faded to a trembling waif. She touched the pin and regained her composure, but within a few moments, it left her again. She shrugged off the coat, unclasped the snowflake, and grasped it in shaky hands.

How would she ever make it through her date tonight? Would Mr. Bonner think she was pretty? She wondered what to wear and entered her closet: a hollow cave filled with unworn sequined cocktail dresses and beaded chiffon gowns. She fingered each one. None of them seemed to fit the occasion.

She drifted to her dresser. On top rested seven identical turquoise leather jewelry boxes. She opened the first, placed the snowflake inside on black satin, and gazed at it. She felt nothing and quickly opened all the other boxes. One by one, she picked up each sparkling treasure—earrings, necklaces, bracelets, and brooches—and held each for a few seconds. The magic lasted only that long. Tenderly she closed the boxes and straightened them in a row, safe now.

She'd skipped lunch and knew Ella would fix her a sandwich if she asked but she couldn't stomach food right now. Her body ached from exhaustion. She curled up to take a nap but wasn't able to sleep so she knitted until she finally yawned, put away her needles and nodded off.

Awhile later Ella knocked on the door. "He'll be here in an hour."

To calm her nerves, Sylvia ran a bubble bath, stepped into the tub with the *Vogue*, and studied all the new jewelry and clothes she wished to buy. She dried off and wrapped a towel around her body. Checking the clock and in a panic, she entered the closet again, closed her eyes, and randomly picked a sapphire blue dress. She put it on. The sequins itched her skin, but she didn't have time to change. With her hair brushed and makeup on, she took the snowflake brooch from the box and returned it to the coat's collar just as the doorbell chimed below. She gasped for air.

Ella knocked and entered the bedroom. "He's here." She appraised Sylvia's choice. "You look charming, dear."

Sylvia glanced at her image in the mirror. Would Mr. Bonner think so?

"It's time." Ella smiled.

Sylvia couldn't breathe, shook her head, and sat on the bed.

"I'm sure you'll have a good time." Ella walked over to her, hand outstretched. Sylvia swallowed, composed herself, and took it. Ella led her to the top of the stairs, placed Sylvia's fingers on the newel, and let go. "You can do it," Ella whispered in her ear.

Sylvia grasped the rail as she descended the stairs. At the landing, she stopped and peeked over the banister. Mr. Bonner, hat in hand, waited for her in the foyer. From the back, he looked nice enough—short brown hair and a sports jacket. But what if he wasn't? Her heartbeat was so loud she thought he might hear it. She turned and ran up the stairs, past Ella and back into the bedroom again.

3

———

*W*here are the Jag keys?" Anne scanned the rack. "He called down ten minutes ago!"

"Not Mr. Duchamp. Let me look." Howard ran his hands along the keys and shook his head. "They're not here."

Anne stuck a hand in her coat pocket and pulled out the key. "Thank God. Found them. Slipped them in here before I got that smarmy guy's Corvette." She read the key-ring tag and sagged her shoulders. "Up north?"

"The lot filled up fast from the convention." Howard held out his hand. "I'll get it. You've taken enough for today; you don't need Duchamp."

"No, it's my turn." Anne ran out into the fog and straight up the hill past the Sears Café. In the next block up, she found the car, jumped inside, and tried to nudge away from the curb into the thick of rush hour traffic. A delivery truck blocked her way though —cones placed behind it with flashers blinking. Anne swerved around the truck and heard a crunch but kept going. In the rearview mirror, she watched as the demolished cone dropped from underneath the Jag and a burly man chased her down the hill. She made it across Post as the light changed from yellow to red and pulled up to the hotel, where Mr. Duchamp waited.

"About time," He growled, got in and threw a dollar bill on the ground. "If you want it, pick it up."

Anne looked at Duchamp, who offered a cocky smile and a wave. She wanted to yell, *Get it yourself*, but with tears in her eyes, she stooped over and picked it up.

Howard put his hand on her shoulder. "Why don't you take the rest of the night off?"

"That's okay. We're too busy." She pulled a tissue from her pocket and dried her eyes.

Anne reached home at 1:00 AM and counted her tips, only now about half of what she needed to pay the rent. She checked her cell, and there was one message from her mom. "Are you using that new moisturizer I sent you? The California sun will wrinkle your face like a raisin." Anne thought about taking off her uniform but instead fell right to sleep.

In the morning, Anne grabbed the only thing left in the kitchen cupboard, a Chips Ahoy! bag, ate the few crumbs left in the bottom, wadded it up, then threw it on the linoleum floor. Out of coffee, she found an opened can of Diet Coke in the fridge and took a sip. It was flat, but she drank it anyway in hopes it had some caffeine left.

She couldn't continue to live like this. What if she got evicted? Maybe Karl would lend her some money or let her stay with him for a while. After all, they'd been seeing each other for almost a year. And the sex was great. He hadn't ever told her he loved her, but she was pretty sure he did. At twenty-eight, she should start being serious about settling down.

She splashed water on her face in the bathroom. Oh my God, was that a wrinkle around her left eye? Maybe her mother was right. Anne pointed at her image in the mirror. "Okay! I'm giving you six more months. If you're not making ends meet by then, you have to move home."

From a chair, she picked up her coat, pulled the old brass key from the pocket, and set it on her wealth and prosperity altar for good luck. Anne rubbed the Buddha's belly, looped rosary beads around its neck, bowed to the Shiva statue, and lit a gardenia votive candle. Its scent wafted throughout the small space.

She had the morning free and knew she should really spend it working but didn't feel much like it. Back on the unmade bed, she picked up a vintage *Life* magazine with Grace Kelly on the cover and began to skim through the black-and-white photos. The ads for slide projectors, encyclopedias, and cars bored her. But Anne especially liked the women's advertisements: Maidenform bras, Ponds Angel Skin, and Clairol hair products. Maybe she'd do a series on those sometime.

She perused page after page until a photo of another blonde beauty caught her eye. Anne paused and stared at the picture. The woman had on a swing coat similar to the one Anne had bought yesterday at the thrift shop. She leaned in closer and peered at something on its collar. Could it be a snowflake pin? It sure looked like it. That would be quite a coincidence.

Next to the woman, a pencil-mustached man held her elbow in one hand and a cigarette in the other. He had a smirk on his face. The pair stood behind a long white Cadillac. This picture might make an amazing photo transfer.

Anne carried the magazine over to her used-but-still-working computer equipment and scanned the photo. Then she flipped the copy upside down on the paper and taped the corners down to make sure they wouldn't move. Her heart zoomed. Starting a new piece always gave her a rush. She held her breath. With a clear marker, she rubbed hard back and forth diagonally over the copy. Transparent liquid seeped dark ink through on fresh paper underneath. Sometimes this process worked, and other times it didn't. With caution, she pulled tape from a corner and peeked.

"Yay!" The woman's head was clearly visible. Anne lifted the entire copy to reveal the couple's eerie gray image. Cadillac fins stuck out fiercely like treacherous sharks'. The transfer looked fabulous, spooky and romantic all at the same time.

To let it dry, she tacked it to the wall across from the daybed. Then she relaxed back on a pillow and studied her work. The picture had a lot to tell. The woman's tight-lipped smile seemed false. Was it a mask covering fear? You could see it in her eyes. They stared straight ahead and maybe blinked at a camera flash that had caught her by surprise. The man's smug expression included one raised eyebrow. He seemed to be squeezing her arm.

Anne returned to the *Life* magazine and read the caption below the photo:

SYLVIA VAN DAM *and fiancé, Ricardo Lorenzo Lopez,*
leaving their engagement party at the St. Francis.

Right here in San Francisco! This woman lived right here, and the coat, pin, and key could really have been hers. Anne looked at the transfer again. Maybe Sylvia had been afraid of her fiancé, with his smoothed-back hair and that menacing sneer. The pair appeared to be opposites, light and dark, sun and moon. Her pale face looked frozen as if she had seen a poltergeist.

Anne's imagination ran wild. She Googled *Sylvia Van Dam.* Several items from the Netherlands popped up in Dutch gobbledygook. To narrow it down, Anne typed in *San Francisco,* and some interesting biographical information appeared. There had been a Van Dam Shipping Company in the late 1930s. A Sylvia Van Dam born in San Francisco in 1942 had lost her parents in a 1955 plane crash. How sad. She would have been just a teen. Anne looked up at the photo transfer. How would Sylvia have gotten along without them? Anne had lost her own father at a young age, but at least she had her mother. The article went on to say that Sylvia's named guardians, Preston and Pauline Palmer, also perished in the accident. Their son Paul Palmer, twenty-four, who had recently joined his father's law firm, became responsible for her.

Anne clicked on an article about a dance at the San Francisco Yacht Club, skimmed the item, and found in the last paragraph a reference to the woman:

> In attendance at the Valentine's dance were club members Jay
> Allen, Patricia Swanson, and Carolyn Grant. Escorted by Paul
> Palmer, Esquire, a stunning Sylvia Van Dam wore pink chiffon.
> Ricardo Lorenzo Lopez, recently from Acapulco, was a standout
> on the dance floor.

Anne checked the *Life* magazine's date: April 10, 1963—two months after that dance. Ricardo Lopez wasn't Sylvia's date that night, but he had been there. Maybe that was when she met him. But how could they have been engaged so quickly? Anne looked at the coat tossed over a chair and studied the snowflake pin.

This was all too surreal and serendipitous. Could Sylvia Van Dam really have owned this coat? These thoughts were crazy. She sat on the daybed and tried to peruse the magazines again. But her mind wouldn't cooperate. She glanced back at the photo transfer and felt goose bumps rise on her arms. Sylvia Van Dam and Ricardo Lorenzo Lopez stared back at her.

4

*S*ylvia smelled the gardenia corsage on her wrist and laid her hand on Paul's shoulder. How sweet of him to remember her favorite blossom. She felt the heat from the bright spotlight bounce off her shoulders as they danced to a crooner singing "Night and Day." Pink and red paper hearts hung over the dance floor, which was packed with club members in formal attire.

A brunette and her date glided near them. The buxom woman's low-cut crimson gown accentuated her cleavage. Sylvia almost wore her own red dress but changed at the last minute, too afraid people might stare. The lace blush-rose piece she chose concealed all.

The song ended and the crowd applauded as the band left to take a break. Paul escorted her to their table, where martinis waited. She took a sip and pursed her lips together to keep her pink lipstick from fading. Then she glanced at Paul. His sky blue eyes stared at her.

"What?" she asked, while pushing a loose bobby pin into her blonde swirl. She had put her hair up into a French twist, thinking it made her look more adult.

Paul put his hand over hers, then quickly pulled it back. "I'm glad you came tonight."

She squinted. "Did Ella put you up to it?"

"No, it was my idea." He leaned back in his chair, debonair in a crew cut and white tux.

"Are you certain?"

"I'm not just your guardian. I'm your friend too."

"Oh?" It had been a long time since she'd thought of him that way. They used to be such great pals. Now though, he didn't visit very often, but he continued to keep track of the trust fund. That was his job, but she felt certain he really did care about her.

She thought back to the first Thanksgiving she could remember: she was six years old, and the Palmer's were over for dinner. Ella had started to serve the pumpkin pie.

Paul sat across the table from her. A big teenager, ten years older—she pretended he was her brother. It would be fun to have one. He didn't have any brothers or sisters either. Paul gently kicked her under the table. She tried to kick back but couldn't reach and slid down on her chair, almost falling to the floor.

Her mother snapped, "Sylvia! Sit up straight or no dessert." She thought her mama was the most beautiful woman in the whole world, with blonde hair piled high on her head and neck sparkling with jewels.

Sylvia pulled herself back up into the chair, and Paul winked.

Her mother grit her teeth. "Get your elbows off the table." Sylvia folded her hands. She wanted to please her mama. Plus she didn't want to miss out on Ella's yummy pie.

Paul's father, Mr. Palmer, The Van Dam Shipping Company's attorney, looked over. Her father frowned at her with caterpillar eyebrows. Then the two men returned to talking about boring business stuff.

Her mother and Mrs. Pauline Palmer, dear friends from the club, returned to their gossip about the other members. After they had eaten the pie, Paul tilted his head toward the open door with a smile.

"Mama, can we be excused?" Sylvia asked.

"May we?"

"Mother, may we please be excused?" She smiled sweetly.

"Yes, dear."

The youngsters ran to the library and sorted through the games in a low cupboard below the bookshelves. "Chess or Scrabble?" Paul held up the games.

"I don't know how to play those."

"I'll teach you." He put the Scrabble box on the hassock and set up the board. "Shake the tiles in this little bag." They started to play, and he helped her spell words. Her favorites that night were "sweet" and "heart."

Over the years, they played Scrabble many times. When she wasn't certain of a word, he'd show her how to look it up in the dictionary. He came up with the most ridiculously long words, so she never understood how she always seemed to beat him. Now, as she looked at him across the table, it dawned on her that all those times, he had probably let her win. Her heart tugged with sadness. Suddenly this past year, he had become so serious. Was it from the strain of his responsibility for her?

"Any shopping trips lately?" he asked.

She fondled her beaded clutch, shook her head, and lied, "No." If she told him about the snowflake pin, it would spoil the evening. She would suffer the consequences later when he saw the bill. Hopefully he wouldn't get too mad at her.

"Good for you." He nodded and drank some of his martini.

She smiled as her stomach tightened with guilt.

At the next table, Patricia Swanson, a plump dowager, wore amethyst teardrop earrings on flabby lobes. Sylvia resisted the urge to lean over and touch the jewels that sparkled in the light. Instead she touched her own pearls then sipped her drink.

The crowd across the room laughed as a tall man, the center of attention, moved his arms overhead as he spoke. They were too far away and she couldn't hear a word, but a glow emanated from him, an electric heat she could almost feel, even from a distance. From the goo-goo eyes and open mouths of the women in tight dresses encircling him, Sylvia could tell they felt it too. Ella would call those girls "floozies." The man looked over at their table and waved at Paul.

"Who's that?" Sylvia asked, trying to sound nonchalant.

Paul frowned. "Ricardo Lorenzo Lopez."

Sylvia nodded. "Right. I've seen his picture in the paper. How do you know him?"

"We played golf once." Paul's voice sounded gruff.

"What's he like?" she asked.

"He's a dipsomaniac."

She giggled. "A what, Mr. Dictionary? That can't be a real word."

"It means he's inclined to excessive drinking."

"You made that up." She turned her gaze back toward Ricardo just as he removed a silver flask from his tuxedo jacket and took a swig. Sylvia and Paul looked at each other and laughed.

"You might be right." She gazed back toward Ricardo. He was so suave. "Tell me more about him." She wanted to know everything.

"He's from Mexico." Paul paused.

"And?"

"And he's a ladies man."

She nodded. "I believe that. He's so dreamy."

Paul's face reddened. "But he's not to be trusted."

"What do you mean?"

The band returned from their break and picked up their instruments.

"I just have a feeling about him," Paul said slowly. Obviously he didn't want to talk about Ricardo anymore.

"What kind of feeling?"

"He's furtive. Like when we played golf. I saw him tap the ball with his foot to get a better shot."

"That's not much." She took another sip of her martini.

The dance floor began to fill up again, and Ricardo pulled a curvy redhead toward him in a tight embrace.

Paul lowered his voice. "I've also heard rumors."

"Like what?" Sylvia whispered, leaning toward him.

He looked across the room, then back at her. "It is just hearsay." He paused.

"What?" She grabbed his elbow.

"It's too black." He shook his head. "I don't want to scare you. Anyway, it can't be true."

She wished Paul would spill all, but he was not the kind to gossip. In fact, she'd never heard him say a bad word about anyone. "You can tell me."

"Let's dance." He stood and put his hands on the back of her chair.

"Excuse me, Mr. Palmer." The maître d' set a long-corded telephone on their table. "You have a phone call."

Paul sat, took the receiver, and mouthed, *Sorry*, to Sylvia. He listened for a few minutes while she watched Ricardo twirl the redhead and dip her down into his arms.

"I see. I'll be right there." Paul hung up the phone and stood. "We've got to go."

"Why?" She wanted to stay and watch Ricardo all night.

"Work emergency." Paul stood.

"Can't I even finish my drink?" She tried not to whine.

"Got to spring someone from the slammer," he said in a deep voice.

Sylvia scrunched up her lips to hold back a laugh. "You don't even do that kind of law."

"Actually it's an estate client in some hot water."

"Can't I stay?"

"By yourself?" His eyes grew wide.

"I'm enjoying the music." She swayed with the rhythm.

He looked around the room. "I don't know."

"Please?" She clasped her hands toward him. "Milo can pick me up."

Paul shrugged. "Well, I don't see why not. I'll notify Milo."

"Thanks. Call me tomorrow." She leaned her cheek toward him for a kiss, watched until he was gone, pulled a cigarette from her clutch, and lit up just like she had practiced.

She sat alone smoking her Lucky Strike, not feeling very lucky. She had only set eyes on Ricardo less than an hour ago, and her heart felt as if it might explode with excitement. Was this what they meant by love at first sight? Even if it were, he wouldn't ever be interested in someone plain like her. In the society columns, he was described as "dashing" this and "playboy" that. She took a drag of the Lucky Strike, curled her lips, and blew smoke out through her nostrils like she'd seen actresses do in the movies.

Ricardo stared across the dance floor. Her throat felt dry. With a jittery hand, she put the martini to her lips and swallowed a mouthful. She should have gone with Paul. Hands shaking, she snubbed out her cigarette and gripped the pearls around her neck. As Ricardo drew closer, his dark good looks became more pro-nounced. His caramel-colored skin was offset by light brown eyes that penetrated hers. A mysterious crescent-shaped scar adorned his right cheek.

Even though her legs felt like Jell-O, somehow she found the power to stand and turned to escape. But he grasped her and brushed his lips over her hand, the thin mustache tickling her smooth skin.

"*Muy bonita*," he said with one raised eyebrow.

Certain her face was as red as the pimento of her martini's

olive, she looked down, pulled her hand back, and played with the pearls again. "*Gracias*," she whispered, having studied a little Spanish in school.

"Would you care to dance?" His accent was thick, exotic.

She peeked at him and stammered, "Not tonight." The band was playing "Sincerely," a slow romantic number, and the thought of him holding her close made her feel lightheaded.

"*Lo siento.*" He shrugged and sauntered away.

Sylvia sat back down and watched as he took the redhead by the hand and led her to the dance floor again, holding her close. Sylvia wished she had the courage to dance with him like that. To be cradled in his arms would be thrilling.

The band switched rhythms to a rousing rumba version of "Rock Around the Clock," the marimba playing the melody. Ricardo swayed with one hand on his hip and the other out-stretched. The redhead wiggled her body, and three more women joined in to dance around Ricardo. He tossed his jacket over a nearby chair, exposing a slim waist nuzzled by a red cummerbund. The satin shone like garnets, and Sylvia wanted to rub her hands flat along its slick surface. She nibbled her martini olive and sucked juices from the toothpick.

Ricardo caught her eye and flirted back with a wry smile. She turned her head. The bandleader's ruffled sleeves and maracas were shaking wildly and so were the dancers' hips. Sylvia rolled her eyes. The tawdry women giggled as Ricardo swiveled to the music's rhythm. *Who does he think he is, Elvis?*

The crowd hooted and clapped. Sylvia frowned, angry and disgusted, with him for being such a show-off and at herself for thinking he was sexy. She downed the rest of her drink, grabbed her white fox fur, and rushed out into the night.

The foggy air seeped over her warm body, cooling it. Milo opened the Rolls door for her, and she slid inside.

"Have fun?" He turned on the ignition and smiled at her in the rearview mirror.

"Guess so." She didn't want to talk about it. The Rolls climbed into the shrouded hills that matched her gloom. A crescent moon, like Ricardo's scar, hung barely visible in the misty sky. She pulled off her pearls and clutched them. Then she closed her eyes and tried to banish Ricardo from her brain.

Once home, she mixed a Kahlúa and cream and carried it up to bed. She sipped it slowly, hoping it would calm her. But instead she grew hot, threw off the covers, and kept thinking of him. His dark slick-backed hair, shiny waist, and rhythmic dancing feet swirled in her mind.

5

The next morning, Anne had another message from her mom. "I told Tootie and Pootie you're probably moving home, and they're so excited!" When Anne was a baby and had started to talk, she couldn't pronounce *Trudy*, her father's sister's name, so she had called her "Aunt Tootie" instead, and the name stuck. A year later, Tootie gave birth to Prudence, and everyone called her "Pootie" for consistency.

Anne remembered her visit home last summer. As soon as she stepped off the plane at Saginaw Airport into the dreadful humidity, she felt like she'd landed on another planet. The sky was a pale blue, with not a cloud.

Aunt Tootie, cousin Pootie, and her mom held up signs that read, "Welcome Home, Artist." Despite the heat, Anne enthusiastically hugged each in turn. In the parking lot, Pootie and Anne climbed in the backseat of the green Ford Fairlane, and her mom pulled out for the hour-and-a-half drive north.

"Sure you don't wanna stop at the mall while we're down here?" Pootie teased.

"Very funny." Anne shoved her cousin's arm. Most girls, while growing up, tired of the Oscoda Walmart, would beg their parents to take them down to the Penney's or Target in the big city. But not

Anne; she would only wear clothes she found at Second Chances Thrift Shop on Main. No wonder no one had ever asked her to prom.

Heading toward the highway, they drove by an empty industrial park and a neighborhood that had every other house boarded up.

Tootie, riding shotgun, asked, "Sold any art lately?"

Anne shook her head. "I hear you're having a drought."

"Did you know Jimmy Johnson moved back to Oscoda?" Her mom glanced at Anne in the rearview mirror.

"Who's he?"

"You know, Jennifer Collin's cousin by marriage. He had moved to Florida but now says 'There's no place like home.' Brought a new wife with him. She's smitten with the mitten now too." Her mom held up her hand to show the shape of Michigan.

The women continued to gab nonstop. They passed the Au Gres Marina and Campground, where Anne lost her virginity to Danny Murphy from college after consuming a box of wine. A smooth Lake Huron appeared on the right, and the rhythm of the car made Anne drowsy. "Are we there yet?" She yawned and nodded off.

"Wake up!" Pootie yelled, and she shoved Anne's arm. She opened her eyes just in time to see a great blue heron stretch out its question mark-shaped neck as it flew overhead. The two girls used to sit on the dock for hours just hoping for a glimpse of one.

"Look, there's even a Mexico restaurant in Tawas now," her mom pointed out.

"Cuatrooo Amigooos," Trudy read. "What's that mean?"

Anne grinned. "Four friends."

Soon they passed Tootie and Pootie's house, and then, two doors down, the car pulled into the drive of the yellow house, the only one on the street not white. A sign in front on the browned-out lawn read, *Avon's Skin-So-Soft Sold Here.* The hydrangeas drooped, and even the maple tree in front of Anne's gable window looked thirsty.

"Supper in half an hour," her mother called as Tootie followed her inside, the screen door slamming behind them. Anne put down her duffel bag and sat on the porch swing.

"Wanna go fish off the pier?" Pootie asked.

"It's too hot." Anne picked up an Avon brochure and used it as a fan.

"Let's play rummy then." Pootie sat across from her cousin and dealt the cards. "Who are you seeing?"

"A guy named Karl. He runs a family hardware store. How about you?"

"Nope, nobody," Pootie sighed.

Anne felt sorry for her cousin. She'd never had a boyfriend.

After a while, Aunt Tootie yelled from the kitchen, "Come and get it, or we'll feed it to the hogs!"

Plates filled with steak, potatoes, and corn on the cob were set up on TV trays in the living room. Anne ate her corn and picked at the mashed potatoes, avoiding the meat. She didn't want to remind them she didn't eat meat because she knew they would tease her.

They watched an episode of Anne's least favorite show, *The Bachelor*, until a Brian's Heating and Air Conditioning ad cut in. It was the same cheesy ad that had run on television for years but had been reshot with Brian, instead of his father, Brian Senior. Brian's familiar deep voice resonated: "One hundred degrees and your air conditioner broke down? Don't start cryin'. Just call Brian." He looked even better now than the last time she had seen him five years before—his smile wide and his arm muscles expanded under the company T-shirt. Seeing him up on the screen, Anne felt the same tough yearning she had in high school. Not even Pootie had known how she had felt about him.

"Boy, that Brian is such a hunk!" Pootie cried.

Anne nodded. "Is he married yet?" She squinted to see if he had on a ring.

"No." Aunt Tootie shook her head.

"Maybe he's gay."

"Mother!" Anne had never gotten those vibes from him.

Her mother defended herself. "I heard it directly from his own mother. Gwen Youngman, their neighbor, said that his mother said that she's frustrated because he never takes anyone out."

"Maybe he's just shy." Pootie picked up an Avon sample, squirted out some lotion, and rubbed it on her thin legs.

Aunt Tootie smiled at her daughter. "Yes. He might be a late bloomer like somebody else we know."

"He did take Jessica Jones to senior prom." Anne had been heartbroken he hadn't asked her. She had thought maybe he would because he always said hello to her in the hallway when passing by.

"Only because she called him." Pootie handed the lotion to her cousin.

Anne hadn't heard that. "If he were gay, he would have moved out of town by now." She dabbed some lotion in her hand and sniffed the orange scent.

Anne's mom shook her head. "Oh no. He needs to take over the family business."

Yes, no known gays in Oscoda. Unlike San Francisco, Oscoda was all white. No ethnic flavors here, no Latinos or Chinese. Except maybe Sue Ellen Eigner—she always bragged about being a quarter Native American. Which might have been true, with her shiny dark hair and eyes.

"Let's go home, Pootie. I have to get up early for the parade." Aunt Tootie leaned over and kissed the top of Anne's head. "It's great to have you here."

Anne and her mother cleaned up the dinner mess and then climbed the stairs to their own rooms. Even though it was nine o'clock, it wasn't quite dark yet, and Anne, still on California time, found it impossible to sleep. She began to clean out a junk drawer and picked up the "magic wand" Aunt Tootie had given her for her fifth birthday. Anne ran her fingers over the plastic star. She had loved that wand and had used it to cast spells—for it to stop raining so she could go out to play, for Nana's cough to go away (it worked for awhile), and for Daddy to come back from Iraq. He did come back, but in a wooden box with the red, white, and blue flag draped over it. God must not have understood her magic prayers, and from then on, she tried hard not to wish for anything too much, or it might come true but in the wrong way.

As the casket was lowered into the ground at the cemetery, her mother had held her so tight that Anne could barely breathe. Tootie sobbed also, having lost her own brother, and she told Anne, "Your Daddy's in a better place now." But Anne had known the truth. He was in the box underground in the dirt. How could that be a better place?

She now waved the wand and wished to make enough money to be able to stay in California. She loved her family and home but never felt as if she quite belonged.

The next morning, Pootie called upstairs, "Ready?" No one in Oscoda ever locked their doors.

"In a minute." Anne had barely slept. An invisible mosquito, as loud as a 747, had woken her in the middle of the night. She had jumped on the bed and swatted at it for half an hour. When she had finally fallen back to sleep, a thunder-and-lightning storm had woken her. She had curled up and listened to the much-needed rain pound on the roof.

She grabbed a blue floppy hat, stepped onto the porch, and let the screen door slam behind her. Sweat already dribbled down her back, adhering her white eyelet sundress to her body.

"Where's the red?" Pootie frowned. Her outfit, a traditional

Fourth of July affair with red-and-white striped T-shirt and denim short shorts fit her lithe body perfectly. She had also stuck a miniature American flag into her ponytail.

"My lipstick, see!" Anne puckered her lips and fish-kissed them at her cousin.

Pootie rolled her eyes. "Come on! Let's hurry. We don't want to miss it."

They walked the two blocks to Main, where kids sat on curbs in front of their parents and oldsters relaxed in folding chairs. The cousins pushed their way to a place in the shade across from the post office right before the city police and county sheriffs turned on their sirens and led the parade. Everyone stood and put their hands on their hearts as the American flag passed along with the Oscoda Marching Band. The Knights of Columbus in capes and plumed hats stood erect in the back of a truck, and elderly VFW men in their medal-covered uniforms waved.

When Brian strutted toward her, beside the Air Conditioning and Heating van, Anne's heart felt like one of the footballs he had punted over the goalpost in high school.

"Annie," he yelled, lobbing a Tootsie Roll at her. She fumbled it then bent over to pick it up, and her hat fell off, which exposed her sweaty, squished hair. As fast as possible, she put the hat back on and looked up in time to see him pass with a smile.

"There they are!" Pootie howled at the flatbed truck with the banner that read: *Oscoda Garden Club Digs You!*

"Hey, girls!" Anne's mom called, waving her shovel. "Groovy, huh?"

The eight women riding the flatbed all wore bellbottom jumpsuits and wigs adorned with daisies and were dancing the hitchhiker.

"They must be hot in those huge wigs," a woman behind Anne said.

As the fire trucks closed off the end of the parade, Pootie asked, "Ice cream?"

"You know I'll never say no to that." Anne smiled, and they waddled in the heat down Main to Oscoda Cones.

"I'll have a scoop of dark chocolate and another of chocolate mint." Anne dabbed her damp chest with a napkin and watched the attendant fill the giant-sized waffle-cone.

Skinny Pootie ordered a lime sherbet in a cup. They stepped out of the shop as the ice cream dripped down Anne's hand. She licked at it, but the top scoop popped off and fell into her cleavage. "Oh my God!"

"That should cool you off," Pootie laughed.

"Hi, Annie." Brian stood before her, his mischievous smile as big as Lake Huron.

Anne reached out to shake his hand but then pulled the sticky mess back. She tossed the rest of the cone in a trashcan. "Excuse me," she said, and she raced back into the ice cream shop and grabbed a pile of napkins. Through the window, she could see Brian fix the flag in Pootie's hair. Anne bit her lip to hold back tears. She wanted to be happy that someone was paying attention to her cousin, but did it have to be Brian?

Now, thinking back to that day made Anne more determined than ever to stay in San Francisco. She decided her next step would be to put herself out there and do some networking.

6

$\mathcal{T}$he next afternoon, Anne forced herself to attend the opening at Gallery Noir on Sutter Street. She shook her umbrella, left it at the door, and followed the crowd inside the bright space, where tony dressers chatted and nibbled appetizers around belly-bars.

San Francisco Color and Light—Anne read the poster description and began to walk the perimeter of the space. Large paintings in a variety of hues from orange to blue hung on the walls: the Golden Gate, Coit Tower, cable cars, etc. She stood in front of the Chinatown painting for a few moments.

A handsome man in a dark suit stepped next to her and smiled.

"Hi, I'm Anne McFarland." She reached out her hand. He shook it, then glanced at her feet and hurried away. In the velvet coat she thought no one would notice her sweatpants and sneakers. She hated to dress up and couldn't wear heels walking the city's hills.

Anne scanned the crowd again. Across the room in an elegant silk tunic, she spotted Lila, the artist, as she touched her long straight hair woven with feathers. Fortunately, it didn't look like Joan, from their creative support group, had arrived yet. Anne wandered over to Lila and waited her turn for a hug. "How sweet of you to come. I've missed you at group."

"I know. Been busy." Anne had quit going not because of the dark church basement or even the $10 fee but because of Joan.

At one meeting, Anne had excitedly shared about selling three pieces at a farmers' market, but Joan had responded, "Don't tell anyone; no one will ever take your work seriously." Another time, Anne had brought up that she had a gallery offer to display her Mogul series for only a $100 monthly fee. "That's outrageous!" Joan had cried. "Why would they be motivated to sell your work if you are paying their rent?"

The other members had nodded in agreement, and Lila had said, "She's right. You should never have to pay to show your work." The group seemed to be able to tell her what not to do but never shared what to do in order to make it.

Raymond Block, the gallery owner, stepped in front of Anne. "Lila, darling! Simply marvelous." He kissed both her cheeks.

"Thank you. This is my dear friend, A . . . A . . ."

"Anne McFarland." Anne held out her hand to him. "Don't you remember? I showed you my Mogul series a year ago."

Anne itched to reach out and straighten his Andy Warhol-esque silver-gray wig that was slightly askew. He adjusted his thick glasses illuminating owlish eyes as he shook his head, grabbed Lila's elbow, and led her away. "You must meet Stephan and Kiki Sodenburg, my biggest clients. They are simply captivated by your work."

Feeling as small as a Michigan gnat, Anne watched Lila greet the Sodenburgs. Kiki smoothed down her Cleopatra hair while Stephan shook Lila's hand. Stout with salt-and-pepper gray hair, he wore a blue sports coat and a red polka-dotted ascot at his neck.

Anne decided to quickly get a bite to eat and leave. "Fancy some champagne?" A woman with short spiked hair held up a glass.

Anne accepted it and took a sip.

"How did you hear about our exhibition?" The woman had a lovely British accent.

"I know Lila."

"Are you an artist too?"

Anne filled a plate with shrimp, stuffed mushrooms, and cheese and said, "Mostly collage and mixed media."

"Wicked! Why don't you tote some in here for us to see?"

"I have. Mr. Block didn't seem to like my style."

"Try again." The woman smiled at her.

"Thanks." Anne doubted she would. Just as she nibbled a shrimp, Joan and some other members of the group walked in. Anne escaped into the restroom. Sitting in a stall, she stuffed a roll in her pocket with a little piece of cheese for tomorrow's breakfast and gobbled the rest down. Then she slipped out of the gallery through a back door.

Hiking up toward her apartment, she heard a cable car clang beside her and considered taking it the rest of the way. But she decided to walk instead—it was a good butt workout anyway. With these hills, she never needed to join a gym. It started to rain, but she had left her umbrella at the gallery.

"Don't you look fancy?" A squeaky voice called.

Anne looked down at the homeless woman huddled in the doorway with a sleeping bag around her shoulders. "No, you're the fancy one, Mata Hari."

The woman wore a gold turban and long black gloves. Last week, on Anne's way back from a Halloween party, she had felt sorry for the shivering woman and bestowed her the dramatic costume pieces.

"Why aren't you at the shelter?" Anne asked.

"I prefer the fresh air." The woman's weather-beaten face made it hard to tell exactly how old she was. Perhaps in better days, with those large eyes, she had been as beautiful as Garbo.

"Did you eat there at least?"

"They ran out." Mata shrugged.

"Too bad." Anne's heart tightened.

Mata smiled a jack-o-lantern missing-tooth smile and ran her tongue over chapped lips.

From her pocket Anne pulled the roll with cheese and handed them to Mata. "Here you go. Bon appétit."

Back at her apartment, she took the key from her coat pocket and put it on the altar. It sure hadn't brought her any luck tonight.

She checked her messages. "Hi, babe. Can't make it now. Let's get together tomorrow instead." This wasn't the first time Karl had postponed a date. She didn't want to see him anyway! She really needed to talk to him though. She curled up on the daybed and gazed at the photo transfer tacked to the wall. Sylvia's dramatic face looked down at her.

Anne opened the newspaper and skimmed an article about Obama's plan to get the troops out of Afghanistan and another about the homeless population in San Francisco. She then read an interesting piece about the Cliff House's disasters: fires, dynamite explosions, and even shipwrecks. It had undergone several transformations over the years. Karl had taken her to brunch there for their six-month anniversary, and the view was to die for. It had been a society hangout in its heyday; she thought she had a postcard of it somewhere in her collection.

She lugged the basket of cards from under the coffee table and plopped it in front of her. The cards were old and new, from vintage shops or sent by friends. She flipped through the pile: the Empire State Building, the Painted Desert, Monument Valley. Then there it was. She ran her hand over the Cliff House's photo and caught a whiff of the sea. She could have sworn it was the same smell the key had given off the other day! She rubbed the card once more and then again, but no smells were emitted.

She studied the postcard; the Cliff House's wood-and-brick building dangled over a white-capped ocean, the sort of place Sylvia Van Dam might have frequented.

Anne wondered why she had become so intrigued by her. She turned over the postcard and read the date: March 1963. A scribbled cursive note read, *Great view. You would like the seals.* It was signed by R. Anne set it on the coffee table and planned to use it for another collage soon.

7

$\mathscr{R}$ icardo and Sylvia gazed through the Cliff House's picture window and watched lazy seals sunbathe on rocks beyond. A thick fog had burned off to make way for a sparkling Pacific with a spectacular view down the coast. Waves crashed on the boulders below. Their date had been for lunch, but he hadn't even picked her up until half past one, so the crowd had thinned out.

With a glint in his light brown eyes, Ricardo asked, "Have you ever had a margarita?"

Sylvia shook her head and stared at him, unable to breathe, completely in awe to be on a date with Ricardo Lorenzo Lopez. Since the Valentine's dance, she hadn't been able to think of anything but him. So a week later when he called, she actually had the power to accept his invitation.

She had asked, "How did you get my number?"

And he had replied, "I have my ways."

Ever since that call, she'd been nervous and unable to sleep, weighing the pros of cons of going out with him. She knew Paul wouldn't approve but thought maybe Ella would just be glad she had accepted a date. Sylvia had guessed wrong.

Ella's face glowered when she opened the door and saw Ricardo standing there in his dark sports coat. "Deliveries in back," she had said.

He stuck out his hand. "*Hola*, I'm Ricardo Lorenzo Lopez."

"Ella Elizabeth Connelly Curtis." She accepted his hand and pumped it several times. Sylvia had never been so embarrassed but didn't know if it was for Ella or Ricardo.

Now Sylvia didn't care what anyone thought and didn't even want to look at the coastal view. She just wished to stare at this man. He was so unlike anyone she'd ever met. How God could make one man so handsome, tall, dark, and . . .

"That's what we drink in Acapulco. Two margaritas with salt, *por favor*." He snapped his fingers at a passing waiter.

Sylvia flinched at Ricardo's rudeness but realized it must have been a Mexican custom, like a flamenco dancer snapping castanets. She wanted to know more about his exotic customs but was too shy to ask.

She crossed her legs under the small table, and their knees bumped. Her face grew hot. She pulled her long legs back and smoothed down her dress. It was one of her favorites, a sophisticated look—a form-fitted bodice with a flared skirt in a red-rose print.

With shaky hands, she opened her purse, extracted a pack of Lucky Strikes, and tapped out a cigarette. She leaned over for him to light it but quickly sat up straight when she realized he was looking at her cleavage. It made her tingle inside to know he thought of her in that way.

"I'm surprised you came with me." He took the cigarette from her mouth, put it into his own and lit it, then handed it back to her.

She tried not to think about his sexy lips touching something going into her own mouth and inhaled her Lucky. "Really? Why?"

He shrugged. "Isn't Paul Palmer *tu novio?*"

She adored it when he spoke Spanish even if she didn't understand all the words. "My what?"

"Your sweetheart." Teasing, Ricardo puckered his lips at her and made a smacking sound.

She laughed. "No, he's just a family friend."

"I saw you dance with him at the club. And the way he looked at you?" Ricardo raised an eyebrow.

"We're just friends."

"You sure?"

Sylvia nodded and watched another couple being escorted to a nearby table by the hostess. Her high bouffant reminded Sylvia of her mother's, and she ran a hand up the back of her own hairdo. She returned her attention back to Ricardo. "I was stunned when you called."

"*Por qué?*"

"Heard you have a girlfriend in Acapulco." Sylvia puffed her cigarette and blew smoke to the side, trying to appear nonchalant.

"I did. Not anymore." He shook his head, tapped a cigarette out of her pack, and lit it.

"What happened?"

"*Que lástima,*" he said with a passing shadow on his face.

Sylvia felt sorry for him.

"She was too young. Her parents told me to wait a few years."

"Are you going to?"

"I thought maybe." He paused, leaned forward, and took her hand. "Then I saw you."

She pulled her hand back from his electric heat and looked down, not able to return his gaze. The ring on his little finger, a thin gold band with a diamond chip, caught her eye. She wanted to pinch the stone and trace her fingers around it. Instead she puffed her cigarette and stubbed it out in the ashtray.

The waiter began to pick up after the lunch crowd, and plates clattered and glasses clinked.

"Sylvia, how long have you lived in San Francisco?"

"My whole life."

"I've heard your parents are dead." He flicked ashes into the ashtray.

"Yes, several years ago." She felt a knot in the pit of her stomach. That was the last thing she wanted to talk about.

"Do you live in that big house all alone?"

She shook her head. "No, Ella and her husband, Milo, are there with me."

He paused. "And who takes care of all the details?"

She frowned, confused.

He rubbed two fingers together.

"You mean with the bank?"

He nodded. "Who makes sure you have enough?"

This must be another Mexican custom. She was raised never to talk about death or money in polite company. "Paul Palmer."

"Really?"

She nodded. "His firm manages my parents' estate." Again she tried to change the subject. "Why did you move to San Francisco?"

Ricardo looked out at the ocean. "Business."

"What business are you in?"

He hesitated then said, "Import. Export."

"Interesting. What type?"

His eyes shifted. "Um, materials."

"Oh, materials. Like fabric?"

"*Si.*" He nodded and shrugged.

Sylvia visualized him talking to prospective clients with colorful handwoven Mexican textiles draped over his arm. "I bet you're very successful."

"*Como no!*" He shrugged again.

Sylvia gazed at him and wished he'd tell her more. But he remained silent. The waiter set the drinks on the table.

"We'll each have the sole." He pointed to the menu and handed it to the waiter.

"Certainly." He nodded and left.

Sylvia peeled off her gloves, tasted the margarita, and lightly smacked her lips. "Mmm. Sweet. Like lemonade."

Ricardo took a gulp. "*Bueno. Sí.*" He stared at her, and there was a lull in the conversation.

Ella had told her to flirt and act interested if you wanted a man to like you. Sylvia pointed to Seal Rock. "Look, he has a mustache just like you!"

They watched a seal slide into the water. Ricardo smoothed his thin mustache then cracked a smile. The sun shone through the plate glass window accentuating the slight scar, just a nick on his cheek, a curved tiny bolt of lightning. She wanted to caress it and ask how he got it, but instead she toyed with the pearls around her neck and peered at the jagged boulders below.

"It's sure a long way down."

"You should see the Acapulco cliffs. They're much taller than this. I dive there."

"What?" Her eyes widened.

"Cliff diving. My friend dared me to jump into the narrow cove." Ricardo looked deep into her eyes. "Every time before diving, my heart beats really hard." He tapped a fist on his chest several times in rhythm, "*Bum, bum. Bum, bum. Bum, bum.*"

She imagined his lean body standing erect on the cliff in a tight bathing suit, beads of water glistening on his tanned skin like glitter, wet hair shiny in the sun. She took a quick sip of her drink and gulped it down.

Ricardo continued, "I look down and wait for the wave to come in. If I don't dive at just the right moment . . . " He paused and looked at her with one eyebrow raised.

Sylvia held her breath.

"Then I straighten up with my arms together above my head, push off, pointing my toes." He arched his back. "Aim out away from the cliff, close my eyes, and pretend I'm flying. Hitting the water always surprises me. I think I might stay in the air forever."

She imagined his straight nimble body gliding into a choppy sea. "How did you ever have the courage?"

"*Muy fácil.*" He shrugged.

Sylvia licked salt off the rim of her glass.

"You missed something." He leaned over and brushed her upper lip.

"Oh!"

"It's *mole*," he said in a soft voice.

She pushed his hand away. "That's not a mole. It's my beauty mark!" At least that's what Ella always called it.

"*Sí*, it's true. You are very beautiful." He licked his lips.

She couldn't believe he had called her "beautiful."

"Mexican *mole* is a special kind of chocolate." He raised an eyebrow. "I'd like to kiss that tiny chocolate drop right off you."

She swallowed and tried to smile. It would feel wonderful to have him do that. Those lips would be warm against hers.

His eyes drifted behind her. She turned around to follow his gaze and saw two men being seated at a nearby table.

Ricardo grabbed her arm and whispered, "Don't look."

She pulled back. "What's wrong?"

He squinted at the window, then pulled sunglasses from his top pocket and slipped them on. "It's too bright. Aren't you hot?"

"I'm fine."

The men behind her ordered scotch on the rocks.

Ricardo's gaze moved behind her again.

"Do you know them?" she asked.

"Quiet." He looked down and licked salt from the edge of his glass. "No."

She wanted to draw his attention back to her. "You missed something too." She reached over and fingered his mustache. Salt sprinkled onto his black sport coat like snow.

He pulled back, brushed it off, and scowled. "*Ay, déjame!* You messed up my shirt."

"Sorry." She cringed with embarrassment.

His eyes sailed to the table behind her again. "I'll need to have it cleaned." Even though he looked immaculate, he gazed down and continued to brush it off.

Sylvia sipped her margarita. The ice had melted, and the salt was gone. The tangy taste had disappeared into a tepid slush.

Ricardo waved the waiter over. "Move us. The sun's too hot."

"Sorry, Sir. We're setting up for dinner. I could lower the shade for you."

"Never mind! *La cuenta, por favor.*" Ricardo stood and pulled out her chair. "Let's go."

"But we haven't even eaten."

He glanced at his watch. "Forgot. I need to be somewhere." With a scowl he threw money on the table, rushed her to his white Cadillac, settled her into the passenger seat, and slammed the door. Confused at his mood change, she sat there in a quandary. He jumped in beside her, kissed the Madonna hanging from his rearview mirror, revved the motor, and raced off. Sylvia held on tight to the dashboard. He wheeled fast around corners and kept looking out the back window as if they were being chased.

She yelled, "Slow down." But he didn't. Exciting and terrifying at the same time, her stomach flip-flopped as they rode up and down over the hills like on a roller coaster. Milo never drove that fast. What had come over Ricardo?

He screeched into the circular drive, came to a halt, and parked. As they walked up the stairs, she tried to find her balance from the dizzy ride, and he caught her arm. At the door, he leaned toward her for a kiss.

She pushed him away and pretended to be angry. "Why did you drive like such a maniac?" He tried to kiss her again, but she turned her head and backed through the door. "You are so wild." She closed the door and caught her breath. If he called, would she dare go out with him again?

8

——

*Y*ou shaved off your beard!" For the first time, Anne could see Karl's rugged face complete with cleft chin and steep cheekbones.

He turned his head to the side. A curly ponytail still bounced to his shoulders. "Handsome, right?"

The heat of his brown eyes made her want to either suffocate or kiss him. "You're a hunk, a hunk of burning love!" She hugged him and inhaled his familiar cinnamon scent, then pulled away. They needed to talk, and she didn't want to get distracted.

He put a bottle of wine on the counter and pulled her onto the daybed. She admired his freshly shaven face again, couldn't resist any longer, and put her palms flat on his cheeks. The texture felt smooth as tumbled rock. She wanted to stay this way all night, just kissing his clean-shaven face, but she needed to resist so in a husky voice said, "Let's go."

"What's the rush?" He wrapped his arms around her.

"I want to talk."

"Later." He kissed her again.

"Is this just a bootie call?"

"Maybe." He laughed and nuzzled her breasts.

With a smile she thought of the first time they were together and he dubbed them "thee cantaloupes."

Letting go, he surveyed the messy apartment. "It's beginning to look like *Hoarders* in here."

"Sorry." She picked up some newspapers from off the floor and put them on the coffee table. "If you don't like it here, then why don't you have me come over to your house?"

"I've told you before. Alameda is too far away, and besides, I'm over here for work anyway." He pointed to a new shelf she'd recently put up. "What's all that junk?"

She straightened a ceramic kitty tilted on its side. "It's not junk. These are found objects for my art. Check this out, though." Anne grabbed her coat from the daybed, slipped it on, and spun around. "Only cost me seventy bucks."

He grimaced. "A thrift-shop buy? Why don't you ever wear that Ralph Lauren I bought you?"

"I'm saving it for a special occasion." Even though it cost him a mint, she couldn't bring herself to wear something so preppy. She wouldn't mention that the black lace blouse she wore now was from a resale shop too.

She picked up the key from her altar. "Look what was in the coat's pocket!"

He read the label, "Sea Cliff."

"Yes, I think Sylvia lived there."

He frowned. "Who's Sylvia?"

"The woman who owned the coat."

"What? How do you know? I thought you got it at a thrift shop."

"I found a picture of her wearing it in a *Life* magazine. Here—Sylvia Van Dam." She showed him the magazine article.

He studied the photo with a confused look on his face.

Anne held up the coat and pointed at the snowflake pin in the photo. "Look, it even has a pin on it like this one."

"You're kidding?"

"Don't you think it's more than a coincidence?"

He smirked. "It's not even a coincidence. It's ludicrous."

"I made a photo transfer of it. Look how cool it turned out."

He inspected the piece tacked to the wall and fingered his cleft chin. "Quite the hobby you've got, babe."

"It's not just a hobby." Why couldn't he be more supportive? After all, when they first met, she was selling her work at the farmers' market, and he really seemed to like it.

"Well, it's not a real job."

She took the key from him. "Maybe I'll try and find Sea Cliff. I've done some Internet searching about Sylvia. She was a wealthy heiress who lived here in the early sixties."

He nodded, but his eyes glazed over. "I'm glad you've found something to keep you busy."

"I'm starved." She moved toward the door. "How about we go to that new café on Polk?"

"Yelp said it was a dump." He checked his watch. "Let's call downstairs and order a pizza." His gaze landed on her kitchen table strewn with art materials. "I guess we'll need to eat down there."

She loved pizza, and maybe there would be leftovers. "I'll straighten up, and we can even move the table out onto the deck."

Karl called for the pizza. Anne cleared off the table and they carried it through the little door out onto the rooftop deck. He hefted out two chairs while she opened the rosé bottle he'd brought and then poured two glasses and put them on the table. Just then the sun began to go down, lighting up the sky.

They heard Val begin his evening warm-ups in the apartment below. "Oh what a lo-o-vely day."

Anne pointed to the scaffolding that covered a Victorian townhouse across the street. All over San Francisco, these Painted Ladies were being renovated. She wondered which pastel hues would be used on this one: pink, peach, lilac, sky blue, or lime green.

"At least something in this neighborhood is getting fixed up." Karl frowned at the peeling paint on her building and the buckling shingle rooftop. "If I owned this property, I could do wonders with it."

She'd heard this before and nodded, composing the right questions she needed to ask about their future together. She leaned across the table and took his hands. "We've been together almost a year now."

He nodded. "Yes. Pretty cool, huh?"

"Where do you think this is going?"

He squinted. "Going?"

Her throat felt dry, and she finally got the question out. "Do you ever see us in a committed relationship?"

"We are in a committed relationship. I'm committed to really wanting you." He leaned forward and put his hands on her shoulders.

"That's not what I meant."

Karl pulled his hands away.

A chill set in under the darkening sky, and she snuggled into her coat and said softly, "I know it wasn't love at first sight, at least not for you, but I was sure by now you loved me."

"It's not that I don't love you. There's more to it than that."

"What?"

"It's hard to explain."

"Try."

Karl sipped his wine. "Since I filed for divorce . . ."

Anne sat up straight and raised her voice. "What divorce?"

"I separated about a year ago. About the same time I met you."

She felt as if she couldn't breathe. "You're married! I've been sleeping with a married man all this time?"

"It's not like that at all."

"Why didn't you tell me?"

Karl scowled. "I did."

She shook her head. "No, you didn't."

"You must not have ever asked."

"Then you misled me." She tried to keep her voice down. "What else haven't you told me? That you have five kids?"

"Only one, Luke, a son." Karl looked away.

She stared at him with her mouth open. "How old is he?"

"One."

"One?" He would have been born right around the time they met. She sat back and squinted at him. If she had that magic wand with her, she'd wish him to disappear right now.

"How often do you see him?"

"Every day."

"How far away does he live from you?"

Karl paused. "They still live with me."

"What?" Anne jumped up, her chair dropping on the ground. Now it all made sense: the constant checking of his phone, the afternoon quickies, and when he did spend the night, he'd always get up at 3:00 AM to leave "for work." And when she had asked him why a hardware store would need him there that early, he always had some excuse: inventory, delivery, or a big sale.

Karl continued. "She can't afford to move out yet."

"You've been sleeping together all this time?"

"Of course not! She's been sleeping in Luke's room."

"You're kidding." With his sex drive, she didn't believe him.

"It's true. I swear. As soon as the divorce is final, she will move out. Then you can move in with me, and we can start to plan our wedding. Luke can stay with us on weekends."

"Quite a proposal!" She had always imagined a romantic evening with candlelight and maybe even violins. "You need to leave."

"You're just being silly." He reached for her hand.

She pulled it away. "Go now."

"Fine. But you're making a big deal out of nothing." He tried to kiss her on the head. "I'll call you tomorrow after you calm down." He closed the door and headed down the stairs just as the door buzzed again.

She pushed the button. "Yes?"

"Pizza!"

She let the delivery guy in, then pulled out some money to pay him but he said it had already been taken care of. At least Karl had done something good! She carried the box outside, set it on the table and opened it. Pepperoni covered the entire pizza. Darn it! She would just have to pick the stinky stuff off. As she went to get another glass of wine she grew angrier and angrier. How could he not even remember that she didn't eat meat? She raced back to the roof, kicked the table, and the pizza pieces flew upside-down and fell onto the tarpapered roof beside her. She picked up one of the gravel-covered slices, threw it down again, ran to her daybed, and broke into tears.

How could she have been so stupid? Why did she keep falling for the wrong guys? Brian, who hardly even knew she had existed, Danny, the college boyfriend who would rather fish than be with her, and then Harley-riding Trevor in his sexy black chaps who wanted her to hang out with him in biker bars. And now this lying, stinking, married Karl.

She picked up the phone and dialed Dottie, her college roommate and best friend. "Please call me back. I need to talk to you. Karl is married!"

9

     ylvia lounged under her white canopy surrounded by pink and purple hydrangea wallpaper. A Whitman's Sampler, sent this morning from Ricardo, rested on her stomach. She pulled out a piece, nibbled, and cringed. Ick, coconut. She tossed it back and picked up another. Mmm, dark creamy chocolate. Savoring the sweet, she sat back on a deep pillow and continued reading *Peyton Place*. The characters were so daring, even having sex without being married. Sylvia wished she had the nerve to follow her impulses like that.

     Sure, she'd been kissed on the cheek before, but she had never necked with a man. The mechanics of sex were a mystery to her. She'd thought of asking Ella how it actually worked, but had been too embarrassed. It had something to do with making babies though. Sylvia knew that much.

     She looked over at the carnations on the vanity. What a shame —they were starting to wilt. When they were delivered last week, Ella had said, "Why not roses?" And she read the card aloud, "*Lo siento*. What's that supposed to mean?"

     Sylvia hadn't told her about the crazy ride home from the Cliff House. Or anything else about Ricardo Lorenzo Lopez. Ella wouldn't have approved. Baffled about what happened on their date, Sylvia thought he would never call again. Besides, she thought she'd be too nervous to go out with him again anyway. But then there were the flowers.

"Miss Sylvie, honey," Ella now rapped on the door.

Sylvia slid the novel under her comforter and picked up some knitting.

Ella poked her head in. "That Mr. Lopez is on the phone again."

Sylvia paused. "Tell him I'm unavailable."

Ella stepped into the room with a frown. "It's the third time he's called this afternoon. Just tell him you're not interested so he'll stop calling."

"You tell him. I'm busy," Sylvia said with a sweet voice, and continued to slide the needles through her yarn.

"Playing hard to get?" Ella teased.

"No, I just don't like him."

"Good." Ella put her hands in her pockets and waited.

Sylvia kept knitting.

"He's not your kind anyway. Why don't you go out with that nice Mr. Bonner?"

Thinking of him made Sylvia cold inside, and she didn't answer.

"He called again yesterday."

"So?"

Ella harrumphed. "Maybe you could go to the next dance with Mr. Paul again."

Sylvia decided to ignore her and hoped that maybe she'd go away. Ella waited for a reply, then shook her head and left the door open. Sylvia got up and closed it with a bang. Why did she care what Ella thought anyway? A mature woman should be able to do what she wanted. She slipped *Peyton Place* out from under the comforter and tried to continue reading.

Paul had told her Ricardo was trouble. She knew she shouldn't waste her time or thoughts on him because he wasn't the marrying kind, and maybe Ella was right, it was time to get married.

In order to have a career, one needed an education. She had barely made it through high school, and college had been a catastrophe. At Mills, she felt so out of place. All the other girls were so self-assured and outgoing. She had tried to make friends, but once, when she walked over to visit the girls in the dorm room next door, they were talking about her.

"That Van Dam girl is just odd," one said. "All that glamour can't be real."

"Do you think she wears falsies?" another asked.

"Probably. She can't be a true blonde. Maybe she puts out too." The girls snickered. Sylvia quietly tiptoed back to her room and cried her eyes out.

Soon thereafter, she had practiced her Speech 101 presentation in front of the mirror until it was flawless. But up at the podium, her cards fell out of order, her throat went dry, and she couldn't get a word out. As she ran out of the class, she could hear all the girls laughing. When Milo picked her up that afternoon for a visit home, she never returned.

Sylvia thought it might be fun to work in a jewelry store, but then that would be too tempting. Besides, girls in her station didn't really work. Yes, marriage was the only option. She should really try and date acceptable prospects. Ella was right.

But just the same, Ricardo intrigued her. Charming one moment and tempestuous the next, his moods changed quickly from playful to serious, hot to cold, *caliente y frío*. Good girls didn't spend time with men like that. They dated the right kind of men from the club or church from the right kind of families. She turned a page of the novel, but she hadn't comprehended a word.

It would be wonderful to follow her desires, feel Ricardo's

arms around her, his lips on hers. With him, she was terrified of what might happen. If they went too far, there could be conse-quences. If she got "pg" like the woman in *Peyton Place*, Sylvia's life would be ruined. She stuck out her lower lip and decided to resist him no matter what.

She heard music outside her window, rushed over, and pulled back the curtains. In the garden below, Ricardo strummed a guitar. His slicked-back hair shone dark as onyx. He wore a black suit with silver buttons along the pant legs and a red satin kerchief around his neck. Grinning up at her, he struck a serious frown then strummed a Flamenco chord and began to sing. His tenor voice was full, the accent captivating:

Señorita Van Dam
Está muy bonita.
I would like you to sita
By my side.

You are the one for me
Soon you will see
There's no escapee
I love yee-e-e.

She ran with excitement, tripped over a chair, pulled a carnation from the vase, and tossed it down to him. The flower landed in front of the tips of his black boots. He raised an eyebrow at her and continued to play.

Her pedal pushers fit snugly and showed off her figure. She slipped into flats, pulled her hair back into a clip, and pinched her cheeks. In a flash, she daubed makeup on her face and applied lipstick. From a jewelry box, she grabbed the snowflake pin for courage and held it tightly as she ran down the stairs, skipping two at a time.

Ella stood on the porch, shaking her head. Sylvia stopped next to her and grasped the wrought iron railing. "Isn't he wonderful?" Sylvia waved at him.

"He's a cad." Ella grumbled.

Ricardo tossed his head back and resumed the vocal serenade:

Sylvia, mi amor,

Just flew out the door.

You know it is her I adore

Come here and I will tell you more.

"The man can't even decide which language to use."

"He's just being romantic," Sylvia tittered, gazing at him.

"Your parents would never have approved."

Sylvia didn't care what Ella or even the neighbors thought, and she raced toward him. He slid the instrument onto the grass, and she dashed into his arms, almost pushing him over.

He kissed her firmly on the mouth, his moustache tickling her upper lip. She grew lightheaded. Everything around them disappeared, and she fantasized they were alone together in the universe, just the two of them.

Sylvia closed her eyes and saw diamonds. This was more exciting than shopping at Tiffany's. With her body against his, she kissed him back and wanted to buy out the whole store. But like her last shopping spree, this trip could cost more than her trust fund would allow. So she pulled back, looked around, and pushed him away. He pulled her once more into his arms and kissed her again.

10

*H*oward ran off to get another car as Anne put a key on the rack. The mad lunch rush had finally quieted down. She used a truck window's reflection to smooth out her frizzy hair, damp from parking cars all morning in the fog. "Hey, girl!" a gorgeous blonde squealed and ran toward her.

"Crissy?" If not for her shrill laugh, Anne would never have recognized her. "What are you doing here?"

Crissy hugged her with an overpowering scent of perfumes, as if she had been testing samples in a department store. "Honeymoon!" She wiggled her ring finger to display an enormous marquise diamond.

"My mom told me you were engaged. Best wishes!"

"Stopped here on our way to Hawaii to pick up a few little things. Your Union Square sure beats the Walmart back home."

Anne studied her friend. In high school, they had called her Skinny Minnie, but under that pink Juicy Couture sweat suit, Crissy had filled out in ways that didn't even seem possible. In ridiculously high Jimmy Choo's, she looked like a voluptuous Victoria's Secret model. Anne smiled. "Look at you!"

"I got a trainer. And you!"

Howard might have enjoyed wearing their work uniforms, but Anne sure didn't. She knew she appeared god-awful in the white ruffled blouse underneath a maroon vest that clashed with her auburn hair. Men's Goodwill polyester pants and wingtips completed the ensemble. "Who's the lucky groom? Someone from college?" Anne asked.

"No!" Crissy whipped out her iPhone. "Here's Jonathan."

Anne squinted. Funny—the man in the photo looked a lot like Crissy's father. "Handsome. Where did you meet?"

"At a Ducks Unlimited dinner." Crissy giggled her piercing screech then lowered her voice. "He's a bit older." She held Neiman Marcus shopping bags up with a shrug. "But then, why not?"

Anne looked around. "Where is he? I'd love to meet him."

"Got tired of watching me shop and went up to take a nap."

"You're staying here then?" Anne glanced up at the hotel.

Crissy nodded. "Pretty sweet, huh?"

Yes, at $500 a night.

"And what are you doing here?"

Anne smiled. "I live here, remember?"

"No, I mean here, here." Crissy studied Anne's uniform. "Going to an Austin Powers party?"

Anne tried not to let her shoulders sag. "I park cars. Just temporarily. To help out a friend."

"Thoughtful as always. And your art?" Crissy fluffed her blonde hair. "We all knew you'd do great things. Which galleries are you in? "

Anne hesitated. "I'm between shows now."

"We'll come to your studio then. I'd love to see where you work and for Jonathan to see your collages. He's an art fan. Never know—might even buy a piece. Tomorrow?"

"I think I have a meeting." The last thing Anne wanted was for Crissy to see her dinky studio, and besides, they probably wouldn't really like her collages anyway. They were too modern for the Midwest. "Do you still paint?"

"I'm getting back to it now that the wedding is over. Jonathan loves my ducks. I use his decoys as models. We've converted the carriage house into a studio for me. Isn't that great?"

Anne nodded. "Just ducky."

Crissy pointed at her and rang out with laughter again.

Ms. Woods, a regular customer and generous tipper, handed Anne a parking stub. "Excuse me, but I'm in a rush!" Her black velvet dress and seed pearl necklaces were exquisite.

"Certainly. Right away." Anne hugged her friend. "Great to see you."

"Here's my number." Crissy handed her a card. "Call if you have time. We'll be in town a few more days."

Anne rushed to get the woman's car, wondering what Crissy would think if she knew what a bust her art career had been. Anne found the BMW, jumped inside, and swung it to the front of the hotel. She hopped out and held the door open for the owner.

"That was quick." Ms. Woods handed her a $20 bill.

"I'll get change."

"No. Keep it!"

Anne couldn't believe it. "Thanks so much!"

Ms. Woods smiled at her, slipped in the car, and drove off.

At the end of her shift, Anne put on her coat and a knit cap and headed toward home. A bus cruised by as she ascended a hill. Along California Street, she searched for Mata Hari but didn't see her. When she entered the apartment building, Mrs. Ladenheim stepped onto her doorstep, hair in curlers with a sad face that drooped like a basset hound's. "Rent's due."

"I know. You'll have it soon."

She checked her phone and saw that Karl had been texting her all day. What a jerk! She should just block his number.

She added her tips to the cash box, lit the gardenia candle, rang her chimes, and touched the key sitting nearby. It felt cool on her fingers. She drifted to her computer and typed in *Sylvia Van Dam* again.

Why was she so fascinated by her? Maybe because she lived during Anne's favorite era, the early 1960s, or perhaps because Sylvia had been orphaned. Anne liked it when a subject called to her, but right now, she needed to focus on pieces she could make a quick buck on, and turned off the computer.

She had it down to a science: one sixteen-by-sixteen-inch still life equaled $100. If she worked all night, she could finish a few to take to tomorrow's farmers' market. She pulled a mango from a bowl, rubbed the smooth peel on her cheek, and then set it on the dinette table. Next she squished a glob of phthalo green paint directly onto a canvas and used a wet brush to provide a pale background wash.

The shower went on in Val's apartment below her. He must have just returned home from the night's performance. Anne turned on the Gipsy Kings, cranked up the volume, and wiggled her hips to the sounds of their rhythmic beat. With a knife, she peeled back some skin from another mango and took a bite. The pulp was juicy. She wished she could paint a taste, tangy and fresh. To produce the mango's magenta hue, she mixed red and blue together and added a smidgen of beige buff to soften the color. Her energy kicked in, and within an hour, she had completed a piece.

She bit into the luscious mango again and stood back to inspect the painting. The color contrast worked; other than that, it was pretty boring. But boring was what usually sold. She squinted and felt a tingle in her chest, a yearning not to be resisted. The basket of postcards on the coffee table called to her. As if in a trance, she moved to the basket, closed her eyes, and pulled out a card. A dark-haired man and blonde woman in a turquoise swimsuit sat on a white sandy beach, an aqua ocean behind them. The pair leaned toward each other. A warm breeze flew into the room, and Anne thought she smelled salty sea air again. She walked over to the altar and looked at the key. It just sat there. She glanced at the window, but it was fully shut.

These aromatic apparitions were becoming downright weird. No one would believe her if she told them. She'd be locked in a loony bin for sure. But even so, they seemed to be connected to the art somehow.

She scanned the beach couple's image onto the computer, enlarged it, and printed it onto thin rice paper. The copy was faint but legible. Anne carefully tore off the sharp corners around the beachgoers, dipped a brush into matte medium, and adhered the couple onto the canvas as if they were sitting atop the freshly painted mango. Getting a whiff of that salty sea air again, Anne paused and studied her new piece. She would paint more plain fruit to sell, but maybe "People on Fruit" would become her next series. She took another bite of mango. The stringy pulp twisted around her tongue and tasted sweet. Too quirky—probably no one at the market would buy it, but she was glad she had done it anyway.

II
——

*T*he sky above Ocean Beach shone a brilliant blue. A heat wave had hit, unusual for San Francisco in March. The coastline here, known for its frigidity, had heated up to eighty degrees.

Sylvia looked up at the Cliff House in the distance, where they had had their first date two weeks before. Ricardo unfurled her blanket into a secluded spot between two crags. Way down the beach, another couple sunbathed.

"Boy, is it hot." Sylvia daintily sat on the blanket, kicked off silver sandals, and stuck her feet in the warm sand.

"*Sí.*" Ricardo leaned over and pulled a Tecate from his red cooler. "*Una cerveza?*"

"No, thanks." She shook her head and fingered the floral sequins on her straw tote.

He opened the beer with his pocketknife, and a foamy gush spewed from the bottle. He took a big swallow. "Grrr," he growled, rolling his r's. Smiling at her, he tugged off his shirt and plopped beside her. Then he lay flat on his back, closed his eyes, and hummed the serenade tune.

She hoped her sunglasses hid her stare, tried not to look at his almost-naked body, lounged back on her elbows, eyes toward the sea, but couldn't resist and peeked back. He was so sexy—dark skin and long narrow waist. Hair swirled around his nipples, but the rest of his chest was totally smooth. However, a trail of dark curls below his bellybutton paraded down his abdomen and disappeared into his tight red swim trunks. She wanted to touch him but instead drew her hand across her own brow. She felt feverish but wasn't sure if it was from the sun or from perusing Ricardo.

He opened one eye, caught her staring at him, and grinned. She turned away and busied her red fingernails by checking the back of her French twist. He put his moist hand on her thigh. She pulled her leg away, sat up, and stared at the crashing waves, their sound matching the pounding of her nervous heart. His body glowed like a bonfire on the beach, beautiful to look at but too dangerous to touch.

She wished he had agreed to go to the club instead. It was safer there, not as isolated. Here alone with Ricardo, anything could happen. He could ravage her, and no one would see. Paul might have even been at the club. She always felt safe when he was near. But then, he would have seen her with Ricardo and probably would have been disappointed at her for going out with him.

She eyed Ricardo again. His flat stomach moved up and down. Had he dozed off already?

She grabbed a bathing cap from her tote and pulled it on, tucking in stray wisps of hair. Maybe a dip would cool her down. She pulled off her white lace cover-up and folded it on the blanket. Yanking Ricardo's big toe, she yelled, "Last one in is a rotten egg!" and she raced toward the ocean.

Ricardo chased her down to the shore. "I'm gonna get you," he hollered.

She ran into the lapping waves, clasped the bathing-cap strap under her chin, and dove in. The icy water shocked her system, but after she got used to it, it felt refreshing. With long, steady strokes, she swam away from Ricardo out past the breakers. There the sun sparkled on what looked like a bed of emeralds. Her fingers tried to catch them, but they disappeared.

Ricardo, shivering and executing a type of dog paddle, took a long time to reach her. When he did, he grabbed her arms and kissed her, long and slow. She could feel it all the way down to her legs that were scissoring back and forth. He tasted of salt and beer. Delicious! He pulled her to him. She could feel his hardness, a new and thrilling sensation, but too scary.

Twirling around she swam toward shore, until a giant wave crashed over her, and she let the momentum push her body to the beach. She sprinted to the blanket and wrapped herself in a towel. Out of breath, she pulled a Coke from the cooler, opened it, and took a sip.

It took Ricardo a while to drift onto the beach. He sauntered up the sand, rubbed a towel along his backside, then drank another beer. She peeled off the bathing cap. A few loose bobby pins fell onto the blanket, and she began to pin her hair back up.

"Leave it." He settled beside her, pulled out the rest of the pins, and ran his fingers through her shoulder-length tresses. Then he fluffed it gently. "That's better."

"*Gracias,*" she stuttered, and she pulled the towel tight against the goose bumps on her arms while thinking of their ocean embrace.

"In Acapulco, it is sunny *todos los días.* The water is hot like a bath."

"Really?"

"The color of your swim outfit."

"Turquoise."

"*Sí.*" He pulled her towel off and flung it over his shoulder, like a matador, letting it drop onto the sand.

She giggled and tugged up the top of her suit so her cleavage wouldn't show. The sun was warm on her shoulders. Ricardo slicked back his wet hair. She wanted to run her hands over it.

He stretched out on his side, closed his eyes, and hummed again.

She wondered what Ella would say if she knew they were here alone at the beach. "Don't burn," is the least she'd say, and so Sylvia pulled Sea and Ski from her tote and spread it on her pale legs, which were turning pink. Ricardo took the bottle, squirted lotion on her back, and massaged it. His hands were cool. He squeezed some lotion onto her chest and began to rub it in.

She turned and brushed his hand away. "I'll do that myself, mister."

He gazed at her, and the scar on his cheek glistened in the sunlight. She touched it. "How did you get that?"

He looked out at the ocean. "Sailing in Acapulco."

"Oh?"

"The big thing, what do you call it?" He swung his arm around.

"Mast? Boom?"

He nodded. "Sí. Boom. On a windy day, the boom flew around fast and hit me. My lips were so fat I couldn't even kiss for two weeks." He laughed. "My eyes were black and blue. I looked like I'd been in a fight."

She shuddered thinking how much pain he must have been in. "Didn't it hurt?"

"No mucho." Ricardo pulled a piece of fruit from his cooler, leaned forward, and handed it to her.

"What's this?" She held it to the light and rubbed the yellow-orange skin with her fingertips.

"A mango." He raised an eyebrow. "They say it's a sexual fruit."

"Oh!" She dropped it in her lap as if it were hot, then scooped it up fast and handed it back to him.

"We have many of these in Acapulco." He grinned. "An amigo brought this one to me from across the border.

"I've never seen one." She shook her head.

"They grow on trees outside my villa. From the veranda overlooking the ocean, I can reach out and pick them." He plucked the air. "We have a whole orchard."

"Sounds like Shangri-La." She thought of being alone with him in Mexico by the sea and hoped to stand there with him on the veranda some day.

She had never been further than Napa Valley or Santa Cruz except when she was ten. Her grandmother had died, and so Sylvia had gotten to ride in the back of the limo with her mama all the way to Fresno for the funeral. Daddy had to work and hadn't been able to come. Most of the countryside had been boring though. She did remember how funny those baby telephone poles looked.

"Those hold the grapevines," Milo had laughed behind the wheel.

Her mama had looked exquisite, in a black suit with shiny diamond-like buttons. "Yes, it's your duty to go to the services when a parent passes away." Her voice had sounded sweet as a bell. "Sylvia, it's important to marry the right man. If I had settled for Charles from the farm next door, I'd still be living in this god-awful place. Pee-u, smell those cows!"

Ricardo broke into Sylvia's reverie. "*Espera.* I'll prove to you it's the fruit of love."

He crossed his legs and held the mango in his hand. She tried not to gape at the bulge in his swimsuit. With his other hand, he used his pocketknife and cut the fruit in half and pulled it apart. He carefully serrated around the pit and dropped it into the sand. Then he scored it like a checkerboard, stabbed at a piece, and put it in his mouth. As he chewed, juice trickled out over his chin. She wanted to lick it off but instead took a corner of her towel and wiped it off for him.

"Here, taste. Suck out the juices." He extended a piece toward her on his knife and watched as Sylvia released the slice with her fingers and slipped it in her mouth.

With lips closed, she chewed and swallowed. "Mmm."

"*Sí*," he mumbled, still chewing.

The tangy nectar clung to Sylvia's lips, and she felt a tingly sensation. Ricardo leaned over and kissed her. His tongue slid inside her mouth and licked around as if searching for leftover juices.

Sylvia began to liquefy. She felt as soft as the ripe fruit, trembled all over, and kissed him back, sticking her tongue into his mouth, exploring for nectar too. His hand glided from her knee up her thigh and toward the edge of her swimsuit. Her breath quickened, and she wondered what it would feel like to have him touch her there, all the way up inside her suit. But nice girls didn't let men touch them there. And because she was a nice girl, even though she wanted him to keep going, she pushed his hand away. "Let's go. It's getting late." She started to stand on wobbly legs. His strong arms enveloped her, and he kissed her again. She gasped for air. "Ella is expecting me home for dinner."

"Let's stay and watch the sunset." He tugged her to him again, then rolled on top of her, covering her neck with kisses.

She could feel him again through their swimsuits. They had to stop. Panting, she pushed him off and yelled, "No!"

"Why?" He shook his head and sat up.

"I don't want to." She looked down. "I'm afraid."

He gently pulled up her chin to meet his eyes. "But I love you."

"You do?" She had waited her whole life for someone to say that to her.

"Yes." He nodded, and they began to reach for each other, but

Ricardo looked beyond her shoulder to the cliffs above them. She followed his gaze to where a man peered at them through binoculars.

Ricardo stood. "You're right, let's go."

"What?" she asked, confused and disappointed. "Who's that man?"

"Probably just someone watching for sharks." Ricardo scowled.

She looked out to where they had been swimming. "Really?"

"Come on." He quickly gathered their things, helped her up, and rushed her down the beach back to the Cadillac.

12

    *A*nne squeaked Tweety, her canary yellow Karmann Ghia, out of the parking garage and drove down Polk. Even though the chilly morning fog dropped dew, Anne left the car's top down to accommodate the folding table, chair, and mango paintings. Gloves, a knit cap, and her velvet coat kept her warm. With the price of gas and maintenance, she didn't drive the Volkswagen often.

In high school, she had sold her paintings and collaged boxes at Oscoda's Annual Souper Bowl Supper & Art Show and also set up a table on Route 23 during Paul Bunyan Days for the passing tourists. It had taken her two years to save up enough to buy the car.

She zigzagged along the early morning streets toward Sunset and pulled into the set-up market on Irving near Golden Gate. She found her assigned spot and unpacked the car.

"Be back in a few minutes. Could you please keep an eye on my stuff?" Anne smiled at the raven-haired woman setting up a jewelry display beside her.

"Don't worry, I'll keep watch." Her heavily made-up eyes were dark and exotic. She draped a fringed shawl over her peasant blouse, then reached for the snowflake pin on Anne's coat and tapped it with red nails. "Gorgeous."

"Thanks." Anne climbed into her car and parked a few blocks

away. Walking back between the stalls, she admired the fresh colors of ripe red tomatoes, cadmium yellow corn, and green leafy lettuce being unloaded and displayed. The usual African sculptures, Children of Chiapas embroidered purses, and hippie tie-died-T-shirt dealers were setting up too. From the Java Joe stand, Anne splurged on a mocha, then held the cup in her hands and licked the whipped cream off the top with her tongue. Customers began to arrive, so she rushed back to her space.

"Thanks." She nodded to the jeweler.

"My pleasure."

Anne threw a periwinkle blue cloth over her table and set three mango paintings atop small easels. On a large one she placed *Mango with People on Top*. Why had she brought it anyway? No one would buy it. Maybe to cheer her up and remind her what fun it had been to make.

She sat on her folding chair, grasped the key in her pocket, and closed her eyes. She'd brought it for luck and silently prayed a favorite affirmation: *I am abundant with plenty.* She opened her eyes, and a young woman pushing a toddler in a stroller stopped and admired the paintings.

"Mommy, what's that?"

"Peach, baby. Say *peach*."

"Each."

Anne smiled at the cherub-faced boy and looked at the mom. "It's actually a mango."

The woman raised her shoulders. "Sorry."

"Buy it, Mommy."

The mother brushed the boy's curly hair from his eyes. "No, sweetie."

"Please, Mommy. Want it."

She sighed. "How much?"

"$100."

"That much?"

"I'll give it to you for $90. An early bird special."

"Birdie." The little boy squealed in delight.

"Okay." The mother took out a checkbook from her backpack.

"I'd prefer cash."

The woman frowned. "But I don't have enough."

"Never mind. Just make it out to Anne McFarland." She accepted the check and handed the canvas to the woman.

"Mango. Can you say *mango?*" The mother prompted.

"Ango." The boy clapped his hands then waved his fingers. "Bye. Bye."

Anne replaced the painting with another. For the next two hours, several people stopped and looked at her work, but she made no more sales. Business boomed at the jeweler's next door though. She sure knew how to hustle.

By eleven, the fog had burned off. Anne set her coat on the back of the chair and took off her cap. "May I?" She stepped in front of the jeweler's mirror.

"Certainly." Anne fluffed her locks then tried to smooth her hair down as best she could. She perused the display case stuffed to the brim with an assortment of antique jewelry. Sapphires, emeralds, and amethysts caught the light and sparkled.

"I'm Jewels." The woman beamed at Anne and held up a hefty ruby necklace. "This would be gorgeous with your hair." She had a thick European accent, perhaps Russian.

Anne shook her head. "No, thanks."

"You must try it on." Jewels swung it around Anne's neck, clasped it behind, and smoothed down the back of Anne's hair. "My best piece."

Anne fingered the gems and admired herself in the mirror. It really was gorgeous. "Sorry. I just can't."

"Very old. Bought it years ago in Constantinople."

Anne shook her head, handed it back to Jewels, and returned to her seat.

"Maybe if you sell another painting?"

Anne nodded. The rest of the morning dragged on. By noon, the sun shifted, blinding her. She dug in her bag for her sunglasses. She must have left them at home, so she scooted her chair over to get some shade from Jewels' overhead tarp. She admired an adorable beagle puppy scrambling along next to its owners. Anne watched while the pair of identical twins tried on matching pearl necklaces. "Lovely on you." Anne tried to help.

"Think so?" They said simultaneously. They admired each other, then paid Jewels. "Today's our birthday. We always buy something special."

Ms. Woods, that generous tipper from work, walked down the aisle toward Anne. The woman always wore the most unusual jewelry. Today a turquoise conch belt encircled her waist over a casual black dress and low boots. Maybe she would purchase that ruby necklace for herself.

At the stall across from Anne, Ms. Woods picked through a pile of crocheted handbags, chose one, and paid for it. She then strolled over and scanned each of the mango pieces, then stopped at *Mango with People on Top* and exploded into a fit of laughter.

Anne stood. "It's nice to see you, Ms. Woods."

"Anne? Fancy meeting you here. Is this your work?"

"Yes." Anne nodded.

Ms. Woods smiled at her. "And to think you were under my nose all this time." She handed her a card:

Freddie Woods Gallery
Canyon Road
Santa Fe, New Mexico

Anne read it, felt weak, and sat back down. "What a coincidence!"

Ms. Woods laughed as her eyes returned to *Mango with People on Top*. "I really like this one. I sensed there was more to you than parking cars. May I?"

"Sure. I like to use a lot of texture."

Ms. Woods ran her palm over the couple in their swimsuits. "Collage? I love collage! Where did you get the photo?"

"From a vintage postcard."

"Very impressive." Ms. Woods flipped over the price tag. "Five hundred dollars." She didn't even flinch. "That's fair." She took a wad of cash from her wallet and counted five $100 dollar bills into Anne's hand.

Anne almost fell off her chair. The price had been so high because she thought no one would really buy it. "Gee, thanks." Anne accepted the cash and resisted the urge to jump up and down and hug the woman.

Ms. Woods studied the other mangos again, then pointed to the collaged piece. "Do you have more like this?"

"Not here, but I've completed a couple of other series."

"I'd really like to see them."

"You would? I mean, great!"

"Please deliver this one to my hotel room tomorrow night and bring your portfolio with you. Does seven o'clock work?" Ms. Woods extended her hand.

Anne stood and shook it. "Yes. Thank you for your business. I'll see you then."

She watched Ms. Woods resume her shopping spree down the aisle as Jewels sidled over to Anne with the necklace again. "Special deal for you today, $350."

"No can do. I've gotta pay my rent."

Jewels scowled. "Perfect for you."

"Sorry, but my funds are tight." Anne looked at her watch. "Time to pack up."

Jewels picked up one of the mango paintings. "End-of-day discount?"

"Okay. For you, $90."

Jewels smirked. "Eighty-five?"

"Sure." Anne took the cash and handed Jewels a card along with the painting. "Pleasure doing business with you."

Jewels gave her a brochure. "Let me know if you change your mind about the necklace. Hope to see you next time."

After letting herself inside her apartment, Anne kissed the key and set it on her altar, adding a mango beside it. She counted out all her saved cash and added in the money from her wares. With the woman's check, now she just had enough to cover the rent.

13

*E*lla entered the library, with lemonade and gingersnaps on a silver tray. Ricardo lifted a cookie and popped it in his mouth before she could even set the refreshments down.

"Mr. Lopez, give me a moment!" Ella put the tray on the desk and picked up the pitcher. "Lemonade, miss?" Ella asked.

Sylvia shook her head. "No, thanks."

Ella glared at Ricardo and left the library, pushing the doors wide open. He shut them again and brushed cookie crumbs from his white dress shirt, which was unbuttoned and revealed his smooth chest. A thin gold chain rested there. He sauntered back to Sylvia and embraced her. "Finally, it's just us."

She leaned against the sofa and gazed into his eyes, light brown, the color of the *café con leche* he had taught her to drink. She felt a sexual tension, a swirling of hot desire all over her body.

He ran his fingers through her hair and whispered, "Love you, chocolate drop," then kissed the little mole on her upper lip. She crinkled up her nose then smiled, grateful he had taught her to appreciate the round dot. He leaned in and nibbled her neck until they heard the doorbell ring. "Damn, what now?"

She started to pull away, but he held her close. "Let the maid get it. That's what servants are for."

Ella's footsteps could be heard scuffling along the marble

foyer, and then there were muffled voices. "Mr. Paul, you don't want to go in there!" Ella's voice was firm as the library doors pushed open.

At that moment, Ricardo kissed Sylvia straight on the lips, turned his head, and grinned at the intruders frozen in the doorway. Ella's hand clung to Paul's elbow as she tried to hold him back. Paul bent his knees to keep from dropping the hatbox-sized present in his arms.

Sylvia felt her face turn red. She knew he wouldn't approve of her dating Ricardo, not to mention that kiss, but after all, she could do what she wanted now. She was an adult. She decided to show Paul how much so by gliding toward him with outstretched arms, the legs of her white silk jumpsuit flying like sails in the wind. "Darling, you remembered."

"Remembered what?" Ricardo slumped down on the couch.

She dropped her arms down and looked at Ricardo. "You silly. My birthday! Isn't that why you were being so romantic today?"

"Of course. Just teasing you." His eyes shifted. "I'll give you your surprise later." He snarled at Paul, who stared back at him with tornado-blue eyes. Ella crossed her arms and looked on.

Sylvia frowned at her. "Would you please make us some more lemonade?" It would be tricky enough to get these men to become friends without an audience.

Ella left the library without closing the doors behind her. "Oh my stars and garters," she huffed as she scuffled away.

Sylvia took the gift from Paul. "Oooh, it's heavy." She feigned a grimace and alit on a hassock. "You men know each other."

Ricardo grunted. Paul clenched his fists and asked, "How long have you been seeing each other?"

"For a while. I know you will become great pals." She stared at each of them in turn. Paul managed a smile, and Ricardo exposed his white teeth.

"That's better." She nodded and peered at the blue-and-white package on her lap. How sweet of Paul to buy something from her favorite store. What if it was that tiara from the display case? Her throat became dry, and a shiver sped down her spine. She swallowed and lifted the box. Fortunately, the package seemed too heavy for that. She tipped it again.

Tiny yelps could be heard. Sylvia ripped off the bow and tore through the paper, and a small black nose poked out through the tissue. She pushed the wrapping aside, and innocent brown eyes blinked up at her. They were rimmed in black, like the eyes of an Egyptian princess lined in kohl.

"This is the cutest thing I've ever seen." Sylvia picked up the whimpering dog and set it on her lap. "Shhh, honey," she cooed, and stroked the puppy until it quieted. The dark fur felt as smooth as velvet.

Paul crouched down and scratched behind the dog's ears. "I recollect that as a child, you always wanted one."

"That's right, and Mama said no every time." Sylvia fingered the pink rhinestone collar around the dog's neck. "What kind is he?"

"She. She's a beagle-basset." Paul continued to pet her.

Ricardo smirked. "Not a pure breed? In my country, I have purebred Labradors."

Paul stood and faced Ricardo. His usually calm voice sounded terse. "Mixes have better temperaments."

"I think she's just perfect." Sylvia moved between the men, holding the puppy in her arms. "Thanks, Paul. You are such a sweetheart." She kissed him on the cheek.

Ricardo looked at Paul with flared nostrils. She held the dog toward Ricardo. "Isn't she a darling?"

He raised an eyebrow. "Beagles are stubborn and bassets are fat."

"Any dog can be trained with patience." Paul smiled down at the cute ball of fur.

"We'll see." Ricardo leered at Paul.

"Yes, we will."

"Sylvia offered the puppy to Ricardo again. "Here, hold her?" Certain he would melt over time, she said, "See what a doll she is?"

Ricardo shook his head. He started to reach his hand toward her but caught himself and turned away.

"Don't be so grumpy." Sylvia backed up, sat on the hassock again, cuddled the puppy, and turned to Paul. "What's her name?"

He took the puppy and held her in his palms. "Doesn't have one yet." He relaxed into a nearby chair. "You get to name her."

"Um. Let's see." Sylvia looked at her. "She's tricolored, but her head is covered in red fur. How about Lucy?"

"Clever." Paul nodded.

"What?" Ricardo asked.

Sylvia moved over and sat next to him. "You know, after *I Love Lucy* on television. Lucy Ricardo."

"Ricardo?" He grinned, but she could tell he didn't really understand. They probably had different TV shows in Mexico.

Paul set the puppy on the oriental carpet, and she ran around in circles on short legs, her roly-poly body going every which way. She soon tired and stretched her body all the way out, long and narrow like a sausage, and tucked her head under her paws.

"Now I see the basset in her!" Sylvia cried.

Lucy jumped back up and started to run around again.

"Looks like she needs a walk." Paul pulled a pink leash from his coat pocket and hooked it onto her matching collar.

"Let's go." Sylvia held her hand out to Ricardo.

He ignored it and got up. "Goodbye."

"Where are you going?" she asked.

"Business meeting."

"But it's my birthday."

Ricardo kissed her directly on the mouth, looked over at Paul, and laughed. Then he hustled from the library and shouted, "*Adiós!* I'll be back at eight with your present."

"Ta-ta, then," Sylvia called as they followed him to the front door. Outside, clouds had begun to roll in, and she grabbed her black coat from the front hall closet. She stood on the porch and watched as Ricardo rushed down the steps, hopped into his Cadillac, revved the motor, and skidded around the corner out of view. From the curb across the street, a green Pontiac pulled away, made a U-turn, and followed Ricardo's car down the hill.

"I can't believe you're seeing him!" Paul held Lucy's leash, and they followed her down the front steps and strolled along the sidewalk in front of Bay Breeze.

Sylvia wanted to downplay Ricardo's quirks. "He can be a bit moody, can't he?"

Lucy followed her nose, sniffing the grass along the curb.

"That's an understatement. How can you just laugh off his odious temperament?"

She put her arm through Paul's. "He was just teasing."

"You call that teasing? He's an ignoramus."

"No, he's just from another culture and doesn't understand the American way."

"Have you told him about the inheritance?"

"What?" She let go of Paul's arm.

"I've heard he's in financial hot water."

Sylvia waved her hand, dismissing the idea. "No, he's not. He's rich; he owns a sailboat and a Mexican villa and travels to exotic places. You've seen that fancy Cadillac."

"That doesn't prove a thing. He might just be after your money."

She stopped and looked at the ground. "Are you saying I'm not desirable?"

"That's not what I mean." He lifted her chin and looked into her eyes. Did she see pity or fear there? "Not at all. I . . ."

"What?"

His forehead creased as he tried to speak.

Lucy jumped up and down on the leash. Paul handed it to Sylvia and shook his head. "He's just not right for you."

"Do you see anyone else on the horizon?" Lucy tugged on the leash, and Sylvia began to walk again.

Paul put his hand on her shoulder, stopped her, and paused.

She waited. "Well?"

He looked away, and they continued along the circular drive beside the rose garden filled with blossoms.

"Not Ricardo."

"Why not?"

Paul shook his head. "Dear, haven't you heard the stories?" He opened the gate to the side yard overlooking the sea. White caps curved and bounced on the choppy waves beyond.

Paul closed the gate while Sylvia leaned over, unclasped Lucy's leash, and let her revel around on the grass. Lucy flipped onto her back, and Sylvia rubbed her tummy. "You mean about that girl in Acapulco? He told me all about her. They broke up."

"I've heard otherwise."

"What?" A slight breeze rustled Sylvia's hair.

Paul paused and looked at her. "It might scare you."

"Tell me. It can't be that bad."

"It is."

"I'm an adult now. You can tell me anything."

"He harmed a girl," Paul said quickly.

She gaped at him. "You can't be serious. Who told you that?"

"I have a source." He frowned.

"Your source is wrong. You're trying to get me to break up with him. But it won't work. I love him."

Paul raised his voice. "But how long have you known him?"

"Over a month."

"Is that long enough to love someone?" The crease between his eyes deepened.

Clouds floated in over the Golden Gate. "How long does it take?"

"I forbid it! Not just as a friend but as your lawyer." His voice grew louder. "Your parents would never have approved."

"They've been gone a long time, and I need to live my life as I see fit."

"But—"

She stomped her foot. "I'm going to marry him."

"Marry him?" Paul yelled. "Don't be ridiculous. You're still too young."

"According to Ella, I'm almost an old maid." Sylvia's eyes welled with tears.

He handed her a pressed white handkerchief from his pocket. "You have plenty of time."

"But I want him." She wiped a tear from her eye. "Don't you want me to be happy?"

He lowered his voice and picked up Lucy. "Of course I do."

"Let's not quarrel." She pet the puppy's back. "After all, it is my birthday."

"Yes. I'm sorry."

"I know you feel responsible for me and that you care."

He put his palm on her cheek. "Maybe I care too much."

14

—

$\mathcal{A}$nne didn't have time to nuke the spaghetti and nibbled a few bites right out of the fridge. She needed to hurry or she'd be late to deliver the collage to Ms. Woods. How serendipitous that she owned a gallery. Anne flipped through her portfolio. Would the woman like the Diva or Moguls? They were so different than *Mango with People on Top*. Anne wished she had more like that one. What if she added people to the other mango paintings? But that wouldn't be as funny. The joke had already been told. Anne chewed some more spaghetti and looked over at the Sylvia and Ricardo piece. Ms. Woods might like that one, but it wasn't finished yet.

Anne put the rest of the spaghetti in the fridge, inserted the collage into her portfolio, and rushed out the door. Arriving at the hotel, she checked Ms. Woods's room number written on the back of her card and rode the elevator up to her room.

She answered the door in a hotel robe with a towel wrapped around her head. "Come on in! Put it anywhere. I'll be out in a jiff," she said, disappearing into the bathroom.

Anne had never been inside a St. Francis room before. This, a corner suite, was probably bigger than her entire apartment. The king-size bed had been crisply made, but papers were piled on a desk, and bubble-wrapped canvases were stacked along the walls.

Setting the collage on the dresser, she stood back to admire it. To imagine that someone had liked it enough to spend $500 on it filled her with pride. She clung to her portfolio in hopes that Ms. Woods might also be interested in some of those pieces too.

A hairdryer started to whir in the bathroom. Outside, the neon lights began to pop on and beckoned Anne to read the Union Square store names: Saks, Macy's, Neiman's, Tiffany's. The *Victory* goddess at eye level now seemed to be waving her trident at Anne. Down below, even though it was only mid-November, Christmas decorations bordered the rink where an ice skater twirled, sped up, and then fell. She looked down at the hotel's front entrance and thought about the picture from the *Life* magazine photo taken there many years ago.

Anne checked her watch. She had a half hour until she had to report for her shift, but she still wished Ms. Woods would hurry out. The hairdryer stopped, and Anne watched the door expectantly, but then Ms. Woods said, "Yes, I said sixty percent." And soon the hairdryer started up once more.

Flipping through the stacked paintings, Anne read their taped labels: Disraeli, Janpers, Forgo. All three local artists were well known and highly regarded. No way could she ever compete with them. But Ms. Woods really seemed to like her collage. Or perhaps she was just being nice to the parking valet? Could she have really only bought it to help her out? Anne started to feel as if the walls were closing in on her. She glanced toward the bathroom again, then rushed out the door and down to the garage.

She parked and delivered cars for about an hour, but when Howard handed her the keys to Ms. Woods's car, she said, "Howard, I'd prefer you take care of this one."

"But I thought you were buds?"

She begged, "Please, I'll explain later."

"Okay. Don't mind her good tips."

Anne watched for Ms. Woods to come out of the hotel and then hid behind a truck as Howard pulled up in the BMW.

Trudging home up California Street, Anne passed the Mark Hopkins and then Grace Cathedral, with its stained glass windows all lit up. A crazy guy with wild hair and eyes preached on the sidewalk in front of it. Storm clouds gathered, and she hoped they wouldn't let go until after she made it down the hill and into her apartment.

Vaulting over Mata in the doorway, she said, "Be right back." Anne pulled the note off of her door, recognizing Mrs. Ladenheim's spiky handwriting. She started to open it but then remembered Mata, put the leftover spaghetti in a pot on the stove, added mushrooms and a jalapeño to make it go further, and sprinkled on some Parmesan cheese for protein. She delivered it to Mata in a paper cup with a plastic fork. "Take out for you."

Mata sniffed and took a taste. "Snappy!" She nibbled tiny bites and swallowed with a smile as if she were the Queen of England.

Back in the apartment, Anne read the landlady's note: *Your rent check did not clear. Please remedy this, or you will need to vacate within thirty days.*

What happened? She started to cry. The farmers' market check must have bounced. Had she been duped by that sweet young mother and her cutie-patootie son? To check her account, Anne turned on her computer. There was an email from Jewels checking in to tell her that the ruby necklace was still available, and then a Facebook post from Dottie popped up. In the photo, Dottie looked as if she had died her hair black, and the notice said, *OMG! I'm having a solo show at New York's Punctured Gallery.*

Anne felt like a bucket of paint had been thrown on her. *Dottie's having a solo show!* She tried to be happy for her dear friend, but all Anne could feel was anger. Why wasn't she the one getting the solo show? Maybe that's why Dottie hadn't called back when she left that message about Karl. She might have been trying to spare her feelings.

She thought back to the first day they met. Dottie's dishwater blonde hair had been pulled back in a ponytail, and nerdy glasses had been perched on her nose. She had arrived late and had struggled to set up her easel, but the contraption wouldn't cooperate. Anne had come to the rescue and showed her how to do it.

They became fast buddies, with Dottie always following Anne's lead. Anne taught her tricks like how to use the end of the paintbrush to etch out paint and mixing in matte medium to make the paint go further. By the time they graduated, they'd been roommates for two years, sharing an apartment off campus. Anne had tried to get her to move to San Francisco with her, but Dottie decided to move back to Alabama with her folks for a while. Six months ago though, she had called and said, "I'm moving to New York." Anne just couldn't believe it.

She squeezed her eyes shut, and Dottie's primary colors came to mind, mostly of clowns in motion: running, jumping, juggling, etc. She had loved to paint dots and said it made sense because of her name. The dots became part of the clowns' costumes. For her senior project, she had transitioned to other circus acts of elephants, acrobats, tightrope walkers, and lion tamers. Not the Cirque du Soleil pastel style, but old-fashioned Vargas or Ringling Brothers. They looked like something you might find on a nursery wall. Anne hated to be catty, but Dottie's technique had been mediocre at best. How did she get a solo show in New York when Anne couldn't even break into the San Francisco art scene?

She started to type in a reply to Dottie: *Congrats! You deserve it.* It wasn't even close to sincere, and Anne erased it. "I will not let the green-eyed monster overpower me!" she yelled, and she slammed her computer closed and slumped on the daybed with a pout.

How could she have run out on Ms. Woods like that? It might have been a good opportunity. Anne was going nowhere fast. She should just give up now and move home. It wouldn't be so bad. She would only take what could fit in Tweety for the drive back. The furniture could be sold on eBay, and castoff clothes could be given to Mata and the homeless shelter. Her artwork sold at the farmers' market at cut-rate prices. Maybe she had been too hasty in letting Karl go. Perhaps marriage was the answer. Actually, he had been leaving messages for her every day, which she had been ignoring.

She went over to her altar and rang her Tibetan chimes. The sound echoed, hung in the air, then faded away. She picked up the key and yelled at it: "You are supposed to be good luck." Her brain felt as if bees buzzed around in it. Maybe she should try to meditate again. She settled cross-legged on a sheepskin and turned on her iPod. Carlos Nakai's Native American flute music drowned the sound of late-night traffic. With eyes closed, twisting the key's label in her fingers, she inhaled and exhaled, willing her jabbering mind to shut up.

15

*S*ylvia entered the Top of the Mark and rushed toward Paul. When he saw her, his smile seemed to emanate from the center of his whole being. It had been almost a month since they had argued about Ricardo. Paul had checked in by phone often but hadn't dropped by like he used to. Seeing his kind face now, she realized she had missed him.

"I got here as fast as I could." She tried to seem nonchalant. "What's this all about?"

"Have a drink first." Paul waved to the waitress. Then he pulled a chair out for Sylvia at the wraparound bar overlooking the city and the bay beyond with the sun shining on it.

She played with the graduated pearls around her neck.

"Great suit color." He smiled and pointed to his gray suit, the same shade as hers. "You look so grown up."

"Well, I am."

"Don't be so defensive. I meant it as a compliment."

She could tell he was trying to sweet-talk her. "I don't have much time," Sylvia started.

The waitress delivered their highballs. Paul frowned. "What's the rush?"

"I've got a meeting." She wished he would get right to the point. When he called this afternoon, he sounded like his pants were on fire, but now he seemed relaxed and calm. She pulled off her kid gloves, laid them on the bar, and tasted her drink, leaving a blood-orange lipstick smear on the glass. "Well?" She raised her eyebrows and looked at him.

"Dear, I can't let you marry Ricardo." Paul's voice was soft and deep.

She tried not to lose her temper. "We've been over this. It's really not that complicated. The engagement party is tomorrow night, and the wedding is in two weeks. It's love. And you can't stop me."

Their eyes locked until she lost her nerve and turned her head, gazing out the window to the city below. Shadows began to overwhelm the buildings as the sun moved west to set. She inhaled and then let the air out. Even though she'd been here many times, the panoramic view always calmed her. She tried a different tact. "Haven't you ever been in love?"

He hesitated. "Yes, but that's beside the point. You're a bright girl. I'm surprised you've been so charmed by him."

"Enough! I know he drinks like a marlin, but he's so, so much fun." She stared at Paul's shiny gold tie clasp then reached out and ran her fingers over it. He put his hand on hers gently. She tugged his red dotted necktie aside as if to strangle him. "You infuriate me!"

He started to laugh and clutched her hand while trying to loosen his tie.

She let go and sat back. He would never be convinced she was old enough to get married if she didn't start acting more serious. She pulled a Lucky Strike from her clutch and leaned over for him to light it.

He blinked and held out his lighter. "When did you start smoking?" She took a deep drag and slowly blew smoke to one side.

"Oh. It's been ages now." She waved the cigarette, tapped it on a crystal ashtray, and let the ashes drop. "I know it's all a bit of a rush."

In fact, she had suggested a longer engagement, but Ricardo had scoffed, wanting a big to-do. When she complained there wasn't enough time, he said, "You have connections and money. You can work it out." To please him, she acquiesced and hired a consultant to help with all the details.

Paul's brow furrowed. "Sylvia, he's dangerous."

"Those rumors aren't true. There's no proof."

The waitress stopped by, but Paul motioned her away. "Yes there is."

"What?" Sylvia looked at him.

"I needed to know for sure, so I sent someone down to Mexico."

Her eyes widened "You didn't."

"Sylvia, I couldn't let you ruin your life." He put his hand on hers.

She pulled it away and returned her gaze to the horizon as the Golden Gate's lights blinked on. "Well. What did you find out?" She took another drag of her cigarette and stubbed it out.

"First of all, he's broke. He owes money all over Mexico."

Her heart thudded. "Are you certain?" Just last week, Ricardo told her he had to check out of the St. Francis because they were booked and needed his room. Maybe that wasn't quite true. Perhaps she shouldn't have let him move into the family beach cottage after all.

Paul continued, "And he has a record."

"What?" She grabbed her pearls.

"Two years ago, he was arrested."

"Why?"

Paul's eyes turned to iron. "Murder."

Sylvia reached for his arm and shook her head. "No," she whispered. "That can't be true." Yes, Ricardo did have a temper, but murder? She thought he would be kinder to her when he grew to love her more. Sometimes he did raise his voice, but he had never hurt her physically. Like the other night when he threw the bottle in the sink—he didn't hit her, although the wild look in his eyes told her he wanted to. "I don't believe it."

"See for yourself." Paul slid a manila envelope toward her.

She opened it and spilled the contents onto the bar. With trembling hands, she studied a black-and-white photo of a younger Ricardo, with no mustache but wearing his usual slicked back hair and all-teeth grin. His arm was wrapped around a Mexican girl. Her white peasant blouse scooped low, exposing voluptuous breasts. Between them, a silver onyx necklace dangled. A sequined skirt hugged her tiny waist and flared to sandaled feet. Sylvia grew warm as she flipped the picture over and read the printing on the back:

Ricardo Lopez and Julieta Garcia
10 Febrero, 1959
Casa de la Juarez

With a cocktail napkin, Sylvia dabbed beads of sweat from her forehead and upper lip. Paul handed her a police report. "I had the detective translate it into English."

Acapulco Police Department
5:00 PM
2-11-59
Report by: Officer Jose Dominguez

Julieta Garcia's parents contacted us because she hadn't returned home the previous night from a date with Ricardo

Lorenzo Lopez. It was determined that they had attended a party at the home of Juan Juarez. When interviewed, the host stated that Miss Garcia and Mr. Lopez had argued around 10:00 PM. He had asked them to leave, and they exited onto the beach. Police searched the beach but found no clues. At 11:00 AM, officers finally found Mr. Lopez at his home. A scratch was visible on his left cheek, and his lips were swollen.

The report continued, but Sylvia choked up and looked out the window. A thick fog rolled in, covering the city. She could no longer see the Golden Gate or its lights. A deep sorrow mixed with fear settled in her chest.

She handed Paul the report and pointed to where she left off. She asked, "Then what happened? Just tell me."

"Ricardo was put in jail and extensively interviewed. He said he dropped Julieta off at home around midnight. A week later, police had to release him due to lack of evidence."

Sylvia shivered, looked at the picture again, and asked, "What happened to the girl?"

"No one knows." Paul gently held Sylvia's elbow. "She was never seen again."

16

$\mathcal{R}$aindrops plopped on the canvas top as Anne chugged Tweety over the San Francisco hills and cruised down Balboa. She turned on the windshield wipers, glad that she had recently changed them. Traffic lessened near the coastline. Wind buffeted Tweety as Anne turned left at the Cliff House then whipped south along the Great Highway above Ocean Beach, where whitecaps zigzagged out in the navy blue sea. The small beach houses she had seen in long-ago photos had been bulldozed to make way for condos. Sea Cliff was probably gone too. She continued to drive toward Golden Gate Park until she spied a small cottage between two huge buildings. This might be it.

She made a U-turn, pulled Tweety to the curb, and parked. The dilapidated sign under an arbor said *Sea Cliff*. It was hard to believe this was it. Sylvia would have lived in a mansion. Perhaps this was just a summer home.

Its white paint looked dull gray under a cloudy sky, and the green trim had faded. Lace curtains in the front windows were drawn. The cottage appeared deserted. She grasped the key and waited a few minutes for the rain to abate. Did she dare go up to the door? Heart pounding, she got out of her car and glided up the three short steps to the porch. Trembling on the threshold, she knocked and waited.

She heard a noise behind her and twirled around, but it was only rain dripping off the eaves. She rapped again then cried out, "Hello?" She took a deep breath, waited a beat, and slid the key in the lock.

It fit perfectly!

She turned the knob, pushed the door open, and stepped over the threshold. It was misty dark inside and smelled of salty sea breezes, as if after so many years it had penetrated the walls. She closed the door behind her, stepped out of her wet shoes, and advanced with caution onto the thick carpet that swept the entry. The ocean's crashing waves could be heard. Unable to see ahead of her, she walked down the hall, grazing her hands along the smooth walls to steady and guide her disoriented body.

She turned a corner and switched on a light. The kitchen appeared to be straight out of *I Love Lucy*. Black-and-white squares covered the kitchen floor like a giant chessboard. The rounded Frigidaire hummed a steady moan. She opened it and smiled at the six-pack of Corona, with one missing. In the cupboard, white Lenox dishes rimmed with eggshell blue flowers rested. A toaster sat on the counter, but no microwave was in view. Everything looked neat and orderly.

The danger of being a trespasser excited and scared her at the same time. She knew she should leave now before someone showed up, but she wanted to see more.

In the bathroom, she flipped on the light. What appeared to be droplets of blood—bright and stark—shone in the white pedestal sink. She felt queasy, drew closer, and realized it wasn't blood at all but dried nail polish. A broken bottle with slivers of glass glistened in the drain. In the mirror she saw her pale and wide-eyed face.

The bedroom door was ajar and she pushed it open. Tossed like an angry sea, the aqua silk sheets were twisted and the pillows askew. Pieces from a smashed turquoise lamp were strewn on the floor. Drawers had been rummaged through. Had there been a fight?

Haphazardly thrown on a chair was a silver satin formal. Picking up the slinky dress, she ran her hand over the smooth bodice, its neckline torn. She opened the closet door and, not finding a light switch, she grabbed blindly toward the ceiling and pulled a string down, illuminating the space. Hanging in the back, ghost-like, was a clear plastic bag. She lifted it up to reveal an ivory wedding gown. A net veil with intricate embroidery of white beads and tiny pearls had been draped over the hanger. Peau de soie pumps stood beneath. Anne slipped her feet inside, surprised that they fit. The stiff edges were evidence that they had never been worn. She removed the plastic from the wedding dress and carried it into the bedroom to examine it more closely. Beads and sequins on a lace bodice sparkled in the light, like the sun shining on a still pond.

She couldn't help holding it under her chin and viewing the reflection in the mirror, a stark contrast between her auburn hair and the off-white gown. It was the most elegant dress she'd ever seen. She glanced around, shrugged off her black velvet coat and turtleneck, and threw them to the ground. The gown smelled clean like Ivory soap as she wiggled it down over her head. She stepped out of her jeans, straightened the dress around her hips, and struggled to close the side zipper. Then she leaned forward and adjusted the bodice to reveal her deep cleavage. The dress fit as if it were made for her. Picking up the veil, Anne placed the band on her head, pulled the netting over her face.

"Very dramatic." She walked toward the mirror like a bride holding an imaginary bouquet. Step touch, step touch, step touch . . .

"Congratulations!" her cousin Pootie's voice yelled, and all of a sudden, the mirror shimmered and flipped over, and on the other side, Anne stood in her emerald green cocktail dress. The one she'd bought several months ago at Rescued Relics but had never had the chance to wear. It had a tulle-skirted flounce over a satin A-line and made her look like a cover girl. Her hair had been twisted up into a magnificent updo. Harp music played. And she found herself in a brightly lit gallery surrounded by all her smiling friends and family, and her own colorful artwork covered the walls.

Rain battering on the roof woke Anne from her dream. Body snug in the daybed, she tried to go back to sleep. It had all felt so real and wonderful.

17

<hr>

*S*ylvia sat in the beach cottage's window seat and gazed out to sea. Large waves, as turbulent as the emotions that roiled inside her heart, crashed on the shore. How could she have been so naive to think Ricardo truly loved her? Now she knew the truth. That he had been counting on her wealth to keep him in his lavish lifestyle.

Her whole body shook with fear. From the bedroom, she got the velvet coat and put it beside her in case she needed the snowflake pin for courage. She should have listened to Ella. "He's not good enough for you," she'd cried. Even Milo, always on Sylvia's side, had stepped in and tried to make her see reason. She had been spending a lot of time at the cottage to avoid their constant barrage.

Sylvia never should have let Ricardo move into the cottage. He had convinced her that it would be the perfect romantic hideaway from Ella's watchful eyes. Now Sylvia knew he hadn't paid his bills and that was why the St. Francis had asked him to leave.

How was she going to tell Ricardo the marriage was off? Could she wait and tell him after the engagement party tonight? But it would probably be better to tell him before. Then Paul could announce at the event that the wedding had been canceled. Sure, there would be a scandal, but that wouldn't be as bad as a life of misery with a monster. She'd rather be lonely forever.

At least she hadn't given herself to Ricardo. Tempted many times, she really wanted to, but she decided to wait for their wedding night. As the girls at Mills used to say, "Why buy the cow when you're getting free milk?"

Too bad her jewelry boxes weren't here. She would open each one and touch all the shiny pieces. That might calm her nerves. Or if Lucy were here, she could stroke her smooth back for comfort. Too bad Ricardo never did warm up to the puppy. He called her Fat Burrito and teased her with treats that he ate himself.

Out the window, Sylvia fingered the snowflake pin as Ricardo screeched up and parked his Cadillac in front of the cottage.

He sprinted up the steps and opened the door. "*Hola, mi amor.*" He tossed the keys on the coffee table and kissed her cheek, smelling of cigars and rum. "Excited about the fiesta tonight?" His usually slicked-back hair was disheveled, and his T-shirt was stained. He plopped into an easy chair and put his shiny boots on the table. "*Una cerveza, por favor.*"

She stood on wobbly knees and made her way into the kitchen. From the icebox, she took out a Corona, flipped it open, and poured herself a glass of lemonade. She put the drinks on the coffee table and sat on the sofa across from him. He guzzled down the beer with closed eyes.

Her throat felt dry, and she took a sip of her lemonade; it was sticky and tart. "Ricardo. We need to talk."

"Not now. I'm napping."

"But it's important."

He opened his bloodshot eyes and stared at her. "What?"

She grasped the pin. "We c-c-can't get m-m-married," she stuttered.

"What do you mean?" He sat up straight. His eyes became slits as thin as knives.

"I just can't marry you."

"Why not? Everything's set." He clunked his boots to the ground, leaned across the table, and grabbed her shoulders. "It's that Paul. He was snooping around. Wasn't he?"

"No."

Ricardo snatched her wrists, twisted them toward him, and shook her. "You're in love with him, aren't you? Aren't you?"

"Nothing like that!"

With Ricardo's nose an inch from her face, he yelled, "I'll kill you if you try to get out of it."

"Stop! You're hurting me." She started to cry. "I-I-I'm just not ready. That's all." He let go, and she collapsed onto the couch, breathing hard, massaging her wrists.

He watched her cry for a moment. "Quiet!"

She felt evil emanating from his pores and knew for certain the things she'd heard about him had been true. He was capable of murder.

But then that evil suddenly evaporated, and he moved next to her on the couch. "Sorry, chocolate drop. I would never hurt you." He took a kerchief from his pocket and handed it to her.

She dabbed at her face.

"You're afraid of the wedding night. Aren't you?"

She looked at him. "Yes, yes. That's it."

"I'll be gentle. I promise." He petted her head. "So we're all right, now?"

She nodded.

He kissed her, and even though she cringed inside, she kissed him back. She had to pretend everything was okay.

"We'll have a wonderful life together. Got it?"

She nodded again and looked at her watch. "Better take me home so I can get ready for tonight."

"You're not going anywhere."

It felt like a heavy rock beat in her chest.

"Your dress is in the closet."

"Oh, yes." She had hoped he had forgotten. Stupidly, she had brought it here in order to avoid another row with Ella.

He raised an eyebrow at her. "We're getting married. Understand?"

Sylvia managed a smile.

He closed his eyes, pulled the flask from his pocket, and lifted it to his lips. "Damn. Empty." He shook it. "Gotta have rum for tonight."

He slipped into the bedroom and came back out a few moments later with his coat. She followed him to the door.

"Back in five." He kissed her slowly, gazed at her, and said gently. "Start getting ready. You have a lot to do."

She watched him pull away from the curb, ran into the bedroom, threw herself on the satin sheets, and wept. She felt like she was in an abyss so deep she would never be able to climb out. The tears continued, but she realized that time was precious. Ricardo would be back soon. She needed to pull herself together and try to reach Paul or Milo to come get her. Sitting up, she opened the nightstand's top drawer and grabbed for a tissue. Her fingers felt something hard and metal. She sat up and looked in the drawer.

Her heart careened as she peered at a gun, so small it looked like a toy. She delicately picked it up, held the pearl handle, and tapped her red-polished fingernails on the cool metal shaft. Was it Ricardo's, or had it been her father's? Was it loaded? Cautiously, she peeked into the barrel but couldn't tell. She heard a noise. The gun grew heavy in her hand. She started to put it back in the drawer then changed her mind and slipped it into her pocketbook on the nightstand instead. She waited and listened. There was only silence.

With shaky hands, she grabbed the phone to call Paul, but

there was no dial tone. She clicked the top mechanism up and down, and then her eyes opened wide as she saw that the cord had been severed. Sprinting to the living room, she looked out the window and considered running out onto the coast drive, but the traffic moved fast, and she knew Ricardo would still track her down wherever she went. Her thoughts raced considering options, but it was like a labyrinth, with each turn leading to a dead end.

Sobbing, she lay on the couch and realized that she just had to go to the party with Ricardo, see Paul there, and ask him to protect her.

She ran a hot bath, locked the door, and climbed in, the warm water soothing her chilly body. Her wrists were turning black and blue. Fortunately, gloves would hide the bruises.

She knew now that nothing Ricardo had told her was true. He told lies and made up stories to impress and deceive. She closed her eyes and heard his voice, "My villa in Acapulco is *muy grande*." "Sorry I was late; I got called away on business." What business? She realized now that he probably didn't even have a job.

She stepped out of the tub, wrapped a towel around her, and entered the closet. As she slipped into the silver satin evening gown, the wedding dress caught her eye—the one she would never wear. She lifted the plastic cover and touched all the shiny beads and pearls. It calmed her for a moment, but then her nerves unraveled.

She had to compose herself. Hands trembling, she twisted her hair up and used a hand mirror to check out the back. She put a cool washcloth over her swollen eyes for a minute and then applied heavy foundation. Love is blind was the saying. Well, Sylvia's eyes were fully open now. She picked up a pencil and redrew her eyebrows.

She clasped a diamond and emerald necklace around her neck, a birthday gift from Ricardo, remembering that night at Ernie's just after Paul had brought Lucy to Bay Breeze: A sommelier poured the last drop of burgundy as Ricardo slid the velvet box across the table toward her. "You like shiny things. Go ahead, open it." She lifted the lid, and her heart somersaulted. The lavaliere cluster of shiny baguettes and emeralds released a soothing sensation in her stomach as she ran her fingers over it.

"Let me put it on you." Ricardo leapt up and connected the clasp at the back of her neck. "Something to match your eyes."

She had chosen not to correct him and spoil the moment, even though her eyes were blue. Then he had kissed her, right in front of all the other diners. She should have known then that it was all a charade. Less than a week later, he had asked to borrow $10,000. She didn't even bother to request it from Paul, knowing he'd refuse the loan. Ricardo had argued, "But we'll be married soon anyway. What does it matter?"

She touched the necklace now, hoping it would help relax her, but its power had lost effect. Could there have been a connection between the necklace and that money?

She put on red lipstick and practiced her smiles: lucky, sparkly eyes; gracious, closed-mouth grin; radiant, white teeth exposed. Adding a last touch of polish to a chipped nail, she heard the key in the lock and, startled, dropped the bottle in the sink. It broke, and the red liquid oozed onto the white porcelain. No time to clean it up now.

What if Ricardo grew hostile again? She rushed to the bedroom and slipped the gun from her purse into the deep pocket of her black velvet swing coat. Uncertain how long she could keep up the charade, she greeted him with one of her fake smiles.

"You look ravishing," he said, and he pecked her on the cheek.

She gritted her teeth and kissed him back, wondering if she'd ever be able to get away from him alive.

18

*I*t was almost noon, and the rain continued to pound on Anne's roof. Rolling over in bed, the key, cottage, and flashing mirror of the dream came back to her, and she thought about the wedding dress. Did it mean she should forgive Karl and move in with him after his divorce and plan a wedding with him? No way; she would never be able to marry someone she didn't trust. It wasn't only that he had been married but that he had misled her. She didn't think she could ever get over that.

The green dress, harp music, and gallery images floated into her mind. She relived the thrill of having her collages on display and celebrating with all her friends. Did it signify that she was supposed to go for it and get her work out there and someday maybe even have her own solo show too, just like Lila and Dottie? But then reality jumped into her mind, she remembered that her rent check hadn't gone through, and she sat up. She needed to get some money fast. Remembering Crissy's interest in coming to see her work, she found her card on the coffee table, picked up the phone, and dialed her number. They might actually like the mangos.

"Aloha!"

Anne could barely hear Crissy due to all the garbled noise in the background. "Aloha?" she yelled. "It's me, Anne."

"Great to see you the other day!"

"Want to bring Jonathan over to my studio for a glass of wine this evening?" Anne looked around her apartment. She'd have enough time to straighten up before then.

"But we're in Hawaii," Crissy giggled. "On the beach right now. Listen."

Anne could hear the crash of waves and imagined Crissy's voluptuous body in a passionate pink bikini, holding a cell phone aimed at the ocean.

"A little more right here, honey."

"What?" Anne asked.

"Jonathan is lathering me up. Bought a Wyland this morning."

Anne scrunched up her nose. That would go great with the ducks. "How nice. Of a whale, right?"

Crissy giggled. "How did you know?"

"Psychic. Let's rendezvous when you come back through on your way home."

"We're flying through L.A. I'll call next time we come to town."

Anne hung up the phone. They probably wouldn't like the pieces anyway. Her work was a far cry from ducks and whales. But she wouldn't let this get her down. Brushing her teeth, she thought of that nice woman at Gallery Noir who had encouraged her to bring in work again. At group, Lila had told her The Divas series had a unique content, balance of colors just right and textures intriguing. But were they strong enough to get displayed on the walls of a gallery? Lila had thought the Mogul series was pretty good too, but no one had wanted them. Anne had no desire to brave the rejections again, but she had to at least try.

Perhaps if she had an irresistible statement, someone would show them. She sat on the daybed, picked up her journal and pen, and started writing:

THE DIVAS

Eva Peron, Madame Mao, and Imelda Marcos helped their husbands rise to political heights. These women claimed to be "for the people" when actually they spent the people's money on their own luxuries. While creating this work, I kept asking myself, What would I have done in their situations?

"What's the use?" She sighed and threw down her pen. *Buck up, girl!* Closing her eyes, she inhaled and then let it go. The she typed up the statement, printed it out, and slipped it into her portfolio. As an attempt to look professional, she donned work slacks, that Ralph Lauren jacket, and her wing tips. Taming her hair, she stuck it up in a scrunchie and attempted to twist it on top of her head like in the dream, but it wouldn't stay in place.

To give herself a confidence boost, she turned on her iPod and set it to "Unforgettable"—Natalie Cole's duet version with her father—and, looking in the mirror, Anne sang along with the sultry voice, an invisible microphone in hand. "In every way." At the last minute, she took the Sylvia and Ricardo photo transfer, added it to her portfolio, and walked out the door.

At Gallery Noir, Fay greeted her with a smile. She wore a terrific red vintage number. "Anne, right?"

Anne nodded.

"It's good to see you again. I see you've brought your portfolio. Put it here on the counter, and I'll go get Mr. Block."

Anne set her portfolio down feeling woozy, and she looked around. Lila's fabulous show was still up, and Anne wasn't surprised to notice many red dots on the painting labels denoting sales.

As Mr. Block followed Fay from his back office, he said, "We're not really taking new artists right now." He adjusted his glasses, opened the portfolio, and began to flip through it. "But Fay insisted I take a look." He held the Imelda piece up for Fay to see. "Collage? That's not real art. Kindergarten cut-and-paste." He picked at the edges of the matte finish that held down the cutout little shoes. "See what I mean?"

Anne wanted to refute him, but it wouldn't do any good. He tossed the piece down, went back to his office, and banged the door behind him. She had tried to just be a painter, but her pieces never felt finished until she glued on a few photos or words to add texture. She didn't look at Fay as she held back tears, stacked her work, and walked toward the exit.

Fay followed and kept her voice low. "Don't worry about him." She glanced at his closed door. "He's full of rubbish."

"You mean you don't agree?"

"He's just a wanker. I dare not say anything, or I could lose my job. Those Divas are fabulous!"

"You really think so?"

"Certainly." Fay took the portfolio from Anne and leafed through the Mogul series.

"Have you worked here long?" Anne asked.

"God, no!" Fay shook her head. "Only two months. I used to manage the Circle Gallery on Union Square, but they went out of business."

"I'm sorry."

Fay sighed. "So am I. We were doing okay, but then the landlord raised the rent. In this economy, the owner knew we wouldn't be able to make up the difference."

"Have you thought of opening your own gallery?"

"I would if I had the quid."

"Squid?"

"Quid." Fay laughed. "Money!"

"I hear you. I can barely pay the rent."

Fay nodded. "This one's interesting." She pointed to the Sylvia and Ricardo piece.

"It's not finished yet. I'm just starting a new series."

She wanted to tell Fay about the coat, the snowflake pin, and the key, but she wasn't sure she'd understand. In fact, she might even think she was crazy.

"Yes. You might want to add some color to it. Looks very interesting though." Fay slipped one of Anne's cards from the portfolio, retied it, and handed it to her. "Try Howard Dean's down near the square and Global Beginnings, too. In a pinch, you can always display at a farmers' market."

Anne hugged the portfolio to her. "Isn't that bad for my reputation? That's what someone in my artist's group said."

"Who would know?" Fay shook her head.

"I would."

"Many artists start out in untraditional ways. There's no shame in that."

"I guess you're right."

She handed Anne her card. "Keep in touch. I'd love to hear how it's going for you."

"Let me know if you have any more ideas. If worse comes to worst, I can move home to Michigan.

Fay's mouth opened. "Blimey! You can't leave. Keep at it."

"I can still be an artist and live in Oscoda. Artsy Crafty, where I worked in high school, told me I can work there again anytime."

"But you'd be going backward in life instead of forward. I can spot talent, and you've got it!"

"Thanks for the encouragement." Anne smiled then she walked out the door and headed down the street. Mr. Block didn't like her work, but Fay did, and she had style. Anne thought again of the gallery dream sequence and knew she needed to do all she could to stay in San Francisco. Even shoot for a solo show too. But it was the gallery owner that made all the final decisions, even if he didn't have style, and she wasn't sure how to get him to accept her work without giving up her desire to make pieces that called to her.

19

——

$\mathcal{I}$n his pressed tux but wearing a five-o'clock shadow, Ricardo steered Sylvia into the St. Francis ballroom. Her heavily made-up eyes, accented with brown lines and scads of mascara, disguised her turmoil. She concealed the terror she felt behind a fake smile, all a show for the high-society crowd. Ricardo had insisted that they invite all the San Franciscan elite. Looking around the room, she didn't even recognize all the guests sipping champagne—men in tuxes, women in colorful sequined gowns.

Long gloves hid the bruises on Sylvia's wrists. She ran a hand along the side of her snug satin gown and fingered her diamond-and-emerald necklace, but it was impossible to capture a soothing effect through her gloves. Besides, since she realized Ricardo had probably gotten the piece through some kind of shady deal, the necklace's sheen had faded for her.

The hotel's consultant had done a wonderful job. Tables glowed with candles and bouquets of baby's breath, lilies, and white roses—white for virginal and naive. She was a virgin still, but she wasn't naive anymore. She knew firsthand how violent Ricardo could be. As they moved through the packed ballroom, she struggled to keep her composure, nodding to well-wishers, dabbing a scarf to her moist, hot face and chest. She wanted to scream, *It's all a sham. Help me! He's dangerous.* She had to keep her composure and find Paul.

The orchestra began to play "What a Difference a Day Makes." On the dance floor, Ricardo held her close, one hand on her lower back and the other tight around her wrist. The bruise underneath throbbed within his grasp as if he would never let her go. Faces passed while he twirled her to the center of the floor beneath the chandelier, and the slow dance sped up with Ricardo's reckless rhythm. All eyes were on them, but she remained certain no one in the crowd could see her desperation.

Sylvia saw Paul as he watched from the outskirts of the throng. Each time they turned, he was there. He started to move toward them, like a beam from a lighthouse, a beacon of safety in the stormy sea of people. She wanted to rush to him and plead for protection, but Ricardo held tight. Then the music stopped.

"Damn it," Ricardo said when he noticed Paul approach.

"I'm next." Paul tapped Ricardo on the shoulder.

But Ricardo shook his head. "No!"

Paul firmly tapped again. Suzie Jones and Rochester Smythe along with other nearby couples stared, and only then did Ricardo step away.

"Just one," he sneered, and he sauntered off to light a cigarette and then grabbed a drink off a tray being passed.

"Uncouth, as usual." Paul shook his head and took Sylvia in his arms. His fresh lime scent began to quiet her rapid heartbeat, and they started to move to the music, both keeping an eye on Ricardo as he stood on the dance floor's edge.

The tenor at the microphone started to sing "The Very Thought of You." His smooth voice led the orchestra while Sylvia and Paul watched Ricardo watching them. After a few moments, he narrowed his eyes at Paul, flicked his ashes into his glass, and drifted over to the bar.

Sylvia whispered into Paul's ear. "We need to talk."

"What?"

Suzie and Rochester danced next to them. Sylvia, afraid they might overhear, said, "Let's go out on the veranda. I need air." Paul led her over to an open doorway, and they slipped outside, where the night sky cooled her nerves.

"What's wrong?" he asked.

"We haven't much time."

"You can't marry him." Paul's firm voice let her know he was ready for another argument.

"You're right. I'm . . . I'm scared."

"What happened?" Paul's eyes filled with concern.

"I'll show you." She glanced around to make certain they were alone and began to pull down her gloves.

"Here's your drink, chocolate drop." Ricardo came up from behind them, handed her a glass of champagne, put his arm around her waist, and pulled her close.

Paul stepped toward him.

"We'd better get the dinner started," Sylvia interrupted and looked at him with wide, warning eyes.

"You sure?" Paul frowned.

She nodded.

"Well, I'm sure," Ricardo said, and he turned Sylvia back into the ballroom. Paul approached the stage and motioned the bandleader to wind it down. At the table, Ricardo sat down without pulling out a chair for her. Sylvia pulled one out herself, slid onto it, and put a napkin in her lap. Across the table, Carolyn Swanson apparently noticed and quickly covered a disapproving frown with her hand. The amethyst earrings, the same ones she had worn at the Valentine's dance, caught the light. Sylvia thought of that night and wished it had never happened.

As the partygoers settled at their tables, Paul stepped onto the stage and spoke into the microphone. "May I have your attention?" The crowd continued to babble.

Ricardo clinked his glass with a fork.

Paul said again, a little louder, "May I have your attention, please?"

Guests hushed each other until the room quieted. Paul began, "Ladies and gentlemen, I'd like to propose a toast." Sylvia thought Paul appeared attractive up there. He had what they called good stage presence, and she understood now why he had won those court cases. Everyone in the room raised their champagne glasses. Paul's deep voice sounded self-assured but sad as he read from his notes:

"To Ricardo and Sylvia.

Two weeks hence, these two shall wed,

that lucky guy, I wish it were me instead.

I wish them well,

only time will tell!"

The crowd laughed, raised their glasses, and sipped. They wouldn't have thought it funny if they'd known the truth.

"Now, let's eat!" Paul descended the stairs and sat on the other side of Sylvia.

Ricardo nodded at him and then finished his champagne and raised his hand for a waiter to pour him some more.

As dinner was served, Sylvia's nerves expanded and her stomach churned. She pushed food around on her plate and managed to swallow some mashed potatoes. In between bites, Carolyn talked nonstop and didn't even pause for Sylvia to answer questions: "You must be so thrilled. Who designed your wedding gown? Where will the honeymoon be?" Dr. Griffith on Carolyn's left smiled at Sylvia and rolled his eyes.

Sylvia pretended to listen but couldn't concentrate. She wished Milo and Ella were there. "You can't invite the help,"

Ricardo had said. She hoped the couple would forgive her recent attitude. She had said some horrible things to them.

The orchestra began to play again, and Ricardo grabbed her hand. "Let's dance." He pulled her up and hustled her onto the floor. "Unforgettable, in many ways." He sang along loudly with the crooner. Ricardo twirled her around and almost bashed into another couple.

During the next song, "Embraceable You," Paul tapped Ricardo on the shoulder again. "Cutting in."

"Ricardo, please." Sylvia tried to keep the urgency out of her voice. But he ignored Paul and steered her to the opposite end of the dance floor. Soon she couldn't stand being pressed against Ricardo anymore and excused herself to the powder room.

She squeezed her way through the congratulatory crowd. "Many years of bliss! Best wishes," they called, but Sylvia couldn't focus on any of their faces as she searched for Paul in the bustling ballroom.

Out of breath, she entered the powder room, dampened a cloth, and patted her cheeks and forehead with cool water. She sank onto a settee and struggled to figure out what to do. Should she try to get Paul's attention again? No, the crowd was too big. She would sneak out through the kitchen and find her way home to Bay Breeze.

She touched up her makeup, taking time to gather the nerve to sneak out. But when she stepped into the hallway, Ricardo stood there waiting. "Took you long enough." His voice sounded rough.

"I'm not well. I want to go home."

"More champagne should help." He held up a bottle. "This party's a bore. Let's go. We can drink it at the cottage."

Sylvia didn't want to be alone with him ever again and tried to pull away, but he held tight. Fear overpowered her as she struggled to breathe. They traveled back through the ballroom. There, the walls, the tables, the lights, and the guests seemed to close in around her, and she felt as if she might suffocate. They were almost to the exit when she crumpled to the floor in a faint.

When she opened her eyes, Sylvia saw Paul kneeling over her. She had no idea how long she had been out.

"Stand back." Paul cradled her head and held a glass of water to her lips. "Drink this, darling."

She took a sip and looked up at all the gaping spectators. "Sorry, too much champagne," she explained weakly. Ricardo stood back, smoking a cigarette.

"Let me through." Dr. Griffith shone a light into her eyes then held a stethoscope to her chest. "She's fine. Must have been all the excitement." He stuffed the equipment back into his black bag. "You should go home and get some rest."

"I'll take you," Paul said as he gently helped her up. Someone handed him Sylvia's black coat, and he held it out and she slid into it.

"She's riding with me." Ricardo nudged Paul away and grabbed her arm.

Sylvia's eyes met Paul's as Ricardo pulled her into the lobby. Paul stepped in front of them. "You've had plenty to drink. Let me drive you both."

"No, she's mine and coming with me."

Outside the St. Francis, while they waited for the car, Ricardo lit another cigarette. A photographer snapped their picture, and the bright flash blinded Sylvia for a moment. A valet pulled the Cadillac to the curb. Ricardo opened the door and shoved Sylvia in.

"I'm going to drive you," Paul said, and he stepped over to the driver's side, but Ricardo pushed him out of the way and climbed in. Paul ran around toward the passenger door and yelled, "Sylvia, get out!"

She reached for the locked handle, but without even kissing

the Madonna, Ricardo revved the motor and screeched the car onto Powell. Sylvia watched out the back window as Paul ran after the car, but Ricardo picked up speed, and Paul couldn't catch up. Sylvia waved to him and tried hard not to cry. Ricardo put his hand on her leg and squeezed. "We're alone now, baby."

"Not to the cottage. Please take me home."

"Forget it," he said, and he drove toward the ocean, weaving in and out of the lonely midnight traffic.

20

⸺

*E*ven though the full moon glowed like an opal, darkness consumed the white Cadillac as it careened around a corner past the Cliff House and almost flew over the edge. Ricardo took another swig from his flask and picked up speed along the straightaway of the high-cliff drive.

Certain they were going to crash, Sylvia grabbed the dashboard. "Slow down!"

His laugh pierced the cool night air as he pressed even harder on the gas pedal. She closed her eyes and prayed, "Our Father, who art in heaven, hallowed be thy name."

A siren screamed behind them, and a blinding light flooded the rear window, which forced Ricardo to slow down and pull over. "Damn it." He stuck the flask under the seat and smoothed back his hair.

The black-and-white police car parked behind them. A stocky officer got out, walked to the driver's side of the Cadillac, and shone a flashlight into Ricardo's eyes.

He squinted with an innocent expression. "Something the matter, sir?"

"Do you know how fast you were going?"

With wide eyes, Sylvia, behind Ricardo's back, tried to catch the officer's attention. He shone the light into her face, grinned, and looked at her cleavage. To her dismay, she realized he thought she was flirting with him.

"No, sir. Was I going over the limit?" Ricardo asked.

"Way over."

Ricardo tapped the speedometer. "This thing must be broken."

The officer sniffed. "Have you been drinking?"

"Just a little glass of champagne to celebrate. You see, we just got engaged."

"Consider this a warning then. Slow down." He started to walk back to his car.

Sylvia couldn't let this opportunity pass. "Officer!"

Ricardo placed his hand on her thigh and squeezed.

The officer returned. "What?"

"Have a good night," she said with a quavering voice.

"Night." With a confused look on his face, he strode back to his car, and within a couple of minutes, he pulled away.

Ricardo let go of her leg. "We'll just wait until he's long gone."

Sylvia felt despondent. If she jumped out of the car and started to run, Ricardo might plow her down—there was no telling what he was capable of. Sick to her stomach, she unrolled the window and looked out at the tumbling waves offshore. A distant foghorn reverberated in the clear sky.

Ricardo turned on the ignition. Sylvia put her hand on his arm. "I'm not well."

"You'll be okay once we get to the cottage."

"I mean, I might get sick."

"Not in my Cadillac!" he yelled. "Get out."

She opened her door and stepped onto the graveled shoulder. "All I need is a little fresh air."

Ricardo got out, leaned against the Cadillac, and lit a cigarette. Not only did her stomach hurt, but she also felt stiff. "I'd like to stretch my legs." She started to walk along the road. A car honked and skidded by.

"Let's go down on the beach. It might help."

"Okay." She wasn't sure she wanted to climb down there. But it would be safer than another wild ride with his maniacal driving.

They scaled the cliff down to the deserted beach, removed their shoes, and tossed them on the rocks. She unhooked her nylons, pulled them off, and laid them aside too. The sand felt cool between her toes. She lifted the hem of her gown and draped it over an arm. Her blonde hair loosened as it blew around her face.

They walked toward the water, and Ricardo sipped from his flask again. Beads of rum clung to his mustache. He licked them off and offered her a sip. "Want some?"

She put her hand out to take it, to keep him from drinking more. But he snickered, raised the flask out of her reach, and stuck it in his coat pocket.

They walked along the shoreline, where the hard sand made a steady path for her feet. She inhaled the cool salt air, welcomed by her queasy stomach. The wind picked up, and she huddled into her velvet coat. "I'm okay now. Let's go back up."

At the water's edge, Ricardo rolled up his tux legs, waded in, and turned around. "Come on."

She shivered. "No. It's too cold."

He splashed toward her and beckoned. "Feels great!" Coming closer, he grasped her coat lapels and kissed her with his stinky breath.

"Leave me alone," she cried over the sound of the waves. Pushing him away, she turned and started to walk back up the beach toward the cliffs.

He scrambled after her, grabbed a bruised wrist, and yanked her into the frigid water up to her knees. Cold spray flew around her.

"Let go!"

"Don't worry. I won't drown you." He had a wicked glint in his eyes.

More frightened than she'd ever been in her life, she thought of the girl in Mexico. Is this how she had disappeared? Would Sylvia be his next victim?

As she tugged away, he tripped and almost fell.

"You bitch!" he yelled, rushing toward her again, his hand ready to punch her.

Certain that he was going to kill her, she backed up onto the sand, reached into the pocket of her swing coat, drew the gun, held it in the air, then aimed it at his chest. "Stop," she screamed.

He laughed at her, a deep hollow laugh. "You'd never shoot me, *mi amor*," he taunted.

How could she have ever thought she loved him? That hadn't been love—it had been charm and lust—but now this was just intimidation and fear. Even still, as he lunged toward her, she was shocked when she pulled the trigger. *Bam! Bam! Bam!*

With a surprised look on his face, he stumbled, then fell back into the foamy wash.

She caught her balance from the kickback and stood motionless, trying to catch her breath, not believing what she had done. She stared at his body as it bobbed on top of a shallow swell. A crest approached, and with a pounding roar, it enveloped him and ebbed out toward the breakers.

A loud wave crashed on shore, and she watched as Ricardo's body floated out further into the ocean. "*Adiós,*" she whispered at a rush of waves with tears in her eyes, saddened for the love she had thought she had and then lost. Mesmerized, she watched his dark form mingle with the midnight blue water and disappear from sight. The frothy tide lapped her bare feet, which broke the spell and alerted her senses. She shuddered, felt the weight of the gun in her hand, and tossed it into the water. It caught on a clump of seaweed. A fresh wave released it, set it free, and pulled it out and down into the watery silt.

Afraid Ricardo would rise up and come after her, she wanted to get as far away as possible and ran up the beach. Like in a dream, the fog began to roll in, and with each step, her bare feet sank deeper into the sand.

By the time she reached the rocks, exhaustion had set in, but somehow she summoned the strength to grab her shoes and nylons and scale the rocks, scraping her feet and the silver gown's hem on the crags. Hot from exertion, she tugged off her coat and tossed it on the car's hood. She opened the heavy door, climbed inside, and reached under the seat for the keys, where he always kept them. Her toes couldn't touch the pedals, and she struggled to pull the seat up, turned the key in the ignition, shifted the car into reverse, and pushed on the gas.

Emerging out of the fog, a truck barreled down the road and honked. She slammed on the brakes and pulled forward just in time. Parked again, she began to shake. She put her head on the steering wheel and sobbed long and loud. Ten minutes had passed before Sylvia leaned over and grabbed tissues from the glove box.

She clasped Ricardo's Madonna that hung from the rearview mirror and blinked a silent prayer before she slowly backed out again and drove toward the cottage.

Paul had taught her to drive. On her nineteenth birthday, he had insisted. "I know you're nervous, but now's the time."

"But Milo takes me everywhere." She had stuck out her lip and pouted toward Paul.

"Yes, but you never know when you'll need to make a quick getaway," Paul had teased back. It had been scary at first, but once she got the hang of it, driving had been exhilarating—whizzing by grapevines, wind blowing her hair, dust flying.

At the cottage, she parked in front and ran up the stairs, the hem of her gown heavy with damp sand. Her bare shoulders dotted with goose bumps, she let herself in. In the entry mirror, she examined her pale, tear-streaked face and asked her image, "What have I done?"

She dropped her necklace and earrings inside her handbag. The side zipper of her dress stuck, so she ripped it off and threw it on a bedroom chair. Then she slipped on slacks and a cashmere sweater. She wanted to stop and catch her breath but looked around the room. The satin-sheeted bed where Ricardo last slept reminded her of him, and she ran out the door and back to the Cadillac.

Navigating through the now dense fog on deserted streets, she finally pulled into the circular drive and around to the back of her house. Her watch said two thirty. Without a sound, she opened the back door and tiptoed up the rear steps, careful not to wake Ella and Milo. Lucy rushed toward her, whimpering with excitement.

"Hush, girl," Sylvia whispered, and she scooped the puppy up. "Yes, I've missed you too."

She pushed open the bedroom door, entered the darkness, and alit on the edge of her bed. With Lucy in her lap, Sylvia caressed the puppy's smooth fur until anxiety began to subside and her eyelids fluttered closed, but then they opened again. Ricardo probably would have killed her if she hadn't killed him first. The police would never believe that. Either way, she was the one who pulled the trigger and ran away. If his body washed up on the beach, they would come, handcuff her, and take her to jail. A plan had to be formulated—she needed to escape.

21

Her mother's voice on the phone sounded frantic: "We heard there has been a windstorm in Phoenix. Are you all right?"

"Mom, San Francisco is nowhere near there." Anne yawned and curled up on the daybed. She had spent the whole exhausting day parking cars. "I'm fine," Anne said slowly. Mr. Block's critique yesterday had put her in a funk, but she didn't want to share any of it with her mother. If it hadn't been for Fay, Anne probably would have jumped off the Golden Gate.

"You sound down." Her mother always tried to cheer her. "I wish you could come home for Thanksgiving next week."

"Me too." This would be the first time she'd ever been on her own for that holiday, and she volunteered to cover at the hotel so Howard could be with his family.

"I suppose you'll be spending the day with Karl."

"Not exactly." Even though he kept calling, she hadn't spoken to him since that night.

"Did you have a spat?"

She didn't want to tell her mother the gory details. "Something like that."

"I'm sorry, dear. If you want to move home, the card table is still set up."

"Thanks, Mom." Anne hung up thinking about their long-ago

fight after her mother had asked her to clean up the art materials from the dining room for the umpteenth time:

"But I'm not finished with this project." Anne stamped her middle-schooler foot.

"I've told you to move it to the basement." She raised her voice. "You can have the whole place to yourself."

Anne started to cry. "I can't. It's too dark."

"Set up an extra floor lamp."

"That won't help. I need natural light. Can I set up a table in my bedroom?"

"Okay. Get the card table from the garage." And so she did. That year, Anne decoupaged everything she could lay her hands on: cigar boxes, tackle boxes, trunks.

Her mother would come in and inspect the work: "You should put some more pink on this one and some sparkles on that one."

Anne really hoped she wouldn't need to move home. Thank heavens that when she talked to the bank, the mango check had cleared, and that when she handed Mrs. Ladenheim a new check, she had only responded, "Let's just not ever let it happen again."

Anne's phone buzzed, and there was a text from Dottie: *Did you see the postings about my show?*

Anne swallowed and texted back: *I'm so proud of you. How did it happen?*

Dottie: *Met this hunk at a party who owns a gallery.*

Anne: *Still painting circus acts?*

Dottie: *Yes, but you might say I've turned everything upside down.*

Anne: *I'm happy for you.*

Dottie: *Please come.*

Anne: *Too tight right now.* She wished she could. It had been almost a year since Dottie had been there to visit. Anne picked up the key from the altar and played with it.

Dottie: *Introduce gallery owners to you. Come.*

Anne: *Can't*

Dottie: *Jet Blue has good deal on red-eye. Book it or fare might go up.
I'll reimburse you half.*

Anne: *You can't afford that.*

Dottie: *Sure I can. Think about it.*

No way could Anne run off to New York in two weeks. With a
sigh, she dialed Fay to thank her for being so nice yesterday.

"Glad you called. I've got some news. I can hang your
Hitchcock piece."

Anne's pulse raced. "What about Mr. Block?"

"The plonker warned it's a one-off."

"A what?"

"One time only. It's a dark spot in the back, but everyone
needs to go by it sooner or later to get to the loo. Can you drop it
off soon? I want to get it up before the holiday weekend."

"Certainly! I'll slip it in a frame and deliver it to you tomorrow
on my way to work."

"That would be great." Fay paused. "Where do you work?"

"At the St. Francis, parking cars."

"Really? Do you like it?"

"Sometimes. I like the other staff, and I meet interesting
people. It can be tiring though, and there are a lot of night shifts."

"Customers just came in. See you tomorrow."

Anne hung up. She wanted to tell Dottie the good news, but it
was nothing compared to a solo show. Anne took a good shot of
the piece and sat at the computer to do a Facebook post but then
stopped and thought about it. Who was she trying to kid? A little
piece back by the loo.

She took the photo transfer out of her portfolio and tacked it
back up on the wall then Googled for more information on Sylvia

Van Dam. An *Arizona Sun* newspaper article popped up. There on page three in large print blazed, *Heiress and Fiancé Missing*. A larger version of her engagement announcement picture—pearls around her neck, hair perfectly coiffed, and smile wide—ran with it. Unlike the party photo with Ricardo, this face had a childlike innocence. At twenty-one, she appeared much too young to get married, but in those days, things were different.

Anne printed out the image. On white rag paper, Anne flipped the copy upside down and moved the special marker back and forth over it. She pulled away the sheet to reveal, like magic, Sylvia's countenance in shades of gray, her beauty barely visible. Anne picked up a small paintbrush and carefully dabbed in a little watercolor to give Sylvia's features pizzazz: baby blue for the eyes, a pale pink for the lips, and off-white creams for the pearls and hair.

Anne had been afraid that adding these tints might ruin the transfer's effect and mar the socialite's exquisiteness, but they only enhanced her visage. With a smile, she pinned the piece to the wall, picked up a red pencil, and wrote below the transfer, *Sylvia, where are you?* A whiff of gardenia scented the air. Stunned Anne sat on the daybed and inhaled. It was as if the woman was communicating with her.

22

$\mathscr{S}$ylvia waited until dawn and watched shadows cast across the wood floor as the sun began to make its way into her bedroom. Visions had raced through her mind all night in a kaleidoscope of fear and raw emotion, making it impossible to sleep. Lucy climbed out from under the covers and crawled over Sylvia. With plans finalized, Sylvia started to tremble, forced herself out of bed, and opened the safe behind her closet door. She pulled out all the cash, counted it, and slipped it into her handbag.

Sipping an Alka-Seltzer, she packed: a dressing gown, under-garments, a skirt, and a blouse, tossing them into a floral satchel. She needed to travel light. With her navy suit donned and her hair twisted up, she took a quick look around, trying not to cry. She might not ever see her room again. Lucy scampered behind as Sylvia turned the crystal knob and tiptoed down the stairs.

She stopped and watched Ella rattling in the kitchen while she fried bacon. Soon sunny-side up eggs would be set on a Haviland plate for her. Sylvia wished she could turn back the clock, before Ricardo and before all the trouble began. She wanted to run to Ella and apologize, feel those strong arms around her. But instead, she quietly crossed the marble foyer. She couldn't face Ella, not this morning.

Lucy followed Sylvia out the door, scrambled onto the lawn, and rolled around. A dewy haze enveloped the front yard and dripped off the roses. "Mr. Lincoln," Milo's favorite bloom, had unfurled last week and would soon lose its petals. Milo was polishing the hood ornament on the Rolls Royce parked in the driveway. Too bad the flying lady wasn't real. Sylvia wished she could climb on its back and be flown far from San Francisco.

She put her satchel down, and Milo looked up. His eyes filled with affection. "Mornin', Miss Sylvie. Going somewhere?"

"Yes, Milo, I need a ride."

"What about Mr. Lopez?"

"I broke it off." She hated to lie. "He's gone."

Milo grinned. "Finally come to your senses."

His words made her queasy with guilt. She walked over to Lucy, who had rolled onto her back to have her tummy rubbed. Tears flicked from Sylvia's lashes as she crouched down to whisper, "Bye, sweet girl." Then she trudged back to the Rolls.

Milo opened the door for Sylvia, but Lucy jumped in first. He reached for the puppy, but she scooted across the seat to the other side. "You sack of sugar!" Milo scolded, and he hurried around to the other door.

"Let her come along for the ride," Sylvia suggested.

"You sure?"

"It'll be okay." She climbed in, and he set the satchel next to her on the seat. Lucy crawled around it and settled into Sylvia's lap. Worried her suit might get mussed, she started to push Lucy off but changed her mind and let her stay. Her warmth and sweet murmurs were a comfort.

"Where to?"

"The train depot."

He nodded and pulled out of the drive. "Heard it was some party last night."

"Sure was." She rested her head back on the leather seat. She remembered the Cadillac parked behind the house and thought of Ricardo. His face loomed in her mind, his surprised expression when she shot him. She broke out in a sweat and closed her eyes tight, willing his visage away. Paul's blue eyes appeared and looked at her with concern. She wanted to go to him now and tell him what had happened, but he would try and convince her to turn herself in, and she didn't want to go to jail. The police would never believe it was an accident. She didn't even know what she was doing.

She opened her eyes, and Grace Cathedral, with its tall towers, emerged. "Stop at the church." She pulled a scarf from her handbag, put it over her head, and flipped the ends around to the back of her neck. Then she pulled out dark glasses and put them on. Milo glided the Rolls to the curb. She slid Lucy off her lap, got out of the car, and looked around to make sure no one would see her. "I'll be just a moment."

She pushed open the cathedral's heavy doors and stepped inside. It was cool, dark, and deserted. She removed her sunglasses and put them in a pocket. Her heels echoed on the tile as she walked down the aisle toward the altar—the same aisle she had planned to walk down on her wedding day, a day that now would never come.

Light from the stained glass windows reflected onto the side of her suit and pale face: ruby, sapphire, and emerald. Alone at the front of the church, she lit a votive and closed her eyes. "Please forgive me. I have sinned." She paused and wondered if God really listened.

She didn't know for sure if she believed, but if there really was a God, why would He allow someone as evil as Ricardo to walk the earth? Well, he certainly wasn't doing that anymore. Would that God forgive her for killing Ricardo? She hoped so. It had been an accident, a reactive impulse.

She moved to the front pew and sat on a cushion, remembering her parents' funeral years before. On that stormy day, it seemed as if the service would never end. The priest's voice had droned on and on about their sacred lives. Sylvia hadn't been able to cry or even pray.

In fact, she felt relief at their deaths. She'd never been able to be the good girl they wanted. "Sylvia, stop giggling and put your hands in your lap." She could hear her mother's high-pitched voice now. Maybe if her parents had lived longer, they would have grown to love her. She wondered again if they were in heaven and what kind of God would take a young girl's parents from her.

A door slammed, which broke her reverie, and the memory flitted away. A tall priest appeared from behind the altar and moved toward her. She raced down the aisle and out the door.

Rushing to the Rolls she slammed the door behind her. Milo woke up and yawned. "Just restin' my eyes." He looked at her in the rearview mirror. "You okay?"

"Fine," she said, but she really wasn't. Her hands shook while she lit a cigarette. "To the train depot."

He started the motor and pulled from the curb. "Yes, ma'am."

As they drove, she said a silent goodbye to her hometown, as if she might not ever return: Coit Tower, ornate pillar of strength; Alcatraz, floating isle of seclusion; Golden Gate, span of crystals across the bay. At the station, Milo pulled the Rolls into the small lot, came around, and opened her door. She slid out and glanced around.

"Where do you want to go? Shall I get you a ticket?"

"No, thanks. I'll be right back." Inside the depot, she located the ticket window and got in line.

The woman in front of her eyed Sylvia and asked, "Haven't I seen you somewhere before?" She wore a mink stole and shiny diamond earrings.

Sylvia shook her head and said with a quivering voice, "No. You must have me confused with someone else."

"I think I saw your picture in the paper. Aren't you the one who just got engaged?"

"That's not me." Sylvia swallowed. "It must just be someone who looks like me."

The woman stepped forward and spoke to the clerk in a low voice, and then his eyes drifted over to look at her. Sylvia quickly pulled her sunglasses from her pocket and slipped them on.

After purchasing her ticket, the woman smiled. "Have a great trip. And congratulations!" she said, and she exited the building.

"When's the next train?" Sylvia asked the clerk, keeping her head lowered.

He looked at the clock. "Ten minutes."

"Where's it going?"

"Los Angeles."

She paused. "That's not very far."

"From there you can catch the Super Chief all the way to Chickagoooo."

She liked the sound of that. She'd always wanted to see Chicago. "Are there private cars?"

"The Super Chief even has roomettes. First class all the way."

"Sounds expensive."

"$50."

That sounded like a lot. She opened her handbag and looked in her wallet. The cash wouldn't last long. "Do you have any other trains leaving in the next half hour or so?"

He shook his head. "Afraid not."

In Chicago, she could always contact Paul to wire money if need be. She counted out the fare and accepted the tickets. Then she hurried back to Milo, who was waiting for her beside the car and holding her satchel.

"Please don't tell anyone you brought me here."

"Don't worry. Mr. Lopez won't know a thing." Milo's large brown eyes reflected her tension. "Anything else I can do?"

"No. Thank you." She hugged him, for the first time since she was a young girl.

"I'd like to help."

She pulled back and took off her glasses. "There is something."

"Anything."

"Move Ricardo's Cadillac from behind the house. The keys are under the seat."

"Where do you think he'd like to pick it up?"

Sylvia paused. "Park it in front of the cottage. He'll get it there." Again, she hated to lie to Milo, but the less he knew, the better.

"Okey dokey." He helped her locate the first-class car, carried the satchel to the train, and handed it to the porter.

Sylvia climbed the steel stairs, turned, and smiled at Milo then followed the porter to a tiny compartment, where he put down the satchel. "This is heavy. What have you got in here, the crown jewels?"

She handed him a quarter, and he left. Safe inside, she locked the door, slipped off her pumps, and rubbed her stocking feet. The cozy space, cool in the late morning, would do just fine.

Outside, the porter yelled, "All aboard!" A whistle blew, and the train pulled out of the station. From the little window seat, Sylvia saw Milo watching the train depart. Even though she wasn't sure if he could see her, as she passed him, she waved anyway. Now, really all alone, she wiped a tear. The train soon picked up speed and headed south.

A strange noise—a whimper—escaped from the satchel next to her. She opened it, and the beagle-basset blinked up at her.

"Oh, Lucy! You stowaway!" Sylvia pulled her out of the bag. "I didn't buy you a ticket. I don't even know if you're allowed."

A folded piece of paper had been stuck in Lucy's rhinestone collar. Sylvia opened it and read:

So you won't be alone.

Take care, Milo.

She embraced Lucy. "I'm sure glad you're here."

Soon the puppy snored in tempo with the train's rhythm. With each mile further away from San Francisco, Sylvia became more relaxed. She watched as buildings and houses disappeared into grapevines and orange groves. She continued to stroke Lucy's furry back, as smooth as her own velvet coat. Sylvia sat up straight. Where was it? She remembered setting it on the Cadillac's hood before pulling onto the road last night. It must have blown off! How could she have been so stupid? That and the snowflake pin could be traced back to her.

23

*T*he train picked up speed, and Sylvia heard a knock on the compartment door. "Need anything, miss? How about a newspaper?"

"Leave it outside the door, please."

She waited for the porter's footsteps to recede, stuck her hand out, and grabbed *The San Francisco Examiner*. She flipped to the society column. This must have been the photo the woman in the station had seen. The headline above her engagement photo said *Upcoming Nuptials*. In the professional shot, she posed, her eyes glowing and smile bright, the picture reflecting a face of joy, just the opposite of how she felt now.

Lucy started to whine.

"Oh, sweetheart. You must be hungry again." Sylvia tied the scarf on her head, donned the dark glasses, and picked up her handbag. Then she spread some newspaper pages on the floor. "Be a good puppy." Sylvia left the compartment, pulling the door securely closed behind her.

The train's swaying forced her to use both hands to keep from stumbling as she navigated the narrow corridor. In the dining car, only one other person, a bald-headed man, sat at a table. She took a seat as far away from him as possible and ordered coffee and a sandwich.

He glanced up from his newspaper and smiled at her. Would he be the type to read the society news? She looked down and sipped her coffee. When lunch came, she took a few bites, then made sure the man wasn't looking before she folded pieces of ham and cheese into a napkin and slipped them into her purse.

He moseyed over. "May I join you?" he asked.

She grabbed her pearls and shook her head.

"You look familiar. Have we met?"

"No." She tried to keep her voice nonchalant.

"I bet you have beautiful eyes under those glasses. Why don't you take them off so I can have a better look?"

"Light gives me a headache." She put a hand on her damp forehead, tossed some cash on the table, and stood. "Excuse me, I'm not well." She pushed past him and hurried back toward her compartment. Before opening the door, she glanced over her shoulder. Inside, she collapsed onto the seat, reached over, and locked the door. Lucy jumped up beside her. It took Sylvia a few moments to catch her breath, and then she removed her glasses and scarf.

It didn't make sense that someone would be looking for her so soon. Was he just flirting? Had he just seen the picture in the paper and wanted to know more about her? Anyway, he was plain creepy.

Noticing the damp newsprint spread on the ground, she smiled at Lucy. "What a good girl you are!" Sylvia crinkled her nose, and tightly rolled up the paper and jammed it into the trashcan.

Sylvia watched as the train passed miles and miles of orange groves. Soon the sky clouded over, and rain dripped down the window. She felt exhausted and wanted to nap, but every time she closed her eyes, Ricardo's face would loom before her.

Lucy sniffed the purse and gobbled up the scraps as fast as Sylvia fed her, though Sylvia saved a few for later. The rain stopped; the scenery changed to small houses, then apartments and tall office buildings. The train entered a dark cavern, and with a screeching of brakes, it slowed down and came to a halt. Bright lights illuminated the Union Station platform filled with people.

Sylvia kissed Lucy's red head and loaded her back into the satchel. Someone knocked at the door. "Los Angeles, ma'am. Do you need help with your bags?" the porter asked.

"No, thanks. I can manage." Sylvia called.

"The Super Chief is on the right. Track Two. Just follow the signs."

With all her might, she picked up the satchel, heavy now with Lucy. She carefully exited the stairs and followed the crowd to the right along the dank depot. Up ahead, she spotted the bald man, stopped while lighting a cigarette. She stepped back behind an alcove and waited for him to move on.

She walked at a steady pace again toward the Super Chief. Her feet clicked along the tiled floor, and soon her arm grew heavy. She put the bag down and switched hands. She stood back up and thought she saw the man walking back toward her. But then she realized it hadn't been him after all, and she quickly followed the signs and boarded her train.

A porter reached for the satchel just as Lucy started to whimper.

"I've got it!" Sylvia raised her voice to cover up the dog's noises.

"Suit yourself." The porter escorted her to a roomette.

"Thank you." She tipped him one dollar. "I'd rather not be disturbed."

He smiled at her. "Yes, ma'am."

She locked the door and looked around the compartment, amazed at its luxury: a double-sized bed with a full bath.

Lucy whined.

"Sorry, girl." Sylvia unzipped the bag, pulled Lucy out, and set her on the ground. She fed her another morsel, filled a soap dish with water, and laid it on the ground for Lucy to lap up. When the dish was empty, she filled it again.

A whistle blew, and the locomotive started to move. Sylvia lowered the shades as the train left the station. They would be far from danger soon.

Later, a whistle woke her from a deep sleep. Lucy was curled up beside her. Sylvia yawned and sat up as the train rolled to a stop. She peeked around the window shade, the sky dark outside except for a dimly lit sign that said they were in Barstow. She watched as the porter hopped out onto the platform, followed by the bald man. Too bad he hadn't stayed in Los Angeles. He walked toward her window. She let go of the shade, and only when certain he must have passed, she peeked out again.

The porter talked to two men in hats and overcoats. One of them showed him what seemed to be a photo. The porter studied it, gazed at her window, but then shook his head. Good thing she had given him that tip. Maybe someone at the depot had told the police where she had been headed.

The men in overcoats watched the last passengers depart the train and then climbed aboard. She quickly checked her lock and grabbed Lucy. There were footsteps in the hallway and a knock on a nearby door.

She heard it open. "Have you seen this woman?" a man asked.

"Nope." Then the door closed again.

The men moved to her compartment and knocked. The rapid beat of her heart raced as she closed her eyes and held Lucy tight. The puppy started to whimper, so Sylvia gently grasped her mouth shut.

She imagined opening the door and yelling, "Here I am, Sylvia

Van Dam. I killed Ricardo Lopez. Shot him three times. You'll find his body near Ocean Beach." She pictured holding her arms in front of her and being handcuffed. It would be a relief to get it over with.

There was another knock on her door, louder this time. She held her breath until the porter said, "That one is empty."

"Okay." Footsteps moved down the corridor.

She waited until it became quiet, then let Lucy go. "Sorry, sweetie."

Lucy licked Sylvia's hand and was fed another leftover snack. Sylvia spied around the shade again until the men left the train. When the Super Chief finally pulled out of the station, Sylvia sat back and exhaled fully, safe for now.

Outside Barstow, Sylvia opened the shades and watched the darkness pass and listened to the *clickety-clack* of the train. It stopped for a few minutes at Needles and then soon picked up speed again and continued on.

She removed her suit, laid it neatly at the foot of the bed, and crawled under the covers in her white lace slip. Lucy plopped down beside her. Soon the black night, rocking train, and warm blankets lulled them both to sleep. Lucy began to snore loudly. It always amazed Sylvia how a little dog could make such a racket. She nudged her. Lucy snorted and grew quiet. When Sylvia fell asleep, she dreamed of crashing waves, pulling the trigger again and again and again, and Ricardo falling back into the surf.

A knock woke her. Sylvia bolted up but stayed quiet. Outside the window, she caught sight of a magenta sunrise and the tips of tall pines. They were far from San Francisco now.

She heard another knock. "Mornin', miss."

She swallowed with relief. It was just the porter.

"Coffee and juice. Fresh squeezed. Paper, too."

Sylvia threw on a silk wrapper from her satchel, stuffed Lucy back inside, and opened the door. "Thanks for not telling those men about me."

"You'd asked not to be disturbed. Our Super guests come first." He laughed. "Besides, a sweet thing like you couldn't do anything so bad."

She tried to smile.

"Those folks are still searching for you though. One is still on this train."

Who was being so persistent? Paul had hired detectives before. Would he do it again? Should she get off the train at the next stop?

"Yep, better still lie low."

Lucy popped her head out of the satchel with a whimper.

"Who's this?" The porter took a cracker from his pocket and fed it to her. "Hey, cutie."

"That's Lucy."

"Ma'am, you are sure full of surprises."

The puppy licked his hand and whined again.

"You both must be hungry."

Sylvia's stomach growled. "Famished."

"Breakfast is served in the Turquoise Lounge." He frowned. "May I bring you something?"

"You wouldn't mind?"

"That's my job. Can I do anything else for you?"

She handed him the trashcan. "Please empty this." The porter took the can and left. Lucy whimpered and scratched at the door, then she ran around in circles in the small space. Poor girl. Her nature wanted freedom to roll in the grass. The roomette became stuffy, and the walls seemed to recede. As the train began to slow, breathtaking white-capped peaks shone in the distance. Sylvia wanted to reach out and touch them.

24

___

*A*nne spotted Mata Hari curled up in a doorway across from the Food-o-rama and smiled at her. "Haven't seen you for a few days."

"I tried to live with my daughter." Mata tugged on her turban that had begun to lose its shine. "But she tried to take away my hat."

"Do you sleep in it too?"

The homeless woman nodded. "My grandkids listen to that crazy rap. It's not music; it's just a cacophony of noise, noise, and noise."

"I hear you, sister." Anne nodded and handed her a cookie from her pocket.

Mata gobbled it up. "Delicious!"

"It's sure going to get cold tonight." Anne frowned and considered inviting her to sleep on the floor of her apartment, but then she'd get evicted for sure. "I sure wish you'd go to a shelter."

"I'm not crazy."

"I didn't say you were."

"My daughter thinks so."

Anne nodded again.

Mata pointed to the sky. "I like sleeping out here in the fresh air. I can breathe better." She inhaled.

"But don't the police bother you?"

"They try. I just move to the block they just came from and settle back in for the night. The cold keeps me looking young. They say sun can damage your skin, but moon glow makes it smooth and shiny. See?" Mata looked up at the full moon and ran a hand along her wrinkled cheek. "You should try it."

"Not tonight." Anne yawned and sauntered down the hill toward her apartment.

As soon as she opened the door, her cell went off with a text from Fay: *I sold your Hitchcock!*

Anne jumped on the daybed and kicked her feet as she dialed Fay. "You're kidding me. That was fast!" They had just hung it two days before. "Who bought it?"

"Movie buffs from L.A. Congratulations!"

"That's wonderful! Are you ready for another piece?"

"Mr. Blockhead says not yet. Keep working on that new series though."

"I will!" Anne hung up and danced a jig around her apartment. "I've sold a piece in a gallery! I've sold a piece in a gallery!"

Val from below echoed a reply. "You've sold a piece in a gallery. Good for you."

"Thanks!" she yelled back

Mr. Block had to come around and show more of her work now. Even if it wasn't up his alley, it was up his customers' alleys. But though Fay had sold that one little piece, there was no guarantee Mr. Block would ever agree to showing more. He could be so stubborn.

Dottie had sent a text too: *Are you coming?*

Now that Anne had sold a piece, could she afford to go to New York? She picked up the stack of bills from the counter and sorted them into piles again: pay off, pay down, ignore. Gas and electric and cell service in one, Visa and MasterCard in another. Online, she paid the minimums on each, then she checked out Jet Blue prices. The sale of her piece would cover half the flight. She wondered if it would be right to take her friend's offer to reimburse her for half and thought of all the times in college she had treated Dottie to groceries, movies, and weekend getaways. This wouldn't be that much different than that.

Anne had always wanted to go to New York. She would have such fun with Dottie exploring the museums and galleries. Maybe even go to a Broadway musical. Besides, she might make some new art contacts for her career, and every artist should see New York. But she had to work at the hotel, and she had also promised herself not to use her credit cards for a while—and she needed to stick to that. So she told herself no. No New York. At least not right now.

Instead, she looked up at her newest piece about Sylvia missing. She heeded Fay's advice to continue to work on the new series, and Googled Sylvia again until she found a short item in the *Arizona Star* that said Sylvia might have been spotted in Flagstaff.

Could she have traveled all the way to Arizona? Maybe she went there on her honeymoon. No—a 1960s rich heiress would go somewhere romantic like Paris, Rome, or Hawaii.

Anne rummaged through her basket for the postcards Karl had sent last spring on his motorcycle trip to the Southwest. She sequenced them by postmark dates, then studied his all-cap print, neat and legible.

DROVE THROUGH NORTHERN ARIZONA UNIVERSITY TODAY. HERE IS NAU'S MASCOT. DOESN'T HE LOOK LIKE ME?

She turned the card over and laughed out loud at the giant snarling lumberjack holding a huge axe poised to strike. It reminded her of the Paul Bunyan statue back home in Oscoda. It did look like Karl, at least when he had his beard.

Another with a picture of the Meteor Crater read:

WHAT HAPPENED HERE?

Snowy mountains with pine trees graced one of the other cards.

Anne flipped it over to read the caption:

The San Francisco Peaks above Flagstaff, Arizona, at 12,611 feet, are the highest in the Southwest. They looked stunning. Karl's note read:

NOT OUR SF. HIKED TO THE TOP TODAY. SHOULD HAVE HEARD ME YODEL. LOVE YOU.

She remembered when she received this one. They had only been seeing each other for a few months, and it had been the first mention of the word *love*. She had read the card over and over to feel its warm effects. Then she had stuck it in her bathroom mirror, but it dampened and started to mildew, so she placed it in the basket with the others.

She picked up the last postcard of Old Flagstaff and inspected it. The buildings were brick and no more than four stories. The Hotel Monte Vista had a neon sign on the roof bearing its name.

With the cards placed side by side on the dinette table, Anne studied them again. She set a fresh canvas on her easel and brushed a quick sky blue wash over it. Then she left it alone to dry.

From the atlas off the shelf, she located the Arizona map, photocopied and cut around it. She glued the map to the canvas and then pressed the edges down flat with a brayer. She taped the postcards so they could be flipped up and read, upside down.

Her hand caressed the picture of the peaks as she thought of Karl's first use of the word *love* to her. At that moment, a pine scent seemed to emanate from the card into the room, fresh and clean. There went her crazy sense of smell again. Suddenly she missed him terribly and started to cry. Even if he was a liar, she was tempted to call him, but she knew she shouldn't. She missed her best friend Dottie too and cried even more. Anne blew her nose and looked at the Jet Blue flight info again. She held her breath and booked it!

25

As they rolled into Flagstaff, Arizona, Sylvia held the satchel with Lucy tucked inside, waiting for the train to roll to a stop. Despite a bright sun, the door slid open to a frigid blast of air. She scanned the platform, descended the steps, and hid behind a pillar to make sure no one had followed her. An old man and a young couple departed, but that was all. She watched others board the train but didn't move until the whistle blew and the train pulled out of the station again. Her whole body felt lighter as soon as the rear of the caboose was visible moving down the tracks toward Chicago.

She scanned her surroundings. Nearby pine trees were covered with snow, and to the north, the white-peaked mountains rose high above. She wondered what it would feel like to be way up there.

Lucy scrambled out of the satchel, ran around in circles, and hopped through the snowy patches. The glistening crystal glints mesmerized Sylvia. She had never seen snow before, and she reached down to touch the marvel of cold powdered sugar. Looking up, she spotted Lucy racing down the road as she bounced in the white drifts.

Sylvia followed, her heels squished into a pile of mush, and cold seeped through to her toes. Her body temperature began to drop, and, lightheaded, she wasn't sure where to go or what to do, so she just kept moving. Before crossing the highway, she scooped Lucy up and walked into town. A man stared when her heel caught in a slat of the wooden sidewalk. Freezing, she coveted his sheepskin coat and hefty boots. She put Lucy down and carefully stepped along the sidewalk, admiring the quaint buildings that lined both sides of the street: a saddle shop, a café, the post office.

In a pawnshop window, a silver candelabra with half-burned candles caught Sylvia's eye. Like her, it seemed odd in this rugged settlement too. Who here would need something that elegant?

Out of breath, cold and curious, she opened the door and entered. It smelled of pine needles. Patsy Cline's heartachy voice broadcasted from a radio; "Crazy, I'm crazy for feeling so lonely." Sylvia set the satchel down and picked Lucy up again.

A burly man came out from a back room. "Howdy."

"Hello." She'd heard people in small towns were friendly. "Brrr. It's cold."

"Last snowstorm of the season, we hope. Spring should be here soon." He spoke in a heavy western drawl. "Anything special today?"

"Just browsing."

"Suit yerself." He sat on a stool, scratching his scraggly muttonchops. His shoulder-length hair needed a good washing.

She didn't like the way he eyed her. Had he seen her picture in a newspaper? She kept her head down and studied a glass case filled to the brim. This certainly wasn't Tiffany's. An odd assortment of old jewelry and trinkets lined the shelves: a squash blossom necklace, a cameo brooch, and jet-black earrings. A Haviland plate with purple flowers on it, just like the ones at home, leaned against a tarnished silver tray.

Lucy began to squirm in Sylvia's arms. She put the puppy down, but the dog ran around and sniffed all the items.

"Lucy, behave!"

"She's fine." The man's eyes softened as he watched Lucy circle herself, drop down, and fall asleep on a faded rug.

"I kin tell you're not from around here."

Sylvia nodded. "Correct."

"Where you from?"

"California." Sylvia wished she had thought to make something up.

"Ooo, whee! Hollywood?"

"No." She turned her back to him and examined more items. A shiny brass trombone was displayed on a top shelf. She'd never been in a pawnshop before. She had often walked by the one near Union Square, with its cobwebbed, grimy windows, but had been too afraid to go inside. Here, though, everything seemed polished to its utmost.

She didn't understand how pawn sales really worked. "Interesting collection you have here."

"Yes'm. Many people down on their luck."

"What do you mean?" She turned around and looked at him.

He held up a turquoise-and-silver belt. "Take this dead pawn here."

"What?" Her hand clutched her pearls.

"Dropped off by a Navajo two years ago for cash. Said he'd be back for it at the end of the month. Never did."

She swallowed. "Does that mean he died?"

"No, no." The shopkeeper guffawed and shook his head. "Saw him drunk out on the reservation just last week. He's fine."

She didn't drink much but was truly down on her luck too. Perhaps that was the answer. Sylvia unzipped the center section of her pocketbook, pulled out the necklace, and draped it over her arm. She didn't like touching it now because it had been from Ricardo. "How much for this?"

The shopkeeper's eyes lit up as bright as the diamonds and emeralds she held. He took the necklace and used a jewelry loupe to examine it, occasionally looking up at her with a glower.

"It's paste. I'll give you ten bucks for it."

"Sir, you must be mistaken." She shouldn't have been surprised that it might have been a fake. Everything else about Ricardo had been. She blinked back tears and grabbed a lace hanky from her purse.

"Sorry, ma'am." He frowned. "Don't cry. I'll give you twenty-five."

"That's not very much."

He watched her wipe a tear. "Okay. I'll give you a hundred bucks for it."

"And the earrings?" She pulled them out and handed them to him.

"Another twenty."

That wasn't nearly enough to sustain Lucy and her. Maybe she should try and sell her watch too.

"How about I escort you around Flag this evening? Treat you to dinner.

Sylvia felt a knot in her stomach. She started to say no but then thought that if she were nice to him, perhaps she'd get a better deal. "Okay." She ran her fingers over the diamond-chipped watchband. She'd bought it on one of her shopping sprees last year. "How about this?" She unclasped the timepiece and handed it to him. It was a Cartier. There'd be no mistake about its authenticity.

He used the loupe again and inspected it, looked up at her with a smile, and then looked back down at the piece. "She's a beaut! Three hundred bucks."

The amount had begun to add up. She looked in her handbag and pulled out a brush.

He shook his head no.

"This?" She held up a lipstick.

Again no.

She started to rummage through the satchel.

He suggested, "How about them pearls?"

She touched the smooth beads around her neck. Paul had given them to her when she turned sixteen, and she didn't want to let them go. The thought of him made her lonesome. Maybe she should have gone to him instead of running away. Her hands shook as she unhooked the necklace and handed it to the shopkeeper.

He amazed Sylvia by rubbing the pearls over his front teeth and then examined them. "Now, these are the real McCoy."

Of course Paul wouldn't buy her anything but the best.

"Yep. I'll give you $400 for them."

She gulped and nodded with relief. "That should do it for now."

"Okay, little lady, here you go." He counted the stack into her palm. Feeling the cash piled there gave her a sense of security for a brief moment.

"Where may I pick you up?"

She hated to lead him on but smiled anyway. "I'll just meet you here."

He smiled. "Around five thirty then."

"Five thirty." She nodded, gathered up the satchel, and hurried out the door with Lucy frolicking behind her. Sylvia planned to never to see that man again.

26

———

A few days later, Anne stood in Mr. Block's office doorway at Gallery Noir. "Good afternoon, sir. I'm here to pick up my check."

He stared at her through his thick glasses. "Any moron knows you don't get paid until the end of the month. Oh, I forgot, you're from Podunkville. That explains it."

Anne wanted to tell him that Oscoda was a very nice little town, thank you very much, but instead she hung her head and closed his door quietly.

Fay came over, put her hand on Anne's shoulder, and escorted her to the door with a whisper, "Sorry about that. He's such a punter."

Anne frowned. "A what?"

"A John. Prostitute's client."

Anne gaped at her and then laughed. "You crack me up."

"Buy you a cup of coffee?"

"That would be great." Anne felt better already.

"Grab a table next door, and I'll be there in a jiff."

The Coffee Cup Café's walls were covered in paintings of— What else?—coffee cups. Behind the counter, the barista in a samurai topknot tapped along on his cell. The only other customer, a tattooed teen, typed on his laptop at one of seven small round tables. Anne sat down and checked her phone and listened to Karl's hundredth message: "She's moved out! The coast is clear. Call me." Anne rolled her eyes. It was too late now. She turned off her cell and watched the busy traffic going down Sutter through the bay window.

"Mocha?" Fay called as she came in.

"My favorite!" Anne admired Fay's funky outfit of a periwinkle shift underneath a long sweater coat and cowgirl boots. As she stood at the counter, the barista ignored her and kept scrolling through his phone. She got his attention, and he fixed their drinks.

After getting their order she set the paper cups with two scones down and pulled up a chair. "Here you go. This new place is cool. I think it might do well."

Anne nodded and then licked the whipped cream off the top of her mocha. "How humiliating all that was with Mr. Block. He'll never show any of my work again."

"Don't be preposterous! I've told you before, you've got talent. Give it more time, he'll come around."

The teen glared over and put his earplugs in.

Fay grinned at him. "Does he think this is his private office?" She focused on Anne. "How's the new series?"

"I'm really on a roll."

"When can I see some of it?"

"Not until I'm further along. I don't want to jinx it." Anne said a silent prayer, pulled a piece off the scone, and took a nibble.

"Let me know when you're ready."

"I will. Have you ever heard of Fredricka Woods?"

Fay nodded with a smile. "Interesting you should mention her. Just the other day, she came into the Noir and looked around. Mr. Block chatted her up in his office for a while. Why do you ask?"

"She stays at the hotel, and I park her car."

Fay's dark eyebrows shot up. "You know her then. Her gallery is the best in Santa Fe. Have you ever shown her your work?"

"Actually she bought one of my pieces at the farmers' market."

"Blimey! Told you that's not a bad place to sell."

"A mixed-media piece." Anne pulled a photo up on her cell and showed it to Fay.

She laughed, "That's the dog's bollocks!"

Anne smiled. "She asked to see my portfolio."

"What did she say?" Fay dunked her teabag up and down and put it on a napkin.

"I didn't show it to her." Anne was too embarrassed to tell her about running out of the hotel room that night.

"Why the bloody hell not?"

"Because she won't like my other finished pieces like the Moguls or Divas. They're different than the mango one."

Fay scrunched up her red lips. "Anne, if someone wants to see your portfolio, you show them your portfolio!"

"But what if she rejects me?" Anne folded her arms and slouched in her chair.

"So what? You need to grow a thicker skin. Get your work to Fredricka."

"It's too late—she checked out yesterday."

"Email her a nice note along with some photos."

"Maybe. Right now I have other issues."

"Money, huh?"

Anne nodded. "Always short of cash."

"Listen. I could use a day off every now and then. Would you be interested in sitting the gallery for me?" Fay blew on her tea and then sipped it.

"What about Mr. Block?"

"He's rarely there on weekends and said I could hire someone to cover occasionally, agreeing to pay ten bucks an hour and maybe a little commission if something sells."

"Okay. I'd like that. Every little bit helps. Just let me know when."

"How about the first weekend in December?"

Anne frowned. "My best friend is having a show opening in New York. I splurged and am going."

"Really! I love New York. It can be so romantic." Fay checked her watch and picked up her tea. "I'd better get back before you-know-who himself gets his knickers in a twist."

Anne smiled, waved goodbye, put half the scone in her pocket in case she ran into Mata, walked down to the hotel, and checked in with Howard.

"It's been a dead afternoon." He pointed to the empty key rack.

"Bored?"

"Not really. I've been people-watching." He looked at a tall brunette strut by. "I saw your boyfriend Karl last night."

"Really? Where?"

"On the dance floor at Rhinestone Ruby's. I figured you must have been working in your studio."

"Was he with anyone?"

"He was dancing the two-step with a curvaceous babe."

Anne's heart stiffened like papier-mâché. She thought she would be over him by now, and still, it really hurt. She tried to keep her tears at bay.

Howard looked at her with concern. "You okay?"

"We broke up a few weeks ago."

"I'm sorry, I didn't know."

"Didn't want to talk about it and still don't."

"Are you sure?" He looked at her with concern.

She nodded. "Since it's slow can I just go home?"

"No problem. I can cover. Take care."

"Thanks." She ran out of the parking garage as a cold wind blew scattered clouds overhead and a Cheshire Cat moon appeared to be laughing down at her. Trying to beat the rain before her own wet tears began to fall, she ran up the hill toward her apartment. How could Karl be out there so fast?

From in front of Grace Cathedral, Mata waved from a doorsill and yelled, "Man troubles, Missy?"

Anne crossed the street, brushing away the tears that drifted down her cheeks. "Yes."

"That's all I've ever had. I suggest you call him and apologize."

Anne handed the scone to Mata. "But I didn't do anything wrong."

"That's not the point."

Anne walked the rest of the way down the hill toward her apartment and let herself in. She listened to a message from her mom. "Pootie's got a boyfriend. Pootie's got a boyfriend. That nice Brian from Heating and Air Conditioning. I just found out they've been seeing each other since July!"

That would have started during the ice cream episode when Anne was home for the Fourth. Grabbing a box of Kleenex, she plopped on the daybed, and though she tried to stop them, her sobs wouldn't subside. She knew Karl wasn't good for her and yes he was a jerk, but she was lonely and had an overpowering desire to feel his arms around her. She wanted to resist, but after awhile, she pulled herself together, drank a glass of water, and called his number. He didn't answer. Again she dialed and this time left a message. "Please call back. It's urgent. I think I'm dying."

A minute later, her phone buzzed. "Anne?"

She began to cry again so hard she couldn't catch her breath.

"Babe?" His voice sounded very far away.

"I'm having a meltdown." She sniffled and reached for another tissue, but the box was empty. "And I'm all out of Kleenex!"

"Where are you?"

"My apartment."

"Be there in half an hour."

She took a bath, held a cool cloth on swollen eyes, brushed her wild hair, slipped into a sexy red nightie, and waited all night for him to arrive. But he never did.

27

———

$\mathcal{T}$he bathroom wall heater's orange coils hummed. Sylvia, naked except for a towel wrapped around her shoulders, stood at the sink, sighed at her image in the mirror, and combed fingers through her blonde shoulder-length hair. Yesterday she had left the pawnshop with a newfound sense of self-confidence, bought fresh clothes at the mercantile, and checked into the Hotel Monte Vista. Knowing it was only a matter of time before the police started looking for her, she had a desire to go incognito with a whole new look. "Here goes." She opened a drugstore sack and placed the contents on the vanity table: scissors, comb, timer, dye, and *Vogue*.

Picking up the scissors, she captured a handful of hair, gritted her teeth, snipped, and threw the clump into the trashcan below the sink. Strands floated like ashes onto the tile floor. She held another section and clipped again, throwing away the bundle. Quickening her speed, she continued until her hair was quite short, a pixie cut, like Mary Martin in Peter Pan. Sylvia thought she had done a pretty good job, leaving short bangs and feathery sides.

She picked up the Miss Clairol box of dye and studied the lovely redhead on the front. Sylvia read the directions, poured the inky liquid into a hotel glass, and stirred in hot water from the tap.

"Does she . . . or doesn't she?" Sylvia said to herself. "Well, she does now!"

If she didn't mix correctly, her hair might turn as bright as Lucille Ball's. She poured the brew onto her scalp, massaged it into her hair, and then combed it through. With the back of her hand, she wiped drips off her forehead and dabbed some onto her eyebrows. She set the timer, put the lid down on the commode, and sat there, trying to read the *Vogue*, but she kept checking the timer. What if she left it on too long and all her hair fell out? That had happened to a Mills girl, one of the mean ones, so at the time, Sylvia thought it kind of humorous.

Ten minutes later, the timer rang. She rinsed her hair out in the sink and let the water run, but even so, dark stains remained around the drain. She dressed in her new clothes: Lee Rider jeans, a light blue shirt with pearl snap buttons, and cowboy boots.

She smiled at the transformation reflected in the mirror and ran her fingers through the new auburn do. Without its weight, her hair curled into light wisps. No one would recognize her now, not even Ricardo—and then she shook her head, remembering that he was gone. Even though she was weighed down with guilt, she felt relieved he was out of her life.

She opened the bathroom door. Lucy jumped off the bed and growled.

"It's me. Sylvia. Or should I say, the new me?"

At the sound of her voice, Lucy grew quiet and barked.

Sylvia sat on the edge of the bed and murmured a made-up song:

Are you ready to start a new life?
Travel the road?
Let go of the strife
and our heavy load?
Lucy howled as if singing along.

Sylvia patted next to her on the white chenille bedspread. The puppy leapt up and put her head on Sylvia's thigh while she petted her for a few moments. Then she put on the new plaid Pendleton jacket, grabbed her purse, and slipped out the door.

She ordered breakfast at the coffee shop next door, but when she unfurled and skimmed the *Arizona Sun* newspaper, on page three, *Heiress and Fiancé Missing* blazed in large print. Accompanying the article was the same photo that had run with the engagement announcement, only this time, it had been blown up twice the size and splashed across the page. She felt faint, folded her arms on the table, and rested her head.

Lucy crawled over and licked her hand while the waitress brought a fresh glass of water. After Sylvia's dizziness subsided and her head had cleared, she returned to the article. It described the engagement party. And it even mentioned that they might be traveling with a small beagle.

Sylvia needed air and exited the diner with Lucy at her heels. A wide-brimmed cowgirl hat, also a mercantile purchase, shielded her eyes from the sun's rays that streamed out from behind billowy white clouds. She looked up at the peaks and felt a calmness she'd never known before, a sense of quiet beauty. Unlike her hometown, Flagstaff had been built on flat land below the hills instead of on them. The dry air was clearer here without the damp sea breezes and fog. Perhaps she'd stay in this town for a while. Her disguise should keep her safe.

Lucy sniffed ahead, nose to the ground. Water sparkled and dripped off the pine trees, making a tiny river along the street's edge. Sylvia clomped along the wooden sidewalk in her Western boots. Besides being practical, they were much more comfortable than the pumps she usually wore.

At this time of morning in San Francisco, cars would be speeding down the streets and inhabitants would rush by on their way to work, errands, and shopping. She listened: no honking horns or yelling voices—not even a barking dog. A bluebird flew down and landed in a nest under the eaves of a nearby café. Down the street, a shopkeeper opened his door, swept the front, and put out a welcome mat.

She glanced across the street, and her heart skidded. She reached for her pearl necklace, but of course it wasn't there. The man from the pawnshop stood looking at her. He stared at Lucy and then at Sylvia again. She froze, not sure what to do.

He crossed the street and asked, "Hey! Where's your friend?"

Sylvia hoped her new look would be successful camouflage. She picked up Lucy and put her hand over the pink rhinestone collar. "What friend?" Sylvia tried to disguise her voice with a high-pitched twang.

"The puppy's owner."

"Lucky is mine."

"You sure?" He squinted and stroked his beard. "Have you seen another dog like that around?"

"Nope." Sylvia shook her head.

"Could be from the same litter." He leaned over and tried to pet Lucy, but she yapped at him.

The man backed up, "Snarly little thing!" He studied Sylvia. "You do look familiar."

She bucked her teeth over her bottom lip. "Think so?"

"Guess not." He shook his head, walked down the street, and entered the Monte Vista.

She let her body ease, but it tensed again as it dawned on her she had better leave town before he discovered the truth. Good thing she had paid for her room in advance. She didn't really need the satchel and those old clothes anyway. At least she had her handbag.

"Okay, girl, let's go back to the station and check schedules."

The thought of getting on another stuffy train made Sylvia nauseous. At the highway, with Lucy still in her arms, she waited while several cars whisked by, then crossed and entered the station. The taped note on the empty ticket window said that the next train wouldn't depart until 9:00 PM.

She looked at her watch—it was only ten in the morning. She went back to the highway and looked left, then right. Down the road, high in the sky, a red, white, and blue sign said:

MARTY'S CARS

SEMI-NEW AND USED

You Try 'em then Buy 'em

She walked toward the sign. In the muddy lot, several vehicles were lined up: a Studebaker, a Rambler station wagon, and an Edsel. At a turquoise car, she paused. She'd never been interested in cars like Ricardo had been, but she had admired the Thunderbird advertised in magazines. Now up close, she knew it was the most adorable car she'd ever seen, with tiny fins and white trim. Behind it, a travel trailer's rounded body glistened in the sun. She wandered over and admired the car's leather interior.

"Hey, girlie girl." A short man in a tall cowboy hat approached her.

"Beg your pardon?"

He cleared his throat and began again. "I'm Marty. Kin' I help you?"

She touched the car hood in awe. "How much is it?" Lucy squirmed, and Sylvia set her down.

"Fabulous, huh? Came in yesterday." He rested his pudgy hands on his stomach, which protruded over a shiny belt buckle. "Before we start dealing, you gotta drive this baby."

"I don't know." She shook her head.

"You can. Gotta unhitch the bullet first." He pointed behind the T-Bird. She'd never seen inside a real trailer before. "May I peek?"

"All rightie." He pulled a chock-full key ring from his belt loop and opened the door. Lucy ran in first, and then Sylvia and Marty stepped inside. Neat as a pin with red gingham curtains hanging in the windows, it smelled of oranges and cloves. It had a toilet, shower, refrigerator, and sink. Books lined the shelves too.

Marty spread his arms wide. "Give you a package deal. This sixteen-footer Bambi is well stocked and has all the comforts of home. See, a lounge bed with blankets and another one that pulls out." He tugged on a folding bed to display a foam mattress and opened an upper cupboard. "Even a sleeping bag in case you want to commune out under the stars. Complete with lots of camping equipment. Live in nature. Not see a soul for weeks."

That was exactly what she needed. No one would find her in here. Being in nature would be nice. She did like flowers.

She stepped outside and studied the T-Bird and trailer hook up. "Is it difficult to drive?"

"Naw. It's a cinch."

"I don't know." She shook her head, afraid of the challenge.

"I could teach you."

"Really?"

"Come on, hop in." He opened the driver's door. She lifted Lucy into the tiny back area before slipping into the driver's seat. Marty tossed his hat upside down beside Lucy, squeezed into the seat, and handed Sylvia the key.

She inserted it and turned on the ignition. The car sputtered and died. Giggling nervously, she tried again, and this time the car leapt forward. "Damn!" She put her hand to her mouth and looked at him. "Sorry."

"Nothing I haven't heard before. Check the rearview mirror to make certain the trailer is straight. Keep aware of the other traffic. Now nudge on the gas pedal."

She did so, and the T-Bird inched onto the highway. A horn honked as a pickup swerved just in time. Sylvia pressed on the brakes and Marty grabbed the dashboard. "Careful!"

She pulled over to the side of the road and tried to catch her breath. Remembering the freedom of those days when Paul first taught her to drive, she wanted to lick this too and said, "Let me give it another try."

"You sure?"

She nodded. "Now what?"

Marty wiped his brow with a kerchief.

She took a deep breath and cruised back out onto Route 66, curving east. The travel trailer wove back and forth behind them like a tinfoil zeppelin. It felt as if it might topple over. She gripped the steering wheel and tried to keep it steady. Soon the T-Bird's motion smoothed out, and the trailer coasted right behind. The cars in the left-hand lane drove past with ease.

"That's right. You're getting the hang of it now."

Along the two-lane highway, pine trees lined the road, and a few cars passed in the opposite direction. She felt more confident and sped up.

"Slow down, girl!" Marty grabbed the dashboard again. "That's better. Now, past the Texaco station ahead, turn left onto the college campus. There'll be less traffic." She nodded and turned left. The trailer wobbled behind, but she was able to get it back on course.

Marty rolled down the window. "Yes, this baby has power steering, brakes, and windows." He continued with a rapid voice, "Two hundred and twenty-five horsepower and a V8 engine—you could drive anywhere you wanted to go in no time."

Satisfied this had to be the perfect setup, she drove through the campus filled with brick buildings with the first genuine smile she'd felt in days. Then she steered back out along Route 66, pulled into the lot, and turned off the motor. She hoped it wouldn't be too expensive.

Marty lugged himself out of the car. He grabbed his hat from the backseat and stared at the chewed brim. "What the heck?"

"How could you?" Sylvia snapped the puppy up in her arms. Lucy blinked at them both with innocent brown eyes.

"That's okay, miss."

"I'll pay for a new one."

"Forget it. She's just a puppy. Step into my office here, and we'll talk business." They entered the closet-like room. Sylvia carefully sat in the chair he pulled out for her with a missing back and cracked leather.

He moved behind his desk. "Let's see how I can get you to buy this today." He wrote a number on a piece of paper and slid it across the desk to her. She had just that much cash, but then nothing would be left. She crossed out Marty's number and wrote a much, much smaller one, hoping he'd accept it.

He hesitated, wrote another number, and passed it to her.

"Deal." She nodded with a smile.

He shook her hand, pulled a clipboard from under a pile on his desk, and handed it to her. "Fill out these forms, and I'll also need your driver's license."

She stood. "Is that really necessary? I'm kinda in a rush."

"You're not on the lam, are you?" he joked.

She swallowed a lump in her throat. "No, nothing like that." She took the clipboard and filled in the form with made-up data, hoping that wasn't illegal. "Sorry, but I don't have my license with me."

"Well, we have regulations here. I can't let you . . ."

She pulled a wad of money from her purse. "I can bring it by later."

He eyed the cash, "Okay. By four thirty, closing time," then nodded with a wink as she counted it into his hand.

"Here's a little extra to replace your hat," she smiled.

He walked her to the car, and she set Lucy in the passenger seat. "Thanks, Marty. For everything."

He shook her hand again. "Now be careful not to go uphill for too long. There's just so much hauling the T-bird can do in one day." As she pulled out of the parking lot, he yelled, "Enjoy your land yacht!"

28

On Highway 66 driving out of town, evergreens stood tall like sentinels along the roadside. In the T-Bird with the trailer behind, Sylvia pushed hard on the gas pedal. She had no idea where she was going and decided to just keep heading east. But no matter how far away from San Francisco she got, the truth would never change—she had shot Ricardo. How would she ever find forgiveness for that?

With the heavy rig behind her, she felt powerful, and she wondered what Paul would think if he could see her. At least she knew he would tease her about the haircut and color. He must be mad with worry though, and she planned to drop him a line soon, as well as one to Milo and Ella too. How would they all feel about her though if they found out about what happened to Ricardo?

Sylvia switched on the radio. Elvis Presley's voice blurted, "You ain't nothing but a hound dog." Lucy awoke from the passenger seat and blinked.

"Yes, Lucy, he's singing your song." Sylvia just loved Elvis. She had seen him on the *Ed Sullivan Show*. Ella pretended not to like him but would always sit and watch. Afterward, Milo would make them laugh by doing his funny impersonations by rolling his hips around and singing into an invisible microphone. Because it was

Sunday, "the really big show" would be on tonight. Sylvia felt sad they would be watching without her.

After driving for an hour, she grew thirsty and pulled into the Wikiup Trading Post. Looking in the rearview mirror to freshen up, the new hairdo caught her by surprise, and she laughed. While applying lipstick, she noticed a woman watching through the store's dusty window.

Sylvia got out of the T-Bird and said to Lucy, "Be right back, sweetie." On the store's porch, Sylvia selected a bottle of Coca-Cola from the fridge. A little bell tinkled as she opened the trading post's door, and the Indian woman behind the counter nodded.

Sylvia put her soda on the counter and picked up a news-paper. She glanced at the front page. Thank heavens her picture wasn't on it. It felt good to stretch her legs as she browsed the stuffy shop. Kachina dolls, rubber tomahawks, and conch belts lined the shelves. She unfolded a T-shirt that said *Navajo Land* with dancing warriors on the front. Another top had the Grand Canyon and mules printed on it, and still another had Monument Valley, which she put over her arm. She looked up and saw that the woman still watched her. Sylvia folded the other T-shirts and put them back on the shelf neatly.

Even though the Grand Canyon was nearby, she had no desire to visit it. She craved wide-open spaces, rock formations, mesas, and geysers, tall things from nature that reached toward the sky. Not unlike the man-made structures she had lived with all her life —such as Coit Tower, the Golden Gate Bridge, and Grace Cathe-dral. But imagine seeing sky-high gifts from God—like Monument Valley. Was it nearby? She had seen pictures of it in Western films. Enormous tabletops—some spiky, some rounded—reaching for the sky like an outlaw raising his arms in surrender. Twirling a postcard rack, she grinned at the rabbit with antlers, a mythical creature called a jackalope. Paul would get a kick out of it. Maybe if she made him laugh he'd forgive her for leaving town without telling him. For Milo and Ella, she selected a card with a young Indian girl on it. Her sweet innocent face might help them forget all the disrespectful things Sylvia had said to them lately.

In order to camp, she needed provisions. The store had a small selection of grocery items. What would Ella choose? She would certainly advise as always, "Choose nutritious. That's delicious."

Sylvia tossed the T-shirt, Ritz Crackers, peanut butter and apples, and several canned goods—Spam (she'd never tried it before and had always been curious), Campbell's Tomato Soup, and Friskies—into a basket. At the cash register, the woman nodded at her again and started to total up the prices. Sylvia added an Arizona map to the pile.

A basket of pendants sat on the counter. Sylvia picked one up and admired the lovely golden brown. It had a fly trapped inside! She grimaced and tossed it back in the basket.

"Amber. Good luck." The woman's voice was deep. "Buy one." Her gray hair was pulled back into a low braid, and wrinkles lined her ruddy face. She could have been anywhere from thirty to fifty years old. The name badge pinned to her Mickey Mouse T-shirt read *Betty Lou*. "Very powerful." She pushed the basket closer to Sylvia.

She shivered. "No, thanks."

Betty Lou flipped off the soda cap and handed it to Sylvia. The Indian woman's dark eyes inspected her then looked out the window and upward. "Rains coming."

There wasn't a cloud in the sky.

She clutched an amber piece on a gold chain and held it toward Sylvia. "Buy one. You need it."

"No." Sylvia's hands trembled as she paid and collected her sack of goods. She pushed the door open, and the bell tinkled her escape.

Was that woman crazy? Did she bother all customers that way? Sylvia put the sack in the trunk, climbed into the T-Bird, and put the key in the ignition. She touched Lucy's head to shake off the eerie feeling.

"Here, for you." Betty Lou all of a sudden stood next to the car. She dangled the nugget in front of Sylvia's face. "Take it."

"I couldn't." Sylvia's voice quivered.

"Please. It's for good fortune." Betty Lou nodded and grinned at Lucy in the passenger seat. The puppy barked at her.

Sylvia grasped the light chain, squinted, and held the amber, bigger than a quarter, up to the sunlight. At least this one didn't have an insect inside. She ran her fingers over the smooth surface, and her tense body relaxed. The yellow-orange translucent sap shone glossy, the color of honey. Black lines, like delicate ink strokes, sparkled.

"It's from nature and will keep you safe."

Trancelike, Sylvia clasped the chain behind her neck and pressed the pendant to her chest. It felt cool. She reached for her purse.

"A present for you. It's lucky."

No one had ever given Sylvia something for luck. Maybe it would really work. She drove away with a sense that the woman knew all about her. Perhaps Betty Lou had seen her picture in a newspaper and recognized her. But that would have been impossible—Sylvia looked so different now. Whatever the case, she sensed this woman had been on her side.

Back on the road, Sylvia felt something inside her breaking lose and melting away, something old and restricting. A month ago, she would never have accepted something from a stranger or have worn anything so cheap. But this was a new life, a new persona, and she needed all the luck she could get.

29

The jet screeched, bounced, and finally stopped on JFK's tarmac three hours late due to a winter storm. The red-eye from hell was almost over. Squished in a window seat, the bulky man seated beside Anne took up the whole armrest, and a baby behind her had screamed the entire flight.

The movie had been *Bridesmaids*, which she had already seen twice and opted not to watch. The romantic parts might remind her too much of Karl (that jerk!).

Girlfriend time with Dottie was just what Anne needed. She couldn't wait to tell her all about Karl and her new art series inspiration. Dottie had always been so supportive and an enthusiastic sounding board. Lately though, Anne had been worried about her. On the phone she'd seemed rushed and distant. Her Facebook posts had gotten weirder and weirder. Like the one where she showed a close-up of her newly pierced nose, and others of her partying with people who looked like characters from *The Rocky Horror Picture Show*. And then there was something about a name change?

"You may turn on your electronic devices," the flight attendant announced over the intercom.

Anne dialed Dottie's cell.

"Hello." Her friend's voice sounded slurry.

"I'm here! Just landed. I'll meet you at the baggage area."

"I got tied up."

"What? You mean you aren't even here at the airport?"

"Sorry. I got tied up with the installation. Just hop on the Air Train to Jamaica Station and then get off and transfer to the LIRR and take it to Penn Station. I'll meet you there."

Anne's head started to swim. "I can't. All by myself."

"Grow up. Take a taxi then. Call me when you get into the city. Get dropped at Penn station, and I'll meet you just inside the Eighth Avenue entrance."

Anne jammed the phone in her pocket, rolled her suitcase down the plane's aisle, exited the Jetway, and followed the passengers to ground transportation. She'd never seen so many people scurrying here and there in her life. Stepping outside to a cold blast of air, she was grateful for her velvet coat. Then she stood in line for a taxi, climbed inside one, and soon exhaustion overpowered her and she quickly fell asleep.

She awoke to a view of Manhattan's outline. Bridges spanned onto it, and she made out the Chrysler and Empire State buildings. Then the excitement hit. New York, the Big Apple, Times Square, Broadway, the Met! She couldn't wait to see it all, dialed Dottie, and notified her she was almost there.

At Penn Station, Anne paid the taxi driver the $45 flat-rate fare and added in some tip, and there went her spending money. No problem. Dottie would reimburse her for half the flight. With her heart thudding crazily, Anne rolled her suitcase into the crowded concourse and stopped to get her bearings. She studied the blue pillars decorated with twinkle lights, watched people hurrying by, and then looked around but found no clues as to where the Eighth Avenue entrance might be. She asked a man walking by for directions, then followed where he pointed, but when she arrived, Dottie was nowhere to be seen. Anne stepped outside for a moment into the cold once more and looked around, but Dottie wasn't there either, so she called her friend again. "Where are you?"

"Be right there." Dottie yawned and hung up.

When she finally arrived thirty minutes later, Anne almost didn't recognize her friend. Her light hair had been died jet-black and cut into a Mohawk. "Nice to see ya." Her usually enthusiastic voice sounded cool, and she gave Anne a little hug.

She tried not to be angry with Dottie for being so late and hugged her back. "I've missed you."

"Great coat." Dottie rubbed Anne's velvet-covered arm.

"There's a story to it. I can't wait to tell you all about it, but we'll save it for later." She popped up the suitcase handle and rolled it along beside her. "I'm starved. Let's get something to eat."

"Not now. I need to get back to the apartment." She took Anne's suitcase and pulled it for her.

"Do you have a boyfriend now? You were so mysterious on the phone."

Dottie nodded. "I've been seeing someone a bit. You'll meet him tonight. I'm glad you dumped that Karl. What a geek." She had met him when she visited San Francisco last year right after Anne started seeing him.

"I thought you liked him."

"Yuck! What about that beard?"

"He shaved it off."

"Did he look any better?" Dottie laughed, and Anne saw her old friend for a second.

"Much!" Anne sadly thought off his smooth face. Too bad he didn't shave it off earlier in their relationship. For some reason though, she didn't feel like telling Dottie all about the breakup like she thought she would.

Neither said another word as they walked the busy sidewalk the few blocks to Dottie's home. Anne wondered what had happened to the Dottie she knew. Had she been kidnapped by New York?

The SoHo loft, a long narrow rectangle in an old building, was located on a seedy street. "Where can I put my suitcase?"

The counter was strewn with unopened paint supplies and empty canvases. Dottie pointed to the coffee table, and Anne pushed aside some old issues of *Punk Planet* and set her case on top. The room smelled of skunkweed and dead flowers mixed together. "Let's open a window." Anne strode over to a grimy one, which overlooked a trash-filled alley.

"Can't. It's stuck." Dottie plopped down on the stained couch underneath a Jimi Hendrix poster. She picked up a bong, lit it, and inhaled. Then she passed it over to Anne.

"No, thanks." As roommates, the only times they ever argued had been when they were high. Karl didn't like the stuff, so Anne hadn't even had any in almost a year.

"Come on. Let's celebrate. You're finally here." Dottie took another toke and offered it again. "It's good stuff."

Anne sat beside her on the couch and took a drag. It burned on its way into her lungs, and she regretted the decision. "Dottie, you seem so different."

"Don't call me Dottie. I go by Dorothea now."

"Since when?" Anne asked.

"Since I met Trevor from the gallery. He said it sounds more sophisticated."

The smoke started to bother Anne's eyes, so she moved to a mustard yellow beanbag chair across from the table and studied her dear friend. She looked anything but sophisticated. Besides the Mohawk and nose ring, her eyes were bloodshot and rimmed with too-thick liner. The baggy pants and tee she wore weren't vintage. They just looked old and dirty. "You have really changed."

Dottie shrugged. "Don't like it, huh?"

"I didn't say that." Anne decided to change the subject. "My mom thinks I should move home."

"Why?"

"I'm having a hard time making ends meet."

Dottie ran her hand over her Mohawk. "Maybe your mom's right. Not everyone is meant to be an artist."

"But you always said if I couldn't make it, no one could."

"I must have been wrong. Some people are meant to move back with mom."

"You've moved home for awhile." Anne felt stung, held back tears, and turned away.

"That was just temporarily. Tell me about your coat?" Dottie took another toke.

Anne had really looked forward to telling her all about it, but now she didn't even want to. Her stomach churned. "Later. I need something to eat."

"Help yourself." Dottie pointed to the rusty fridge.

It was empty inside except for an unidentifiable moldy vegetable in a drawer. "Not much here. Can we go to a nearby restaurant?"

"I don't have time. There's a deli across the street. Go ahead."

"Can you pay me back now?"

Dottie squinted at her. "For what?"

"The plane ticket."

"Oh, that." She took her wallet from a back pocket and opened it. "Don't have any cash right now. Get it to you later."

That was supposed to be Anne's spending money. There was nothing left in her ATM. She spied Dottie's money jar sitting on the counter. "May I at least use your change?" When they'd roomed together, they'd raided their jar for special occasions.

"Sure, knock yourself out."

Anne dumped the coins onto the counter.

Dottie pulled herself up off the couch. "I need to get to the gallery to finish up a few details."

Anne looked at her watch. "But the opening doesn't start for hours. You mean I came all this way, and now you don't even want to spend time with me?"

Dottie shrugged. "I'm sorry. Do you want to come with me now?"

"Can you use my help?"

"Not really."

Anne didn't want to navigate her way across town by herself later tonight, but her body swayed with hunger and jetlag. She needed to get something to eat and to lie down for a while. Unzipping her suitcase, she pulled out the green dress. "What do you think?" She held it up under her neck. "Is it too much for tonight?"

Dottie shook her head. "It's lovely. I should change too." She turned around and pulled off her T-shirt, revealing a tattoo that covered most of her back. The curvy letters formed words that were difficult to make out. Anne's stomach roiled as she deciphered the words "death" and "doom" before Dottie slid into a see-through black blouse. Her Dottie really had been kidnapped by New York.

30

——

$\mathcal{S}$ylvia decided to drive north up the mountain into the indigo sky, decorated with a few wispy white clouds. After an hour, the T-Bird's engine started to make a funny sound. *Cha-chung. Cha-chung.* She thought about Marty's warning but wanted to make it to the top of the peak, so she tried to ignore it and just kept going. Then the noise got faster and louder, *chung, chung, chung.*

No way would she like to get stranded by the side of the road, so she looked for a place to pull over. Spotting a *Campground Ahead* sign, she followed the arrow down a dirt road to a copse of pines next to a stream. It even had a picnic table. Yes, this quiet campground would be the perfect place to hole up for a few days. No one would find them here.

She parked, lifted Lucy to the ground, and carried the sack from the trunk into the Airstream. The closed-up space still smelled of cloves with a hint of oranges. Lucy ran around outside for a few minutes then dashed into the trailer, sat down, and stared at Sylvia.

"You're right. It's suppertime!" She continued to unload the groceries, but Lucy kept jumping on her.

"Hold your horses, girl." Sylvia found a bowl in the cupboard and picked up a can of Friskies. She rummaged through the drawers for an opener but couldn't find one. "Wait a sec." Slicing an apple, she offered a piece to Lucy, who took it in her mouth, grimaced, and spit it out. Sylvia opened the Ritz Crackers, located a knife, and spread some peanut butter on one. Lucy gobbled this treat right down. Sylvia fixed one for herself and ate it and then made another for Lucy. She wished she had some of Ella's grape jelly to add some flavor. They ate this way for a while, standing at the counter until Sylvia was full.

When she spread the map out on the bed, Lucy dove into it, ripping the center. "Stop!" Sylvia yelled. Lucy froze, kicked it again, then sank on a pillow for a nap.

Sylvia straightened the map out again and thought of Milo. She recited the rhyme, making the motions he had taught her long ago. "North, south, east, and west. But here at home is the very best." She pointed way to the left of the Arizona map toward San Francisco and began to study the possible routes she could take. They might be able to continue north, up higher into the mountains, but the T-Bird probably couldn't make it. At least, not with the trailer on it, but she wasn't about to try and unhook them. She decided that after resting here a day or two, she would head out to Monument Valley. She found it on the map and put her finger on it, tracing the route. On the way, maybe she would spend time in the Painted Desert too. She liked that name and imagined jewel-tone colored sand.

Sylvia stepped out of the trailer and closed the door, breathing in deeply. How did these pines smell so fresh? Was it a chemical reaction from the slight breeze touching them, or would they give off an odor even in the stillest air? The aroma made her body and mind feel clean. She sat at the picnic table, lit a Lucky, and inhaled. The acrid smoke tarnished the nearby forest scent. She tossed the cigarette to the ground and crushed it under her boot, thinking she might quit.

The silhouetted pines on the hill and gathering clouds above resembled an artist's rendition of a Western scene. She could just sit here for the rest of the afternoon enjoying the view. A bush rustled, and something moved out from behind it. It was the most beautiful creature she had ever seen, and it stood only about ten yards away. Sylvia froze as tears sprang to her eyes. It was a good thing Lucy slept in the trailer; she would have scared it away.

The deer had a white tail and two budding antlers. Sylvia wished she could reach out and touch its brown fur. Her fingers imagined its hemp-like texture. It strode along on an uphill path away from her. With as little movement as possible, Sylvia tiptoed on a lower parallel walkway. She followed the deer for several minutes until it turned a long neck toward her, bounced down a gully, and disappeared out of sight.

What a gift! Sylvia felt full of gratitude to God for allowing her to witness this living animal, but then guilt settled in again, knowing that she'd killed a living creature too. She touched the amulet around her neck and looked toward the sky. "Please, God, forgive me."

Surprised that being in the wilderness didn't scare her, she realized it actually had a calming effect, probably because she felt safe from whoever might be out there looking for her. However, she felt an underlying itch of loneliness.

Paul had told her how much he liked to watch animals up at his mountain cabin. She'd thought he was crazy, but now she understood what he meant. If he were here, she would tell him all about the deer.

As she walked back toward the trailer, Lucy scratched at the door, and Sylvia hurried to release her. While unpacking the rest of the groceries, she heard a pinging noise on the tin roof as rain fell in large drops. She stuck her head out the door and laughed as her puppy ran up the trailer steps for cover. She had a wet-rat look about her and seemed angry too, as if it had been Sylvia's fault she'd gotten caught in the cloudburst. Sylvia threw a towel over the puppy and dried her soaked fur. The rain continued to pound and drip down the windows. It abated slowly and then stopped altogether. The sun came out, and it appeared as if the rain had never happened.

Outside, an owl hooted and swept toward the trailer and into the top of a tall pine. Sylvia wondered if it had a nest up there. As dusk set in, she searched the cupboards and found a Coleman lantern tucked away in the back of one. She took the lighter from her purse, lifted the glass globe, and tried to ignite the wick, but it didn't work. There seemed to be a canister in the bottom, and she shook it, hearing the oil splatter inside. She turned a knob, attempted again, and this time it lit. The lantern light cast a soothing glow around the trailer and onto the floor. Outside it grew dark.

She hung the lantern on a hook over the bed, crawled beside a dozing Lucy, and picked up the jackalope postcard. With a magazine underneath and pen in her hand, she began to write:

Dear Paul,
I'm okay. Are you?

She thought that sounded stupid and crossed it out, then got mad at herself for ruining the postcard. She scrounged in her purse to find the notepad and envelope she'd taken from the Monte Vista.

Dear Paul,
I saw a deer today. It looked at me. I'm sorry.

She thought it best to try and be funny and started again:

Dear Mr. Dictionary,
Sorry I left without saying goodbye. It was necessary. I'm okay.
I'll be gone for a while. (Don't worry; I'm not buying any
jewelry!) Take care of Milo and Ella and yourself. Don't try and
find me. I need to be alone.
Sincerely,
Sylvia

She yawned. In the morning, she'd write to Milo and Ella. She folded the top edge of the blue paper back and forth and carefully ripped off the hotel's name. The note to Paul slid with ease into the envelope. She licked it, and with the pen she scratched out the hotel insignia and wrote Paul's office address. In the next town, she'd buy stamps and drop the letter in a mailbox.

She turned off the lantern, and the trailer became pitch black. Then she realized that the postmark would reveal her location. Were the police checking the mail? Did they really do that sort of thing?

31

___

*A*nne rode the elevator to the third floor, stepped out, and followed the voices down a hall to the gallery. She'd had to pour on the makeup to cover puffy, jetlagged eyes. But she felt voluptuous in the green dress, velvet jacket, and upswept do. This time, she'd made three ponytails, twisted them together, and used plenty of bobby pins to keep it all up. Too bad her slingback heels were already killing her. She pushed through a couple making out in the doorway and entered the large space jam-packed with people, where techno music played.

Giant canvases hung on the walls painted in bold colors such as the ones that come in kindergarten paint boxes. Yes, these were Dottie's, all right. Circus characters at play: red-nosed clowns in polka-dotted costumes, a blue-tutu-wearing dancer on an elephant's back, acrobats juggling balls.

They seemed like ordinary pieces you might find in a child's room, except they appeared to have been painted upside down. It was obvious to Anne that they had been created right side up and then just turned around and displayed upside down. As her mind twisted them around, they seemed so familiar. Then she realized they were the same paintings Dottie had shown at her senior college exhibition—only tonight they had been hung upside down!

Anne leaned in and looked at the acrobat's price card: *Juggling Your Way Through Life*, $10,000. "Yowser!"

"What do you think?" Dottie put her hand on Anne's shoulder.

If she let on that she knew her friend's secret, how would she react? Laugh? Deny it? Anne studied Dottie's heavily made-up eyes for a clue. "Intriguing."

"Yes, everyone says so. That lady over there just bought one."

Anne forced out a smile. "Congratulations." Unbelievable!

A guy with a red bandana tied around his head and a beer belly underneath his leather jacket nodded at Dottie from the doorway.

"See you later." She moved toward him as if he were a magnet.

In the change jar there had only been enough for one slice of pizza. Now Anne's stomach gurgled with hunger, and she wandered through the horde to the appetizers. She dropped a few limp carrot sticks along with watery Ranch Dip on a tiny paper plate and ignored the bowl of Cheetos—their orange covering would stain her hands and mouth. Not a slice of cheese or even a little quiche was to be found, and no dessert either. What happened to sweet and salty? And to think she had planned to have dinner here.

For her own solo show, she envisioned an elegant affair—a cloth-covered table, champagne or martinis, delicious canapés, and, of course, chocolate. Anne looked across the room at her friend. If Dottie could do it, so could she.

Anne nibbled a carrot stick and panned the room looking for a place to sit, but no chairs were to be found. All the other guests wore black from head to toe—knit hats, turtlenecks, dresses, leggings, and combat boots. The Kelly green cocktail dress with the tulle skirt made her stick out like the Incredible Hulk. Why hadn't Dottie told her not to wear it? At least Anne had on her black coat. She touched the snowflake pin, also pretty sparkly for this crowd.

"Well?" A man moved next to her.

"Well, what?" she asked.

"What about the paintings?" He too, of course, wore shades of black: a handsome charcoal suit with a gray tee underneath. Curly dark hair was pushed back behind his ears, accentuating a Roman nose and chiseled cheeks.

"Interesting." She didn't want to badmouth Dottie. "What do you think?"

He paused for a moment. "They're colorful."

Had he guessed her secret too? Anne grew warm and wanted to take off the coat but didn't wish to expose more of the bright dress. "Do you know Dottie?" She nodded toward her friend in the corner surrounded by a Goth group of people.

"Who?"

"Dorothea."

"No. Do you?" He poured wine from a box into a plastic glass.

"College roommates." Anne nodded. "I guess she's really an artist now."

"What do you mean?" He tasted the wine and set it down with a grimace.

"We had a professor once who didn't think you were a true artist until you'd had a solo show."

The man smiled at her now, revealing beautiful white teeth. "Nonsense. I believe someone's an artist the moment one picks up a paintbrush."

"What about training?"

A woman stepped in front of them to get to the wine, and the man put his hand on Anne's back and moved them out of the way. "Maybe someday, but the act of simply creating makes one an artist." He popped an olive into his mouth and chewed.

"But don't you need to have your work chosen by a gallery in order to be bona fide?"

"No. A true artist doesn't need to please anyone but themself."
Anne smiled at him. "You must be an artist too."

"Not exactly, but I do follow the trends. Where did you girls
go to school?"

"U of M."

He looked confused. "Missouri, Montana?"

"No, Michigan." She stuck another carrot in her mouth.

"Are you a true artist?" Someone had turned up the music,
and he had to yell to be heard.

She finished chewing and said, "Yes and no, according to your
definition. Occasionally when I'm in the zone, I forget to remember
to care if others like my work."

He laughed. "Maybe someday you won't care at all. What
medium?"

"Mixed media."

He nodded. "Are you showing here in New York too?"

"I live in San Francisco." She put down her plate. "Trying to
break into the field."

"Sergio." He put out his hand.

She clasped his firm grip and didn't want to let go of his
smooth palm. "Anne, Anne McFarland."

"Irish?"

"With a bit of Scotch. You're *Italiano*."

"Sì. Speaking of Scotch, would you like to leave this party and
get some? Or perhaps an Irish coffee?" His eyes sparkled at her.
They were practically burnt sienna, her favorite brown hue.

"How about a Chianti for you?" She couldn't believe she was
being such a flirt. It would be fun though to have a fling while here
in New York.

"Anne!" A shriek could be heard from across the room, and
Crissy swept forward, her blonde curls pinned up into an exquisite
coiffure and perfectly painted nails that only an afternoon at a

salon could achieve. Her knockout body was accentuated by a black mini-dress.

"Aren't you all gussied up?" Crissy giggled her high-pitched laugh and gave Anne a big hug. "How's California? Anything in the Getty yet?"

Embarrassed, Anne frowned. "Not yet."

"Who's this hunk?" Crissy grabbed Sergio's bicep and lifted her eyes to Anne.

"Sergio. This is Crissy."

He shook her hand. "Glad to meet you."

"Charmed. I'm sure."

"How in the heck do you know Dottie?" Anne asked.

"Who?"

"Dorothea."

"We're Facebook friends through you." Crissy giggled.

"You came all this way to see her show?"

"We're hunting for an apartment."

"But I thought you lived in Michigan."

"We do, silly. Our second home will be here. Johnny." Crissy pulled her husband from the appetizers. "Here's Anne from high school. I've told you how we all knew she'd hit it big. Remember, she lives in San Francisco now and does collage, all that gluey stuff?"

He bowed and shook Anne's hand. "Jonathan." With his silver hair and button-down shirt, he really did look like Crissy's father.

"I'm glad to finally meet you." Anne smiled at him.

Sergio asked, "Crissy, are you an artist too?"

Jonathan placed his hands on her shoulders. "Her ducks are superb."

Sergio looked at Crissy's cleavage with confusion. "Ducks?"

Jonathan grinned. "It's amazing how real they look."

"I see." Sergio suppressed a smile and glanced at Anne out of the corner of his eye.

Crissy pointed to a painting of a seal holding a beach ball. The upside-down animal looked like it was balancing on top of the ball. "Johnny, let's buy that one for the new apartment."

"Anything you want, sugar!" Jonathan kissed her cheek.

Crissy giggled. "We're opening a gallery here."

"Maybe you'll show Anne's work?" Sergio suggested.

"Oh, dear me, no! Her stuff is too modern." Crissy giggled again.

Anne felt her face turn red. The black-clad bodies made her start to feel as if she were at a funeral.

"We'll mostly show landscapes. You know, trees, lakes. And, of course, my ducks. Midwestern themes."

Anne had heard enough. "Gotta go." She felt Sergio's eyes on her as she walked to the exit and left without even saying goodbye to Dottie.

Anne tottered down the hall in her tight heels, rode the elevator down, and stepped out into the cold evening. The wind flounced tree branches to look like dancing arms, and crowds of people bustled by on their way to maybe other gallery openings, theatres, or restaurants. A parade of taxis drove by, but she didn't have the money to hail one.

Snuggling into her coat, she hiked uptown toward the apartment. After a block and a half, she stopped to check the street signs to make sure she had been going the right way. Oh, great. Twenty-third Street, only twenty more blocks to go. Her feet stung, and her toes felt as if they were getting frostbitten. She should have worn her wingtips or clunky boots even if they didn't go with her cocktail ensemble. Either would have fit in more with the gallery crowd anyway.

She tottered down the sidewalk again, but her shoe caught in a grate. "Aaah!" She tugged her foot, but the heel popped off and fell down into the sewer. Peering into the abyss, she realized that even if she could retrieve the heel, who knew what it would be covered in? She tried not to think about it and continued along the sidewalk: Up down, up down, up down. No way would she be able to walk all the way back to the apartment now.

It began to rain, but the drops quickly turned to sleet. This weather was one of the main reasons she had moved from Michigan. The icy blast soaked her hair and started to seep down the coat onto her shoulders. Sheltering under a Laundromat's awning, she leaned against the door and looked for a bus stop. Then she spotted a subway entrance across the street and felt for the leftover change in her pocket. She'd heard horror stories about the New York subway but didn't really have much choice and crossed the street toward the entrance.

32

*I*n the morning, Sylvia thought she'd whip up some Spam for breakfast. From the blue can's back, she pulled the key, inserted it, and rolled back the top. At least an opener hadn't been necessary. Yuck! The Spam smelled like dead baloney. She located a frying pan and looked out the door to check on Lucy romping outside under a baby blue sky. Sylvia inhaled the fresh pine scent, trying to mask the Spam's odor. She turned the knob on the range but nothing happened; then bent over and inspected it. Why didn't it work? She used her lighter and turned the knob, but it still wouldn't go on.

Lucy rushed in with a hungry whine. Sylvia scooped some of the Spam into the bowl and set it on the ground. The puppy gobbled it right up. The odor didn't seem to bother her. Sylvia thought she would try it too and examined a glob on a spoon. It looked a lot like pâté. She held her nostrils shut with one hand, stuck out her tongue, and licked a small amount off the spoon. It tasted disgusting! She spit it in the sink.

Ella would know how to make it edible. She would sit on her high stepstool in the kitchen and read the *Joy of Cooking* as if it were a romance novel. "Hey, Sylvie! How about persimmon pumpkin pudding or chestnut soufflé with chocolate caramel sauce?" What Sylvia wouldn't do for one of Ella's home-cooked meals now.

Sylvia's stomach now felt a little queasy from the Spam episode, so she decided to take a stroll before a peanut-butter-on-Ritz breakfast. She stepped into the sunshine, where nearby boulders had been cleansed to a lustrous sheen. An adorable rabbit with a cotton-ball tail nibbled grass nearby. Lucy shot out of the trailer and chased it down the path out of sight.

"Come back!" Sylvia ran after her but couldn't keep up. "Lucy!" she called. Out of breath, Sylvia slowed down and continued to pursue Lucy's bark. Soon the pines grew dense, blocking the sun. The smell of bacon overpowered the pine scent, and Sylvia followed it into a clearing, where a station wagon and small tent stood. A cook stove with frying bacon and eggs sat on a picnic table.

A manly kind of woman with broad shoulders and stocky legs held out a piece of bacon. "Sit, girl." Lucy obeyed with her tongue hanging out and accepted the bacon crumble.

Sylvia was astounded by Lucy's response to a stranger. Usually it took her a while to warm up to someone, but she guessed that with bacon, anyone could be Lucy's friend.

"Hi-dee-ho." The woman waved then wiped her hands on her shorts. "Come join me. Doris is my name." Her buzz-cut brown hair was plain, but it showed off her teardrop diamond earrings that sparkled in the light.

Sylvia felt surprised she didn't want to touch them. In fact, she hadn't had a desire to touch anything sparkly since she'd sold her jewelry.

"I'm S . . . Susie Stevens." Sylvia shook the woman's outstretched hand.

Lucy whined and jumped up on Doris.

"Lucy, don't beg." Sylvia felt herself grow red.

"Sit." Doris held out the rest of the bacon strip. Lucy sat and was rewarded with the whole leftover piece. "Susie, you have a seat too."

Sylvia parked herself at the picnic table and felt the warm sun on her back. The Spam taste long forgotten, her mouth now watered from the bacon smell.

"Had breakfast yet? Just scrambling some eggs."

Sylvia shook her head. "No."

Doris heaped food on two plates and handed one to Sylvia. Lucy jumped up and put her paws on the bench.

"Lucy, down." Doris's voice was rigid.

Lucy sat and stared at the food. Sylvia had never been so ravenous and took a big bite. Somehow the food tasted better than anything she'd ever eaten before. "Delicious."

"It's the fresh air. Weaves itself into the vittles."

Sylvia believed her. She swallowed the last of her eggs, started on the bacon, and pulled off a little bit. "Lucy, sit."

Lucy hurried over and leapt on Sylvia's leg.

Doris directed: "Be firm and honest."

"Lucy, sit." Sylvia made her voice sound deep and serious. Lucy sat. Sylvia giggled and gave her the snippet.

"Where you from?" Doris asked.

Sylvia took another bite of bacon and swallowed. "Flag. You?"

"Kentucky."

Sylvia watched as Doris poured water from the stove into a tub and rinsed the dishes.

"May I help?" Sylvia asked.

"Nope." Doris flipped them upside down on a towel. "They air dry."

"What's Kentucky like?" Sylvia thought she might want to go there too.

"Mostly farming. Not much to speak of." Doris sighed and looked up at a tall pine. "Going home today."

Disappointed, Sylvia thought she could learn a lot from this pro, and she watched her take down the tent and pack it up.

"Sure you don't need any help?"

"Got it."

Sylvia admired the keen way Doris folded over and rolled up her sleeping bag. It had been hard enough for Sylvia to refold the map again. "Doris, do you happen to have an extra can opener?"

"Sure do! And more. I can't fit anything back in my car; it's filled to the gills." She laughed. "I've collected too many rocks and Indian keepsakes. How about the stove too?"

"That would be great!" Sylvia liked the idea of learning to cook outside. She could still smell the fresh bacon and eggs.

Doris piled everything, including cans of Spam, on the table.

"Thanks, but I don't need the Spam." Sylvia felt nauseated just looking at it. "But I'll take everything else." She played with the amulet, then had another idea. "Would you do me another small favor?"

"Probably."

"Mail a letter for me when you get to Kentucky?"

Doris eyed her curiously.

Sylvia fibbed: "I don't want my boyfriend to know where I am. He might try and find me."

"Oh, a Dear John letter."

"Something like that."

Doris grinned. "Been there before. Yep, be happy to."

Sylvia lugged the stove to the trailer. She grabbed the envelope and delivered it to Doris with some coins for postage. "I really appreciate it."

She studied the address. "I thought you said you were from Flagstaff."

Sylvia's stomach tottered. "I am. But my boyfriend is from California. That's one reason I've changed my mind about him."

"Can't blame you. There's nothing like Arizona."

"Nope." Sylvia smiled.

"You take care now."

"Thanks!" Sylvia called and waved as Doris pulled out and drove down the dirt road. Lucy rolled around in some pine needles under a tree. It would be nice to stay here another night or two. Sylvia might see the deer again.

33

Up down, up down. Anne hobbled down the subway entrance's broken escalator stairs. She considered taking her shoes off but didn't want to step on the grimy surfaces. As she approached the depths of the subway's cavernous space, her body broke out into a sweat. The depot smelled of urine and fast-food hamburgers. She reached the bottom, found a spot to stand, turned her back to the crowd, and focused on a pastel mosaic that adorned the wall. She tried to do some deep breathing, but the noxious odors and her anxiety made it impossible.

A train whizzed into the station, and she turned, around feeling the vibrations from the large engine. It halted, doors opened, riders pushed in and out of the cars, and the train continued on its way with a strong wind-like gust.

At the other end of the station, a tuxedoed girl played saxophone. Her dreadlocked head moved back and forth in rhythm. A man strode by and tossed coins into the empty case at the musician's feet. Anne listened to the jazz version of Beethoven's Fifth and let it help her body unwind.

She hopped over to the subway diagram posted on the wall and tried to figure out which line to take back to Dottie's. It was quite confusing, but Anne finally thought she knew which one would get her there. She read the ticket instructions and scrounged in her pocket for change but didn't have enough.

Should she ask the saxophonist for a loan? Did Anne possess a talent someone would pay to see? Painting here would be out of the question, but how about her modern dance routine from high school? Pootie had dared her to sign up for the course and Anne had done so in hopes of improving her coordination. She now could flip over that fast-food box, put it in front of her to accept coins, and perform her dance.

She closed her eyes, put the "Bootylicious" song in her heart, and tried to recount the choreography. She knew she hadn't been very good, but her mother, Tootie, and Pootie had sat in the front row and, when her performance was over, hooted with a standing O. The saxophone interfered with Anne's concentration and kept her from recalling the right moves. Should she do an interpretive dance instead to the sax?

A tap on her shoulder took her by surprise, and she opened her eyes with a start.

"Ready for that scotch now?" Sergio grinned at her. His wool herringbone overcoat made him look even more handsome than before. "I know a place a few stops down."

She held up her foot and pointed to her missing heel. "But I've had a little mishap."

"I can see that." He grasped her elbow and helped her balance.

"How did you find me?"

"It wasn't hard. I followed you. Boy, you have big feet!"

She laughed. "Gee, thanks."

"Take them off."

"Ick. I don't want to walk on this floor!"

"Take them off." He held up a palm and stared at her, which made her apprehensions start to melt and want to do anything he asked. "Trust me." His voice softened.

She pulled the heels off and handed both to him. He tossed them one at a time into a nearby trashcan, then bent down and scooped her up into his arms. She held onto his neck, snuggled into him, and wiggled her deliciously freed toes.

A screeching sound from another train could be heard as it approached the station.

"In my right pocket, you'll find a ticket," Sergio instructed.

Anne slipped her hand inside and retrieved it. He carried her to the turnstile and tilted her a bit. "Now slide the ticket in the slot."

She did, and he lifted her up high and walked them through the metal bars. The train halted, doors opened, and Sergio pushed inside a car. There were no visible seats to spare, but he finally found one, sat down, and pulled her onto his lap just as the car took off again.

She batted her eyelashes at him. "My hero."

An old lady with blue hair sat across from them clutching her handbag.

Sergio traced circles on Anne's back. She rested her head on his shoulder and inhaled the warmth of him, like honeysuckle on a summer day. The subway lights flickered off and on as the train moved along the tracks. The car's rhythm lulled her, and she closed her eyes.

The train halted, and Sergio slid her onto his seat, turned around, and pulled her to his back. He trudged out and carried her piggyback-style to the escalator. Fortunately, this one worked. She rode with him up it and out onto the sidewalk.

"Let's skip the drink and go back to your hotel," he whispered in her ear.

"Don't think so, mister. Besides, I'm staying at Dottie's. I mean, Dorothea's."

He bounced Anne on his back along the busy sidewalk and

into a packed Irish pub. "Is all of her furniture upside down too?" He pushed his way to the bar and set Anne down on the only vacant stool.

She twirled the seat around with a laugh and put her arms around him again. "Yes. We wear antigravity boots to walk around, hold on tight to chairs, and use a seat belt to sleep."

"When she works, does the paint drip onto the floor?"

Anne resisted the urge to kiss the top of his strong nose. She ordered a Baileys and coffee, he a Chivas on the rocks. They sipped them slowly and ate three bowls of peanuts. A jazz trio started to set up in a corner.

"Tell me more about your work." His eyes shone dark in the dim light.

"I use old things to inspire me."

"Like what?"

"Mostly photos. I love vintage magazines." It felt good to talk with someone about her work. He really seemed interested.

"Another round?" the bartender took their glasses.

"No, thanks." Anne yawned and shook her head. "Didn't get much sleep last night."

Sergio glanced at his watch. "But it's only 9:00 PM in California. One more?"

"Okay, just one."

When they were almost done with their second round, she swung her arm around him and said, "You are so sexy."

"Want to find out how sexy I really am?"

She giggled. "Maybe someday."

Outside, the traffic had thinned. He hailed a taxi, slipped Anne inside, and climbed in next to her. As soon as it left the curb, Sergio didn't waste any time, and he pulled Anne to him and kissed her. She could taste the husky liquor and salty peanuts. His fingers played with the lace hem of her dress where it rested on her thighs. His warm hand inched up under her skirt toward her panties. Her breath quickened.

The cab pulled up at Dottie's, and Sergio asked, "Sure you don't you want me to come up?"

Anne couldn't imagine someone as refined as him in that revolting loft and kissed him again. "She'll probably be asleep."

"My place, then?"

She considered it for a moment then shook her head. "Better not."

He kissed her. "Sure?"

She opened the car door. "Not really. But thanks for the rides and drinks."

"Can I show you around tomorrow?" He made circles on her back again.

"I need to spend the day with Dottie, Dorothea."

He scribbled down his number on the back of a receipt. "Call me. I want to see you again before you go."

"Probably won't have time. I leave day after tomorrow."

"But you just got here."

"I have to get back to work."

He smiled. "That's right, you're an artist."

She nodded and held up a finger. "Yes. I pick up a paintbrush, and therefore I am!"

She kissed him, pulled herself away, and climbed out of the cab. It had begun to snow. The frozen sidewalk was cold on her bare feet, and she sprinted up to the building, but then turned back around, ran to the cab, and kissed Sergio one last time. Returning to the apartment door, she punched in the code and rode the elevator up to the loft.

Dottie wasn't even home yet. Shivering, Anne tried the knob on the radiator, but it wouldn't budge. She texted Dottie but got no reply. Too cold to even get undressed, Anne crawled under a scratchy blanket on the lumpy couch that smelled of weed. She closed her eyes and tried to fall asleep. The fridge burbled and coughed. Rolling over onto her back, she stared at the stained ceiling.

Sergio probably had a queen-size bed, or rather a king with comfy pillows and smooth sheets. They would have made love and spooned all night. In the morning, they'd sleep in, and he'd fix her a bountiful breakfast. Should she call him now and ask him to come back and get her? It would only be for this one night.

34

*I*n the Painted Desert on fine sand, Sylvia spread out a sleeping bag and sat on top. The trailer had been stuffy, so she planned to sleep outside. Lucy wandered off, her nose low to the ground. Sylvia yawned, tired from driving for hours, then scanned the horizon.

They had spent a heavenly two weeks in the mountain campground. But a noisy family had moved into a nearby site, and Sylvia's rations had run low, so she pulled out and stopped in Tuba City to restock on supplies: a flashlight, clean clothes, groceries. She then followed the map into the desert to a new camping spot on a mound of compact sand. A different kind of beauty spread before her. Instead of lush trees, here the expanding terrain spread out stark and bleak all the way to the horizon; a vivid blue sky contrasted with an ivory ground. Strange jagged and twisty growth dotted the land.

In the mountains, she had enjoyed wearing the same T-shirt every day without needing to impress anyone with her fashion sense or overcome her shyness. Under an oak, she read aloud a book of Robert Frost poems left in the trailer. Over and over again, she recited until she knew each by heart, the words lifting off her tongue and soothing her soul. Daily she walked the path of soft pine needles, Lucy in tow, skipping in and out of the stream. Most afternoons, the deer made an appearance, and Sylvia watched quietly from afar.

She observed all the natural wonders, so in awe of what God had created. Her loneliness started to abate because she knew she wasn't alone now. God was with her. She didn't know if he had forgiven her for shooting Ricardo, but she was, however, certain of God's love.

But would she ever forgive herself for shooting Ricardo? His death still haunted her. Every time she closed her eyes, his last expression filled her mind like a movie film breaking as it flips through the reel, over and over and over again until it suddenly stops. Would she ever forgive herself for not listening to the ones who really cared for her and for allowing a man like that to harm and deceive her?

Fresh desert air now swirled around her. Some people were afraid to sleep outside by themselves, but not Sylvia. She embraced the chance to sleep out in nature for the first time. It had been too cold to do so in the mountains. As a little girl, she had wanted to go camping with her father, but her mother had said, "No! Sophisticated girls don't camp."

Lucy had wandered way off in the distance. Sylvia yelled, "Snack!" and the puppy dashed toward her as fast as her little legs could carry her.

"Sit." Sylvia held up a cracker, and Lucy waved her tail. With a firmer voice, Sylvia demanded, "Sit!" This time, Lucy set her round behind on the ground, received the treat, and then settled under a nearby shrub.

Dusk kissed the silver trailer with a pink tourmaline wash. Shadows fell, and a lizard slid across the sand. At first, Sylvia flinched, then, fascinated, she watched as it scurried into a rocky crevice. As a young girl, Sylvia had been terrified of lizards. Scads of them lived in the rose garden at home under the boulders and sunbathed on top. Her fear of them had kept her from collecting the quartz and other shiny stones that hid nearby in the damp soil.

Milo once caught a lizard for her, put it in a shoebox, and poked holes in the lid. "Sylvie, you've always wanted a pet, and now's your chance."

They named her Lizzie and kept the box beneath the garden tools in the garage. They gathered grass, and Milo snatched flies to feed her. He held her for Sylvia while she learned to pet her scaly back, which felt like mama's alligator purse. Milo would hold Lizzie to his lips, pretend to kiss her, then pull back with a grimace as if she had bit him. Once, Milo picked her up and her tail fell off, but it kept wiggling. Sylvia giggled so hard she almost wet her pants.

Then one morning, they opened the box, and Lizzie was gone. "She must have escaped." Milo frowned. "Hope she didn't run into the house. Your mama wouldn't like that much, and neither would Ella." The thought of that made her laugh and not be so sad that Lizzie had run away.

A quail now skirted by and called for its mate. Sylvia had never seen a real one before, but she recognized it because a porcelain replica sat on a desk in the library at home.

"A sophisticated girl wouldn't do this either," Sylvia spoke out loud and stuck her fingers in the sand, moving them back and forth through the gritty texture. She brushed her hands off, admiring her short-clipped easy-care nails. Then she touched a soft white plant, brought her fingers to her nose, and inhaled the sweet aroma. What had she missed by not camping with her father? Would he have loved her more? Known her better? She thought of her mother and felt a knot in her chest. Her mother's goal had been to mold Sylvia into the perfect child, who would become a woman who could "catch a man."

Sylvia had caught a man, all right, but he happened to be the wrong one. Maybe here in Arizona, his death would begin to fade from her mind. She felt grateful to be in nature. The freedom and open spaces of the desert had to be the opposite of jail. Maybe out here on the road, she would figure it all out.

She picked up a rock, a simple one, with gray streaks into black like Ella's hair and coarse to the touch. Not shiny, but striking just the same. She thought of Milo and Ella again and hoped they had forgiven her for running away.

By being in nature, Sylvia had begun to discover that life had more to offer than shopping and marriage. She changed herself on the outside with a new hairdo and clothes. Was it possible to recreate herself on the inside too? She had a desire to try.

The temperature began to drop, and it grew dark. Fluffing her pillow, she nestled into the sleeping bag and pulled off her jeans to sleep in her T-shirt and panties. Lucy poked her nose into the bag. Sylvia lifted the flap, and the beagle-basset crawled inside and burrowed down to the bottom. "Night, night." Sylvia rubbed her feet on Lucy's back, glad again the stowaway had joined her on the journey. Lucy snorted and grew quiet.

No moon tonight, Sylvia looked up at the dark sky filled with stars. She had never seen so many. She found the Big Dipper, and followed it with her fingers, counting the stars of the ladle, three stars along the handle and four for the cup. What were some of the other constellations? She wished she had paid more attention that night at the Valentine's dance. On the club's deck, Paul had tried to point the stars out to her, but she had been distracted by the music and Ricardo's dancing.

Paul had pointed and said, "There's the North Star. If you find and follow it, you'll never get lost." She looked for it now, certain it was somewhere near the Dipper but not sure which one.

Paul would love the sky here. Tears formed in her eyes, and she realized how much she missed him. He had always been a part of her life. As her guardian, he had been kind but firm. Like when he had been concerned about her spending.

He had asked, "What monthly amount would be enough for you?" She had given him a number but hadn't been able to abide by it. Even so, he never really got angry with her. How could she have been so shallow and taken him for granted? He always had her best interest at heart. If she had told him the truth about Ricardo's death, he would have supported her. She knew that now. Paul had always been on her side. He should have received her letter by now, and she hoped he would forgive her too.

A bright star dropped from the sky, left a streak, and disappeared. With a wish for guidance and safety, Sylvia closed her eyes and touched the smooth amulet on her chest. She remembered the strange Indian woman who gave it to her, and smiled. Maybe the pendant would bring her luck as the woman had foretold.

Sylvia inhaled the sweet-smelling nearby bush again, and quiet surrounded her. As she drifted off to sleep, diamonds sprinkled from the sky onto the sleeping bag, covering her in grace, giving her pleasant dreams of wishes fulfilled, wishes she hadn't even known she had. Gentle winds lifted her up. The sleeping bag spiraled into the air. Shiny stars twirled around. Like an envelope caressing a letter, the sleeping bag flew, sending warm thoughts to Paul across the miles.

All of a sudden, Lucy scrambled out of the sleeping bag and woke Sylvia, who rolled over and floated on the edge of sleep, remembering strange dreams of Paul. Emotions for him billowed through and around her, caressed her, seeped in, and she sat up. It was only a dream. He would never think of her in that way!

Lucy yelped and stood at attention, staring off into the distance. Sylvia's eyes followed her gaze out into the dark but didn't see anything. She grabbed the flashlight and turned it on.

The puppy barked and then stopped. There must be something out there!

"Lucy, come," Sylvia called, and the two ran up the steps into the trailer and closed the door behind them. Sylvia tried to secure the door, but the lock jammed. With the flashlight pointed out the window, Sylvia swept the beam back and forth. She caught a nearby movement, but it was only a bush trembling in the wind.

The air cold and blanket thin, Sylvia wished she had grabbed the sleeping bag, but no way would she go back out there for it. She turned off the flashlight to save the battery and twisted on the lantern. Its beam cast an eerie shadow on the trailer's walls.

And then a sound came from outside. "*Yip-yip-yip-yowl*."

Lucy jumped onto the bed beside Sylvia.

"*Yip-yip*." And then again from outside, "*Yip-yip*."

Lucy barked.

"Hush, girl." Sylvia pulled Lucy to her, and they huddled together. "What big animals are out there?" Sylvia whispered. "Wolves? Bears?"

Then a cacophony of howls echoed off the trailer. Could whatever was out there pull open the door and get in? She had never been so frightened in her life. The lantern sputtered and blew out. She reached above her head and shook it. The oil canister seemed to be dry. She should have bought more in Tuba City. Sylvia turned the flashlight back on and pointed it at the ceiling, trying to get as much of a glow as possible.

The howling began again. "Yip, yip, yowl." It sounded otherworldly, perhaps ghosts or maybe even creatures from outer space. Wasn't there a recent *Twilight Zone* about a flying saucer landing in the desert? She could hear the show's theme song now: *Do, do, do, do*.

The flashlight in her hand began to flicker. She shook it, and the ray steadied for a moment, then died. The trailer grew as dark and cold as obsidian.

35

$\mathscr{A}$nne had decided not to call Sergio and stayed in the apartment to wait for Dottie, but she never showed up or even texted. Here Anne was in the arts capital of the country with no money and ditched by her ex-best friend. The freezing apartment and bumpy couch kept Anne from getting a good night's rest. Her stomach grumbled, but she didn't even have enough cash to buy breakfast. Dottie must have had money hidden in the loft somewhere.

Anne removed the couch cushions and found three quarters, a dime, and a magenta bra. Anne peeked under the magazines on the coffee table and then inside the stash box.

She thought she heard a noise and turned to the door. What would Dottie say if she caught her? It grew quiet. Anne looked in the sugar bowl, the freezer, and the top cupboards. Stuffed under the sink in the back, she discovered a collage she had made Dottie for college graduation: a photo transfer of the two of them, big smiles with arms around each other. Anne's eyes filled with tears.

She rifled through Dottie's lingerie drawer but still didn't find any cash. She opened a box on the dresser. Voila! Five crisp hundred-dollar bills were folded inside. If she took some, it wouldn't really be stealing. Dottie owed her about half that much anyway. Anne peeled two bills off, slipped them in the zipper part of her daypack, and returned the rest. The door opened, and she slammed the box shut.

Dottie lurched in, her Mohawk awry. "What a night."

"Congratulations!" Anne returned the cushions to the couch and folded the blanket.

"Yeah. Three of my pieces sold."

Anne pumped her arm. "Cha ching."

Dottie rolled her eyes and kicked the radiator two times, and it whooshed on. Then she drifted to the couch.

Anne sat beside her. "I've been waiting for you to get back."

"You have?"

"I helped myself to your box." Anne nodded toward the dresser.

"Yeah, whatever."

"Let's go! I can't wait to see the Big Apple. I've got to change, then I'll be ready." Anne jumped up.

Dottie sighed and picked up her bong. "You go ahead. I'm beat."

"You mean I came all this way, and you don't even want to spend time with me?" Anne felt like she'd been socked in the stomach.

"I just can't go out today."

"Why did you invite me then?"

"I didn't really think you'd come." Dottie closed her eyes and laid her head on the top of the couch. "I have to rest up for a rave tonight." Dottie pulled the blanket over her. "You can come with me if you want."

"You think?" Anne ruffled through her suitcase and threw on jeans, a heavy sweater, and boots. Then she bundled up in winter gear, grabbed her daypack, and slammed the door on her way out. Snow covered the ground, and an overcast sky drooped with cold dark clouds. At the deli across the street, she found an inside café table, dried her eyes, and ravaged a jalapeño with cream cheese bagel.

New York had a whole different vibe than San Francisco that took some getting used to. There, you could get anywhere on foot, cable car, or bus within minutes, easy peasy. But here you could walk forever and never reach the end of it. The colors even seemed different—not as vivid—and fog didn't float in from the water like in San Francisco, only chilled dampness.

Anne pulled Sergio's number from her pocket and itched to call him. In the light of day though, she felt it probably wasn't wise to pursue that relationship. Her hots for him might have just been a rebound attraction, and, after all, he was a GU, a geographical undesirable.

She pulled out her New York City day-by-day map and took notes as she planned her itinerary by bus and on foot. No way would she get back on that subway. Of course she'd go to the Met first, then the Frick, then The Plaza for tea, and then the Whitney. It might even have up their biannual show for emerging artists. She thought someday she might send them a submission.

Even though Anne had the right-of-way, as she crossed the street, a red Ferrari sped around the corner and slammed on its brakes just in time. The driver glared, flipped her off, and yelled, "Dumb broad."

She mouthed, Sorry and backed up to the curb and found the bus to the Met.

The special Matisse collage exhibit awed her with its fabulous multicolored cutout shapes and textures. But when she reached the Egyptian temple, it was so crowded she could barely see a thing. She wanted to read the hieroglyphics at the Egyptian temple but didn't want to squeeze in between bodies.

A walk through Central Park had been cold but invigorating. Bare trees stood guard along pathways that sparkled with softening snow. But at the Sheep Meadow, she must have turned right instead of left, because she ended all the way over on Central Park West and had to circle back to get to the Frick.

The intimate nature of the former mansion built in 1914 warmed and calmed her. She wandered the gallery spaces around a reflecting pool in a central courtyard. The Fragonard Room had four large rococo panels; the romantic series *Progress of Love* had actually been brought over from France. In a large salon, she sat and admired the marbled floors and paintings by Renoir and Gainsborough, two of her favorites.

An hour quickly passed by the time she exited the Frick and wandered toward The Plaza for tea. But when she arrived at the big hotel, the menu prices were so high and the other diners so dressed to the nines she considered skipping it; however, she took one look at the stained glass ceiling and knew she just had to sit under it. The child's menu was only $30. She could order that even though she didn't really like peanut butter and jelly.

In the ladies lounge, she pulled off her cap, grabbed a brush from her pack, and twisted her hair back into a scrunchie. She examined herself in the full-length mirror, flicked lint off her coat, and touched the snowflake pin. This would do; she'd fit right in. No one would guess her outfit was secondhand. On her way back to the restaurant, she stopped to admire the painting of Eloise, from her favorite childhood story about the girl who lived at The Plaza.

At The Palm Court's entrance, Anne waited in line behind a velvet cord until the hostess escorted her to a small table next to a potted fern. The tallest bouquet of gladiolas she'd ever seen stood on a table in the center of the room, and huge arched glass doors surrounded the space. The stained glass from above reflected colors onto the white tablecloth as she studied the menu again: the Classic, the New Yorker, and Eloise. Then she saw the small print:

the child's menu was $50 dollars for adults. Should she slip out now before a waiter came to take her order?

"Ready, ma'am?" A dapper waiter stood beside her, a leather notepad in hand, his short hair gelled back to perfection and tuxedo neatly pressed.

Anne felt her face grow hot. She took a sip of water and smiled at him. "Can I have the Eloise at the child's price?"

He tilted his nose toward the ceiling. "It's against hotel policy."

"Are you sure?"

"I'm sure."

"Please? I'm a starving artist."

"Really? So am I!" His snooty attitude evaporated.

"What type?"

"Starving too!"

She smiled. "What type?"

"I paint modern portraits. What about you?"

"Mixed media. I'm from San Francisco. I don't think I'll get to the Plaza ever again."

He frowned. "I sure hope you do."

"It's so elegant. You must love working here."

Pencil poised, he looked around, then smiled. "The Eloise. That's a good choice."

"Yes, if you please."

The waiter left, and Anne people-watched. The other diners, mostly women, chatted with one another. One matron wore a hat with pheasant feathers that looked like it might have been from the early 1900s, when the hotel had first been built. Thank goodness Dottie wasn't here. Anne grinned and imagined her in the Mohawk as she clutched a cucumber sandwich with black-polished fingernails. In fact, Anne was glad Dottie had been such a flake after all. If she'd been with her, Anne wouldn't have had last evening's magical time with Sergio. And then she'd gone ahead

and found the money. If Dottie had been there, she might not have
ever gotten reimbursed for the plane tickets. And this day had
been absolutely wonderful. She'd been lucky. She felt in her pocket
for the key, brought it out, and kissed it. "Thank you," she whispered.

If Sylvia had ever been to New York, she certainly would have
eaten here. Anne thought about how fun it would be to have the
blonde sit across the table from her sipping tea from a lacy white
cup. Things had been so hectic that Anne hadn't had a chance to
think of the series clearly. Since finding out the heiress might have
been seen in Arizona, Anne had run out of clues. The series was
dwindling to a close, just one more piece or two.

Toward the end of a series, Anne always felt a little disheart-
ened, uncertain what would come next. She gazed around the
restaurant again. The Plaza and New York in general would make a
great series. Ideas bounced in her head, and she grabbed her
journal from the daypack and jotted a few notes:

New York
Era? '20s or '30s (long time ago)
The Plaza
Frick
Central Park
Grand Central Station

She continued to write until the waiter returned with her
meal. But instead of the Eloise, he brought her the Classic on a
silver-tiered tray along with a glass of champagne. Anne devoured
the little sandwiches: truffled quail egg, smoked salmon, and Maine
lobster. She spread lemon curd on a still-warm scone and nibbled it
up. The hazelnut napoleon had been her favorite of all five
desserts, but it didn't stop her from eating them all.

The check came for the most scrumptious meal she'd ever had and at the children's menu price. She left a hefty tip, took a business card from her pack, and wrote on the back, *Thanks! I owe you one if you visit California,* and she slid it underneath the cash.

She made her way to the Whitney, but when she got there, it was closed for renovation. Clouds had begun to gather. She hopped a bus and decided to head back to Dottie's. Fingering Sergio's number in her pocket, she wondered what he had done that day.

36

———

$\mathcal{S}$ylvia looked out the window to the east as the sun peeked over the horizon behind wispy clouds. On the earth, bands of rock changed colors from amethyst to topaz as the shifting light caught the different layers of sand. The landscape that had seemed so ominous the night before became flush with the glow of serene colors. Being in nature could be terrifying one moment and exhilarating the next. Even so, if they made it to Monument Valley today, she would check into a hotel.

Lucy jumped off the bed and scratched at the door. "No, girl." Sylvia still felt afraid of what might be out there. Late into the night, she had listened to the mournful screeches, but when they finally ended, Sylvia still couldn't get to sleep.

Now a horn honked and a Jeep headed their way. Sylvia slid on some jeans as a ranger in a Smokey the Bear uniform stepped out of his vehicle. In fact, he seemed about as big and tall as Smokey might be. "Mornin'," he called.

She opened the door a smidgen and poked her head out. "Hello?"

Lucy flew past her with a bark and lunged at the big man.

He laughed, bent down, and revealed his palm for Lucy to lick. Then he stood up and took off his hat. A rugged but handsome face had been underneath. "Mornin'," he said again, glancing in the trailer. "Who's out here with you?"

"Lucy." Sylvia walked down the stairs and picked her up.

"I see." He nodded. "A big storm's brewing. Could be a flash flood."

She studied the white clouds collecting on the horizon. They seemed harmless. "Thanks for the warning. I'll pull out now."

He frowned. "Better stay here on this rise. It'll be safer." He put his hat back on and climbed into his Jeep.

"Sir. There were some dogs or wolves or something howling last night."

He smiled as if he admired them. "Coyotes, ma'am. The tricksters throw their voices to sound like their prey."

"They're not really dangerous, are they?"

"Don't usually bother people, but keep your wee dog close."

"I will." She swallowed. "They sounded pretty scary. I thought they might even be aliens from UFOs."

"Maybe so." He smiled at her from under his hat. "We do have craters nearby, and no one knows exactly how they got there." He continued, "And don't worry about our black bears—they only live in our mountains."

Lucy squirmed, but Sylvia held tight. She felt relieved they hadn't run into any of those when they were up there.

He kept going, his voice deep and low. "To avoid our scorpions, never reach into dark places or overhead ledges that you can't see in. And make sure to shake out your shoes before putting them on."

She nodded. "Okay."

He wasn't done yet. "And don't worry about our diamondback rattlesnakes. They only strike when surprised."

"Is that all?" She opened her eyes wide.

"There's a lot more, but nothing to be concerned about." His eyes drifted upward toward the clouds again. "Yep, a big storm's coming. Better get back in the trailer and stay put." The dust flew behind him as he drove out along the dirt road.

Sylvia leashed Lucy for a quick walk, then returned to the trailer and closed the door tight. She tried to read a *Vogue* but had already looked at it, and she tossed it on the floor. She picked up the poetry book and practiced her recitations, but her throat became dry. She grabbed a pen and paper to write Paul another note:

Dear Paul,

Sorry, I . . .

She sat back and tried to decide what to say. Her earlier dream floated to her mind, and her cheeks grew hot. How could she have that kind of dream about him? She put the paper aside and looked around the trailer.

The acrid smell of kerosene still lingered, and the space seemed to grow smaller. "I'm not afraid of a little rain. But I am afraid of snakes, scorpions, and space monsters. Let's get out of here and go to Monument Valley."

Sylvia lifted Lucy into the T-Bird. The trailer bobbed behind as they drove out the dirt road and turned east onto the quiet two-lane highway. Ahead stretched the white line, and yellow spiky bushes dotted the vast terrain that seemed to go on for miles.

Sylvia had never felt so free. She flipped on the radio, turned it up, and sang along, her voice full, on key, and high. "Love is a many-splendored thing." Was true love splendored? She had thought her feelings for Ricardo had been true love, and at first, it had seemed splendored.

In the distance, white clouds turned to gray with bulging denim-colored undersides. Sylvia drove toward them, making good time. According to the map, they'd make it to Monument Valley within the next few hours. She looked forward to a hot bath and a good night's sleep in a decent hotel.

She sang again with the radio, Lucy her devoted audience. Sylvia felt elated as if she could drive like this forever. Within a few minutes, the billows turned to onyx, and the wind picked up. A tumbleweed flew in front of the T-Bird, and she swerved to miss it just in time. Reminded of the *Wizard of Oz*, she wondered if they would be pulled up into the sky too.

Far-off lightning flashed, and within a few seconds, thunder called. Lucy hunkered down in the seat. The radio started to cut out. Sylvia moved the dial back and forth but only heard static.

A few drops splashed on the windshield. She considered turning back but decided to keep going. "It's nothing. Just a little wind and a few sprinkles." She turned on the windshield wipers.

More lightning flashed, this time closer, and the thunder roared right after. Drops overflowed in puddles that floated down the glass, making it hard to see. All of a sudden, the rain turned to hail and banged on the T-Bird's roof like ping-pong balls. Sylvia held tight to the steering wheel; her heart seemed to pound as loud as bongo drums.

Though invisible in the rearview mirror, the trailer could still be felt. Water seeped through the convertible's roof. A windshield wiper bounced off the glass, and finally, unable to see more than a foot in front of her, Sylvia pulled to the side of the highway and turned off the motor. A quivering Lucy crawled into Sylvia's lap. Soon a shallow stream rippled underneath the car, and then, as the rain continued to fall, the road filled with water, gushed, and became a river. The T-Bird hitched to the trailer felt like a kite on a string. Sylvia tried to open the car door, but the torrent's force wouldn't allow it. As the deluge deepened, the car began to rock and sway. She felt as if she were on a roller coaster ride.

With a deafening crunch and screech of metal, the T-Bird's bumper separated from the trailer. Sylvia screamed as the car lifted and washed away in the current with them inside. She held her puppy tight and shouted the twenty-third Psalm into the torrential rain: "The Lord is my shepherd; I shall not want. He makes me to lie down in green pastures. Help me God! He leads me beside still waters."

She felt for the amulet and touched its smooth surface, portended to bring her luck. How could she have been so stupid as to drive into a storm? She should have heeded the ranger's warning. Just like she should have listened to Paul, Ella, and Milo when they warned her about Ricardo.

"Please, God! I don't want to die," she yelled. Was he punishing her for killing Ricardo? Would she go to Hell? Would she die before having a chance to tell the ones she loved she was sorry? Rain continued to pound on the roof as the car drifted faster and faster and then spun in a circular motion into the flash flood's whirlpool.

37

_D_espite the lumpy couch, Anne awoke rejuvenated from her nap feeling the lure of possible New York night adventures. Dottie was nowhere to be seen. So Anne broke down and texted Sergio.

He got right back to her: _Big Foot! Did you have a good day?_

Anne: _Fabulous. Can you meet?_

Sergio: _Love to._

Anne: _When? Where?_

Sergio took a few minutes to reply: _7:30. Corner of 6th Avenue and West 51st Street._

She opened the map and found the spot. Then she ruffled through some drawers and slipped a chiffon baby-doll dress over her turtleneck. Dottie had bought it "thrifting" last year on her San Francisco visit. It had fit her like a baggy dress, but on Anne, it looked more like a blouse and hit the top of her thighs. She wore her jeans underneath and looked in a cracked mirror. Not so bad. With her new style, Dottie probably wouldn't wear the thing ever again anyway. Anne donned coat, hat, and gloves, slipped out, and made her way to the bus stop, the snow piled thick along the sidewalk's edge.

As Anne rode the bus toward the designated corner, she removed her gloves in order to fondle the key in her pocket, hoping for a lucky night, and then giggled at her outrageous imagination. Looking out the window, she admired the colorful holiday lights strung on the bare trees and tall buildings. Her favorites were the white ones that looked like stars in a night sky. After a few miles, she jumped off the bus at Armani's. The guidebook rated it as the best pizza in New York. She considered stopping in for a piece but didn't want to chance being late to meet Sergio.

Arriving just in time at their rendezvous corner, long lines stood on the sidewalk coming from two directions. The neon lights above Radio City Music Hall blazed: *The Rockettes Christmas Spectacular!* How exciting! She pushed through the mob scene and walked to each end of the building, staring into people's faces. It was almost 8:00 PM when she finally spotted him standing on the corner right where he said he would be. He wore his wool coat again and a jaunty red tam that would have looked silly on anyone else but was fun and festive on him. He hugged her to him. "I'm so glad to see you."

She gazed up at the neon sign. "I've always wanted to see The Rockettes."

He frowned. "I'm sorry. It's sold out."

"That's okay." She tried to hide her disappointment.

He grinned and held up two tickets. "But I got the last two!"

"Tricked me!" She laughed.

They got in line and followed the crowd into the lobby. The art deco space with the cool chandelier and huge mural would make a great photo collage. She would add it to her New York list.

"Souvenir programs!" With an armful, a teen in an elf costume stood before them. "Only $45."

"Want one?" Sergio asked and pulled out some cash.

She grabbed his elbow and dragged him toward a rack of postcards. "No, thanks. I'd rather have a couple of these instead."

She'd mail one to her mother, Tootie, and Pootie and add the other to her collection. He bought her the postcards of high-kicking chorus lines.

Inside the theatre, he held his hand on the small of her back and guided her to their orchestra seats. Sitting down, she said, "These are great seats. You can see the whole stage from here." She looked up at the arched ceiling and scanned the balcony. "This place is humongous!"

He smiled. "It's one of the biggest in the world, seating almost six thousand."

"No way!" As the lights went down, she held her breath in anticipation, and he squeezed her hand. Soon the music began, and the velvet curtain rose to wild applause. Anne had never seen so many other long-legged women with big feet in her life. They wore reindeer antlers on their heads. How did they keep so synchronized? Anne knew that if she practiced for hours she wouldn't ever be able to dance like that.

She could have done without the 3-D glasses and flying Santa in his sleigh. When it flew toward her, she grabbed Sergio's arm, laughing hysterically, and scrunched down in her seat, certain Santa would crash into her.

In the next scene, a red tour bus rolled onto stage and twirled. The dancers bobbed up and down on the seats and exited the vehicle in sparkly costumes. In another sequence, tin soldiers marched: step touch, step touch, and kick, kick, kick in a long straight line. Sure they could tippy-tap across the stage, but Anne bet they couldn't paint mangos like she could.

During the Nativity sequence, Anne whispered to Sergio, "Are those real camels?"

He nodded yes.

After three curtain calls, Sergio escorted her out through the crowd to the sidewalk. Limos and taxis lined the curb.

"I sure got a kick out of that." Anne said with a straight face.

"Ha! Ha!" Sergio smiled.

She yawned. Despite her nap, the jetlag had finally caught up with her. "I should get back to Dottie's?"

"You can't go back yet." Sergio held her close as theatergoers bustled around them.

"I've got an early flight."

"You sure? How about my place?" He kissed her and looked into her eyes. "I have a great bottle of Chianti."

"Don't think so."

He kissed her again, and she could feel his heat all the way through their layers of clothes she wanted to nestle with him all night. "Okay. One drink, but not at your place. Somewhere public."

"I know a cool spot you'd like."

"Death and Company?"

"How did you hear about that?" He hugged her to him again.

"Saw it online."

"I know an even better place. PDT."

"What does that stand for?"

"Please Don't Tell."

She spoke through the side of her mouth. "You mean if I do you'll have to kill me?"

He laughed. "You're good! There's a subway station down the block?"

She shook her head. "Let's take the bus."

"I've got a better idea."

They walked a few blocks from the theatre crowd, and Sergio hailed a cab. He gave the driver an address. They climbed in just as it started to sprinkle. He dialed to make a reservation then put an arm around her shoulder while raindrops hit the windshield and dripped down the glass.

The cab dropped them off at a hot dog joint. Sergio led her

inside to the front of a long line that snaked out of an old-fashioned telephone booth. "Hi, Salvatore."

"Sergio. My man." The burly bouncer shook his hand and then clasped him on the back and opened the door for them.

Sergio put the receiver to his ear, dialed "1," and said his name.

A wall next to Anne opened up, and they stepped inside a dimly lit speakeasy packed with people. The hostess sat them at the corner of a long bar. Behind it, shiny liquor bottles were displayed.

Sergio handed Anne the cocktail menu. "What do you recommend?" she asked.

"This place is known for their bacon-infused whiskey."

"I don't eat a lot of meat. Just fish."

"Really?"

"I'm a pescetarian."

"A what?"

"It's like a vegetarian, but I do eat seafood."

"Okay." He smiled. "That can be arranged. I don't think they have any fish drinks though. He ran his finger down the menu. "You might like a Witch's Kiss. It's quite a concoction with Irish whiskey. "

She nodded. "Sounds enticing."

He ordered her one and a beer for himself. "Hungry? You probably don't eat hotdogs, but the tater tots are to die for."

"Sure. No onions, just cheese, please." She wanted to remain kissable.

They each sipped their drinks. Sergio touched her snowflake pin and then ran his hand along her coat's arm. "Bella! Wherever did you find it?"

"What?"

"They don't sell coats like that at Bloomingdales anymore."

She took a sip of her drink and hesitated. "I bought it at a thrift shop."

"You're kidding."

"No, really."

A waitress delivered their tots in a paper boat, and Anne dipped one in some cheese and nibbled. "Mmm."

He ran his hand over the jacket's velvet shoulder. "It's so classy. I bet you got a great deal."

"I did." She shrugged off the coat and showed him the label. "A Dior."

"It's perfect for you." As he toyed with a curl that had fallen over her eyes, she felt a connection with him as if she'd known him for a long time, maybe even in a past life. She pulled out the key and opened her hand. "I found this in the pocket."

He took it from her and read the label, "Sea Cliff. Where's that?"

"I think somewhere in San Francisco near Ocean Beach."

"It must have belonged to the coat's former owner."

Anne nodded. "That's what I thought. A few days after I bought it, I saw in an old *Life* magazine a picture of a woman in a coat that looked just like it. It even had a snowflake pin on its collar."

"That's amazing." Sergio's eyes penetrated hers.

"Quite a coincidence."

He shook his head. "My grandmamma says everything happens for a reason."

"Do you believe that?"

"I do." He smiled, pressed the key back into Anne's hand, and kissed it.

"There's even more. Her fiancé was in the picture too. They were leaving their engagement party at the St. Francis. He looked scary."

Sergio nodded.

Anne opened her eyes wide. "I think she was afraid of him."

"Sounds like that picture would be a good one for your artwork."

Anne couldn't believe Sergio had said that. "I thought so too, so I made a photo transfer of it."

"I can't wait to see it. I love that technique."

"You know it?"

"Certainly." He nodded.

"I've become a bit obsessed. I Googled their names and found out that after that party, they went missing."

"Really? What do you think happened?"

"I don't know."

The bartender came over, and Sergio looked at Anne. She nodded, and he held up two fingers. They continued to talk until two o'clock in the morning. Then they left the bar and cuddled in the taxi's backseat. "Big Foot. Please come home with me."

"Better not."

"I just want to be with you as long as I can." His hands searched through the layers and found her bare back.

She gazed into his eyes, and her heart stirred, like a brush mixing paints, then became awash with desire. She smiled and nodded slowly. "Okay."

He grinned and gave the address to the driver. And she floated along in Sergio's arms all the way to his apartment.

38

*S*lumped over the T-Bird's steering wheel, Sylvia regained consciousness with a splitting headache. She must have passed out. The sun, almost straight overhead, shone through the cracked windshield. She stretched her neck, looked in the rearview mirror, and winced as she touched a gash on her forehead. All she could remember was the pounding rain and her scream as the car flew. Silence surrounded the T-Bird; at least the rain had stopped.

Lucy moaned on the passenger-seat floor, and Sylvia picked her up. "You okay, girl?" She gently moved each of the dog's limbs, but when Sylvia manipulated the right front paw, Lucy let out a high-pitched shriek.

Sylvia flinched and kissed Lucy's forehead. "Sorry!"

She looked out at the surroundings: a desert earth drenched a deep sienna and pockets of water pooled throughout. The driver's side of the car tilted into a sandbar. She tried to open the door, but it wouldn't budge. Damp dirt must have piled above the door's bottom edge. She carefully put Lucy on the floor again, leaned over, and pressed the passenger door handle. It clicked but was stuck too. Sylvia crawled up onto her seat, leaned back, and kicked the door with her boot, but no luck. She kicked again, harder this time, and it flew open.

Climbing out of the car, she sunk up to her ankles in deep

sand. She put her purse over an elbow, gathered Lucy in her arms like a baby, careful not to hurt the leg, and looked around the vast landscape. At least there weren't any dark clouds in sight.

Sylvia trudged along for half an hour. The air became warm and dry, the wet sand releasing heat as the moisture evaporated. Her arms grew tired from the puppy's weight, so she sat down on the sand to take a break. Removing her Pendleton she tied it around her waist. A nearby cactus pointed up from the earth. She felt like they were in the center of nowhere and had no clue which way to go to find civilization.

Spying a dip on the horizon up ahead, she gathered Lucy in her arms again, and walked toward the indentation. Step by step, Sylvia's boots pushed into the deep, thick dirt. She slid down a bank into an arroyo, where the ground remained hard. A trickle of red water ran through it. She knew people usually lived near rivers, so she followed the wash upstream.

The afternoon waned and clouds began to gather, but she kept going, one foot in front of the other. With each step, Lucy grew heavier, but Sylvia, determined to take care of her, kept on. Sylvia touched the charm around her neck. "Please bring us luck." Her voice rasped with thirst.

The sky filled with a sunset like she had never seen: orange, purple, and reds, fire colors. Just as it grew dark, exhaustion over-took her, her knees buckled, and she fell onto the sand, unable to get back up.

A half moon shone like a snapped pearl button as it peeked out from behind a tuft of clouds. The sky cleared, and stars beamed. Her body shivered from the cold. To keep them warm, she huddled over the moaning Lucy in her lap. Would they die right here?

Sylvia's head throbbed and her body ached, but she forced herself to stand again with Lucy still in her arms. She climbed to the top of a dune and looked around until she spotted what might be a road and headed toward it, step by step, until she reached the highway.

She'd heard of people hitchhiking (Wasn't there another *Twilight Zone* episode about that?) and thought someone might pick them up. They stood by the side of the road and waited for a car to come by. One approached, and she pointed a free thumb east, but the car passed by. She tried again with the next one, but that sedan kept going too. Sylvia finally collapsed down from exhaustion and nodded off.

A honk woke her as dawn approached and a truck pulled up beside them. "Need a ride?"

Sylvia touched the amulet around her neck as relief washed over her. She plodded to the truck. "Thank God!" She opened the door. "My puppy's hurt."

The driver tugged at her gray braid. "See, amulet work."

"Betty Lou?" Sylvia had been half afraid of her at the trading post but now was thankful to see her.

"I felt you were in trouble." Her almond-shaped eyes showed concern as she looked at Lucy.

"How?" Sylvia asked.

Betty Lou chuckled. "Magic."

Sylvia didn't believe in magic but smiled, grateful for whatever had brought Betty Lou to her.

"Get in." Sylvia handed Lucy to Betty Lou and climbed up into the Ford.

"Got caught in the storm, huh?" The Indian woman scratched Lucy behind the ears. The puppy looked up and blinked at her.

"Yes." Sylvia nodded.

"Where were you going in that deluge?"

Sylvia felt like a little girl being scolded. "I wanted to see Monument Valley."

Betty Lou pulled the blanket from her shoulders and draped it around Sylvia. "Monument Valley is far away." She touched Sylvia's head wound with the blanket's edge.

"Ouch!" Sylvia backed away. "That smarts!"

Betty Lou opened a cold Coke bottle and handed it to Sylvia. "Put it on your head."

Sylvia took a few gulps and held the soda on her throbbing head. "Please take us to a veterinarian. Lucy's really hurt."

Betty Lou stretched out the puppy's legs one at a time. Lucy yelped when the front paw was touched, and the Indian woman stopped and set her on the seat. "No vet necessary." She started the ignition, revved the engine, and pulled out onto the road.

Sylvia frowned and put her hand on top of Lucy's shaky body. "She needs a vet."

"I can fix her." Betty Lou's voice was firm.

Sylvia wanted to believe her. "Where are we going?" she asked.

"To hogan."

"Hogan?" Sylvia finished the Coke, put the bottle down, and looked at Betty Lou.

"My hogan. Home."

"Is it nearby?"

"Just down the road." Betty Lou nodded ahead. "Hungry?" She handed Sylvia an oatmeal cookie. Lucy looked up and sniffed, eyes on the cookie. Sylvia broke off a piece and fed it to her.

As the sun rose, the sky turned rose colored with a smattering of high white clouds. From the truck's rearview mirror, a woven novelty hung; the crystal teardrop in its center glittered in the light. Sylvia was surprised she didn't want to touch the shiny object but instead preferred to watch the landscape glide by. Small grasses poked out of the damp sand, fat barrel-shaped cactus dotted the horizon, and white bushes wafted in the breeze.

They drove for what seemed like hours, but finally, the truck crossed a wooden bridge over a bloodred river and pulled off the highway onto a bumpy road. The jolting movement caused Sylvia's head to throb even more. Betty Lou drove about another mile then stopped. Crows flew over an igloo-shaped building, and half a dozen sheep grazed nearby. A corral held a pinto pony. No other buildings could be seen for miles, just open desert.

Betty Lou tilted her head. "Welcome. Hogan."

Sylvia thought of Bay Breeze. Could someone really live in this primitive structure covered with mud?

She picked up Lucy, followed Betty Lou to the building, and entered past the doorway blanket, where the woman motioned to the right. Stepping inside the muggy building, an enticing aroma of cedar and cooked corn greeted her. The simplistic beauty of the circular dwelling astonished her. It had no windows, but light shone through the smoke hole at the top.

"Sit." Betty Lou picked up a spoon from the stove and pointed it to a sheepskin rug on the earthen floor. Then she stirred the pot on the stove and added a log to its dark potbelly.

Sylvia studied the dirty carpet. Ordinarily, she would have been disgusted, but under these circumstances, she couldn't wait to collapse on it. Her head felt dizzy and her body fluctuated from cold to hot. Careful not to jostle a sleeping Lucy in her arms, she settled onto the soft wool and looked around.

She had expected the structure to be dark with dirt walls, but instead, the interior had been lined with wood, like the cedar closet at home. Framework ceiling poles overlapped each other in a circular fashion. A loom leaned against a wall, strung with an unfinished blanket, red zigzags woven into gray and black.

Sylvia rested her hand on Lucy's back. Betty Lou crouched in front of them and touched the injured leg, and the puppy cried out. Delicately, Betty Lou manipulated her other legs. She returned to the harmed one and instructed. "Sylvia, hold tight."

Grimacing, she did as told. Betty Lou yanked the wounded leg straight out with a jerk that made a loud pop. Lucy screeched and then hummed a low moan.

"Oh, you poor, sweet girl." Sylvia kissed her head.

"Better now." Betty Lou nodded and stood up. "Hungry?"

At the stove, she filled a bowl and placed it on the ground. Lucy perked up, hobbled over, and gobbled all of it all up. Then she lumbered back to Sylvia, plopping down next to her.

Betty Lou smiled at Lucy. "See, didn't need a vet."

Sylvia touched her throbbing head.

"I'll heal it too." Betty Lou pulled a bandana from a basket, sprinkled liquid on it, and wrapped it around Sylvia's head.

Sylvia tried not to stare at the suede pouch that hung on a leather string around Betty Lou's neck and wondered what was inside it. "I don't know what would have happened to us if you hadn't come along. Thank you."

"Knew you were in trouble. I sensed it."

Sylvia didn't really know what that meant but didn't want to be rude and ask. Did this woman have special powers like Glinda the Good Witch? "We'll get out of your way soon. May I use the telephone to call a taxi?" She thought about her wrecked T-Bird with a sigh.

Betty Lou giggled. "There's no phone."

"You live out here without a phone?" Sylvia frowned.

"Yes. No poles on the reservation."

"Reservation?"

"You're on Navajo land now," Betty Lou answered with a deep voice, moved to the stove and stirred the pot.

"Then could you please take us to a hotel?" Sylvia needed a shower and a warm bed.

Betty Lou ladled more thick stew into a tin cup, added herbs, and handed it to Sylvia. "Eat first. Make you better."

The mouthwatering aroma was so enticing that Sylvia couldn't say no, and she took a bite. It tingled her mouth with an assortment of flavors: meat, corn, parsley, and something that tasted like licorice. It was so good that it reminded her of Ella's Goulash.

Betty Lou pulled up another sheepskin and sat across from her. They ate in silence, except for Lucy's gentle snores.

The stew warmed Sylvia's stomach. "This is yummy!"

"Secret Navajo recipe."

Sylvia touched her head. "It actually feels better now." She tossed off the blanket and unbuttoned her jacket.

"Told you so." Betty Lou unwound the bandana. Sylvia set her cup down and relaxed back onto the sheepskin with her elbows for support. Betty Lou's hair appeared as shiny as mica in the soft firelight, her smile crooked and eyes full of mischief. She seemed like a wonderful person, but Sylvia had been a poor judge of character before.

39

     *S*ylvia asked, "Do you live out here all alone?"

"Usually. But sometimes my husband sleeps here." Betty Lou grinned her slanted lips.

"Where is he now?"

"Don't know."

"You don't? Is he on a business trip?"

"Something like that."

Sylvia leaned toward Betty Lou and gazed into those dark eyes. She felt connected to her, as if they'd known each other forever. "Do you love him?"

"I love him more when he's not here." Betty Lou snickered.

Sylvia's eyes opened wide, and she put her hand on Lucy's sleeping body. "Why?"

"He drinks too much. Gets mean and scares me." She leaned toward Sylvia and whispered, "Sometimes makes me want to kill him."

Sylvia gasped and clutched the amulet. "Has he ever hurt you?"

"Plenty." Betty Lou shrugged and rolled back her sleeves revealing red scars. She mocked herself in a high-pitched singsong voice: "Felt butterflies in my stomach. Thought it love."

Sylvia nodded. "I've felt that way before."

The hogan grew dark. From outside, an owl's song, like a low-pitched flute, penetrated the chilly space. Sylvia shivered and pulled the blanket back around her shoulders.

"Still cold?" Betty Lou put another log in the fire. She lit a lantern, hung it on a nearby hook, and sat in front of Sylvia cross-legged. Removing the pouch from around her neck, she dumped the contents into her skirt's lap: clear crystals, a carved turquoise bear, black rocks. Her hand clutched a crystal like the one on the rearview mirror, and she replaced the other pieces in her pouch. With eyes closed, she held her hand toward Sylvia. After a few moments, Betty Lou's fist began to shake.

Sylvia wondered if this was another nightmare or maybe even the *Twilight Zone*. But those would be frightening, and this was not. Calmness settled in on her, and, stretching out her stiff legs, she rested weary arms by her side.

Betty Lou rose, circled Sylvia several times with slow, prancing steps, then began to yip, not unlike the sounds those nighttime coyotes made. But instead of being scared, Sylvia allowed the echoing vibrations to move through her like enormous hugs of power filled with adoration and self-love.

Betty Lou opened her eyes and sat back down. "Butterflies are not real love. After a time, they always fly away." She waved her hands like butterflies, reflecting dark shadows on the wall.

Sylvia imitated her. First she wiggled her right hand and then her left. The shadows shifted, and a flutter of butterflies flew off the wall and into the room; silent pastel wings surrounded them. Mesmerized, Sylvia watched the clear colors flit around the space. They swarmed overhead and landed on her body like soft kisses. Betty Lou clapped her hands twice, and the butterflies evaporated.

Sylvia's hands continued to dance in the firelight. Her right shimmered with fire hues of bright orange, magenta, and ruby; it felt hot but was soothing. Her left hand streamed shades from indigo to violet, the other fire colors, and felt cool and refreshing, but not freezing.

Betty Lou stood up again and with quick steps rubbed her palms together. On impulse, Sylvia jumped up and copied her until fluorescent sparks crackled and hissed and flew high up to the dome-like roof. Lucy hopped up with a bark.

Sylvia felt radiant, rose up, and drifted into the sparks. She became one of them, a red, white, and blue Fourth-of-July firework. Her body vibrated, and she could hear her heartbeat. It had never felt so open.

With a grin, Betty Lou sat back, watching. Sylvia wanted to be near her, and she floated down to her sheepskin. Trance-like, she settled into Betty Lou's eyes for direction. Following Betty Lou's gaze upward, she watched as the sparks dimmed and then disappeared like shooting stars.

Betty Lou paused for a moment then commanded with a mellow voice: "Share your sorrow." She pursed her narrow lips that Sylvia knew could hold a secret.

Sylvia sat tall and alert, her tongue loosened, and she couldn't hold back. "I killed a man," she blurted. Her whole body released from saying it aloud. She searched Betty Lou's face for a reaction, but it remained unchanged, listening eyes encouraging the truth, as if she had already known.

"It must not have been on purpose." Betty Lou folded her hands in her lap. "You're a good girl."

Sylvia became consumed with grief—sorry for Betty Lou and sorry for herself, for the way they'd been mistreated. She tried to hold back, but a flood of tears escaped her, and she couldn't stop. With her body wracked with grief, Sylvia wept while Betty Lou sat guard.

Time passed. It was hard to tell if she had sobbed for a minute or an hour, but the tears finally subsided. Betty Lou handed Sylvia a kerchief. "Blow," she instructed.

Sylvia did and then tried to smile.

"Tell me all." Betty Lou seemed to glow in the dark.

"My fiancé, Ricardo, drank and was mean, too." Once she began, it was impossible to stop. She told Betty Lou everything: Paul's warnings, Ricardo's charm, his deceptions and death.

"It's not your fault." Betty Lou smiled serenely.

"But I shot him."

"There is good and evil. Ricardo was evil."

"But it's a sin to kill."

"Maybe your God did not want him on earth anymore." Betty Lou looked up for a few moments as if listening for a god to speak, then nodded. "I know you are forgiven and blessed."

Sylvia wished she could believe that. Maybe with time, she'd be sure. Drained, she yawned and couldn't keep her eyes open. She didn't want to leave now. Betty Lou made her feel loved and protected. "It must be late. May we stay here with you?"

"Yes, sleep here." She nodded.

Sylvia looked around for a bed. "Where?"

"Here." Betty Lou pulled over more sheepskins.

Sylvia yawned again and caressed the thick fur. She curled up onto her side, body warm with Lucy asleep beside her.

Betty Lou lit a stick of white leaves. She wafted it around the room, spreading a pungent but calming aroma. A sliver of daylight shone under the hogan's blanketed door. It was hard to believe they had been up all night, and Sylvia rolled onto her stomach, feeling as if she were part of the earth, sensing its slow rotation. Betty Lou covered them with a blanket and chanted an Indian lullaby. In its rhythm, like a gentle rain, Sylvia could hear a song of redemption. Betty Lou's low voice massaged Sylvia's body like one of Ella's nighttime back rubs. Feet toward the fire, Sylvia rested, convinced for a moment that God had forgiven her for shooting Ricardo.

40

Walking home, Anne passed a bakery, and the smell of cinnamon reminded her of that morning a week ago when Sergio brought her his secret-recipe spiced donuts with fresh coffee and then joined her back in bed. She almost missed her plane. He seemed to really like to listen to her talk. Not like Karl, who had always changed the subject to his own interests. In their short time together, she felt closer to Sergio than she had to Karl after a whole year. She felt like Sergio might be the one, even though he lived all the way across the country. The day she left, he texted a quick thank-you and she had replied but still hadn't heard back from him again. Maybe it was just a one-night stand.

She pulled the yellow UPS slip off her mailbox. Funny, she hadn't ordered anything lately. The writing indicated that the package had been given to Mrs. Ladenheim. Anne knocked on her landlady's door. At least her rent was paid.

Mrs. Ladenheim answered with her usual hangdog expression. "What?" She twisted a curler in her hair.

"Thanks for accepting my package." Anne put on her best smile.

"What do you mean?"

Anne held up the slip.

"Oh, that." The older woman walked down the hall into a back bedroom.

Anne didn't have the patience for this. She was exhausted. Not only had she worked a morning shift at the St. Francis; she had also covered for Fay at the Noir all afternoon, and it had taken her a few days to get the jetlag out of her system.

The Siamese cat slid by. Anne reached down to pet it, but it hissed and skittered back inside. After a few minutes, Mrs. Ladenheim returned, shaking the box. "Can't hear much. Feels heavy, though."

Anne put out her hands and took it. It wasn't heavy at all. As she clomped up the stairs, she read the return label: *S. Parmeggianno.* She didn't know anyone by that name.

On her daybed, she set the package in her lap, grabbed some scissors, and slit open the tape along the side. She folded back the tissue paper and smiled—shoes just like the ones Sergio had thrown away at the subway station! She looked closer and saw that these were the real thing—not like the knockoffs she had bought on eBay. Real Ferragamos! And brand-new too. They must have cost a fortune. Anne ran her hands over the soft leather, so unlike the stiff insides of her old slingbacks. She pulled off her wingtips and slipped into the new shoes. They were exactly her size.

She rifled through the box for a card, found one, and read:

Big Foot—
You are a delight. Thanks for the kisses. Watch your step in these.
Sergio

How did he guess her exact size and find her mailing address?

Now she knew he had been thinking of her too. She looked at her phone. It was almost ten PM there. She shouldn't call this late.

Her mother had taught her it was rude to call anyone after nine.

Holding up her pant legs, Anne modeled the shoes in the mirror. They sure looked sexy. She considered texting him but really wanted to hear his voice, couldn't wait until morning, and dialed his number.

He answered right away. "Yes?"

"How did you know my size?"

"So good to hear your voice."

She thought about his juicy tongue twisted with hers in the back of the taxi and his warm hand on her thigh in the cool night. "And know the type?"

"I sell shoes for a living."

"You do not!" She thought he was in art too. He had said something about following the trends.

"Yes, I do. The minute I saw you, I thought, *Now, this girl has style.* A size nine. I recognized the designer right away."

"But those weren't even real."

"The intent was there. You deserve the real thing."

She looked at her image in the mirror again. "I can't accept them. They're too much."

"Yes, you can."

"I'm going to send them back."

"Don't you dare! They won't fit me."

She laughed. "But . . ."

"It won't hurt anything for you keep them."

She hadn't owned a new pair of shoes in ages. "I'll think about it. How did you get my address?"

"I have my ways. Any plans to come back to New York soon? I really want to see you again."

"We could Skype." There'd be no harm in that.

He sighed. "Guess that'll have to do for now."

She laid back on the daybed and imagined them dining at

Jardinière, her favorite San Francisco restaurant. He'd probably even go to the ballet with her. There could be no denying that instant connection. "You could come here." It slipped out before she could catch herself.

"Am I invited?"

She paused and looked around her shabby space. He lived in a tony high-rise overlooking a park. She thought about all the work she had ahead of her to complete her series. Fay was coming over next week to see its progress and pick out a piece for a group show. Anne really needed to focus on her career, and he would be quite a distraction. "This isn't really a good time."

"I hope someday it will be."

"Hope so too."

41

"Get up, sleeping head," Betty Lou called to Sylvia.

She hadn't really been asleep, just floating on the sheepskin as if it were a cloud. She touched her once-tender forehead and sat up. Sunlight streamed through the hogan's smoke hole, and memories filtered through Sylvia's confused mind: stew, butterflies, fireworks, confessions, and lullabies. She remembered the flash flood and crunching metal and looked around for Lucy, who was asleep beside her.

"How many hours have we been here?" Sylvia asked.

Betty Lou handed her a cup. "It's been days."

"What! You must be joking."

"Drink tea. You'll feel better."

"But."

Betty Lou waved her hand at Sylvia. "Hush and drink."

Parched, Sylvia smelled the minty concoction and sipped. She rotated her shoulders and neck then asked, "What about the trading post?"

"It's closed."

"Is it a holiday?" She drank the tea, sweet heaven.

"More important to be with you." Betty Lou grinned at her. Neat braids hung over a green 7 Up T-shirt.

Sylvia smiled, comforted to be with someone who cared about her. "Have I really been asleep all this time? I don't understand exactly what happened."

"Don't need to know."

Betty Lou took thin bread from the stove, put it on a plate, and handed it to Sylvia. The color of charred embers, the bread tasted ashy, and she tried to choke it down with tea.

"Oops. Forgot honey." Betty Lou dropped a dollop on the bread. Sylvia tried another bite. The smooth honey masked the bread's blandness.

Lucy perked up and hobbled over for a bite. Betty Lou mixed a bowl and set it in front of Lucy. She quickly ate it up. Then she lay back down and fell back to sleep.

"Sweet, sweet girl, so tired." Betty Lou sat cross-legged in front of Sylvia and looked at her. "Had dream about you."

"Really?" Sylvia nibbled the bread, filling her empty stomach.

"Saw man."

Sylvia touched the amulet in fear. "Was he dark with a scar?"

Better Lou shook her head. "No, soft blue eyes, hair color of lamb's wool."

"Sounds like Paul." Thinking of him made her feel warm inside. She really missed him.

"Very handsome." Betty Lou raised her eyebrows.

"I guess so. What else did you dream?" Sylvia swallowed the last bite, put down the plate, and licked honey from her fingers.

"He cares for you."

"Yes, I've known him my whole life. When my parents died, he became my guardian."

Betty Lou stared into Sylvia's eyes. "Loves you."

"Yes, he's just like a brother." Sylvia nodded.

"Not like that. Wants to marry you."

"That's ridiculous." Sylvia felt her face flush as she remembered that sensual dream she had had in the desert. But Paul would have told her ages ago if he felt that way about her.

"Dream real. Saw white things: handkerchief, gardenia flowers, pearls." Betty Lou started to stand up. "Finish tea. Need to go."

"What else?"

"Little squares with letters." She held up a thumb and forefinger.

"Scrabble tiles. I bet you saw Scrabble tiles!" Sylvia couldn't believe it.

"Time to go."

"Wait. Tell me more." Sylvia, surprised at her raw emotions, felt on the verge of tears.

"What's more to tell?" Betty Lou shrugged. "Good man loves you."

From Betty Lou's firm voice, Sylvia could tell the subject was closed. But she really wanted to hear more.

"Come." Betty Lou motioned for Sylvia to follow.

"Where are we going?" she asked.

"Take you to hotel."

Earlier, Sylvia wanted nothing more, but now she didn't want to leave this wonderful woman. However, she didn't want to impose any longer. She thought about the accident. "I need to take care of the trailer and car."

"Tomorrow another day. First take care of you."

Sylvia rose, picked up her purse, and stretched. A bath would be divine.

They stepped out the blanketed doorway, where a few innocuous clouds drifted in the blue sky above dry sand. Betty Lou's pickup truck was parked next to the hogan. Sylvia felt a soft wind waft around her as she took in the scenery. In the corral, the pinto flicked its mane, sheep nibbled on short grasses, and a hawk flew in circles overhead.

Betty Lou whistled, and Lucy shot out of the hogan behind them. "See, leg better."

Chased by the sheep, she yelped and scurried behind Sylvia with a whimper. The women laughed deep and strong. Then Lucy reversed things and with a wide distance rambled in circles around the sheep.

Betty Lou nodded. "That's one lucky dog." She whistled again, and Lucy ran to her.

"Wish I could do that." Sylvia scooped Lucy up and slid into the truck.

"You can. Easy." Betty Lou climbed in, and they pulled onto the dirt road and back to the highway. Sylvia pursed her lips trying to whistle.

"Yes, a good man loves you," Betty Lou teased.

"Does not!" If Sylvia saw him again, would she feel embarrassed remembering the dreams? Could it be true that he really loved her? She fingered the pendant. What if he knew the truth about Ricardo? Maybe God would forgive her, but would Paul?

As they rode along, Sylvia looked at Betty Lou, her skin the color of the dry sand along the highway. She obviously had special powers. Did she learn them from her family, passed down from generation to generation, or was the magic something she had just been born with?

After a half hour, Betty Lou pulled onto a long gravel drive. Sylvia had expected a ramshackle roadside motel, but instead, they stopped in front of a Spanish hacienda, a desert oasis painted pale pink. "What's such a big hotel doing way out here?"

"Railroad stop. Tracks on other side." Betty Lou turned off the motor. "See those tiles?" She pointed at the red roof. "I helped make them."

"What do you mean?"

"A girl then. Wet the clay, laid it on my leg." Betty Lou

demonstrated on her thigh. "Curve. Pat. Smooth. Smooth. Curve. Pat. Smooth. Smooth."

Sylvia laughed. "You're kidding!"

"No. Different legs, different sizes."

Sylvia nodded. The tiles were varied, but still Sylvia wondered if Betty Lou was just teasing.

"Go on. Get out." Betty Lou handed her a bundle wrapped in a woven blanket. "Pick you up in the morning."

"What time?"

Betty Lou scowled. "Don't know. Sun about there." She pointed in the sky behind the hotel.

Sylvia hopped out of the truck and lifted Lucy down.

Betty Lou nodded. "Rest up." She pulled out the drive and headed down the road.

In the hotel's lobby, a welded jackrabbit held an ashtray. Decorated with Indian rugs and Mexican paintings, the inn looked like the home of a wealthy, but eccentric, ranch family. Much cozier than Bay Breeze, here you could probably slouch on that deep velvet sofa and even put your boots on the coffee table.

A lamp, shaped like a blooming cactus, flickered on the reception desk. Sylvia rang the bell, and a man sporting a vest, bolo tie, and thick mustache came out of the back room. She pulled dark glasses from her handbag and slid them on. With a lisp, he said, "Welcome to La Posada, the Resting Place."

Sylvia hoped it would live up to its name. She put Lucy down.

"Cute puppy!" The man smiled at her. Lucy blinked at him and backed up behind Sylvia.

"I'd like a room."

"Certainly, pretty empty this time of year." He swiveled the guest book around, pushed it forward, and handed her a pen. "Sign the registry."

She hesitated. Usually she took her time and wrote her name

very neatly. She recalled Paul saying, "You can tell a lot about a person by his or her John Hancock." It might have been illegal to sign a fake name though. So with determination, she wrote her name, Sylvia Van Dam, very fast and messy so no one would be able to read it.

The innkeeper squinted. "Miss a . . . a . . . a . . . Dawn? Follow me." He grabbed a skeleton key off a rack, came out from behind the desk, and looked around. "Where's your luggage?"

Sylvia held up the bundle. "Just this." Her boots clicked on the red pavers as she followed him through the lobby. "This inn is lovely."

"She sure is. Even designed by a woman architect. Built in 1929 for the railroad to bring tourists to the desert and see the Indians."

Sylvia's hand grazed the wrought iron railings as they ascended a staircase up to the second floor. At the end of a dark hallway, the man pushed open a door, and she smiled at the lovely room. Lucy jumped onto the bed with the hand-carved headboard. A saint's icon hung above it. Over a stone fireplace, the mantel had been painted with a floral motif. Sylvia peeked into the bathroom and spotted a big clean tub! She handed the man a quarter from her purse. "Perfect."

He laid the key on top of a stamped tin chest and quietly closed the door. She took off the necklace, ran her fingers over the smooth amber, and put it back on. Perhaps it brought her luck after all. She spread the contents of Betty Lou's blanket on the bed: a white blouse and full floral skirt with embroidered roses. How thoughtful of Betty Lou. Sylvia couldn't wait to try on the outfit. But first she needed a bath. It had been at least a month! The fact that she had been in the hogan for many days baffled her. She couldn't even remember exactly what had happened there—just that she still felt a resonating calmness in her chest.

Sylvia tossed her filthy clothes in a pile on the floor, reached to turn on the bathwater, then hesitated. The tub was so clean. She should probably take a shower first to rinse off her grime. Funny, she couldn't ever recollect taking a shower. She opened the door, turned on the water, and stepped in. The frigid water pricked her skin, which released a long-forgotten memory she couldn't quite place but that now began to surface.

She jumped out, wrapped herself in a towel, sat on the bathmat, and tried to piece together her memory. She had been about five and had discovered a shiny tiara hidden in her mother's closet. It was the most beautiful thing Sylvia had ever seen, filled with diamonds that sparkled in the dim light. She had put it on and paraded in front of the mirror, a queen with arms stretched overhead.

Her mother had swept in, shrieking like a wrathful hawk, and ripped the tiara off Sylvia's head.

She cried, "But Mama, I want to be a beauty queen too."

"You are far too plain. Plain, plain, plain. You will never win a contest."

"I want it!" Sylvia reached for the tiara.

"No. And you'll never wear any of my jewels again." Her mama's usually serene face had become twisted and frightening.

But Sylvia wanted the tiara. She rubbed her scalp, wailed, and stamped her feet.

"Nice girls don't have tantrums," her mother had said through clenched teeth. She dragged Sylvia into the bathroom and threw her in a cold shower. Through the door's etched glass, she could see her mama holding the shower closed with a sneer on her face. Sylvia hunched on the tile and cried while icy water pitted her skin like rose thorns from the garden.

It seemed like forever before dear Ella pushed her mother aside and opened the door. "Mrs. Van Dam!" Ella pulled Sylvia out and wrapped her in a soft towel. "She's only a child."

Sylvia had never understood why her mother had been so mean, but looking back now, she realized it might have been jealousy. Sylvia had taken away some of her mother's spotlight. Could her mother's treatment have been why Sylvia held back her emotions all these years, growing up quiet and shy, even after her parents were gone?

Her heart now felt injured as if wrapped in gauze. Ricardo never loved her, but neither had her mother. She now remembered another conversation she had overheard after the funeral. Paul was in the library studying the will with some others and he raised his voice to ask, "All the jewelry to Grace Cathedral's building fund? Not even a keepsake for Sylvia?" Her mother had kept her promise that day with the tiara. It all started to make sense to her now.

42

___

Anne flipped through a *Cowboys and Indians* magazine, cut out some boots, and glued them onto the Arizona map. Then she perused more *National Geographics* in search of places Sylvia may have visited. The photos of natural wonders made Anne wish she had driven through Arizona when she moved to San Francisco instead of through Vegas, where she had dumped a lot of cash into a slot machine. Her apartment now looked like a tsunami had hit: newspapers, magazines, clothes, and art supplies were strewn about, and a pile of dishes sat stacked in the sink. Canvases leaned against the walls, and other pieces had been pinned to them. She had kicked into a last flurry of energy to get ready for Fay.

"Sorry the place is such a mess," Anne apologized as Fay stepped inside.

The gallery manager ran her fingers through her spiked hair. "I'd worry if your studio was tidy."

"Would you like some coffee or tea?"

"No, thanks." Fay slipped on some cat-eyed glasses and examined the pieces pinned to the wall. "This is a new direction for you."

"You don't like them?"

"No, I mean, yes." Fay raised her arms and waved them. "I'm gobsmacked!"

"Really?"

"It's a whole new level. How did you ever come up with the concept?"

"It's like I'm obsessed—working from an intuition stronger than I've ever experienced." She told Fay all about the coat, pin, key, and Sylvia research.

"That's wild. What do you think happened to her?"

"Don't know. That's why I keep researching."

"I love this one of Sylvia's headshot. She sure was a looker."

Fay climbed over a tarp to inspect a whitewashed shadow box on the wall more closely. The assemblage had a glass heart suspended over a pair of tiny silver heels pointing away. Another section held a snowflake pin similar to the one on the velvet coat. "How did you ever come up with this combination of images?"

"Some are from my research, and others are from dreams."

"Your pieces will be the best in the show!" Fay hollered.

Anne felt her heart chakra open with pride. "It's been a magical process."

"I wish we could display all of these instead of including other artists' work."

"But that would be a solo show."

Fay sat on the edge of the daybed. "I know. But Old Blockhead insists on group shows now. He thinks we'll sell more. I don't agree, but he's still the boss."

"When's the reception?"

Fay shook her head. "We're not."

"What do you mean?"

"Mr. Block doesn't want to spend the quid."

"We could do a potluck." Anne pulled over a kitchen chair and sat facing Fay.

"That's a thought. But then there's still the cost of marketing mailers, etc., etc. Where's your price list?"

"Here." Anne handed her the agonized-over-for-hours neatly typed sheet:

Anne McFarland

The Sylvia Series

1.	*Portrait of LIFE*	$275
2.	*Lucky Strike*	$275
3.	*Cliff House, Seal of Approval*	$400
4.	*Missing*	$500
5.	*Pockets of Deep Secrets*	$500
6.	*Walking Away from Love*	$1000
7.	*On the Road in Arizona*	$500
8.	*Full Moon Over Monument Valley*	$500

Fay straightened her glasses, picked up a pencil from the coffee table, and circled numbers on Anne's list. "I'd like to show number 1. That's a twenty by twenty-two, correct?"

Anne nodded. "Yes."

"And 4, 5, and 8."

"Eight isn't finished yet."

"Then finish it!" She laughed.

"But I thought you could only choose one."

Fay took off her glasses and looked at Anne. "Mr. Block has seemed a bit distracted lately. He might not even notice and let them slide in."

"Mr. Micromanager himself?"

Fay nodded. "He asked if I'd be interested in curating future shows."

"Wow! What did you say?"

"That I needed a raise."

Anne laughed. "Did he give you one?"

"He said he'd get back to me, but I don't count my hens before they're hatched." Fay looked back at the list. "These prices are way too low."

"But if I price them too high, they'll never sell."

"That's not true. If you price them too low, they'll be devalued." She crossed out and doubled the cost of each piece. "Of course, we'll need to take a 50 percent commission as usual if anything sells." As she put the pencil down on the table, her eye caught the Ferragamos underneath. She leaned over and picked them up, studying the label. "Where did you get these?"

With a straight face, Anne said, "I bought them."

"On eBay?"

"No, on sale at Neiman's." She took them from Fay, slipped them on, and strutted across the room.

Fay's eyes grew wide, and she swallowed. "How much were they?"

"Only $500. Isn't that a deal?"

"It's probably not any of my business, but should you really spend that kind of money now? Maybe after you sell one of these pieces to celebrate, but . . ."

Anne started laughing. "I'm just teasing!"

"What do you mean? Where did you get them?"

Anne put her hands on her hips and dramatically paraded around. "You were right. New York can be very romantic."

"Tell all!"

"I met a guy there, and he sent them to me."

"Ferragamos? Just like that?"

Anne sat down on the chair again and nodded. "Practically. My heel had broken in a grate, and he threw that old knockoff pair away."

Fay grinned. "Fast work! When's he coming to visit?"

"I'm too busy right now. Plus, he—Sergio—lives too far away." Anne sighed.

"Sergio sounds sexy! I've heard bicoastal relationships can be thrilling."

"We have a Skype date for next week."

"Blimey. Things have changed. I haven't even had a phone call from a man in years."

Anne didn't want to pry. "Sorry."

"Don't be. I had a love once. I gave up on finding another one years ago. Me mom calls me a spinster." Fay checked her watch and kissed Anne on the cheek. "Gotta run. Thanks for sitting the gallery for me the other day. I'll let you know when I need you again. Can you deliver the pieces at the end of next week?"

"Yes. See you then." Anne closed the door, sat on the daybed, and studied the list. If she really could sell something at those prices, it would be amazing. She'd better start working again on that last piece, or it would never be finished in time. It needed many more layers.

To add the final touches on *Full Moon over Monument Valley*, she mixed brown and red paints together and dipped a brush into the smooth texture, and the smell of cinnamon sprang into the air. She sniffed again, but the scent was gone. Anne looked at the portrait, and a chill went down her spine. It was as if Sylvia was really looking at her, trying to tell her something.

43

*B*etty Lou drove the Ford along the highway dressed as if going to a powwow, in a garnet-colored dress and loads of silver and turquoise jewelry. Her hair had been smoothed back and wrapped into an exotic type of loop. Sylvia felt fancy too in her new prairie outfit. Lucy sat on her lap and looked out the window.

This morning, the sandy ground had popped with wildflowers, a coverlet of beauty. The colors more striking than an ocean full of gems: magenta, purple, gold, white. Filled with gratitude, Sylvia could feel God's presence. "Amazing!"

"You're lucky to see. Doesn't last long."

"But it looks like it could last forever."

"Oh, no. Desert is moody. Every day new." Betty Lou handed Sylvia a pair of binoculars. "Try these. They're very powerful."

Sylvia had never used binoculars before. She held them up to her eyes, but everything looked blurry.

"Adjust them here." Betty Lou pointed between the lenses.

Sylvia swiveled the focus, and the vision cleared. Suddenly, a giant cactus seemed to jump right in front of them, and she screamed. She pulled the binoculars down to see that the cactus had actually been very far away. "Boy, do these ever work."

Betty Lou laughed. "Told you."

Sylvia continued to scan the desert with the binoculars. After riding for several miles, she spotted a glint up ahead and yelled, "I've spotted something."

Betty Lou steered off onto the sand and followed Sylvia's directions until she told her to stop. They got out and hiked toward the shiny object. Sylvia tried not to step on any of the wildflowers with her boots, but it was impossible. The women soon reached the trailer, which appeared to be all in one piece. In fact, there was barely a scratch on it—just a loose bumper and flat tires.

"Now what?" Sylvia asked.

"I'll get my husband to help." Betty Lou whistled for Lucy, who had run off. The puppy sprinted back and circled around them.

"Your husband?"

"He'll be back around in a few days."

"Won't someone steal it?"

"Not with those tires. My man will fix."

Sylvia didn't understand how such a wise woman could be so stupid about a man, but then again, she'd made a similar mistake herself.

They trudged to the top of a rise that overlooked a dry riverbed with cracked dark mud. Lucy ran down the slope and out into the desert again. Betty Lou whistled, and Lucy ran straight back toward them. Sylvia puckered her lips and tried to make a sound, but nothing came out except silent air.

"Current seemed to have flowed out that way." Betty Lou followed a wash of curves and searched the horizon with the binoculars, looking for the T-Bird. She frowned and looked at Sylvia. "I think the desert took it."

"What?" Sylvia frowned.

"I told you, desert moody."

Sylvia remembered the first time she saw the T-Bird, smitten with the white top, little round windows, and turquoise hue. The thought of the car fading, rusting, and falling apart like a dead bird saddened her.

"Nope, no sign of it." Betty Lou shook her head. "Sorry. It's probably not meant to be found."

"Can't we keep on looking?"

Betty Lou raised her hand to the sky and glanced toward the sun. "No, it's time to go." As they walked back to the truck, Lucy danced beside them.

"Do you need to get to the trading post?"

"No, we're going to get you home."

"Home? To your hogan?" Sylvia looked forward to spending more time there with Betty Lou.

"No. San Francisco."

Sylvia touched the amulet and shook her head. "I can't go back there."

"You must go back and face the truth."

"I don't have enough money to get back there, and besides, I need to take care of the trailer." They climbed in the truck.

"How about I buy it from you?"

"What'll you do with it?"

"Move near the hogan. My husband can stay there when he snores with too much drink." She made a deep belly laugh.

"How can you be with a man like that?" Sylvia blurted.

"It's my destiny. Your destiny is to go home to Paul."

"But I'm not ready."

"Get ready." Betty Lou's deep voice was firm.

Sylvia fingered the amber. "I might not ever be."

"Yes, you will."

Sylvia wondered how she would ever have the courage. "But what will happen when the police learn I shot Ricardo?"

"Don't know. Paul will help."

"How can I tell him what I did?"

"How can you not?" Betty Lou was right, as usual. She turned on the truck's ignition, pulled out, and headed south for a while and then east.

Sylvia pointed behind them and raised her voice. "Aren't we going to Flagstaff? It's back the other way."

"No, you're flying out of Albuquerque. Bigger planes there."

"How long will it take to get there?"

"A day or two."

"It's that far?"

"No." Betty Lou grinned. "First we're going to Monument Valley."

44

Arriving at their destination, a fog covered Monument Valley so thickly that they couldn't even see the red mounts. The murky air looked similar to the moistness back home, but not with the same salty sea odor—just a hot and sticky evaporation from past rains.

They waited in the truck for an hour chatting, Lucy sleeping on the seat between them, until dark began to set in and Betty Lou shook her head. "Too bad, time to go."

Sylvia touched her amulet and closed her eyes for a few moments. When she opened them again, the mist had cleared, and a full moon rose over the red towers. The butted vista was even more spectacular than she could have ever imagined, those sky-high gifts from God.

Betty Lou lifted Lucy out of the truck to dart around, and the women stood admiring the view. Sylvia remembered the last full moon, which felt like a lifetime ago—on Ocean Beach, as Ricardo's body fell back onto the waves. That memory had begun to fade, and so had the haunting effects. Her guilt had begun to subside, but she doubted she'd ever forgive herself for killing a man. But at least now she knew she didn't have a choice in what she had done. Betty Lou had taught her that much. It had all been part of her destiny.

As it grew colder, Betty Lou whistled for Lucy, lifted her back in, and started up the truck again, and the three of them headed toward Albuquerque.

On the drive further east, she patiently tried to teach Sylvia how to whistle. "Round lips. Blow air from belly and out."

Sylvia blew, but only a little air came out of her mouth. She kept trying until a high squeak finally escaped, but nothing more.

"Don't worry. Keep practicing. You'll get it."

Betty Lou checked them into a hotel, and Sylvia slept more deeply than ever.

In the morning at the airport, Betty Lou gave Sylvia cash for the trailer.

"Do I really have to go? I don't think I'm ready."

Betty Lou looked deeply into Sylvia's eyes. "You are."

Sylvia gazed down at Lucy in her arms. "I'm sure they won't let Lucy on the plane. I'd better take the train."

"You can ask. If they say no, she can just stay here with me."

"No! I couldn't leave her here."

Betty Lou grinned. "Teasing."

Sylvia shook her head and walked to the counter. "I see you have a plane leaving soon for San Francisco. Is there any way I can take my dog with me?"

The clerk's eyes softened under the brim of his cap. "She's such a cute little thing."

"What do you think?" Sylvia held her breath.

"You'll need to pay for her seat and buckle her in."

She paid and returned to Betty Lou, who stood on the tarmac next to the plane, waiting with a smile. "Have a good journey."

Sylvia tried to smile and swallowed back tears. Betty Lou removed a bandana tied to her wrist, handed it to Sylvia, then pulled a small feather from her pouch and held it up. "This feather carries desires. Whisper yours to it, and they will come to you."

Sylvia took it, twirled it in her fingers, and put it in her purse.

"Lucy Lou, I have something for you too." Betty Lou held a lamb rag doll up to the puppy. "Made it special for you. Lucy licked Betty Lou's hand.

"But how can I ever repay you?" Sylvia asked, putting the lamb under her arm.

"No need to. Go home. Get strong, and help someone else someday."

"I don't know how."

Betty Lou nodded. "You will."

"I'm scared. What if the police are looking for me?"

"When you land, go straight to Paul. He will help you."

Sylvia climbed the stairs to the TWA plane, where inside there were twenty plush seats. Finding theirs, she set Lucy down, then reached for the bandana and wiped her own eyes. As the other passengers boarded and walked down the aisle, she must have heard "What a cute puppy" ten times.

The airplane engines revved, and with shaky hands, Sylvia adjusted her strap and then Lucy's and gave her the stuffed lamb. "Sweet girl. There's nothing to worry about." Never having flown before, Sylvia wanted to reassure herself more than Lucy, and she tried not to think about her parent's accident.

She took the feather from her purse and gripped the edge of her seat as the airplane bounced down the runway. It rose, and she leaned back, closed her eyes, and felt her body release. She felt light as the feather she held in her hand, looked down, and fingered the soft black edges.

The plane leveled off, and a stewardess wearing a pillbox hat came down the aisle. "Coffee or tea?"

"Coffee, please."

Out the window, Sylvia could see dry desert sand, tiny round bushes, and a scattering of buildings. Nearby aqueous clouds shone misty white like milk-glass dishes in the cabinet back home. How wonderful it was going to be to see Ella and Milo again.

Sylvia held the feather between her hands and whispered, "Here are my desires: (1) the police are not looking for me; (2) I will have the courage to tell Paul everything; and (3) he will forgive me."

Off in the distance, there must have been rain because a rainbow now appeared across the sky. The multicolored arc symbolized God's promise to Noah that the Earth would never be destroyed by flood again. Sylvia wished she had remembered that story earlier when her whole world seemed to be going underwater.

45

Anne examined herself in the mirror and tried to brush her hair. The thick waves had grown out of control. She really needed a haircut but didn't want to spend the money. Her Skype date was in a few minutes, and Sergio would really think she looked like a yeti now. She twirled her hair into an updo. It seemed too fancy, so she refastened it into a long ponytail and draped it to one side for a more casual look. Then she applied mascara and lipstick. A plain phone call would have been much easier but not as exciting. Besides, she really wanted to see his handsome face again.

She left on her sweats because she'd only be seen from the waist up. Just for fun though, she slid into her Ferragamos. They made her feel sexy. She paused. What if Sergio had a shoe fetish and lurked around galleries in search of the perfect feet? She shook her head. That couldn't be the case. If so, he probably would have needed to look at her feet to get turned on. That night in the back of the cab and then in his apartment, he sure didn't need any help in that regard.

At exactly 6:00 PM San Francisco time and 9:00 PM New York time, they connected. "Can't see you. Move to the center of the screen," he suggested.

She adjusted her chair. "Is this better?"

"You look gorgeous."

"So do you." Even though the image looked fuzzy, his endearing grin made her want to jump through the computer, give him a big hug, and more.

"How goes it, Big Foot?" He smiled.

"Okay. Been doing my art."

"Good girl. Find out more about Sylvia?"

"Not much. Still at it though. Want to see what she looks like?"

"Sure."

Anne took the portrait off the wall, carried it to the computer, and held it up for him to see.

"She was almost as glamorous as you."

"You charmer." Anne smiled and set the portrait on the floor beside her. "What have you been up to?"

"Work."

"Good boy."

"I'll show you mine, if you'll show me yours."

Anne cringed. "No way!" Maybe he was a pervert after all.

"I just meant your shoes." A pant cuff and a man's shoe shot into view on the screen.

"Those Ferragamos too?" she asked.

"My most comfortable pair." His face appeared on the screen again. "I want to make sure the ones I sent fit you really well."

"Okay. Wait a sec." She now regretted her sweatpants choice and pulled them up to her knees. He probably wouldn't be able to tell she hadn't shaved lately. At least the shoes covered her toes that screamed for a pedicure. She stood up, kicked her feet one at a time like a Rockette in front of the computer, struggled to keep her balance, and almost fell into the portrait. "Perfect. See?"

"Perfecto." His laugh was contagious.

"Thanks again." She sat back down and looked at his big smile. "I really like them."

"And I really like you."

"Me too. What a coincidence that we met at that crazy art show and hit it off."

"Not a coincidence. As I told you, my grandmamma says everything happens for a reason." He paused. "She might even say we are meant to be together."

"Do you think so too?" Anne tried to read his expression to see if he was teasing her.

He nodded solemnly. "I do. I miss you. When can I come visit?"

"I'll let you know."

"How about Christmas?"

That would be a sad day this year since she couldn't afford to go home. "I have to work that day, but maybe."

"Let me know."

"I will." She nodded. "I really miss you too."

He grinned at her. "Want to meet me in Milan this summer?"

Anne laughed. "Sure, why not?"

"I'm serious. I'm going over for a buying trip."

"You mean Milan, Italy?" He must be crazy.

"Have you ever been?"

"No." She shook her head.

"Every artist should see Italy. After I'm done with my meetings, we can rent a car and drive to Florence."

"That's where Botticelli's Birth of Venus is!"

He nodded. "Yes. And *David* too."

Imagine seeing *David* with her David. She'd ask him to stand next to the statue and compare them. "I can't."

"Why not?"

"I can't afford it." She sighed.

"No problem. I'll pay for everything."

"I couldn't let you do that."

"Yes you can. After Florence, we can explore the hill towns. I have friends with a vineyard who would love to host us. Think about it."

"Of course. I will. Over and out for now."

"Ciao, Big Foot." He kissed his palm and set it on the computer.

She blew him a kiss and signed off. Italy! She knew she couldn't go, but just in case, she'd apply for a passport anyway. Some serious "woo woo" was needed now. In her relationship corner, which happened to be in the bathroom, she arranged two little heart-shaped stones on the ledge next to her shampoo and conditioners and said a little prayer to help with their romance. Thoughts of him visiting her at Christmas here in San Francisco and a trip to Italy filled her imagination with desire.

46

An afternoon sun bounced off the windows as Sylvia gazed up at the skyscraper. She had been to Paul's office many times before, but from down here on the sidewalk, it was difficult to tell which one was his. Professionals in business attire bustled by and stared at her. Women in downtown San Francisco didn't wear western skirts, boots, and wide-brimmed hats. Still, she felt safer in her new persona. No one should recognize her. But would Paul?

She touched the amulet, closed her eyes, and imagined being back with Betty Lou in the quiet desert. The memory calmed Sylvia's galloping nerves. Her finger counted up twelve stories and moved to the west corner window. That should be it. Was she ready to face him?

Lucy tugged on her leash.

"Okay. Let's go." Sylvia pushed through rotating doors into the building's lobby. The security guard nodded with a smile at Lucy.

Sylvia's boots thumped on the black-and-white mosaic tile floor as she made her way across the lobby. As the otherwise-empty Otis rose, she inspected herself in the smoky-mirrored wall. Her eyes were a tad puffy but otherwise clear. She took off the hat, fluffed her short red hair, and applied pink lipstick. She felt as if she'd been away for years even though it had only been a month. The elevator stopped with a ding, and the door opened. At the end of the hall, she paused in front of the glass-plated door stenciled:

PAUL PALMER

ATTORNEY AT LAW

"Be calm, Lucy." Sylvia held tight to the leash. She took a deep breath, turned the knob, and entered.

"May I help you?" The secretary at the front desk stuck a pencil into the bun on top of her head and turned her nose up when she saw Lucy.

Sylvia swallowed. "Mr. Palmer, please."

The girl gave her the once-over and asked in a nasal tone, "Do you have an appointment?"

"Not exactly."

"He's very busy." The secretary squinted at Sylvia.

"I'm sure he'll want to see me."

"And you are?"

Sylvia paused. "Tell him I'm here to see Mr. Dictionary."

The girl frowned, stared at her, and pushed the intercom. "Mr. Palmer, there's someone here looking for a Mr. Dictionary."

Sylvia held her breath. She couldn't wait to see him.

Paul opened his office door and rushed to her. "You're back!"

"Yes." She smiled at him.

Lucy yelped excitedly. Paul bent down, picked her up, and scratched her behind the ears.

"Patricia, hold my calls," he ordered.

Sylvia followed him into the office. He shut the door behind them, unhooked Lucy's leash, and put her down. Then he reached for Sylvia's hands, but the puppy yipped at his ankles.

Sylvia stepped back and demanded in a firm voice: "Lucy, sit!"

Lucy sat, and Sylvia smiled with pride and gave her a treat. "Good girl!"

"She's grown." He leaned down and let Lucy lick his hand.

"Hey, you." Sylvia touched Paul's back and handed Lucy her lamb. She cuddled up with it on the carpet.

He took Sylvia's hands again and stared at her. His kind eyes were the color of a clear mountain sky. She moved forward and held him tight. The familiar scent of his citrus aftershave filled her with relief. She felt safe now.

Paul pulled back. "I'm so glad you're here."

"Do you think your secretary recognized me?" Sylvia tilted her head toward the door.

"Not with that haircut."

"Hey!" She punched him on the arm.

He reached for her again then stopped, turned red, and moved behind his desk. It dawned on her for the first time how handsome he was with his trimmed crew cut and clean-shaven face.

"My God, Sylvia. I've been so worried."

"I've been in Arizona." She slid into a leather chair across from him while Lucy dropped the lamb and sniffed the perimeter of the room.

He nodded. "Why didn't you tell me you were going?"

"Sorry." Tears rimmed her eyes.

"I thought Ricardo had hurt you. Ella was so frantic that she made Milo break his promise, and he told me that he drove you to the depot. The ticket agent informed me where you were headed." He ran his hand over his crew cut.

"Are you the one who sent detectives to look for me?" she asked.

"We assumed you were running from Ricardo, and I wanted to find you before he did. But then his body washed ashore."

She gasped and grabbed her amulet. "It did?"

Paul nodded. "So. What happened? Why did you go?"

"Just needed time alone." She didn't want to confess about the shooting yet. After that, everything between them would change.

Paul frowned with a crease between his eyes. "But why did you leave without telling me?"

"I just had to. I had done something horrible."

"What could be so bad?"

Her throat went dry, and she swallowed. "If I tell you, is it private?"

"That's right, attorney-client privilege."

"Promise you won't hate me?"

"I could never do that," he said gently.

"Before the engagement party, I tried to break it off, but . . ." She thought she might suffocate and started to cough.

Paul poured a glass of water from a crystal decanter on the sidebar, handed it to her, and sat in a chair beside her. She took a sip and set the glass on the desk. She held up her palms. "Before the party, he twisted my wrists and threatened to kill me if I didn't go through with the wedding."

"That bastard!" Paul raised his voice.

She continued, talking fast. "I believed him. Remember, at the party, I tried to talk to you, but he wouldn't leave us alone?"

Paul nodded. "I knew something was wrong."

"When we pulled away from the St. Francis, he drove like a maniac. I begged him to take me to Bay Breeze, but he refused and sped toward the cottage. I felt certain we were going to fly off the high-cliff drive, until a policeman finally stopped us."

Paul pulled a handkerchief from his pocket and handed it to her. She dabbed at her tears. "But he only gave Ricardo a warning and left us on the road. I felt ill. Ricardo suggested a walk on the beach. I thought it might sober him up, so I agreed. It didn't work. He just kept drinking."

Paul clenched his fists. "Go on."

"He came at me. I thought for sure this time he would overpower me. I warned him, but he wouldn't stop, so I pulled out the gun."

"What gun?" Paul put his hand on Sylvia's arm.

"I found it in a drawer at the cottage. I was afraid Ricardo might use it, so I had put it in my coat pocket."

"My God!" Paul raised his eyebrows.

"I pointed the gun at him, but he just kept coming toward me." She paused. In telling Paul the truth, would he hate her forever?

"Go on." He leaned toward her.

"I shot him."

"Jesus!"

Trembling, she said, "I'll never forget that look on his face. Never." She sobbed into her handkerchief. "I stood on the beach and watched as his body washed out to sea."

"You poor girl. But I don't understand. Why did you leave town?"

"I was confused and scared. I didn't want to go to jail."

"I would never let that happen. You should have come to me."

She nodded. "I'm so sorry. I know that now. Can you ever forgive me?"

"There's nothing to forgive. You did what you felt you needed to do. I'm just so glad you're back, safe and sound. It's all over."

She sat up straight. "But I have to tell the police."

"No you don't. They think some bad business acquaintances killed him. The FBI had been investigating his dealings for quite some time."

She fingered the amulet. "Really?"

"Besides the girl in Acapulco, he'd also been suspected of drug sales and perhaps money laundering too."

Sylvia looked down. "You must hate me now."

Paul stood, pulled her to him, and lifted her chin. "How could I?" He wiped a tear off her cheek with his finger.

"Still, I need to go to the police."

"I won't let you."

"But they need to know the truth."

"The truth is that he was killed for his evil ways, and that's what the police think. They haven't even put much effort into finding whoever shot him. Probably because they believe justice has been done."

"But I'm guilty."

"Look here." Paul raised his voice. "It was self-defense."

"But . . ."

"They'll ask you a lot of questions, and there might even be a trial. Think of the publicity. I can't let you go through all of that. You're not strong enough."

"I'm stronger now than I've ever been before."

"I believe it. You've been through enough already and don't deserve to go through all of that too." Paul took her hand. Lucy scampered over and looked up at Sylvia as if in agreement with Paul.

47

$\mathcal{A}$nne had hoped Mr. Block would be in his office or out of the gallery when she dropped off her pieces, but no such luck. He stood at the counter with another man, flipping through a portfolio. Wearing paint-splattered cargo pants, the man scratched his bowling-ball head and gave her the evil eye. "And what kind of work do you do?"

"This is Anne. She's the next Man Ray," Mr. Block smirked. Anne slipped past them to the back of the room and handed her Bubble-Wrapped pieces over to Fay, who stacked them along the wall. "Ignore them," she whispered, then she grabbed Anne by the arm. "Let's go get some coffee."

The Coffee Cup Café was packed. The top-knotted barista hustled to keep the line moving. Fay and Anne bought their drinks and sat on seats that had been just vacated.

"Things are really heating up with Sergio, and he's coming for Christmas."

Fay touched her cup against Sylvia's. "Cheers! Is he staying through New Year's?"

"He can only come for four days. It's a busy time of the year."

"Better than nothing."

"He's asked me to meet him in Italy this summer. And I'm going."

"Blimey!"

Anne had woken yesterday morning from a delicious dream, certain it was a sign. She had been riding down the Amalfi coast with him in an Alfa Romeo convertible, her profile classy in a chiffon scarf with lose ends blowing in the breeze. Under a racing cap, he smiled at her and steered the wheel with leather-gloved hands into a driveway of a whitewashed villa with a stunning Mediterranean view.

When she woke, she had grabbed the *Condé Nast Traveler* from the coffee table and ripped out the Italian travel pages: hand-painted plates from Siena, a bottle of red wine, a couple walking hand in hand under a bougainvillea-covered trellis. Her scissors had flown while she cut out the images, then she'd used matte medium to adhere them to paper. She had scribbled on it, *Yes, I'll meet you there*, and then had scanned it into her computer and emailed it off to him. Pinning it on the wall above her bed, she hoped it would seep more into her dreams.

Now she opened her spiral notebook and showed her notes to Fay. "I have a plan: Sell, sell, sell! That's how I'm going to get to Italy."

Fay put two packets of sugar in her tea and stirred. "Sell what?"

"Everything. All my art supplies, furniture, and Tweety too."

"Your auto? You won't need that much money."

"Listen." Anne put up her hand. "I'm not done. First I'll sell it all, go to Italy, and then move back home to Oscoda."

"That's not a plan; it's a retreat!"

"No it's not. Life's much simpler there. I'll live with my mom. And besides, it's much closer to New York. I can visit Sergio more often." Anne licked the whipped cream off her mocha. "Don't you see I'm meant to go to Italy? I even had a dream about it."

"But your dream didn't tell you to give everything up."

"How else could I get the money to go?"

"Let Sergio pay."

"I can't do that. Yes, I'll be moving home, but I get to go to Italy first."

Fay shook her head. "But I told Mr. Block about your new series, and he's on the verge of giving you your own show. I thought that was your dream. Not this."

"He won't. You saw how rude he was to me today. I'm tired of waiting around. Tired of having doors closed shut in my face. I've been to every gallery in town, and they've all rejected my work. I'm tired of not knowing if I'll have enough to buy food and pay rent." Anne slammed her notebook closed and pushed it into her pack.

"I can understand your frustration, but give it a little more time."

Anne lifted her chin. "Moving back home is my destiny."

"I don't believe that, and neither do you."

"But it's perfect. I can be an artist there. Even Sergio said that someone is an artist just by picking up a paintbrush."

"He didn't mean for you to move home to do it."

Anne's phone buzzed. "It's Oscoda. Excuse me. I'd better take it. Pootie?"

"Hellooo cousin! When are you moving back?"

Fay swallowed the last of her tea, picked up her purse, and mouthed, "We'll chat more later." She stood up and wound her way out of the café.

Anne waved good bye to Fay and answered Pootie, "Not yet. How are you?"

Pootie screamed, "I'm getting married!"

Anne felt as if the wind had been knocked out of her. "Brian from Heating and Air Conditioning?" She counted backward in her head. "But you've only been seeing him a few months."

"I know, isn't it great? I want you to be my maid of honor."

"Really?" Anne thought about standing at the altar in an ugly dress staring at Brian.

"Two weeks."

A man in a business suit grabbed Fay's chair and moved it to the next table.

"But you always dreamed of a spring wedding on the lake."

"It's a winter wonderland theme," Pootie yelled. "And if I don't get married soon, I won't fit into my mom's wedding gown!"

Anne paused, trying to understand, and then she counted back the months again. "You're having his baby too?"

"Surely not anyone else's. Can you believe it?"

Anne frowned. "Not really."

"Don't worry. We've heard you have money problems, so my mom is paying for your plane ticket. I really need you to be here with me."

"I wouldn't miss it."

"You can wear that green dress you posted on Facebook awhile back that you like so much. Just think, you'll be able to spend Christmas here at home."

"That would be great but . . . Christmas?" But that was when Sergio was coming to visit.

"Yes, it's on Christmas Eve, between services. The church will already be decorated, so we won't need to do it. I have a special snowflake hat for you . . ."

"But . . ." Anne couldn't get a word in edgewise.

"I can't wait! I'll see you then," Pootie said, and she hung up.

Stunned, Anne sat back in her chair. She thought for a minute about inviting Sergio to join her in Michigan. But their romance would be the talk of the town, and besides that, she wasn't ready to introduce him to her crazy feminine family yet. They'd never let her hear the end of it.

48

─

*P*atricia, I'll be gone for the rest of the afternoon." Paul grabbed his hat off a rack. "Cancel my four o'clock and dinner reservations."

In the elevator, Lucy squirmed, and Paul set her on the floor. As they rode down in silence, Sylvia felt peaceful having finally confessed to Paul. They crossed the lobby and exited the rotating doors. Lucy sprinted across the sidewalk into traffic.

Sylvia let out a loud whistle. "Lucy, come!" The puppy turned around and blinked at her as a car honked and skidded to a stop. Sylvia whistled again, and this time, Lucy scurried back toward her. Paul stared at Sylvia in admiration.

"Snickerdoodle!" Milo stepped onto the curb next to Paul's Lincoln and scooped up Lucy. "That was a close one."

"Milo's working for you?" Sylvia asked Paul, and she touched the chauffeur's shoulder to make sure he was really there.

"With you gone traipsing around the world, I had to have something to do," Milo laughed.

"You mean you recognize me?" She turned her head side to side and batted her eyelashes.

Milo bunched his lips, trying not to laugh. "I'd know you anywhere. Even as a carrottopped cowgirl."

"It's so good to see you." She smiled at him and slid onto the smooth backseat—very different from Betty Lou's big truck and her own T-bird.

Paul climbed in next to her. "Let's take her home."

Milo set Lucy on the seat beside him and drove up and over the hills toward the top of San Francisco. Sylvia could see the Golden Gate, majestic along the sparkling bay, and she sat back, feeling grateful to be home again.

As they pulled into the circular drive, Milo honked. The birch tree had new leaves, the roses were in bloom, and a blue jay flittered in the birdbath. Had her yard always been this lovely?

Ella strolled out onto the porch, a hand over her eyes. Sylvia jumped out of the car, let out a big whoop, and ran toward her. With an enormous grin, Ella opened her arms wide. "Welcome home!"

Sylvia gave her a big hug. "I've so missed you."

Lucy frolicked around their feet.

Ella rolled her eyes. "Gentleman. Take that dog for a walk while I get Sylvie settled."

"Yes, ma'am." Milo and Paul answered together. The chauffeur hooked Lucy to her leash, and the three of them took off back down the driveway.

The women headed into the foyer and up the stairs. At the landing, they stopped and stared at the portrait of Sylvia's mother. She probably had been Sylvia's age when it had been painted.

"She was very beautiful."

Ella nodded. "That's for certain."

Sylvia touched the amulet. "But she could be mean, huh?"

Ella sighed. "Quite a temper."

"While I was away, I remembered some things from when I was little." Sylvia touched Ella's arms. "Thanks for being here for me."

"I tried to shield you from her."

"Was I a bad girl?"

Ella linked her arm through Sylvia's and led her up the rest of the stairs. "You were the sweetest child and still are."

"I don't think she ever really loved me."

"She did the best she could."

In her room, Sylvia hopped on her canopy bed and admired the hydrangea wallpaper. Ella sat beside her and took her hand.

"Why didn't you ever have any children?" Sylvia asked.

"God decided not to bless us in that way."

"I'm sorry."

"We're not, because He knows what's best. Instead he blessed us with you."

Sylvia's eyes filled with tears. "You really feel that way?"

"Always have and always will." Ella nodded.

Sylvia fell into those big wide arms and sobbed.

"That's for certain." Ella handed her a lace hanky. "Couldn't love you more than if you came from my own body."

"Sorry if I caused you any worry."

"Never mind about that now. I'm just glad you're home."

Sylvia wiped her eyes and looked around the room. "It's great to be home. I feel like a changed girl."

"You can say that again!" Ella pulled a comb from her apron pocket and tidied Sylvia's hair.

"I should have listened to you from the beginning."

"That's for sure!" Ella laughed. "I'm just relieved you realized the truth about Mr. Lorenzo before it was too late." She shook her head. "Too bad you had to go through all that pain. Guess that's part of growing up these days."

No way could Sylvia ever tell her what really happened. She'd be mortified. "How did you know you loved Milo?"

Ella crossed her arms and shrugged. "I just felt it in my bones."

"What did he say when he asked you to marry him?"

"Not much. He'd been dragging his feet for a long time. I

thought he'd never get on with it, and one day, he noticed Franklin Godswarth eyeing me. Next thing I knew, Milo said, "Miss Ella, it's time we got hitched."

"What did you say?"

"'Yes, sir.' He had been my boss, you know. And I gave him a big smooch that I'd been saving for him for a long time."

Sylvia nodded. "But since then you've been the boss. Haven't you?"

"Not at all! We just try and make each other happy."

"Why do you think Mr. Paul never got married? Is it because the right girl never came along?"

Ella looked at her out of the corner of an eye. "He wouldn't know the right girl if she ran up and kissed him on the mouth."

Sylvia smiled. "Do you think he'll be a bachelor forever?"

"I hope not. He deserves the best."

"Yes, he does." Sylvia yawned.

"You must be beat." Ella helped pull off Sylvia's boots. "Now take a bath and crawl in for a little nap before supper." She gave her another hug and closed the door on her way out.

The turquoise jewelry boxes sat on the dresser as always. Sylvia slipped off the bed and opened each one. In the dim light, the shiny baubles sparkled, but, curiously, she had no desire to pick them up.

She inspected herself in the full-length mirror. Her formerly rail-like body had filled almost into an hourglass figure, and her pale skin now had a rosy glow. She touched her short hair that had started to grow out. Should she keep it red, or go back to being a blonde?

She wandered over to the jewels again. They had represented so many hours of turmoil. Shopping had been her one true passion, but she didn't feel that spark of desire anymore. What did her future hold? Now that she had seen how others lived and felt grateful to God for her own fortune, she wanted to do something more with her life. But what could that be?

She hoped part of that would be marriage to someone wonderful, maybe even to Paul. She pondered the dreams and wondered if they could be true. Could Betty Lou have made all of that stuff up? No, because she knew about the Scrabble tiles.

Did Paul maybe really love her? That relaxed feeling Sylvia had around him couldn't have been love. But then, she had thought her feelings for Ricardo had been. If it had been true love, things would have turned out differently.

Sylvia ran her bath, climbed in, and closed her eyes, thinking more about Paul. Had there been signs that he loved her? She remembered how he gently slid the gardenia corsage on her wrist before the Valentine's dance and how careful he had been not to hold her too close while they danced. And when the band played "Heaven," she caught him as he gazed at her with a pained expression on his face. It all came rushing back to her now, and she realized it might be true. Maybe he really did love her. It was a different kind of love, filled with admiration and consideration.

But what did she feel about him? She inhaled and exhaled, and a calm spread through her body. Her feelings for him were like a restful pond; an occasional ripple might occur, but soon it smoothed out. With Ricardo, it had been just the opposite. Her emotions for him had been like a wild ocean full of crashing waves and undertow. With him, she had found it hard to breathe. That couldn't have been love.

The serenity she felt with Paul might be love—not dullness, but a feeling of safety and completeness. Wouldn't it be wonderful to spend life in that tranquility? But could she imagine kissing him? She summoned his muscled arms and tennis legs to her mind. Come to think of it, he resembled a blonde Rock Hudson. How amazing she hadn't noticed that before!

She examined her narrow feet and long limbs. Her breasts peeked up out of the water, and she wondered what it would be like to have him touch her, like in her dream. She giggled. Maybe she could love him in that way.

49

Aunt Tootie pushed gray strands from her face and drained the water in the sink. "I'm beat. It's nearly midnight."

Anne dried the last plate and stacked it in the sideboard. "Me too."

"Thanks for your help." Tootie moved to her rocker in the living room. "Let's visit awhile."

Anne plopped on the couch across from her. "Our Pootie's married. I can't even believe it."

Her aunt nodded and closed her eyes. "At least the weather held."

Anne looked out the window and watched a squirrel scamper up a tree. The dusting of snow that had fallen that morning had begun to melt. The candlelight service had been lovely, and Pootie's stomach didn't show in her mother's loose-fitting gown. But Anne felt like a doofus.

In her velvet coat and Ferragamos, she thought she'd look like a model. But instead, her mother had said, "You can't wear that coat. It's bad luck to wear black at a wedding." During the ceremony, Anne nearly shivered to death and dropped the bouquet three times. Her mother had Shirley Temple–curled her hair and pinned the huge snowflake headdress on top. Then, as she applied Anne's makeup, she said, "Just think, when you move back home, I can do this for you all the time." Anne hadn't announced yet that she was planning to move home. "Look how radiant." When her mother handed her the mirror, Anne had nearly fainted. Her mother had added a ton of rouge to Anne's cheeks and drawn in Joan Crawford eyebrows.

It was a good thing she hadn't invited Sergio for sure. When she had told him about her sudden change of plans, he hinted to be invited to join her there, but she resisted the notion.

He had said in a soft voice, "We must not be meant to be together right now."

Anne now sighed. "Brian's a great guy."

Tootie rocked back and forth. "It just all happened so fast."

"That's true." Anne wondered if Tootie knew about the baby.

"At least I know she'll be settled close by."

"That must be a comfort to you." For a moment, Anne considered confiding her plans to move back. But anything she told her aunt would get right back to her mom.

"You know, I almost got away." Tootie smiled with a faraway look in her eyes.

"What do you mean?"

"Yep. Got as far as Traverse City, all the way across the state, but I chickened out, turned around, and came back."

"You'd never told me that."

"I never even told Pootie. Always been curious how my life might have turned out." Tootie reached for an Avon lotion sample from the end table, squeezed some out, and rubbed it into her hands.

"You've had a good one though."

"Don't get me wrong. I don't regret my choice." Tootie picked up a photo of her brother from the table. "Your father got away from this Podunk town like he always swore he would. All the way to Iraq." She shook her head. "He always wanted more."

"He did? I'd never heard that before either."

"Your mom got so mad when he signed up."

"She did?"

"Yep, and you are so much like him." Tootie nodded and looked at the photo.

"I am?"

"First of all, you got his hair, wavy like a lion's mane."

Anne touched her hair. "What else?"

"Your laugh. Big as day."

Anne smiled. "Really?"

"You can be stubborn too."

"Am not!"

"Are too." Tootie paused, stared at the picture, and wiped away a tear. "Died for his country."

Anne nodded.

"I'm so proud of him." Tootie looked straight at Anne. "Proud of you too."

"Even though I haven't made it as an artist?"

"Doesn't matter. You are still following your dream. Just keep at it. He did too, even though it killed him." Tootie kissed the photo then put it down.

Anne felt tears flick her eyelashes.

"I'm just glad your dream isn't as dangerous."

"My mom too, I bet."

"Yep, you're different from all the rest of us, all right. Just like him." Tootie sighed.

Anne remembered that parent-teacher conference long ago when she first realized she was different. She had been coloring at her desk while her mom met with Mrs. Couts, the kindergarten teacher.

"Anne's different, all right. I've seen this before. A child without a father will have a hard time coping. Probably will her whole life."

Anne had hung her head. She looked at her socks: one lime green and the other lemon yellow. That morning, she hadn't been able to decide which pair to wear, so she wore one on each foot.

Mrs. Couts had flipped over a piece of paper and put her pointy finger on the page. "See, here are you two, and this must be her father." Anne hadn't been able to see way up there but had known it must have been her rainbow picture. She'd used every color in the crayon box and put her dad way high in a "better place" and also in a crate in the ground. She hadn't known if he could be in two places at once but figured if God was everywhere, her father should be able to be too.

"I suggest you remarry as soon as you can so she'll grow up with a man around," the teacher had continued. Her usually chatty mom hadn't say a word and had just nodded. Maybe that was why, for a time, she had gone out with that Dr. Jones, the dentist with the crooked teeth who smelled of onions. After a few months, he'd quit coming around, and her mom never saw another man after that, at least not to Anne's knowledge.

Her mother had held her hand tight as they walked the two blocks home that day. Even though Mrs. Couts hadn't seemed to like the picture much, her mother still stuck it on the refrigerator, where it stayed for a year.

Now Tootie opened a drawer in the end table and pulled something out. "Here. Your mother asked me to give these to you. She was too emotional to do so herself."

Anne reached across the coffee table, took the dog tags, and ran her fingers over the raised letter and numbers.

"Symbolizes bravery. It's yours now. You've earned it too."

50

Ella knocked on Sylvia's bedroom door. "Mr. Paul will be here soon. Are you ready yet?"

"Almost." Sylvia's hands started to shake, but then she thought of his kind face, and her body calmed. In the last two weeks, he had come over almost every evening but had so far shown no indication that he especially cared for her. They sat in the library while he listened patiently to her travel adventures, and sometimes they played Scrabble. Since she'd told him she'd shot Ricardo, he'd somehow grown pensive. But her feelings for him grew stronger and stronger with every visit, and she was surprised and delighted when he suggested they go out on a dinner date.

Since she'd been back, jeans and boots had become her standard wardrobe. But tonight, she wanted to be alluring, and she examined herself in the full-length mirror. Would he think she looked attractive? She swung her head back and forth dramatically. "If I've only one life, let me live it as a blonde." She'd even had her hair rinsed back to her natural color.

Lucy stood on the bed with a bark.

"Do you like it?"

Sylvia returned to her reflection in the mirror. She touched the stiff bouffant. The loads of hairspray used to keep it in place emitted a tart odor that she hoped would dissipate in the night air.

Her pale pink chiffon A-line flowed in a soft swirl just above the knees. She wished she hadn't pawned the pearls in Flagstaff. The ones Paul had given her. It would have been nice to wear them tonight. Not because she wanted to rub her fingers over them to calm herself, but because they were from him.

Now she applied a little rouge but didn't need much. No thick pancake to mask her emotions tonight. With eyeliner and lipstick on, she felt ready.

"He's here!" Ella knocked and opened the door. Lucy shot out of the room to greet Paul.

Ella shook her head at Lucy then looked Sylvia over. "My baby girl has sure grown up."

"Do you really think so?" Sylvia ran her hand over the bouffant again.

"Mr. Paul won't know what to do."

"What do you mean?"

"He's always been sweet on you."

"He has not!"

"Has so." Ella sat on the edge of the bed. "The real question is, how do you feel about him?"

Sylvia felt her face turn red and touched her cheeks.

"Then we'll just need to wait until he pops the question."

"But he hasn't even kissed me yet."

"That's okay. There's plenty of time for that. Hurry now. You don't want to keep him waiting." Ella took Sylvia's elbow and led her down the hall. At the top of the stairs, Sylvia let go and rushed down toward him. She paused on the landing. "Good evening."

He put Lucy down, turned around, and his smile widened. "You're dazzling!"

Sylvia smiled and strolled down the rest of the stairs, and he handed her a bouquet.

"Thank you, kind sir." She smelled them.

"Real roses!" Ella grinned at Sylvia. "I'll get these in water right away." She took them and hurried toward the kitchen.

Sylvia and Paul stared at each other, not sure what to do next. She'd never seen him look more dashing: gray suit pressed, baby blue tie that matched his eyes knotted below his smooth chin.

"Shall we have a cocktail before we go?"

He looked at his watch. "No, we should go. Our reservations are for seven."

"Aren't we going to the club?"

"I thought it might be nice to go to a restaurant." He helped her into her mink. "Just the two of us."

As he steered the Lincoln out of the driveway, she admired the way his strong hands grasped the wheel. She leaned over, switched on the radio, and turned the knob until she found a favorite. "'Great Balls of Fire!' Oh. I love this one." She leaned back and sang along.

Paul winced. "I don't. Switch it to something more relaxing."

She played with the dial again. Elvis crooned, "Wise men say that fools rush in."

"Is this okay?"

"Perfect." He sang a few words: "That fools rush in . . ." Paul's deep voice blended well with Elvis's. And Sylvia soon joined in with pleasure.

Caesar's wasn't very crowded yet, and they were seated at a private booth. After the wine was delivered, opened, and poured, Paul clinked his wine glass with hers, and they each took a sip. He then pushed a narrow box across the table not unlike the one Ricardo had given her with the emeralds in it.

"What's the occasion?"

"You're home." Paul smiled at her.

"Yes, I am." Not wanting anything shiny tonight, she rubbed her fingers over the velvet case.

"Open it."

With trepidation, she lifted the lid, and tears filled her eyes. They were her pearls. The ones she'd sold in Flagstaff. "Oh, Paul. How did you ever get these back?"

"It wasn't easy." He shook his head.

She thought of that geezer from the pawnshop. "I can't even imagine. Really, how?"

He grinned. "Your friend Betty Lou helped."

"If anyone could wrangle them back, it would have been Betty Lou. I'll need to send her another special thank-you note." Sylvia took them from the box, turned around, and leaned back while Paul clasped them for her. She returned upright and ran her hands over the smooth beads. "You are really so sweet. I'm so glad you got them back."

He smiled. "And I'm so glad you are back too."

She ordered veal scaloppini instead of her favorite spaghetti because she didn't want to spill any on her dress.

"Miss Van Dam?" She looked up from her plate at two men staring at her—the same ones who had rung the bell this afternoon! She had practically forgotten all about it. She had just returned from the beauty shop when the doorbells chimed and had tried to ignore them, but the long Westminster melody tolled again, and she remembered Milo had taken Ella to the market. Sylvia pulled a robe on over her slip, padded to the bedroom across the hall, and peeked down out the curtains.

A lone Plymouth sat on the circular drive, and on the front stoop, two men stood in dark suits, hats in hand. Could they be salesmen? She didn't see any display cases. She swallowed. Could it be the police? Even though Paul felt their interest in her had blown over, she had kept a low profile.

The large man knocked, and the short one pushed the bell again. *Bum, bum, bum, bum. Bum, bum, bum, bum.* She was tempted to answer it, but Paul had advised her not to talk to anyone unless he was there. Besides, she couldn't go down in her robe. She wasn't decent. They rang the bell again and looked up at the window. She stepped away from the window and waited until she heard the car drive off, then exhaled.

"Come with us." The big man with a pockmarked face now reached out his arm to escort her.

Paul stood with a worried line between his eyes. "Who are you? What's this all about?" he demanded.

"Sorry, Mr. Palmer, but we need to ask Miss Van Dam a few questions."

"Right now?"

"The chief wants it done right away." The policeman put his hand out as if to escort her.

"Can't this be done at her home?" Paul asked.

"No. The chief wants her at the station."

Even though her body started to shake, like a fawn learning to stand, Sylvia rose and touched Paul's arm. "It's okay." At the station, Ella and Milo wouldn't see her with these men.

"At least let me drive Miss Van Dam in my car. You can follow us."

The large one paused for a moment then nodded. "All right, sir."

Paul collected her mink stole and held it out as she slipped trembling arms through the sleeves. The maître d', waiters, and other diners gaped at them. Before Paul led her swiftly down the restaurant steps, she whispered to him, "Everything's going to be all right, isn't it?"

But Paul didn't say a word.

51

They were alone in the small room. A bare bulb hung from the low ceiling, reflecting off walls painted the color of fading seaweed.

"I'm scared," Sylvia whispered with wide eyes.

Paul leaned over and put his hand on hers. "Now, remember, keep calm and think of your future."

"I know, but . . ."

The large detective, his brown suit wrinkled, entered the room and put a Coke in front of her. "You must be thirsty."

"Yes, thank you." She nodded and hid her shaky hands under the wooden table.

The detective sat across from them. His puffy eyes had dark circles under them. He sighed, scratched his pockmarked face, and slid a piece of paper in front of her with a date on it. "Were you with Mr. Lopez the night in question?" He pointed at the paper.

She nodded.

"Speak up."

"Yes," she managed to eke out as she glanced over at the large window. Were the chief and others observing her through it like in the movies?

"Where?"

"The St. Francis Hotel."

The detective's voice remained even. "What time did you leave?"

Paul interrupted. "That's all in your file. Just get to the point."

"Mr. Palmer, you know we need to follow procedure." The detective flipped through some pages in a thick folder and looked up at Sylvia. "Tell us what happened after you left the hotel."

"Ricardo had been quite tipsy."

Paul cut in. "He was more than tipsy. He was snockered!"

"Mr. Palmer, you are not the one being questioned. Miss Van Dam?"

"I agree with my lawyer. Mr. Lopez had been quite drunk."

"Then what?"

"He drove like a maniac through the city and out to the cliff drive." She took a sip of her Coke and set the bottle down. "I felt sure we were going to crash. But then an officer pulled us over."

"Yes, I see that's in the report here." He pulled more sheets from the file.

"I tried to get the officer to help me, but he misunderstood." She squeezed her eyes shut.

"What happened next?"

She murmured, "We decided to go down to the beach for a walk."

The detective raised his voice. "In the middle of the night? Wasn't it dark?"

She pulled a hanky from her purse. "I hoped the fresh air might sober him up."

"Did it?" He loosened his tie.

"No." She shook her head. "He kept drinking from his flask."

"Did you see anyone else there?"

"No."

"Did anything else unusual happen on the beach while you were there?"

"No?" She felt lightheaded.

"Like something that would make you leave town fast?"

She looked at her hands and shook her head. "No, nothing."

"Why did you leave then?"

"I was scared."

"Of what?" The detective lit a cigarette, and the smoke drifted toward her.

"Of . . . of . . ." She coughed, sipped some Coke, and looked at Paul. His eyes blinked at her, a beacon of concern. If she spoke the truth, the chance of a normal existence would be dashed. Even if no trial took place, the publicity alone would be with her forever.

Her metal seat squeaked as she turned back to the detective and somehow found the courage to use the words she needed to say. "We had argued." She dabbed at a tear. "I . . ."

The detective hit the table. "Are you sure you didn't see anyone else on the beach that night?"

"There was no one else there." She shook her head.

"Where was Ricardo when you left the beach?"

"As I said, he was very drunk. When he . . ." she paused, "splashed in the water, I took the chance and ran back up to the car."

"Where did you go?"

"To the cottage and then to Bay Breeze."

"How did you get there?"

"I drove the Cadillac."

"Wasn't it Ricardo's?"

"I had Milo, my driver, return it to the cottage so Ricardo could get it later."

"Wasn't that far from where you left him?"

Paul pushed back his chair. "The beach was just up the road. Ricardo could walk to the cottage to get it."

The detective glowered at him then turned back toward her. "Sylvia, Miss Van Dam. Why did you leave town?"

"Because I was afraid he'd follow and find me."

"Who?"

"Ricardo?" Confused, she glanced at Paul. He nodded back at her.

The detective pulled a photo from the file and slid it toward her. The face of a man with beady eyes stared back at her. "Did you see this man down there?"

He looked familiar, but she knew for sure he wasn't on the beach that night. "No."

"Have you ever seen him before?"

She focused on the picture intently and tried to remember.

The detective continued, "His name is Johnny the Rocket, works for the Zamboni clan. Known for doing a job fast as Sputnik."

She studied the picture again and then remembered those spooky eyes. "Yes, I did see him once."

"When?"

"About a week before that night. Ricardo had just left the liquor store with a bottle of rum and climbed back into the Cadillac next to me."

"Did the man speak to you?"

"No. He came to the driver's side of the car and gazed at Ricardo. It must have been for a full minute, but then he just walked away."

"What did Mr. Lopez do?"

"He laughed and said the man must have been *loco*. Then Ricardo turned on the ignition and sped us away."

The detective held up the photo. "Did you ever see this man again? Are you sure he wasn't on the beach that night?"

It would be so easy to nod her head and say yes. But then a man innocent of that crime would be arrested. "I didn't see him then, no." She crossed her arms on the table, broke down, and sobbed into them.

Paul placed his hand on her back. "May I please take her home now?"

"Just a moment." The detective left the room.

"Paul, what should I do?"

He put a finger to his lips and turned toward the mirror.

The detective returned with his colleague, who said, "Some evidence needs further investigation."

"What evidence?" Paul frowned.

The short detective spoke slowly. "The slugs taken from Mr. Lopez's body were from a .32. Gangsters don't usually use a caliber that small. When we searched Johnny, he didn't have one in his possession. Now it's come to light, Miss Van Dam, that your father had registered a .32 many years ago. Do you think you can provide that gun for us?"

She clutched her handkerchief. "I'll try."

"We'll need the one with this serial number." The detective handed her a slip of paper. "It'll be easy. The ballistics will clear you."

"Are you charging her with a crime?"

"No, we're just exploring every lead. Until we have solved the case, everyone involved is a suspect." The large detective eyed Paul and opened the door for them.

52

———

$\mathcal{A}$nne sat back on the daybed while playing with her father's dog tags and realized that as much as she loved her family, she couldn't realistically move home after all. Even though it would be cheaper, she wouldn't be able to breathe. There had to be another way for her to make enough money to get by and also to meet Sergio in Italy.

She wished it could happen through selling her art. She studied the first of the Sylvia series for what seemed the hundredth time. She thought it would be hanging in Gallery Noir by now but Fay had been unable to convince Mr. Block to hang more than one of Anne's pieces in the show. Fay had asked her again if she had contacted Fredricka Woods yet but Anne had changed the subject.

The black frame now set the piece off perfectly. The turquoise background accentuated the *Life* photo of Sylvia and Ricardo leaving their engagement party. *Poor Sylvia, what happened to you?*

Anne read over her research notes:

- *Van Dam shipping business rises*
- *Sylvia's parents' plane crash left her an orphan and heiress at thirteen*

- *Valentine's dance with Paul Palmer*
- *Various society listings of Sylvia with Ricardo*
- *Engagement party*
- *Sylvia missing*
- *Sylvia seen in Arizona*

Then the trail ended. She had thought that when the series had been completed, her Sylvia fixation would be over too, but that wasn't the case. Anne still wanted to find out what had happened to her.

So many thoughts swirled in Anne's head. This obsession was driving her crazy. She glanced at her watch. If she left now, she could make it to Grace Cathedral in time. That might clear her head. She threw on her velvet coat and flew down the stairs. Outside, a late-afternoon sun shone in the sky, but the wind had picked up.

Full of anticipation, she jumped onto a cable car and held on as it headed up California Street. A labyrinth walk usually helped her make decisions, like the time right after she moved here and things were tough. She had been tempted to move home then too and found the labyrinth walk helpful. While meditating to its center, she had had a vision of the snow and everyone knowing her business, and Anne knew she just couldn't go back. Just like she felt right now.

The cable car made its way up and over the hill and soon stopped at the corner. She hopped off, walked across the street, and opened the cathedral's heavy door. Smelling of musty hymnals and dripping candle wax, a Gregorian chant played on the sound system. She dropped a dollar in the donation basket and waited a few seconds for her eyes to adjust. The church was dark inside even though a lingering afternoon light streamed through the stained glass windows and tapers flickered on the altar down the aisle. Colorful mosaics adorned the walls.

A teenage girl wearing a stocking cap and a gray-haired lady already walked the path.

Anne had read all about labyrinths on the Internet. The black-and-white pattern, modeled after the labyrinth at Chartres Cathedral in France, defined lines that continued, doubled back and around, and winded toward the center of a circle and out again. At Chartres, thousands of medieval pilgrims had made it a symbolic journey when going to Jerusalem had not been practical. One article had described the concept this way: "Labyrinths balance the left and right sides of the brain with twists and turns; they help one let go of worries. The path is set, so you don't have to think about it."

She pulled off her boots, set them under a pew, and smiled at her "big feet" in thick socks that would keep her toes warm in the drafty church. Her hands ran down the coat's velvet collar as candlelight bounced off the rhinestone brooch.

At the labyrinth's threshold, she bowed, hands at mid-chest, and closed her eyes to contact her inner self. She took a deep breath, let it out, found a sense of calm, and asked these questions: *Should I continue to search for what happened to Sylvia? Will you guide me?* Anne placed these questions firmly in her heart, opened her eyes, and stepped onto the path.

She walked the narrow strip in search of her own natural pace. The chant floated in the air. Soon, she found a rhythmic beat. The tempo slowed, and she moved in accordance. The teenage girl approached on the opposite path, and they nodded at each other. Anne continued and soon lost sense of time and place. The beat picked up again as she progressed closer and closer and around and around to the center of the labyrinth, the black-and-white path leading the way.

On the path's next rung, the elderly woman draped in a turquoise pashmina walked toward her. She gazed at Anne's pin then looked into her eyes as if she recognized her. Anne thought she seemed familiar, too, but she couldn't remember from where. Tall and elegant, the woman might be seventy. Wrinkles lined her face, but despite that, she remained attractive. Her hair curved up into a French twist.

They passed each other. Who was she? Where had Anne seen her before? She pulled her thoughts in and focused back on the question. *Should I continue to search for what happened to Sylvia?*

At the labyrinth's center, Anne sat on a round cushion and closed her eyes. The Gregorian chant continued, and she inhaled and exhaled slowly. *Here I am tonight. Waiting for a sign.* A chime rang, and she fell deeper into a meditative state.

After a few minutes, the woman took a seat on a nearby cushion, disrupting Anne's reverie, and Anne stood and began to wind her way out of the labyrinth. She picked up her pace, almost dancing, and focused again on this question: *Sylvia, what happened to you?*

Anne sauntered and breathed. The black-and-white tiles, like the *Life* magazine photo, moved fluidly in front of her. As if in a trance, she continued until she wound her way to the end. Back on the threshold, she bowed and stepped out.

She slipped into her boots, glanced up, and caught the woman staring at her from across the labyrinth. She smiled, and Anne felt a warm glow in her chest.

She trailed the woman out of the cathedral into the black, blustery night and watched her slide into the backseat of a Rolls Royce. Anne wondered again why the woman seemed so familiar —perhaps she was from the hotel. But certainly she would have remembered someone as sophisticated as that.

A slick gust hit Anne hard. She decided to splurge, hailed a cab, and relaxed back on the ripped vinyl seat. Her fingers played with the key in her pocket, but she still wasn't any closer to receiving an answer to her questions.

53

———

*A*nne sat in Gallery Noir and watched the fog ooze by, thick as clam chowder. The Feng Shui money plant she had placed in the corner this morning hadn't worked. It was almost closing time, and even though Sutter Street had been crowded all day, no one had been in.

She looked around at the hodgepodge of pieces in the group show on the walls: three large Jackson Pollockish splatter paintings by that bald-headed artist from the other day, several of Lila's gorgeous landscapes, and Anne's mixed-media portrait of Sylvia.

Now she watched as an elderly man with a cane found his way into the gallery. The door closed behind him, blocking out the city noises. He looked around at the varying artwork but froze when he saw her Sylvia portrait piece. Anne thought he probably didn't like it. Older folks rarely understood her work.

"May I help you?" she asked, standing from her folding chair.

"Just browsing."

"If you have any questions, just ask." She sat back down, flipped through a *Studios* magazine, and fantasized about how she would set up her own someday. It would have lots of light, wall space, and color.

She glanced up at the man. From his tweed coat pocket, he

pulled out his glasses and read aloud the words Anne had scrawled across it: "Sylvia, where are you?"

All of a sudden, the man's face turned crimson, and he began to weave back and forth, struggling on his cane for balance. Was he having a heart attack?

"Careful, sir." Anne dragged her chair over and helped him into it.

He wiped his brow with a handkerchief. "Just a little lightheaded," he rasped.

She grabbed an Evian, screwed off the top, and handed it to him. "Are you okay?"

He drank with shaky hands.

"Sir, is there anyone I can call?"

"Just give me a moment." He sat back and held up his hand, trying to catch his breath.

.She put her hand on the phone, ready to dial 911 if necessary.

He took another sip of water, then pointed to the portrait, looked at her, and blinked. "Who did this?"

"I did."

"Where did you find the photo?"

"On the Internet from a newspaper clipping." Did he actually like it?

"Incredible." He handed her the water, got up from his chair, and studied the piece again. "Do you know this Sylvia?" He removed his glasses and looked at Anne with faded blue eyes.

"No." Anne shook her head.

"Why did you make it then?"

Anne handed him the coat from the back of her chair. "I found this at a thrift shop and then saw a picture of Sylvia Van Dam in a *Life* magazine wearing one just like it. It even had a snowflake pin too." Her words tumbled out, excited to talk about the process.

He touched the pin with a frown.

"I became obsessed, Googled *Sylvia Van Dam*, started to make pieces, and couldn't stop."

"You mean there are others?"

She nodded.

"How much is this one?"

She handed him the sheet and pointed out the price. "It's $1000." To make the sale, she considered telling the man the cost was negotiable and cutting out her own portion of it.

He studied her for a moment. "Do you deliver?"

"I suppose so." She kept her voice calm and tried not to sound too eager even though her heart sprinted.

He smiled. "I'll take it."

Now Anne felt as if she might faint, and she grabbed the back of her chair for support. He had seemed like such a normal, sweet old man. But now she thought he might be crazy. "Are you kidding?"

He pulled a checkbook from his jacket pocket.

She wanted to jump up and down. "Sit again, sir. Make it out to Gallery Noir." She pulled a calculator from the counter and added in the tax. "The total comes to $1080."

He didn't even flinch, wrote the check, and handed it to her.

"Thanks." She stared at all those numbers and resisted the urge to give him a big hug. He seemed legit, but what if he were senile and broke?

"Would you be able to make the delivery on Friday? Shall we say, at two?"

"Certainly."

"My address is on the check. I hope you'll stay and have tea with us. I'd like you to meet my wife."

"Sounds nice." Anne glanced at the check again. The address sounded as if it might be located up in Pacific Heights, a lah-de-dah neighborhood. Maybe it was even located near the historic Queen Anne Hotel—that would be a good omen. Anne really would feel like a queen when this check cleared. She decided to think positive thoughts and assume it would.

The gentleman picked up his cane and hobbled out the door. Anne watched as he eased himself into a cab and rode off. She then realized she was barely breathing, exhaled, took in a deep breath, and exhaled again. She waved the check in the air. "Hey, money tree, look at that!"

54

Anne steered Tweety up into the hills in search of the address. She turned a corner, swerved around a curve, and there it was. The historic marker on the gatepost read:

BAY BREEZE

1912

Anne double-checked the number and pulled Tweety into the circular drive that surrounded a flourishing rose garden with a concrete birdbath in the center. She parked and gaped up at the building. Gigantic columns appeared to hold up the mansion that reminded her of the Met, large and stately. She carried the piece wrapped in butcher paper from the passenger seat and climbed up the stairs. On the threshold, she caught her breath and admired the view below as morning clouds dispersed to reveal the Golden Gate Bridge stretched over a phthalo blue bay. Her pinkie pushed the doorbell, and chimes rang inside.

A man with wavy hair brushed up into a pompadour opened the ornately carved wooden door. "Good afternoon, Miss McFarland." He took the piece from her. "You are expected in the library. Follow me."

Anne stepped inside. The largest crystal chandelier she had ever seen was suspended above the marbled foyer. Arched staircases reached from each side up to the second floor, where portraits were hung along the walls. The first landing displayed an oil painting of a young woman; her blonde hair was scooped up into a French twist, and a rose-colored gown clung to her lithe body. At her feet, a small beagle preened on a pillow. Anne wished she could run up the steps to inspect it closer, but she followed the butler down a long hallway and into a library bigger than her entire apartment. He set the piece on a desk and turned to her. "May I take your coat?"

Her hands caressed the velvet in the cold space. "No, thanks."

He tugged down his vest. "Will there be anything else, sir?" he asked the man who sat by the fire.

The older man checked his watch. "Tea in twenty, George."

"Certainly." The butler left.

Mr. Palmer waved to Anne. "Come on over."

"Good to see you again." She shook his soft hand.

"Forgive me for not standing. My legs are a little creaky today."

"I'm sorry to hear that." She wanted to ask if he'd had any more fainting spells but instead pointed to the picture. "Would you like me to open it for you now?"

"Let's wait until after tea." He nodded toward a chair. "My wife will join us soon."

Anne sat across from him and fingered the brass brads along the edge of her seat, suddenly nervous without really knowing why; she looked around the room. A giant oriental carpet accented the wood floor. The high shelves were lined with more books than one could ever read in a lifetime. A grandfather clock, with a sun and moon inside, stood against a wall.

"Thank you for buying my piece."

He blinked and smiled at her. His gray hair shone in the

firelight. "Thank you for being so talented. Your work is quite unique."

"I'm curious, what attracted you to it?"

"You'll see in a moment."

She frowned, puzzled. Not sure what else to say, she remained silent and shifted in her seat. The clock ticked loudly. She looked around again and wondered what it would be like to live in a mansion like this. It would be a far cry from not knowing if you could pay the rent on time.

"Oh, here she is! My wife, Sylvia."

Hearing that name, Anne jumped to her feet. A velvety light glowed around the elderly woman. Her thinning hair was looped up into the distinctive French twist. She wore a small strand of pearls, a turquoise silk blouse, and a pashmina around her thin shoulders, all very stylish, except for the Velcro Nikes on her feet.

A beagle puppy, like the one in the painting, followed her closely then ran to Paul and jumped in his lap. "Hey, Lucky, my boy." He leaned down and let him lick his chin.

Sylvia floated across the room and took Anne's hand.

Anne blurted, "My God, it's you!"

"Yes, I recognized the coat and pin at the cathedral. Thought I was seeing things." Her voice resonated like a singing bowl, and she smelled of gardenias.

"It is you." Anne wondered if she was having another dream.

They held hands. Sylvia's eyes gazed straight into Anne's heart, the connection deep, as if they had known each other for a very long time.

Anne had thought that if she ever found Sylvia, it would feel like lightning had struck, but instead, she felt a calm like never before, a softening of her body and a downshifting of her tense brain. Sylvia smiled and smoothed the back of her hair. She touched the pin on the coat Anne wore. "I still remember the day I bought it."

"Do you want it back? The coat too?" Anne started to take it off.

"Heavens, no! Where ever did you find them?"

"A thrift shop." Anne pulled out the key. "This was in the pocket."

Sylvia took it and twisted it in gnarled fingers. The backs of her hands were spotted with age, but her pink nails were as pretty as the roses in her garden.

Paul called, "Ladies! Time for tea."

George set a tray on the coffee table. Lucky jumped off Paul's lap, stuck his tail in the air, and wagged it back and forth like a paintbrush.

Sylvia laughed. "I think he needs a walk."

George pulled a biscuit from his pocket. "Walk!"

Lucky barked and followed George out of the room.

Sylvia and Anne sat on the sofa, side by side. Paul poured from a floral teapot, handed Sylvia a cup, and then offered one to Anne. "Ginger snap?" he asked.

She didn't think she could eat a thing. To be polite, she picked up a cookie and laid it on her plate. "What a privilege to meet you, Ms. Van Dam. I mean . . ."

"Mrs. Palmer, but you can call me Sylvia." She covered her mouth with her elbow and coughed.

"Sylvia." Anne liked the way it felt in her mouth, smooth and sophisticated. Suddenly it all made sense as her mind put the pieces together. She remembered she had seen the name on the check, Paul Palmer, in the Sylvia research. He had escorted her to the Valentine's Day dance. But Anne had never researched to find out more about him.

"Go ahead and show Sylvia your art piece." Paul's excited voice filled with enthusiasm. He limped over and sat on the other side of his wife on the couch.

Anne held her breath as she unwrapped the paper and handed it to Sylvia.

As the older woman held it, her face fluctuated from frowns to smiles. "It's amazing. Paul had tried to prepare me. 'Sylvia, where are you?'" she read the scrawled question aloud. "I'm right here." She daubed at her eyes with a lace hanky.

Anne stood behind the couch and put a hand on Sylvia's shoulder. "I didn't mean to upset you."

Paul's eyes pooled up too, and he patted Sylvia's hand. "Now, dear. We'll just put it away."

Anne started to reach for the collage. "I'll take it home and return your money."

"No!" Sylvia held the picture to her chest. "I love it."

"But I don't want you to have it if it makes you sad."

"I'm just having a good cry, that's all. It's just these memories." She wiped her eyes. "Some good and some bad, but they made me who I am today. They take me back to the time when I grew up."

"You sure you want to keep it?"

"Of course. And what ingenuity."

Anne smiled as pride enveloped her.

Sylvia pointed above the desk. "We'll remove those botanicals and put it there."

"Shall I hang it for you now? I brought a hammer and nails."

"Not now. This has been enough excitement for one day. Would you mind coming back another time to do that?"

"I'd be happy to." Anne nodded.

"How about next Friday at the same time?"

Anne nodded. "If I'm not prying, what did happen to you? Where were you?"

"Well, dear. It's a long story." Sylvia looked at Paul.

"She went away. When she returned, let's just say we kept our lives private."

Sylvia tugged at the white cloth napkin on her lap. "Yes, and . . ." She held the napkin to her mouth and coughed.

Paul looked at her with worried eyes. "When I saw your work in the gallery, I couldn't believe it." Paul chuckled. "How did my Sylvia get up there on those walls? I almost passed out."

"And scared me half to death." Anne laughed.

"What a perfect gift." Sylvia patted Paul's hand. "Thank you, dear.

They were such a sweet couple. Anne wondered if she would ever have a love like that someday.

55

"How sweet of you to help like this." Sylvia handed Anne an apron.

"No problem. Besides, I'd like to improve my cooking skills, which are nonexistent." Anne slipped the apron on over her head and turned around for Sylvia to tie the sash.

She admired Anne's thick hair, so full of life, just like her—and lovely today, pulled back in that chiffon scarf matching her hazel eyes. Sylvia enjoyed having her near. Ever since they met, just over a month ago, Sylvia's spirits had felt more energetic.

"Start chopping here." She sat on Ella's kitchen stool at the counter and pointed to a cutting board surrounded by fresh tomatoes, bell peppers, and mushrooms. Lucky rushed in and stood at Sylvia's feet. "Go sit on your carpet." He backed up, turned in circles, and obeyed.

Anne picked up a knife and starting hacking at a tomato. "Like this?"

"Slow down." Sylvia took the knife and demonstrated just as Ella had taught her years ago. "This way, and then that way."

Anne retrieved the knife and tried again, this time getting into the rhythm. "How much do we need?"

"Enough for thirty women."

"Thirty! Wouldn't it be easier to make it at the shelter?"

"Can't. They don't have cooking facilities."

"Why not?"

"There's not enough room at the shelter, and besides, kitchens cost a lot to build and maintain." Sylvia put a skillet on the front burner and turned it on. "Now toss it in."

Anne slanted the cutting board toward the skillet. "Oops!" Some pulp plummeted to the marble floor.

"That's okay, just wipe it up. There's a dishcloth in that drawer. Start on the peppers next."

Anne cleaned up the floor and began to chop a green pepper. "How long have you been doing this?"

"Every Monday for almost fifty years." Sylvia shook her head with a smile and thought about her conversation with Paul when she told him she wanted to volunteer at the shelter. It had been a few months after that horrible night with the police questions.

Paul had been over for dinner, and they sat at the card table in the library. He opened the Scrabble board and said, "Sylvia, you need to start getting out more."

"I know." She peeked at the door to make sure Ella wasn't near and lowered her voice. "Is the business with the police over?"

"At least for now. I think they accepted that you just couldn't find that gun." He smiled at her.

"But I still feel so guilty. How can I ever live with it?" She flipped over some Scrabble tiles.

He leaned over and took her hand in his. "When the truth is too much, you can squeeze like this." He pressed his thumb into her palm. She gazed down at their fingers woven together, the smooth sensation of his power evident in his calmness and sincerity. She thought maybe he was finally going to kiss her. Even though she thought he loved her, he still hadn't. But instead, he released her hand and sat back. "It's time you move forward and live your life."

"I know, and I think I've come up with just the thing to occupy my time." She'd been thinking about it for quite some time but wasn't sure he'd approve. "Guess what it is."

He laughed. "I suppose what you've always done. Shop."

She touched her pearls. "I don't want to do that anymore."

He blinked. "You don't? Do you want to go back to school?"

"No."

"Join the Garden Club or Junior League?"

She shook her head.

Paul continued. "Play bridge?"

"Something more meaningful."

"A stock club. I know one that's starting just for women. It's called Dollars for Dolls."

She scrunched up her face.

"What is it then?"

"I've heard the church is starting a women's shelter."

"What's that?"

"A place that provides needy women with whatever they might need. A place to get a good meal, sleep, or maybe even to get away from a bullying husband or one that hits them or . . . It could have been so much worse for me. I have so much and have been so fortunate. What do you think?"

He smiled at her. "I think it's perfect."

So she wrangled Ella into teaching her how to cook, which hadn't been easy. And now, all these years later, Sylvia was showing Anne how to do it.

"I can't believe you make all this sauce from scratch."

"As Ella used to say, 'Don't be hasty. It will be more tasty.'" Sylvia began to stir the pot. How wonderful to have a companion to help her! Even after Ella died, she had continued. Recently though, her stamina had waned, but she just couldn't give it up.

"Here comes some more." Anne scooped up a handful of peppers and dropped them into the sauce.

"You're doing a great job. Keep at it." Sylvia tossed in a handful of herbs and stirred the sauce, and an enticing aroma sprang into the room.

George came in and looked around. "Mr. Palmer says it's almost time to go. Walk?" He looked at Lucky, who jumped up and waited for his leash to be clasped.

Lucky and George left the kitchen, and Anne whispered, "I don't think he likes having me around much. He's always so grumpy."

"That's just his nature. He's had a hard time. He lost his wife last year and then his house too."

"How sad." Anne shook her head.

"We do what we can to make him feel like family."

Anne pushed the last of the mushrooms into the skillet. "That's it." As instructed by Sylvia, she added pasta to the giant pot of boiling water and stirred.

With a spoon, Sylvia scooped up a little sauce, blew on it, and tasted. Lucky scuttled into the kitchen with George and Paul in tow. "Ready?" Paul asked.

"Give it a whirl," Sylvia commanded her husband.

He pulled a noodle from the pot and threw it against the wall, and it stuck. George didn't even crack a smile.

"Hey, let me try it!" Anne tossed a noodle, and it dribbled down the wall. Lucky raced over and gobbled it up.

"No, you gotta give it a good flick." Paul showed her his wrist action. "See?"

Anne tossed another one. This time it held fast, and the room exploded in applause—except for George, who was all business. He used the hot pads, carried the pot over to the sink, and drained out the water. Anne stirred in the sauce.

"Don't forget the parmesan cheese," Sylvia said, and she coughed into her elbow. George grabbed it from the fridge, and they all hurried out to the old Lincoln. Paul sat in the front passenger seat, and the ladies climbed in the back. Sylvia put a dishtowel over her knees, and George set the warm spaghetti pot on them. He rushed to the driver's side, started the engine, and pulled out of the drive.

"Yesterday I made gingersnaps for dessert. But we need to be careful and only give each woman two. Too much sugar isn't healthy. If you'd like, next week, I'll teach you how to make Ella's secret recipe."

"What happens when you go on vacation?" Anne asked as they rode toward downtown.

"I give the center a donation for pizza or some other type of take-out."

When the Lincoln pulled up to the center, there was nowhere to park. George put on his flashers as Anne ran inside, and an assortment of ladies followed her back out to the car.

"Mrs. Palmer, you always bring the best food!" A hefty woman in a rainbow-colored knit cap grabbed the spaghetti pot from her. Still more gathered the salad, cookies, and bottled water from the trunk. "Thank you so much!" they cried. "You're the best."

"No, you are the best!" Sylvia called as Anne helped her out of the car.

"George, we'll see you in an hour." Sylvia grasped Anne's arm for support.

They entered the shelter, and Anne heard a familiar voice. "Missy!" Her homeless friend stood there, with a hand on her hip wearing the worn out turban.

"Mata. Here for a hot meal?"

"You bet. I always come on Mrs. Palmer's night," Mata said, then she hurried to get a spot in line.

56

"Knit one. Purl two. Knit one. Purl two," Sylvia's voice recited in rhythm as she clicked the needles. Turquoise yarn slid back and forth through the loops.

Beside her on the library couch, Anne chanted too. "Knit one. Purl two. Knit one. Purl . . ." The words were meditative, like a mantra.

"Lucky, stop!" Sylvia yelled, and she nudged the beagle away with her Nikes. "Sit."

The puppy sprinted across the room and back again then ran around in circles chasing his tail.

"How are things going?" Sylvia asked.

"I'm frustrated. I just can't seem to make ends meet." Just this morning, Mrs. Ladenheim reminded her that rent was due again.

"In what way?"

"I really want to make it as an artist, but maybe I'm really not good enough. I've tried every gallery in town."

"Not good enough! You are a wonderful artist! Be brave. You must have had courage to move out here in the first place. Now find that courage and persevere!"

Anne sighed. "I go to sleep at night with bravery, but when I wake up in the morning, I've lost it again."

"I make notes to myself." Sylvia held up a knitting needle and wrote in the air. "I write them on sticky notes and post them on my mirror."

"You do?"

"Try it. They have to be positive though. Not *I will be brave*, but instead, *I am the most courageous person in the world.* Is there a particular gallery you want to show in?"

"Gallery Noir, where Paul bought my piece. But Mr. Block, the owner, doesn't like my work."

"What do you mean he doesn't like your work? Who wouldn't?"

Anne shrugged.

"I've learned sometimes you need to tell someone what they'll do instead of ask. Come up with reasons that will convince them. Use the sticky notes. Stand tall, and rehearse in the mirror. Now, how're things with Sergio?"

Anne tried to keep her knitting needles from tangling. "The relationship has cooled off for now. He lives so far away. I've tried to meet someone who lives closer, but no one compares to him." Her last Skype date with him hadn't gone well:

"Sorry, Big Foot, but I can't seem to get the time away. Let's save our time and energy for Italy."

She still planned to go even though she didn't know where she'd get the money. "But that's a few months from now. I miss you."

"I know. Miss you too. I promise to come out sometime before then."

Anne thought maybe he really wasn't very interested in her after all.

"It will all come together when it's meant to. Let's finish these up. I want to deliver them before dinnertime."

Paul walked in without his cane. It must have been one of his good days. "Any telephone calls, telegrams, special-delivery letters?" Lucky yelped and ran over to him.

"Nope. What's new at the club, dear?" Sylvia asked.

He kissed her cheek. "Won ten bucks." Sylvia ran her hands along her arms. Paul picked up the blue pashmina from the back of the sofa and draped it over her. "There you go."

Sylvia patted his hand. "Thank you, dear."

Anne could feel the love between them. Lucky continued to nip at Paul's heels. The old man climbed down onto the carpet and let the dog lick his face and even his ears.

Sylvia paused her knitting needles. "Paul! That's disgusting." He ignored her. "Please!"

"It's good for my arthritis."

"You don't have arthritis on your face. And in front of company."

"But I'm not just company any more." Anne laughed and tried to concentrate on her knitting.

Paul made his way to a chair, and Lucky settled at his feet. "Speaking of that, we have a proposition for you."

Anne looked up.

"How would you like to move in with us?" Paul pulled Lucky into his lap.

"You mean here at Bay Breeze?"

"No, the zoo," Paul chuckled.

Sylvia touched Anne's arm. "You could convert the attic into a studio. Aren't lofts the thing for artists? There's plenty of light up there."

What Anne wouldn't give to see Mrs. Ladenheim's face if she gave notice. "That's a generous offer. Let me think about it. How much would the rent be?"

"Rent? My lands!" Sylvia smiled. "No rent. We'll pay you."

"For what!"

Paul rubbed Lucky's back. "George will still be here, but you can help take care of us youngsters too."

"Please say you'll stay with us. We could really use the help.

My pep's not what it used to be." Sylvia crooked her elbow and coughed into it.

Anne set her knitting on the coffee table, hugged Sylvia, then hopped up and hugged Paul too. "You are both so sweet. How about this? I'll come and help out but won't move in." She realized how much she really liked her small apartment and independence.

"Sounds like a plan." Sylvia cast off her knitting. "Okay. That's it for me."

"Just a sec. I'm almost done too." Anne sat back down and finished up. She counted the assortment of colorful jewel-toned caps as she placed them into a shopping bag. "Fifteen."

"How marvelous! That's almost twice as many as last year. Thanks to you."

"Let's deliver these puppies!" Anne stood and helped Sylvia to her feet.

Lucky barked, and they all laughed.

"Bundle up; it's nippy out there," Paul warned. He sat shotgun next to George with the "girls" both in the back as usual.

When they pulled up at the shelter, Anne hopped out from the car and put her hand out for Sylvia. So that they could finish the hats, pizzas had been delivered.

"Not tonight, dear. You go on in alone." She seemed to be short of breath.

Anne looked at her with concern. "I'll be back out in a few minutes." She ran into the building with the hats and emptied them on a table.

"These are beautiful!"

"I want a blue one."

The women attacked the pile with glee. Anne smiled, then scanned the room with a frown. "Where's Mata?"

"Haven't seen her tonight." One of the women pulled a pink cap down over her head.

As Anne climbed back in the Lincoln, she removed a special hat she had designed from the bag and asked, "Can we drive down California Street?"

George nodded and turned the car around, cruised up and over Knob Hill, and headed down the crest, Anne checking every doorway. Soon she spotted Mata, curled up for the night. "Stop here."

"Hi, Missy." The homeless woman scowled at her. "Haven't seen you around much."

"Been busy. I brought you something." Anne held her breath and showed Mata the hat. Anne had used twisted gold yarn and added a few extra inches to make it more turban-like. For the pièce de résistance, she had sewn on sequins.

Mata stared at it for a moment, took off the old one, tossed it aside, and tugged on the new. She grinned and posed her head to the light of a streetlamp. "I do look like Garbo. Don't I?"

"Of course." Anne jumped back in the Lincoln filled with a sense of accomplishment. "I've been trying to get her to take off that filthy old thing for months now."

"And you did it!" Sylvia patted her hand. "You have a real affinity for helping others."

Anne smiled. "Because I'm learning from the best."

57

*T*ell me more." Sylvia smiled from underneath the canopy as she lounged on her bed.

"When I got out of the Jaguar, Mr. Duchamp tossed a five on the ground with a smirk and told me to pick it up, as usual. I almost did, but instead, I thought of my affirmations: I am proud, I am confident. I am brave." Anne, in her work uniform, demonstrated. "I stood tall, looked him straight in the eyes, and said, 'Get it yourself.'"

"What did he do?"

"He just stared at me. Then I repeated louder, 'Get it yourself.' This time, his face turned red, he jumped in the car, and he drove off. Howard picked up the bill for me and said, 'You go girl.'"

"I'm so proud of you." Sylvia, with her floral caftan loose around her thin body, got up and patted Anne's shoulder.

"I've never felt so empowered in all my life."

"Next you'll need to confront Mr. Block."

"I don't think I can ever do that."

"Yes, you can."

"You seem so together. I'm sure you never had any bad habits or obstacles to overcome."

"That's what you think. Come. I have something to show you." Sylvia opened her closet door and revealed the safe behind it.

She dialed the combination, pulled out a box, and handed it to Anne.

Lifting the lid, Anne's eyes widened. "Vintage jewelry!"

Sylvia nodded. "They're vintage now, but when I bought them, they were new."

Anne fingered the shiny pieces. "I've never seen so much gorgeous stuff!"

"I have four more cases here too."

"There must be at least a million dollars worth." Anne gaped at the stacked boxes.

"Probably more."

"But you don't even wear much jewelry, except your wedding band and pearls."

"I have my secrets." Sylvia winked.

Anne carried the box out of the closet and sat on the edge of the bed.

"In my youth, I shopped at Tiffany's almost every day."

"You're kidding!" Anne looked over at her.

"I was what you'd now call a shopaholic." Sylvia put an elbow to her mouth and coughed.

"No way."

"Paul, my guardian then, wanted me to stick to a budget." Sylvia giggled and sat next to Anne on the bed. "I never could. He tried so hard not to get upset with me."

"But you don't seem like the type." Anne fingered a shiny butterfly brooch.

"You do have that snowflake pin."

"That's true." Anne nodded. "What helped you stop?"

"I killed a man and ran off to the desert."

"Oh, sure." Anne rolled her eyes with a laugh.

Sylvia pursed her lips as if to tell her more but then nodded. "Actually, I did go to the desert. There I learned the truth," she said with a whisper.

"What is it?"

She paused with a wistful look in her eyes. "It's bright stars on a clear night, sharing what you have with the community, and time with the ones you love."

"Sounds about right." Anne tilted her head.

"And you are one of those I love." Sylvia hugged her and held on for a moment.

Since meeting Anne a few months ago, they had grown so close. She had been proud to teach her young friend how to knit, cook, play Scrabble, train Lucky (not with much success), and sing lyrics to Elvis Presley songs. Also, over the short period, she had tried to instill as much confidence in her as possible.

"I love you too. And I'm grateful for all you and Paul have done for me." Both had tears in their eyes.

"You're the one who has done so much for us. You've kept things humming: planning meals, making appointments, etc."

"I've been happy to do it."

"And it does our hearts good to have you with us. Still happy in your apartment, or are you ready to move in?"

"I'm good. The gallery has even sold another one of my pieces, but thanks anyway."

Sylvia started to cough and couldn't stop.

Anne frowned, poured a glass of water from the nightstand, and handed it to her. "You okay?"

Sylvia took a sip and nodded. "Just a little frog in my throat."

Anne's cell phone buzzed. "I've got to get to the hotel."

"Off you go then."

Anne kissed Sylvia on the cheek and walked out the door. Worn out, she rested back on a pillow for a few moments, then returned the box and locked the safe. She looked around the stuffed closet. Whatever possessed her to buy all this junk anyway? It was time to clean out the years of accumulation. Others shouldn't have to do it after she was gone. Her knees cracked as she lowered herself onto a rug. At least fifty pairs of shoes were stacked beneath the clothes.

She reached far in back and pulled out a pair of pale pink pumps. How did she ever wear such high heels, let alone dance in them? She had worn these ages ago to the Valentine's dance at the club, the night she met Ricardo. Her life would have been so different if she had never met that scoundrel. She shook her head and tossed the heels in a box destined for the Goodwill.

Between some shoes, a red scarf had tangled, and she tugged it out. Somewhere there were mittens and a hat that went with it. She had knit a matching set for Paul the Christmas after she returned from her "adventure."

The red wool now soft under her fingers, she thought about that trip up to his mountain cabin. Sylvia's memory now was as crisp as the weather had been that holiday night. Despite the icy air, they chose to sit outside on the porch swing to view the stars. This time, she paid attention to the constellations he pointed out to her. The ground had been covered in white, and snow weighed down the pine branches next to the frozen pond.

Paul cleared his throat. "I'm glad you're here with me safe and sound."

"At least for now."

"I'm relieved they haven't tried to question you again during the holidays." Paul reached for her hand. Betty Lou had been right. He was a good man. Sylvia wondered for the hundredth time what it would be like to kiss him. Would it be like kissing Ricardo? At least Paul didn't have a mustache or a five-o'clock shadow to prick her. He probably wouldn't dart his tongue in and out like a snake as Ricardo had done either.

Paul put his arm around her, and she snuggled in close. It felt comfortable and right to be with him. But when would he ever kiss her?

At that moment, he leaned over and put his lips on hers. He tasted of the hot toddies they had sipped earlier. A heat spread throughout her body and she kissed him back, a different kind of feeling than with Ricardo, not scary at all but still exciting. Paul pulled back and said the three magic words: "I love you."

It was about time. "I love you, too."

"You do?"

"Of course!" She laughed.

He kissed her again, this time long and slow. She crushed up against him and never wanted to let go.

"Marry me?" he asked.

"Oh, yes," she said, and then they kissed again.

A month later, they had a simple wedding at Bay Breeze. A judge presided with Ella, Milo, and Lucy as witnesses. Sylvia wore an ivory-colored suit and carried a gardenia bouquet. When she came down the stairs, she knew by the look on Paul's face that the long journey had been worth it.

Now she picked up a pair of cowboy boots and smiled. She had bought them almost fifty years ago in Flagstaff. She pulled a hanky from her pocket and wiped the sand off until the leather shone, and she thought of that long-ago trip riding the train, stroking Lucy's back, pawning the jewelry, driving the T-Bird and trailer, camping, the flash flood, and Betty Lou. That dear woman —if it hadn't been for her, Sylvia would certainly have perished. It had been ages since their last road trip to visit her. The trading post had closed, the hogan and trailer had been abandoned, and all the animals were gone.

Sylvia pushed herself up and in stocking feet stepped into the boots. They felt floppy. Her feet must have shrunk over the years. She gazed at herself in the full-length mirror and giggled to see how funny she looked in the caftan and boots. Hands out, she sashayed into the bedroom, singing with an Elvis lilt:

A wise woman said
that I was no fool.

Sylvia danced around the hardwood floor.

"What are you doing?" Paul asked, leaning on his cane in the doorway, a grin on his face.

She traveled toward him and raised the volume of her voice:

Like the ocean waves
crashing to the sea
darling our love shows
you're the one for me.

She started to cough.

"Take it easy." Paul scuffled forward and took her elbow. "You know what the doctor said."

Singing again, Sylvia stepped away and waltzed around the room once more:

We were meant to be.

Paul blinked his eyes and chuckled.

Sylvia laughed too. But then a cough overpowered her, and she collapsed into a chair.

"You okay, darling?" He reached for her.

She nodded even though the raspy hack continued, and her eyes welled with tears. Paul poured cough syrup from the nightstand and carried it to her without spilling a drop. She swallowed the cherry liquid, grimaced at the too-sweet taste, and tried to catch her breath. Paul frowned with concern and put his hand on her back. "Come, dear, lie down." He guided her to the bed. They leaned on each other for support. "It's time for your nap anyway."

She knew she would fall asleep soon—there was enough codeine in the medicine to soothe her feisty spirit. That was why she didn't like to take it. Paul slid the boots off her feet and dropped them to the floor.

"Hold me awhile." She patted the bed beside her.

He climbed onto the bed and cuddled her close, tucking his hand into hers. She dug her thumb into his palm. In her young fantasies, she had never imagined a life as fulfilled as this. Soon her eyes fluttered closed as she drifted off to sleep, grateful for his love.

58

Foggy afternoon shadows crossed the library's hardwood floors, and a bright light shone onto the collage that hung over the desk. The room had recently been restored to its previous chaos. This had been the saddest week of Anne's life.

"I still can't believe she is really gone." Paul's eyes watered as he hobbled over and collapsed into his chair, setting the cane beside it. He seemed to have become frailer in the past few days.

"Neither can I." Anne touched his shoulder and sat across from him.

The service had been lovely, with a sprinkling of the ashes at his lake cabin. The first time Anne came to Bay Breeze, she sat in this same chair. "It's you!" she had said when Sylvia had come toward her. She now could hear her mentor's voice filled with compliments and pep talks. Even though they'd only known each other for a few months, they had loved each other unconditionally. But it was all over now.

In her mind, she relived over and over that awful afternoon: The house quiet, with Paul and George playing cards at the club and Lucky asleep curled up on the floor beside the hospital bed that had been cranked up to keep Sylvia's cough at bay. Anne turned the worn pages, reading Frost poems aloud to Sylvia, who mouthed the words from memory. Earlier her sentences had ricocheted from one reminiscent topic to another as her pale skin glistened. Anne paused for a sip of water and listened to Sylvia's rattled breathing.

She seemed to have nodded off, but then she opened her eyes. "Let's just chat awhile."

Anne set the book on the side table and fluffed her friend's pillows. She started to hack again, a deep sound that echoed off the library walls. Anne poured another dose of cough syrup and waited patiently for it to take effect.

"That's better." Sylvia gazed over at her. "You're so precious."

Anne smiled at her. "Why didn't you and Paul ever have any children?"

"God had other plans for me. But for many years, I thought it was for punishment."

"Punishment for what?"

Sylvia swallowed a few times, caught her breath then began, "Remember when I told you I had killed a man?"

Anne nodded with a smile.

"Well, I wasn't joking."

Anne's hand flew to her chest. "What do you mean?"

"Brace yourself: this might be hard for you to hear." Sylvia reached for Anne's hand. "When I was twenty-one, I became engaged to a villain. I thought he loved me, but he only loved himself." She breathed in and out a few times. "He hurt me not only emotionally but also physically. One night, he tormented me. I couldn't help it, and I . . . I shot him."

"No!"

"Yes. That's when I went on my little 'adventure.'" Sylvia nodded toward the collage. "The police suspected me but never had enough evidence to prosecute. Paul's the only one who has ever known. I've held it in all these years."

"How horrible for you! He must have been terrible—a monster—for you to have done something so drastic."

"Yes, but it was a long time ago." Sylvia sighed.

"But . . ." Anne had so many questions she wanted to ask, but Sylvia held up her hand.

"I can't talk any more about it." The older woman closed her eyes. "I just wanted you to know the truth." Her breathing grew shallow, and she patted Anne's hand. "Please go make us some tea now, sweetie."

Boiling the water, Anne thought about how awful it must have been for Sylvia to have gone through and lived with such a nightmare all her life. Anne returned with the tea to find Sylvia with a slight smile on her face as if wrapped in a fabulous dream. The sound of her hoarse breathing couldn't be heard—only the ticking of the grandfather clock. She looked younger, peaceful somehow. Perhaps it was the gravity, but her wrinkles seemed to have disappeared.

Anne set down the tea tray on a table and touched Sylvia's tepid hand, but she didn't respond. Trembling, Anne grasped Sylvia's shoulders, but she was gone. Even though Anne knew it wouldn't do any good, she called 911 and sobbed over her friend until the emergency crew arrived.

Now Paul smiled at Anne. "Please grab that binder on the desk over there for me."

The title read *Sylvia Van Dam Palmer Trust*. Anne didn't want to think about what was in it and only wished Sylvia were still there.

He put on his glasses. "Move a chair over here next to me."

Anne rolled the desk chair beside him as he flipped through the pages. "Let's skip all this mumbo jumbo and all this blah, blah, blah about me." He pointed at a paragraph. "Read aloud starting here."

"The Trustee shall use $10,000,000 to establish a non-endowment fund to expand the San Francisco Episcopal Women's Shelter, which may be used but not be limited to the addition of sleeping space, transitional housing, and a kitchen. The contents of Bay Breeze's bedroom safe shall be sold, and proceeds shall be added to this fund. The SFEWS shall be renamed the Betty Lou Center for Women." This thoughtful gift caught Anne unaware, and she burst into tears.

"Keep going. There's more."

"Anne McFarland shall be the advisor of these funds."

Paul grinned and handed her a handkerchief. "Surprise! It was all Sylvia's idea." He reached into his coat pocket again, pulled out a chain, and handed it to her. "This is for you too."

She ran a finger over the amber pendant's smooth surface. "What's this?" It didn't look like much.

"Sylvia always wore it close to her heart, under her clothes." He chuckled. "She called it her magic amulet."

"Really?" Anne clasped the chain closed around her neck. "Let's see if it works." All of a sudden, her tense body relaxed, she smelled gardenias, and a soft breeze flooded her chest. She felt the older woman's presence, which eased the heartache. She knew Sylvia would always be with her.

59

———

$\mathscr{A}$nne read aloud the sticky notes on her mirror: "I am confident. I am talented. My pieces are the best in San Francisco." She thought about what her aunt had told her about her father's bravery. "I am courageous. It's in my genes."

Since Sylvia had made the suggestion, Anne had focused on sinking these affirmations deeply in her psyche. She picked up a pen, scribbled another, and stuck it beside the others, thinking back to the day a few months before when Mr. Block finally gave her a check for Sylvia's portrait.

"They must have bad taste." He frowned at her.

"Can't he even get a little excited?" she complained to Fay over coffee.

"I did say to him, 'Now you need to give her that solo show.'"

"And . . ."

"He just scowled and shook his head." She mashed her lips together.

"What's he got against me?"

"He thinks you are unproven. He doesn't want to take a chance." Since then, the gallery had sold quite a few of her pieces. She had even been able to save up a bit for her trip to Milan with Sergio.

"We'll see about that!" Anne now said aloud, and then read the Post-its again.

She inspected herself in the full-length mirror. For this mission, she wished she had a power suit, as her mother used to call them when dressing for a big Avon home party. Nevertheless, Anne felt she now looked pretty sharp in the Ferragamos, charcoal slacks, and a red silk blouse underneath the black coat. She touched the snowflake pin.

Downstairs and out the door into the foggy mist, she hoped her updo wouldn't get all frizzy. She marched to the cable car and hopped on. While riding, she rehearsed her affirmations in her head. *I am talented. I create the best work in town. I am a proven artist.* Making the walk to Sutter Street, she recited the affirmations aloud: "I am talented. I create the best work in town. I am a proven artist."

She peeked into Gallery Noir's front window and could see Mr. Block sorting portfolio stacks at the counter. In a corner, Lila held up one of her canvases for Fay to see. Kiki and Stephan Sodenburg stared at an ugly paint-splattered abstract on the wall.

Anne thought maybe she should come back later when Mr. Block was alone. No, Sylvia would have encouraged her to do it now. Anne touched the amber pendant and whispered, "I am talented. I create the best work in town. I am a proven artist." She stood erect, pushed her shoulders back, and opened the gallery door.

"Morning," Fay called, and Lila gave her a little wave. Mr. Block didn't even look up.

Anne put her hands on her hips and headed straight toward him. "Mr. Block, I need to speak with you."

He nodded to her. "Ms. McDonald."

"It is McFarland! Let's go into your office for some privacy."

"No need." He returned his eyes to the portfolios.

She took a deep breath and let it out. "There are three reasons you need to give me a solo show."

He peered at her over his glasses.

She raised a finger and said, "One: I am talented!"

His gray eyebrows shot up.

"Two: My pieces are the best in San Francisco. Every time you've shown my work, it has sold."

"That's true," Fay called out.

"Three: I . . . I have courage."

"What?" A confused grin crossed his lips.

That wasn't the way she'd rehearsed it. Embarrassed, she glanced around the gallery. All eyes were focused on her. Fay smiled, nodded with approval, and moved beside her.

Anne continued with a firm voice: "I have enough courage to walk out this door and never offer my work to you again."

There was silence. Mr. Block just looked at her with that awful smirk on his face. She breathed deeply and counted to ten in her mind. "This is your last chance." She stared at Mr. Block for a moment, then spun on her heels and paced toward the exit.

Her hand almost touched the door when he spoke. "Ms. McFarland." She turned around.

"Do you still have more pieces like the ones that sold?"

She held her head high. "You know I do."

"I'll think about it." He looked down and flipped a portfolio page.

Slumped shoulders, she ran her fingers over the amber. *I do have courage*, she thought. Then she blurted, "No you won't. You'll decide right now." She glared at him and put her hand back on the door.

He glanced around the room. Everyone gave him a frown. He looked back at Anne and nodded slowly. "Okay."

"Okay? When?"

He looked up at the ceiling in thought. "Mid-July?"

"It's a deal." She started to dash to his limp outstretched hand but stopped herself, sauntered over to him, and shook it.

Fay, Lila, and even the Sodenburgs gave a round of applause.

"And another thing: make Fay your curator for God's sake."

Anne glided out the door as if floating on air. The fog had cleared to a periwinkle blue sky. Her mind in a daze, she walked down the street away from the gallery. Then she stopped in amazement. Her own show! She'd done it. She wished she could tell Sylvia, and she looked up into the sky.

Anne counted the few months until mid-July. It was right around the corner. And then she realized that was when she planned to meet Sergio in Italy.

60

Anne walked around the gallery, straightening all the pieces on the wall, and worried that no one would come. At least the weather wouldn't keep them away. It had been a warm summer day, and now, as the sun began to set, the usual fog hadn't even rolled in. Anne inspected herself in Gallery Noir's plate glass window, then separated the tulle skirt of her green dress. She had considered buying a new outfit for the occasion but couldn't find one she liked any better at her usual haunts. She had twisted up her hair, and it had cooperated.

Lights shone over each piece, which made the black-and-white photos and texts more discernible. Crisp turquoise and red hues provided colorful backgrounds. Anne recalled the exhilaration of creating each one: discovering photos, cutting, painting, gluing, drawing, and visualizing what might have happened to Sylvia. When the work had been up in Anne's apartment, she felt as if it were a part of her.

The catering crew had just finished setting up the appetizers and had left. She wandered toward the enticing aromas and gaped at the crab-stuffed mushrooms, baked Brie, bruschetta, crostini, and more stacked into a lavish display, resisting the urge to dig in and ruin the effect.

Mr. Block peered over his glasses at Fay in the back office.

They'd been in there for half an hour. Anne hoped he hadn't decided to give her friend the boot. Something was up though. Besides the opulent spread, he had splurged on fancy postcards and had even snail mailed them to his client list.

She checked her phone again. Of course Sergio was in Italy now, but Anne thought he might at least call or text. The night she had told him she couldn't meet him in Milan, she had called instead of using Skype. She hadn't wanted to see his disappointed face.

"Hi, Big Foot."

"I have good news and bad news. Which do you want first?"

"The good?"

"Mr. Block has agreed to give me a solo show at the Noir."

"Wonderful! That's what you've always wanted. The bad?"

"The opening reception date collides with our trip."

"Can you change the date?"

"No. Mr. Block has it all set. Are you mad at me?"

"Not at all. I can't tell you I'm not disappointed. And my family was so looking forward to meeting you."

"Your family?" He hadn't said anything about his family being there!

"A first solo show is only once in a lifetime. This is an important step for you."

"Can you rearrange your trip and come to San Francisco then?"

"What's the exact date?"

"July sixteenth."

"I'll be in the middle of my meetings." He had paused for a moment. "Let's just face it. Maybe we aren't meant to be together."

She had felt dejected. "Don't be like that." That had been a few months ago, and since then, things between them seem to have fizzled out. She tried to forget about him but instead thought about him all the time: his handsome face, silly hats, and kind words.

She sighed and fluffed her skirt again and hoped people would show up. Mr. Block emerged from his office with a frown, headed for the appetizer table, and heaped a plate. Fay came over to her, looking like a jaguar that had swallowed a macaw.

"What is it?" Anne whispered.

Fay mouthed, *Tell you later.*

A delivery boy came in with his hair gelled up like Bart Simpson's. He carried a huge bouquet of red roses.

Fay led him to the counter next to the guest book. "Put it here." She tipped him, and he left. "Sergio, I presume?" Fay raised her eyebrows at Anne.

Anne reached for the tiny envelope hoping it was addressed to Big Foot, but it only said *To Anne.* She opened the card and read silently.

Congratulations! When are you coming home?
Love,
The Michigan Clan

Anne laughed. She knew they were teasing her this time. "No, from my mom and family." She had tried to get someone from there to come, but no one had been willing to make the trip.

Anne saw a familiar face walk in the door, turned her back, and asked Fay, "What's she doing here?"

"You'll see," Fay said mysteriously.

"There you are, Miss McFarland." Fredricka Woods handed her a small basket of mangoes and glanced around the gallery. "Congratulations! I knew you had promise."

Anne set the offering on the counter and gave her a sheepish grin. "Sorry about running out on you that night."

"No problem. You just weren't ready yet." Fredricka turned to Fay. "Has he told you?"

"Just now. Can I share the news with Anne?"

Fredricka nodded and toyed with her *milagro* bracelet.

Fay grabbed Anne's hands. "Ms. Woods bought an interest in the Noir."

"What?"

"I sure did! Mr. Block needed an infusion of cash. I offered to buy out 75 percent of the business."

"You did?"

"I said only if you let that smart girl help make all the decisions." Fredricka put a hand on Fay's back. "First time we met, I could tell you really knew your stuff."

A shriek came from the entrance as blonde Crissy ran toward Anne. "Surprise!" Jonathan trailed close behind.

"You came!" Anne gave Crissy a big hug.

"Of course." She pecked Anne on the cheek. "Besides, I wanted to come shop in your Union Square. I have plenty to buy for now!" She screeched again and put her hands on the tent dress, over a baby bump.

Anne shook Jonathan's hand. "Congratulations."

He smiled. "Now we'll have a Jonathan IV!"

Lila nudged in and touched Anne's elbow. "I'm here. I'll talk to you again after I have a thorough look around."

"We can't wait to see your work either." Crissy and Jonathan wandered off as Fredricka left to pour herself a glass of wine.

Fay stood with Anne while she watched the door. After a few minutes, Howard arrived straight from work in his ruffled-blouse uniform. A black-clad couple she didn't know walked in, and then the Sodenburgs arrived. Next were George and Paul.

Paul took Anne's hands in his. "She would have been so proud of you tonight."

Anne looked up at the ceiling. "She is!"

"Yes, she is." He spread his arms around the room.

"Paul, here's my friend, Fay."

She shook his hand. "Pleased to meet you. And who is this gorgeous bloke?" Fay asked.

"I'm George." He blushed with a shy smile.

Mr. Block edged over and whispered to Anne, "The Soden-burgs want to talk with you." He grabbed her arm and pulled her toward the chichi couple.

"Tell us the motivation behind your work." Stephan held his wine glass toward her.

"I found a coat with a key in its pocket. Then I saw a picture in a magazine, and did Internet searches. Images arose, and I lost myself in the process."

"Interesting."

"Isn't her work fabulous?" Mr. Block smiled at the couple.

"We'd like to at least purchase this one." Kiki smiled and pointed to a collage. "I think it represents . . ."

Anne's attention began to wander. She watched George help Paul to a chair and deliver a plate of food to him. The butler then returned to Fay with a grin. She held a bunch of grapes to his lips and tried to feed him, and he let her.

Across the room, Anne recognized Jewels from the farmers' market in full gypsy regalia: red headscarf and fringed shawl over a long dress. A critic from *The Examiner* studied Anne's large Monu-ment Valley piece and took notes. Mrs. Ladenheim, wearing a fancy lace dress, stood in the doorway. All gussied up and without her curlers, she actually looked quite nice. Anne couldn't believe she had really come. Mr. Block made a beeline for her with an outstretched hand.

Even though the reception appeared perfect in every way, it felt as if something were missing. She looked around the space again. And then she saw him walk through the door. The fedora on his head reminded her of something out of *The Godfather*. But this guy was no gangster.

Her Ferragamos sprinted forward, and she threw her arms around him. "You're here!"

He kissed her cheek and then the other. "I wouldn't have missed it. Even if I had to come from the other side of the world."

ACKNOWLEDGMENTS

First I would like to thank provocateur Judy Reeves for teaching me to slow down, go deep and write wild. You were there at the beginning and throughout the process with your thousands of prompts, and cheered me to the finishing line. I would not be here without you.

A huge shout of gratitude goes to my comrades and colleagues at San Diego Writers, Ink and especially to all the Brown Baggers and marathon writers who sat beside me while these characters magically appeared on the page and their stories began to unfold. I am deeply indebted to Amy Wallen and her read and critique group that pored over my first typed drafts with patience and encouragement. I also want to thank Jeanne Peterson and those Reeling and Writhers that continued to help me mold the novel as I further honed my craft. To Steve Kowit and Sundays at Liberty Station group, thank you for giving me the respite and confidence I needed to move forward and submit this novel for publication.

I am very appreciative to the editors Victoria Austin-Smith and Tracy Jones for cleaning up my messes, and to coach Marni Freedman for insisting I go back in and rewrite the book for the jillionth time. To Brooke Warner and all those at She Writes Press, thank you so much for being brave and providing this great opportunity of hybrid publishing to women like me.

I am forever grateful to Tanya Peters and Kristen Fogle for literally holding my hand along the way. A huge hug goes to my

Point Loma Book Club for teaching me to be a better reader, listener and friend. A special thank you to The Amigos for their love and support and for demonstrating how to be artists every moment of every day. To Phil Johnson who helped me focus on my goals, ignited my sense of humor and made me laugh.

To my siblings, Todd Greentree, Sandy Greenbaum and Leslie Zwail, you lived through the 1960s with me and are always in my heart. And lastly, I am so grateful to the real Lucy and my hero, Jerry, for being my constant companions. You have made this and all things possible. I don't know why I've been so blessed.

ABOUT THE AUTHOR

photo credit: Daren Scott

JILL G. HALL facilitates creativity groups for artists of all types and curates exhibitions at Inspirations Gallery, NTC at Liberty Station. Her poems have been published in *A Year in Ink, Wild Women, Wild Voices, City Works Press, Serving House Journal,* and *The Avocet.* She resides in San Diego with her husband, Jerry, and beagle-bassett, Lucy. Learn more at www.jillghall.com.

SELECTED TITLES FROM SHE WRITES PRESS

She Writes Press is an independent publishing company
founded to serve women writers everywhere.
Visit us at www.shewritespress.com.

A Cup of Redemption by Carole Bumpus. $16.95, 978-1-938314-90-2.
Three women, each with their own secrets and shames, seek to make
peace with their pasts and carve out new identities for themselves.

Portrait of a Woman in White by Susan Winkler. $16.95,
978-1-938314-83-4. When the Nazis steal a Matisse portrait from the
eccentric, art-loving Rosenswigs, the Parisian family is thrust into the
tumult of war and separation, their fates intertwined with that of their
beloved portrait.

Shanghai Love by Layne Wong. $16.95, 978-1-938314-18-6. The en-
thralling story of an unlikely romance between a Chinese herbalist
and a Jewish refugee in Shanghai during World War II.

The Sweetness by Sande Boritz Berger. $16.95, 978-1-63152-907-8. A
compelling and powerful story of two girls—cousins living on separate
continents—whose strikingly different lives are forever changed when
the Nazis invade Vilna, Lithuania.

The Belief in Angels by J. Dylan Yates. $16.95, 978-1-938314-64-3. From
the Majdonek death camp to a volatile hippie household on the East
Coast, this narrative of tragedy, survival, and hope spans more than
fifty years, from the 1920s to the 1970s.

Hysterical: Anna Freud's Story by Rebecca Coffey. $18.95,
978-1-938314-42-1. An irreverent, fictionalized exploration of the
seemingly contradictory life of Anna Freud—told from her point of
view.